DEFIANCE

The gold Quasi-Robot said extremely clearly, as if explaining to an imbecile: "We hope you have not been hasty. This is serious."

"Don't I know it. I told you, I've made my choice. If you think you have some damn right to give me an alternative like the alternative you gave me, I think I have a right to pick which course I accept. I'll take the desert, and you can take Limbo PD and shove it right up your electronic valves."

I felt I was unfair to those Q-Rs, who were blindly serving the community, or attempting to, as their programming insured they must. But then, how could anyone ask me to be otherwise? Nobody expects the condemned to embrace the axe.

But nobody expected either, at least I don't think they did (certainly I didn't), the cheer that went belting up from the crowd in the Hall. Even the people cheering seemed unnerved. They were cheering me. Not so much for my speech but for that very thing which so appalled them normally. Because I had defied the System, bitten again at the burning sun. . . .

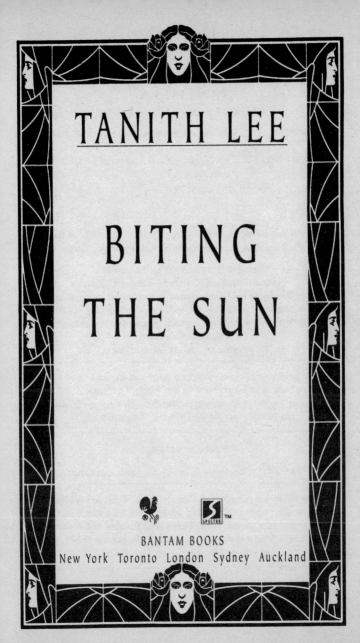

TANITH LEE

BITING
THE SUN

BANTAM BOOKS
New York Toronto London Sydney Auckland

BITING THE SUN

A Bantam Spectra Book / October 1999

DON'T BITE THE SUN was originally published by DAW Books
in February 1976.
DRINKING SAPPHIRE WINE was originally published by DAW Books
in January 1977.

ISBN 0-553-58130-9

Published simultaneously in the United States and Canada

PRINTED IN THE UNITED STATES OF AMERICA

OPM   10 9 8 7 6 5 4 3 2

TRANSCRIBER'S NOTE

Although I have put the Four BEE into equivalent modern English, the Jang slang vocabulary which the writer uses pales in translation. I have therefore left the sixteen or so odd words she employs untouched, and included on the following page a glossary, which provides an adequate, if imperfect, guide to what they mean.

GLOSSARY OF JANG SLANG

attlevey   Hello.

dalika   Violent argument.

derisann   Lovely, beautiful.

droad   Bored out of one's mind.

drumdik   Utterly horrible, the most ghastly thing.

farathoom   Bloody, fucking hell.

floop   Cunt. See also *thalldrap*.

graks   Balls.

groshing   Fabulous, marvelous.

insumatt   Unsurpassable.

onk   Mild ejaculation, e.g., "Bother."

ooma   Darling, honey.

ooma-kasma   Extreme term of affection, e.g., "love of my life," not generally used.

promok   Moron.

selt   Slow on the uptake, easy to fool.

soolka   Well-groomed. Applied by Jang only to non-Jang.

thalldrap   See *floop*.

tosky   Neurotic.

Vixaxn   A word never written in full in the first section of the autobiography. Though spelled fully here, the meaning—though obviously still pretty bad—is also still obscure.

zaradann   Insane, nuts.

GLOSSARY OF GENERAL TERMS

Glar Early Four BEE title, similar to professor. The term hung on as a polite name for Q-R teachers at the hypno-schools, but otherwise was extinct by this time.

mid-*vrek* Middle period of any *vrek,* lasting forty units.

rorl Four BEE equivalent of a century.

split Four BEE minute.

unit Four BEE day.

vrek Period of one hundred units.

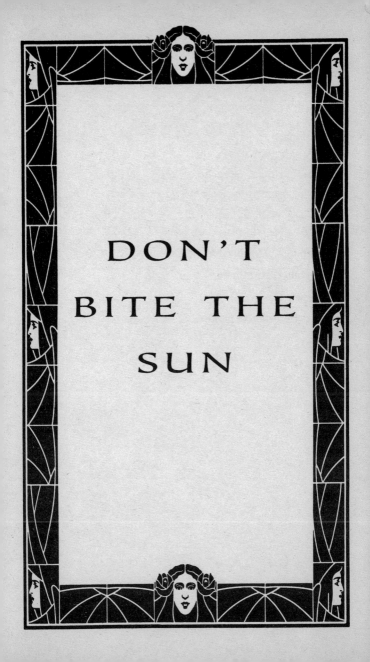

DON'T
BITE THE
SUN

My friend Hergal had killed himself again. This was the fortieth time he had crashed his bird-plane on to the Zeefahr Monument and had to have a new body made. And when I went to visit him at Limbo, I was wandering around for ages before the robot found him for me. He was dark this time, about a foot taller, with very long hair and a mustache, all glittery gold fibers, and these silly wings growing out of his shoulders and ankles.

"*Attlevey,* Hergal," I said.

"*Attlevey,*" said Hergal, and flapped his wings about. "*Groshing,* aren't they? No strength, of course, just for show. Have to get another new bird-plane if I fancy a flight."

"I thought," I remarked, popping a button for a floating chair, even though mannerless old Hergal hadn't bothered, "that the Committee might have canceled your license to fly."

"Ha ha!" gaily chortled Hergal. "Wouldn't dare."

"I do wish, though, you'd pick somewhere else to crash down on top of. It gets rather monotonous, always the boring old Zeefahr. I mean, how about trying the Robotics Museum?

You might even manage to crack the roof, and that *must* be an achievement."

Hergal tugged his mustache.

"Hmm," Hergal said.

"Anyway," I said, giving my messenger bee a good kick—it's always dozing off and falling on me in the street, usually when hordes of people are about—"I've brought you some ecstasy pills and a sixth-dimensional cube to contemplate."

"Oh, good," said Hergal. I could see his mind (?) was on higher things than ecstasy and contemplation. I remembered the nasty time Hergal and I got married for mid-*vrek*, down at the Prism Playgrounds, and then lost each other, and I ended up stealing lots of glass dresses out of confusion, and having my dreams analyzed, and buying a desert animal from Four BOO that was fierce and furry, and snored all the way home in the bubble and then bit me at the last moment, when I'd actually decided I could stand it being fierce and furry, and snoring.

Hergal, of course, just rented a bird-plane and crashed on top of the Zeefahr Monument. That was number nine. What I was trying to say was that Hergal's mind had been on higher things then, or so he said.

"Listen, Hergal," I stated, "I'm afraid I've put in an order to have you officially cut out of my circle of friends. It's not that I don't like you. I mean, you're really lovely, particularly with your—er—wings, but I'm just tired of everyone coming up and saying to me: 'Is it *true* you know that *floop* Hergal? Do tell!' "

"I see," said Hergal. He didn't even have the politeness to cry. Everyone in the Jang always cries when they're officially cut out of circles.

"Oh well, there's nothing more to be said then, Hergal." I got down from the chair and bounced on the crystallize-rubber floor. My bee fell on my head.

"Oh *farathoom*!" I snapped.

Hergal looked a bit surprised, but he didn't bat a gold fiber eyelash until I strode to the doorway.

"Er," he ventured then.

"What did you say?"

"Er," Hergal admitted. "Perhaps you'd tell me what circle you're cutting me out of."

"Mine, you *thalldrap*!" I yelled.

"But . . . who are you exactly?"

Well, I *mean,* I'd had it flashed all over the city that my new body was pale and slim, with knee-length silver hair and antennae. He just didn't try.

Outside, my bee fell on me again, right in front of the Robotics Museum and a crowd of visitors from Four BOO.

I was so depressed I went and drowned myself, for the tenth time, in my bubble. Perhaps I could even get a duplicate of Hergal's body and really drive him *zaradann.*

PART 1

1

Of course, when I woke up in the Limbo Tub I'd changed my mind. Some quasi-robot medicine man was peering in at me.

"Look here, young woman—I see that is what you predominantly are—this has got to be stopped. This is the second time you've been back here in ten units."

"Mmm," I swam around a bit and smiled at him with my emotional response wires.

The Q-R went away, and someone came and asked me what I wanted to come out as, and by then, you see, I'd anti-Hergaled myself. How *drumdik* it would be if people actually thought I *was* Hergall! What with that, and that *floopy* bee swooning in my hair . . . I showed them the new me. As usual it was depressingly lithe and glamorous. Hatta, and lots of other people I know, nearly always makes a point of having a fat body once in a while, or spots or something. Anyhow, this me was willow-waisted, with an exotic bust and long, long scarlet hair. I got into it, and it felt so odd I had to go somewhere quiet and have an ecstasy pill, and forget about it for a while.

Hatta found me not long after.

"*Ooma* Hatta," I purred. Everyone always looks nice when you're in ecstasy, even Hatta, who was being fat *and* spotty just now, with three eyes.

"*Attlevey, ooma. Groshing* again, I see. Don't you ever get a mite ill with it?"

"No," I said.

"I'll take you for a meal. It must be coming up to some eating time or other, isn't it?"

"Well, I'm hungry. I drowned just after meal three, and this new body hadn't had a thing."

We went out, Hatta holding me up—I was extremely ecstatic—and rolled on to the float-bridge. My awful, beastly bee came rushing out after us. I just couldn't get rid of the thing. It fell on Hatta this time.

"*Onk!*" said Hatta, typically and nauseatingly mild about what happens to him. I threw the bee off the bridge, but it came back again. "Let's go to the Fire-Pit."

The Fire-Pit, they say, is absolutely the place to go if you're feeling low. I almost cheered up, but, in the end, just before we got there, my Neurotic Need asserted itself and I had to get off the bridge and go steal something. It was alive, this thing, with long white fur and big orange eyes. Its whiskers got tangled up in my hair, and I gave it to my bee to hold a second or so before I got hysterical.

"Here we are," Hatta said.

We jumped off the bridge, and fell about twenty feet until the electricity wave-net of the Fire-Pit neatly caught us. Hatta looked apologetic. In the Fire-Pit everything burns with scarlet fire. The tables float in flames, non-hot of course, and fireballs bounce gently in the plates. I matched.

"I forgot," Hatta said, "about your hair."

I'd calmed down now anyway, but he shoved another ecstasy pill into my mouth, just in case, and then had to carry me to a couch.

"What will you have, dear?" Hatta asked kindly.

I winced at his un-Jang vocabulary, hoping no one had overheard.

We had a large nut steak on fire, with all sorts of burning fruit stuck out of it on burning skewers. Hatta carved with the molecule needle knife and did it all wrong, but we got something to eat eventually. Ecstasy was wearing off by then.

"I hear," Hatta mumbled through steak, "that you've had Hergal officially cut out."

"Yes," I said.

Hatta went on eating for a while. Our bottle of fire-and-ice arrived and he sniffed it and tasted it and stared up at the fiery ceiling.

"Eight-first Rorl, I shouldn't wonder," Hatta said. I fingered a skewer, but Hatta only murmured: "Er, I really admit you're looking *groshing*."

"Thank you. I can't say the same for you, *ooma*."

"The thing is," Hatta said nervously, "I haven't had love for two units now, and I wondered if perhaps we could get married for the afternoon."

"Not with you looking like that we couldn't," I said. Well, I mean. Outraged pimples and a couple of tons descending on you with three yellow pupil-less eyes to watch the effect.

"Look," Hatta encouraged me, "can't you see that it's an Essential Experience to have love with a body you're not really attracted to?"

"Why?" No, I wasn't going to be bamboozled with Jang Essential Experience jargon, particularly from reactionary old Hatta.

"Well . . ." began Hatta.

We were interrupted. Kley and Danor had arrived with a pet animal that immediately started a fight with my white, stolen thing, and therefore with my bee. In the confusion they drew up floating fire couches and helped themselves to our nut steak. They were both male this time, with long iridescent hair, and Danor had those silly wings like Hergal's and kept knocking things off the table with them.

They vaguely greeted me and began chatting with Hatta.

I stood up, got my white furry animal under one arm, and drained my third goblet of fire-and-ice.

"I must flit, *oomas,*" I said gaily.

"Oh, but—" Hatta began.

"Thank you for a wonderful fourth meal, Hatta," I gushed. "I'll see you next body."

I flitted.

Outside it was one of those depressing blue-crystal-golden-drops-of-sunlight afternoons. The weather is always perfect at Four BEE, but now and then the Jang manage to sabotage something, and we get a *groshing,* howling sand-storm come sweeping in past the barrier beams to cheer us all up. I'll never forget the time Danor and I, both female then, I might add, disabled the robot controller at Lookout 9A and let in a down-pour of volcanic ash from one of the big black mountains outside, floods of it for units and units—every-thing went *zaradann.* They had to deliver food by bird-plane, and the roads were full of robots trying to dig us all out. We even achieved an earthquake once. Nothing fell down, of course, though we all hoped the Robotics Museum would. Hergal and I were sitting in a big crystal tower at the time, unsuccessfully having love telepathically, and it shook like jelly, which was more than we were doing.

I went to a call-post and had my new body flashed out, so my friends (?) would recognize me. I put a scanner on the Zeefahr and waited for ages to see if Hergal would hurtle out of the sky on to it, but he didn't. So I signaled Thinta.

"*Attlevey,*" I said when her three-dimensional female image appeared in front of me. She looked nice, pleasantly plump, with big green eyes and sort of furry hair. She hadn't changed for ages. Stability at last.

"Oh *attlevey, ooma,* I was just making a water dress."

She held it up, greenly opalescent and gently dripping.

"Thinta," I said, "I've just been drowned and come back like this, and I'm absolutely *droad.*"

"Oh, I didn't know it was you," Thinta said. She obvi-ously hadn't seen the flash yet. "Well, *ooma,* why don't you go to one of the Dream Rooms? Wait a split and I'll be with you." She vanished.

Thinta liked the Dream Rooms, though it was reckoned to be pretty anti-Jang really. You always met lots of Older People with "set ideas" who told you you shouldn't be there, but out having love and ecstasy or sex changes or Sense Distortion, like all young people are usually rigidly expected to have. I went into Jade Tower to steal some jewelery while I waited for her to come gamboling down in her miniature safe pink bird-plane.

Stealing is an absolute art, and one of my few simple pleasures.

There's a big dragon in Jade Tower, bred on some farm near Four BAA. It rattles its jade-plated scales at you, and green fire comes out of its mouth and gives you a really invigorating, pine-scented, all-over shower. I've always liked the dragon. It stirs me in an odd romantic way. I once sat in its nice warm mouth for ages and tried to get Kley to rescue me, but he just took an ecstasy pill and rudely collapsed. I think I'd embarrassed him.

"*Attlevey,* dragon," I said.

I got into its right ear for a while—it looks like a shell inside—and thought about what I might like to steal, while the dragon roared and sprayed away at everybody.

2

My bee, clutching my white, furry, stolen pet, followed me as I wandered innocently through Jade Tower. I waited subconsciously for both of them to fall on my head. Other people's bees zoomed by, all efficiency and programmed determination to serve. I felt conspicuous—transparent clothing, chains of gold anemones, toe rings, fingernails as long as my fingers—utterly Jang. And honestly, I never liked wearing it all that much. You feel so naked if you forget to pop a tinselly flower in your navel, and finger-long nails are dangerous.

All the Older People nodded approvingly at me. I was just what a young person should be, tinkling, almost nude, my one-color eyes still dark from ecstasy, and my Jang vocabulary working like a catalyst in everything I said.

I sidled up to a large revolving tray of scent bomb earrings, smoking fragrance, light winking and glittering on their tortured shapes. I stretched out my hand. A floating mirror swam down to me and showed me my new face. I selected a pair of solid-phosphorous things, magnetized them

to my ears, and watched them uncoil and wend lovingly down
my neck, over my shoulders, and sigh to rest on my abdomen.

"Madam looks charming!" sang angelic voices in the
domed, see-through roof.

I knew I'd come at the wrong time. Jang girls usually
trail in in the mornings when the whole place throbs to Jang
upper-ear music, which you can't actually hear consciously
but which sends you into euphoria in seconds. Then they can
sell you practically anything, with machines screaming:
"Simply *groshing*!" and "*Ooma,* how *derisann*!" all around
you.

Then, all at once, I felt light-headed, happy, and abandoned. The older ladies looked bewildered and clapped in
their portable audio-plugs. Upper-Ear had been turned on full
blast. *Zaradann* with joy, I cursed Jade Tower's observation
robots. I removed my spoils, put my hand down among a pile
of junk, and let them go. I brushed back my hair and magnetized about six pairs of coiled, random earrings which I had
just picked up, and which were probably all odd, in the tangle
at the back of my neck. But it was a reflex. I was too ecstatic
to get any sort of satisfaction out of it, really.

I went past this woman on the way out. She was busy
paying, working up into a real frenzy, and I noticed she'd left
her audio-plugs out, so the Upper-Ear could help her along.
Honestly, she must only just have migrated from the Jang
herself.

"It's so *groshing*!" she was crying while the machine,
only going on her clothing and hair, was saying:

"Absolutely charming, madam," and all the time the
vis-take was feeding her enthusiasm into electrodes which
changed emotion into power, and pushed it into Four BEE's
main power station banks.

It was rather sad, somehow. I never pay for anything if I
can help it. I just enthuse ever so unexcitedly, and drive all
the robot assistants *zaradann*.

3

Outside Jade Tower Thinta was waiting for me, looking as impatient as Thinta can look; more patient than ever, in fact.

I took out my earrings and found one pair, four odd. Thinta ignored me. I threw them down the Jade Tower terrace and watched electricity wave-nets catch them at various junctures. My mind bounced between my demagnetized ears, from the retreating aural joy and delight that had ruined my stealing enterprise.

"*Attlevey,* Thinta," I remembered to say. I suddenly realized I'd rather be solo, but here was Thinta and we were going to a Dream Room.

No, really, I liked the Dream Rooms. I'd never let on what dreams I programmed for myself, though Hergal always dreams of flying. I thought Hatta probably dreamed of being some sort of three-headed monster.

"What's that?" Thinta asked, gazing up at my white, stolen pet, kicking and hooting in the clutches of my bee. Thinta's bee moved in to help. Thinta's bee always moves in to help. It gets you down. Thinta tried to stroke my pet, and my pet tried to bite Thinta.

"Stop it!" I shouted at all of them. I felt pretty *tosky,* actually.

We got to Four BEE's Third Sector Dream Rooms more or less all right. Thinta flew safely, and I realized how much I preferred being with Hergal and feeling the blood drain out of my head with fright. Actually when I'm with Hergal I always realize how I prefer being with Thinta and not feeling the blood drain out of my head with fright.

"Here we are!" Thinta cried, and proudly guided us down to a superb landing in one of the nets. I mean, you don't *have* to guide *anything* into a net. They're there to catch you. Oh well.

We got out and on to a movi-rail. There were lots of people buzzing up and down, and crowds of Jang for once. The ones coming out were discussing what they had been dreaming—all symbols and astral projection and so on. I felt a bit small. I usually did. Honestly, I just couldn't feel at home in that place if someone didn't make me feel inferior about what I chose to dream. The average Jang dream ecstasy is to be a mote of pulsing light, sucked to and fro between fiery suns, novas and palely smoking moons, a kind of cosmic, all-over comprehension of having love. No, really, I read it on a flash. Anyhow, Hergal dreamed of flying. Good old Hergal.

The bottom of the shaft is lovely, masses of smoldering pink cloud architecture with rays of gold passing in between, and the whole thing shifting ever so gently. Cloudy robots guided us to little transparent cubicles and helped us drop clothing and anchor ourselves on comfortable air cushions that give you a stimulating tonic massage as you dream.

I waved to Thinta as the walls, ceilings and floor began to smoke up and turn opaque, then settled back and dictated my dream to my robot. The idea is just to give them the skeleton of what you want; they think up the relevant sets, costumes, special effects, and also lots of little twists and surprises to delight you. But I was a bit of a pest. I always have too much imagination to fit inside my head. I've been told, though of course I don't remember consciously, that, during my twentieth of a *rorl* at hypno-school, that was the worst problem my tutors had with me. I could turn a seven-dimensional geometric exercise into an epic adventure, where all the planes and double planes were really the inhabitants of a besieged citadel, fighting off hordes of triple bisectors with paralyzer-beams.

The robot struggled valiantly with my detailed color descriptions, my quick but elaborate costume sketches on the thought-receptive wall-panel, my demands for background music, and the sweeping grandeur of ruined palaces I kept stressing whenever new thought flagged. I think Thinta had been long gone by the time the robot staggered out.

I lay back, closed my eyes, and waited. Suddenly you feel this stroking sensation all over, and then you're there. . . .

Oh, well done!

A sweeping grandeur of ruined palaces, fallen marble blocks and pillars towering upward without roofs, crumbling stairways, and great window spaces through which burning arrows of light streamed and bubbled. Overhead an enormous planet hung low, like a pitted emerald in the pale green sky. Arid desert, faintly glittering, stretched away and away.

I'd just come in sight of this place, after traveling for units without sustenance across the Blazing Waste. It was twilight. The huge creamy-tawny beast I rode stood stock still, its pads planted in the sands, its shaggy-maned head lifted to stare at that baleful planet overhead. I dismounted and climbed one of the crumbling stairways. I was all gold: gold hair, gold skin and eyes, gold tunic and groin-high boots, ancient double-bladed dagger with a gold-plated hilt. I saw my reflection in cracked glass floors and shreds of mirror.

Darkness gathered. Things twittered high in the ruinous roof.

Two red candles up ahead. No, not candles. Eyes, watching me. I could sense, I could tell, there was something in this

place that would hurt me if I wasn't careful. Obviously, I was
fairly weak from my ordeal in the Crystal Deserts, but mine
was an old and noble line, forged like good steel (of course). I
felt no fear (what's that?) but drew my gold-hilt dagger and
went forward through the dense viridian dusk.

The eyes went out.

There ahead was a terrible monster, breathing a poisonous fire that almost scorched me. I uttered ancient mystic
words to protect myself from the flames, and closed with it.
The fighting was long and awful. (Naturally.) But grace was
in my every movement, my blade was swift and certain.
(What else?) Eventually the thing collapsed and blew away
like the desert dust, leaving only a bleached skeleton at my
booted feet. I went on. Nets of bronze dropped down. Too
proud to struggle, I was borne upward through the tall ranks
of pillarheads, to a vast hollow rampart. I found a table of
glass laid out with a feast of exotic foods and sparkling
wines.

"Eat," boomed a voice out of nothing and nowhere.
"Drink. You are weary."

I stepped up to the table and, mistrusting the food despite
my hunger, spoke first a magic charm. At once the whole
thing went up in purple fires (surprise! surprise!) and a clap
of thunder howled around the rampart. Huge winged horrors
flapped down on me. I beat at them until my strength was
almost exhausted, and then, using ancient incantations, managed to drive them into the fire on the table, where they were
consumed. Many more demons attacked me during the long
and terrible night. Blazing meteors screamed from the sky
and exploded far out in the desert wastes, as I slew pythons of
flame and dragons of brass. Temptations were offered me and
countless mirages, all of which I resisted and all of which
proved to be false. At last, toward dawn, when I knew I was
almost too weary to save myself any longer, even though my
beauty and my luster were still undimmed (sort of pale gold
with romantic shadows under my eyes, all swooning and gorgeous) a tall figure appeared at the end of the rampart.

A male. A mythical figure and handsome beyond belief,

dark-eyed and pale-haired, but with evil stamped all over his marvelous face. He drew a long and phosphorescent sword, and we were at it again. Where my extra reserves of strength arrived from was quite beyond dream-me (though real-me knew all right) but, by my *insumatt* skill, I at last had the being at the point of annihilation under my long dagger. But I paused. Something stopped me. His beauty clouded my reason and I could not strike. Ashamed, I flung down my blade, and cried:

"Kill me. I am unworthy to be your opponent." And the great sword lifted and then was gone.

I looked up astonished. My enemy was my enemy no longer. Three times more marvelous, he embraced me, and told me of the ancient and terrible curse that had lain upon this place and upon him. I, by my bravery and beauty, had saved both him and his land. (Splendid!)

He led me down the steps into a wonderful hall of gold and fire, and I saw that the palace was a ruin no longer. There was the glitter, past long windows, of the unlocked rain, and all around the desert was blossoming.

To the tremulous tinkle of fountains bursting from rock, I woke up.

"Who am I?" I often thought that after a dream. "Where am I?"

It doesn't take long to recollect, however. I felt disappointed. Life had been just beginning for me, for us. We had been going to feast and have love, and now I would never know what it was like to—Of course, I could have had that added on to the dream if I'd asked. Only I never do. I know of people who go to a Dream Room just to dream about having love, but what's the point? I mean, you can have love any time you want, really, any way you want, and there are millions of pills and stuff to guarantee results. So why go off and dream about it too?

"You've been ages," said Thinta.

It's not the dream that takes the time—they stretch your time sense or something, and every dream lasts a regulation

ten splits—it was all my pre-dream direction that hung everyone up.

Thinta was drinking silver-water cordial, but I wanted to
go away alone and think about my lover, and the dragons I
had fought.

"I have to dash, Thinta *ooma*," I said. "I have to go
back to Limbo for the first unit checkup on my new body."

It's true. They like to check you if you don't stay in for a
unit or so. Hergal always stays in.

"Of course, *ooma*," Thinta smiled drowsily. Perhaps she
wanted aloneness too. But no. "I'll come too. We have to pay
yet."

Oh *farathoom!* Thinta's such a *bore* about paying for
things.

We trailed along to our pay booths and she was off.

"Thank you, thank you. It was absolutely *groshing,
groshing!* Oh thank you, I'm so happy. It was so *derisann!*
Oh! Oh! Oh!"

Oh shut up.

"Thank you," I droned urbanely.

Machines registered protests, started to encourage me.
The booths were full of people yelling their guts out with
praise and joy. All right, I thought, I'll show you.

I raised my voice.

"Oh thank you," I screamed. I took an ecstasy pill and
soared and soared. I ranted. I screeched until my throat gave
out. I hugged the machinery with unbridled passion, and tears
of love ran down my face.

Thinta helped me outside. She looked approving.

"You've been a very good girl," she congratulated me.

Perfect sunlight hit me in the face and threw the husks of
my vision at my feet. Dragons eddied on the gentle breeze.
My lover faded and was gone.

4

I left Thinta and went to Limbo by Body Displacer. They're efficient, but they tend to make you puke. No one uses them now except Older People, who think they have to be in a hurry about things and have cast platinum stomachs. I got in and threw switches and wished I hadn't. It's quick of course, but really I think you lose so much time being sick at the other end when you get there that you might just as well hop on a float-bridge. Anyhow, I arrived, and I did feel pretty weird, actually, as if I'd left something behind. My head or something.

Robots glared at me. They disapproved. Body Displacers are non-Jang, and non-Jang youth is obnoxious, unreasonable, *tosky, zaradann*.

They gave me my check. I'd lost a small, artistically placed mole in transit, and they grumbled. Otherwise my body was fine. Except I was tired of it.

"I'd like to apply for a new body," I said.

Shocked silence.

"How long does it take?"

"Your request has been registered," the quasi-robot told

me. "Normally you would have to wait for thirty units. It has been marked on your records, however, that you have gone through fourteen bodies in the past *vrek*. You will therefore have to wait for sixty units."

"Can I appeal?"

"Oh yes."

"Will it do any good?"

"None whatsoever."

I went out.

The afternoon was getting more tiresomely lovely with every second.

5

I went down to Peridot Waterway and signaled for my bubble. The water ran past going steeply uphill, a smooth pearly green. Buildings towered up all around me. My bee fell on my head but I was too depressed to swear at it. That white, stolen pet landed in my arms and took a good-sized slice out of me. We slapped each other, and it jumped down to the floating road where a magnetizer caught it and slammed it up against somebody's artistic, eighth-dimensional statue.

The bubble came along and I got in. I dragged the pet in with me, I'm not sure why, I suppose because I had stolen it. I always attach importance to the things I steal, except where my pleasure in getting them is ruined, e.g., Jade Tower. It sat and sneered at me, slitting its big eyes. I rubbed stuff on my hand and the tear healed up. The pet looked disappointed. I set the bubble for home, but I didn't really want to go there. I'll drown again, I thought, and *farathoom* to their sixty units.

I reached for the controls, but before I did anything I thought of the pet. It would probably go *zaradann* with panic; it just wouldn't understand, when the water filled the oxygen locks. It wouldn't like the asthmatic drowsiness of dying, and I couldn't explain.

Oh well, I could always drown tomorrow.

Home. Home is where you tie your bubble, as they say. It was where I tied mine. We went up the moving ramp, me, my bee, and the pet, and under the big gold ornamental lamp in the porch that opens and shuts like one of those ancient flowers. Home. It's all glass, delicately misted up at strategic points and shot through with rainbows. It booms to the echo of tireless mechanical voices, begging to know what they can bring us to eat or drink, or do to make us laugh. Music you could hear (but is it music?) raged around the glass halls, all clicks and tattoos and crashes and chimes. I signaled my makers and took the flying floor to where they were. Older People hardly ever change their bodies, and my makers were the same as they had been for *vreks* and *vreks*. They were both male; they had been male predominantly now for ages, very *soolka* in their dark beards and tasseled sandals, having a simply *groshing,* non-Jang orgy, with lots of older women in terribly sexual, opaque dresses.

"Who are you?" they inquired mildly.

I told them.

"Oh," they turned a few memorizer mirrors on me so they could try to store my image somewhere in the place for future reference.

"Don't bother," I told them, "I'm changing again in sixty units or so."

The flying floor wafted me away from them, and they returned to their antics without a backward glance, even at my hair. I remembered one of them, the one who had been my female maker all those *vreks* and units ago, hated scarlet. Oh well, perhaps she was more tolerant now that she was a male most of the time. I couldn't recall when she'd last been female. Probably not since my post hypno-school period, when the two of them decided to set up home and include me. Usually people don't bother about staying together, but my makers had always been pretty kinky.

Up among the slowly revolving glass turrets, I had to turn on the vacuum drift and be sick. I'd sort of been waiting for it ever since the Body Displacer affair. Then I immediately felt hungry. I'd missed about ten mealtimes, what with one thing and another.

Artistically shaped fruit, toasted snow-whirls and drinks with silver ice in them came whizzing to my aid, even before I'd opened my mouth. My makers had been adding telepathy units while I was out; I'd have to be careful. I wandered into the fur room, my feast following me on dainty crystal trays and singing atrocious little songs about how tasty it was, in case I forgot the filthy stuff was there. I settled in warm, smoky-gold drifts, absentmindedly eating it all up.

I turned on the picture-vision in the ceiling and lay looking up at the most absurd love-rites I'd ever seen. Everyone had about six bodies, and they twined and twined, gorgeous colors, amid the heavy aroma of incense and the slow hiss of cymbals. I turned off the picture-vision and had the ceiling open into a sixth-dimensional cube, but you had to be in the right mood to contemplate. Sometimes you really get going with it, it sucks you in, but when you're low it just looks a mess.

I left the fur room and went to the pool. I injected myself with oxygen and swam for a long while among the waving jungle of exotic weeds at the bottom. I was a lost princess of an ancient line, seeking a monster in the turquoise depths of some forbidden sea.

Crash! That *thalldrap,* Kley, had signaled. The three-dimensional image of Kley and some *tosky* Jang party he was at careered all over the pool.

"Switch on, *ooma,*" Kley called.

"I'm tired," I said. "Go away. Go away."

But they wouldn't go. They were in ecstasy, but with energy pills to make them energetic at the same time. Oh, it was ghastly.

I got out of my ruined, forbidden-sea pool, and the dancing image followed me through our neat gardens, bashing into abstract statues and whatnot, and getting tangled up in the five-dimensional pillars. I found the recluse switch, and the party was gone, exploded out of its nonexistence back to its real existence somewhere or other.

I saw the pet bounding across the gardens, a white blur through the silk-of-aluminum grasses.

I wanted sleep.

I dreamed all night, unprogrammed dreams in which a nebulous, dark being chased me through fires and waters and finally bit me, while overhead the perfect ornamental stars under Four BEE's invisible, domed wave-roof glittered and gleamed.

I remember that time at the Prism Playgrounds I had my dreams analyzed, when Hergal and I lost each other. Not that I understood a word of what the robot told me as I stared into its big electric eyes. I really think I was too busy cursing Hergal to concentrate properly.

In my sleep, I heard an awful crash. I woke up. A flash was blazing over the city. Hergal again. We weren't far from the Zeefahr, and I nearly always heard the impact. I transparalyzed a wall and watched the flame streamers licking the sky.

What an unimaginative pest Hergal was.

But the flash was clearer now, and it wasn't Hergal.

This time it was Thinta.

How utterly *drumdik*.

6

"Hallo, Danor," I said.

He looked pleased. I'd recognized his new body immediately. I'd seen the flash as I gave myself a meal injection. (I can hardly ever face anything more solid first thing in the morning.) He's always so slim and dashing, though, whether male or female, that you couldn't miss him really. He was all long hair and drooping mustache, totally the rage just now, and both absolutely jet black with a sort of sapphire sheen to them, midnight blue eyes, and no wings. Antennae, though.

"Like me?" He turned slowly around, and I admired him. He did look rather effective and was wearing a kind of metallic second skin, with the sort of boots I'd programmed in my dream of the cursed lover.

"*Derisann,*" I said.

It was quite late morning. When I sleep, I sleep on and on, often until Four BEE gets itself dark again and turns on the starlight. Otherwise I knock back my stay-awake pills with everybody else.

"Come and eat," Danor invited. He adored food.

"Couldn't," I said.

"Oh. The Dimension Palace, then. Hatta said there's a new labyrinth on Super-Seven."

He was so enthusiastic, it seemed a pity to put out the flame, so we trailed along to the Palace.

The Committee, which is continuously bringing out reports on everyone and thing in Four BEE, states that the D.P. provides an "essential outlet for negative motivational reflexes." Anyway, that's what it says on the flashes.

The dimensions are, of course, interesting; air can be solid or different colors, or everything be inverted so that, for instance, you look at your nose in a mirror and have a fit because it's growing inward instead of out and you can only see with your eyes shut.

All told, the Dimension Palace really shakes you up. It's very popular. I suppose you don't get many shocks in Four BEE normally, except when an automatic door opens upward instead of down, or something.

Super-Seven was a total nightmare and I didn't last long. I suddenly found myself over in one place, looking back at myself in another, or rather at my body from the hips downward because I'd split in two. It was pretty ghastly. I mean you obviously haven't really split in two or anything. It's just that the law in this particular piece of dimension makes it look as if you had. I could even still experience what my legs and feet felt like, and when I put my hands down to them I could touch my thighs. When I did that I saw my hands appear by my thighs, which was reasonable, but as my thighs were on the other side of the room, it looked a bit *drumdik*. Then I found I'd split again. I was peering back at my far-away hips and legs and feet, and, a little nearer, my willowy waist and exotic bust and shoulders, all with coils of scarlet hair lying neatly about them, but chopped off at neck level. I was just a head presumably. Sweat leaped out all over me, and I could feel it all over me, thank goodness. What would happen if I moved again? I risked it. *Farathoom!* I was staring at my upper body now, and a bit farther off my poor disorientated head, and I was looking, actually, out of my feet.

At that my yells took on form and flapped all over the place; the panic button went off on my belt, and seconds later hordes of robots, oblivious of the ghastliness all around, hurried me back to sanity.

7

Danor and I floated drowsily in our adjacent baths of warm liquid air, still trembling from horror. Once the delicious relief wore off, I knew I was going to feel, as I always did, how futile that kind of nonconstructive terror is. But just now, completely attached to myself, my hair unfurling like a fabled red anemone, I was quite glad I'd come. Danor came drifting to the dividing wall and pulled himself over into my bath. We plunged around and quite soon began kissing each other, and then Danor hauled us on to one of the air cushions.

"Let's have love," he suggested, making the proposition quite appealing.

"You know that's only for Older People," I said. "It's absolutely non-Jang not to marry first."

Danor rolled on to his back and stared at the abstract picture mist on the ceiling.

"Then let's get married," he said, "for mid-*vrek*."

Mid-*vrek* is forty units and that's a long time, but Danor looked hopeful and somewhat tempting, so I agreed.

We took his bubble up Purple Waterway and dashed

through corridors of mauve liquid, with Danor thumping the controls wildly. He seemed in an awful hurry.

The Ivory Dome is a good place to marry. The quasi-robots tend to keep their opinions to themselves, and not remind you all the time that on the last six marriages they did people were more grateful and enthusiastic about paying, before rushing off and having love. In the creamy foyer we bought each other rings, five each for the left hand, and I just didn't have the heart to try to steal mine, with Danor so gallantly bawling himself hoarse in the pay-booth.

We coughed along the moving spiral to a free hall, and got into all the floating white stuff you have to wear. The quasi-robot in a black robe and sparkling headdress took our vows of loyalty to each other for mid-*vrek* with a superb show of interest.

"I promise to have love with you and no other for the period aforesaid, unless I seek annulment, which may be granted on alternate units throughout the marriage, and which must be paid for."

Four BEE's power station banks do rather well out of this, actually, because long-term liaisons nearly always fade away quicker than the participants have reckoned. Four BEE covers itself on short-term alliances, too: If you only marry for a unit or an afternoon, which naturally falls short of the annulment period, you have to pay both before *and* after your stay together.

Danor and I exchanged the ten rings without dropping any. (Hergal usually dropped every single one and they made a terrible row, crashing and rolling all over that marble.) Then, together with our robot, we paid our "thank yous," after which Danor dragged me out of Ivory Dome and into the bubble again, and we splash-dashed away to a floater.

The floaters, which drift gently in the sky and are made of plastic-reinforced cloud mass, are favorites with newly-weds. I'd been in them quite often, but their niceness seldom palls.

Danor pushed me gently but firmly on to a large, soft but

adjustable bed of gold and purple storm-drift, and ran a
melter over my clothing and his.

"I find your body most attractive," he breathed. "It's
one of the best you've ever designed."

Flattered, I smoldered under his caresses, and was rather
shocked when he suddenly drew away and sat up.

"What's wrong, Danor?"

Danor looked sad.

"It's no use," he said. "I thought, with you, it might be,
but it isn't."

We tried again, however, in various positions, and it began to get dark, and we were tired of it all by then. We rested
and drank love-potions, and swallowed ecstasy and energy
pills, and finally lay side by side, panting with unproductive
fatigue.

"If only," Danor murmured, "we could have had love at
the Dimension Palace, I know it would have been all right.
It's all this delay. It's always the delay." He peered at me
soulfully. "I haven't had love now, successfully, for ten
vreks."

I was horrified. Poor Danor.

"Surely," I said, hiding my disappointment rather well, I
thought, "it's just that you're predominantly female, the
same as I am. Possibly more so. When I was male last and
Kley was female, everything went splendidly. But you've
been male for ages. I expect you need a change."

"Unfortunately," Danor said, "it's no use then, either.
Just easier to pretend it is, when I'm a girl."

I tried to think of some bright encouraging sentence, but
none came.

Danor went to a cloud wall and turned on the pressure so
that a large oval window appeared. He looked at twilit Four
BEE, glittering underneath.

"Goodbye," he said. And he jumped out and fell hundreds of feet into the city. It stunned me. He looked as though
he meant it, even though it was a pointless act when they'd
only shove him in a new body ten splits after he hit the
ground. A most weird feeling went over me, like when you

meet the dragon in a dream—only not like that because that's enjoyable terror and this wasn't—and I struggled and tried not to let the feeling fill me up. And suddenly I recollected we'd married for entire mid-*vrek,* and now I'd have to pay for the annulment tomorrow. So a warm reassuring anger came instead. Annulment is something you can't steal, and you can't marry anyone else, even for half an hour, until you've bought it.

I fumed and fussed around the floater all night; I punched at those silly clouds and shouted at them when they served up this *groshing* meal I didn't want.

I faced the dawn disheveled, not wanting to stay up there and hating the thought of all that thanking I was going to have to do at Ivory Dome, with the quasi-robot probably looking disapproving that we'd lasted such a ridiculously short time.

"Attlevey, ooma," said a voice, and I saw the signal light was on, and there in the room with me was the three-dimensional image of this gorgeous girl, with a body very like mine, except for jet black hair with a sapphire sheen to it.

"It's me, Danor," she said.

"Groshing," I said. And a little cold bead rattled in my mind, but I was fed up to my back pearly teeth, wasn't I? And I soon forgot it.

"I thought you'd like to know," Danor said calmly, "that I'm going up to Ivory Dome now, to pay for the annulment."

"Thanks," I barked, and flicked the recluse switch.

8

I wandered around Four BEE all day, then felt a bit odd and realized that I hadn't eaten again, and had a meal injection.

I met Thinta near the Robotics Museum. She actually *likes* it in there. I didn't know her at first in her new body, but she was just the same in fact, underneath the soft gray fur, and her eyes, although without any whites now, were the usual clear green.

"It was the Dream Rooms," Thinta explained as we drank snow-in-gold at an underwater restaurant. "I always dream I'm some sort of cat thing. I wanted them to make me a cat's body, but they refused. The fur's only a compromise, really." She started to grumble about the Committee and the way they hadn't let her have a built-in purring system, and I got away as soon as I could.

I honestly wanted to cut every single friend out of my circle, I was suddenly feeling so *droad* and alien with all of them, but in the end I officially cut myself out, which was easier and then I sat on the steps of Jade Tower under the dragon roars and sprays, and cried.

I mean, it's polite to cry when you're cut out of anyone's circle, even if it's your own. But it went on and on. I couldn't stop.

I think I cried all night.

PART 2

1

I got home about morning, and found my makers were in the act of splitting up.

"Home is yours," they said kindly, "we've made our own arrangements." Older People can do that—just pack up and leave each other and go off with someone else whenever they like. They were both still male.

Robots were moving out their stuff. It felt odd, seeing them go, just like that, not that we'd ever been close or anything. You never are with makers, even if they *do* stay in the same place with you after hypno-school is finished.

"Don't worry about the home-payments to the Committee every third *vrek*," they added. "We know how you hate paying, so we've made provision to pay for you, alternately. It seems only right, after so long."

I was almost glad when they'd finally gone. I felt so peculiar about it all.

And home sort of . . . echoed. I don't know.

Hatta signaled me ages afterward, or perhaps not so long, really, it just seemed ages. His voice invaded my privacy, but without any image—probably just as well, knowing Hatta.

"*Attlevey,* Hatta," I sighed.

"What's all this," Hatta demanded, "about cutting yourself out of your own circle? You can't. It's not—well—it's not ethical."

"Oh," I said.

"No," said Hatta. "Are you feeling low because of the annulment with Danor?"

"No," I said; I wasn't sure.

"You need cheering up," Hatta told me. "I'll take you for a meal."

"No. Thank you."

"Well, the Adventure Palace, then? There's a new Upper-Ear symphony in Fourth Sector. Fire-riding?"

"Really, Hatta. I honestly can't—"

"Look, *ooma,* I'm serious," said Hatta seriously. I cursed him, but rather wearily. "I'd like so much to marry you. Just for the afternoon."

"Let's see you," I said coldly.

"Well, er," said Hatta.

"Your image," I said. "Now."

"There's something wrong with the control. I can't seem to get an image through to you—"

"Nothing ever goes wrong with the control," I said. Well, it doesn't. Hatta muttered. And then, there he was.

"Oh Hatta!" I shouted. "You utter *thalldrap!* You *floop!* Oh go away!"

He was huge, bluish, shiny, lumpy, but it was the two heads that really got me down.

"But *ooma*—"

"No. Nonononono! If you want me so much, get yourself a reasonable body." He hung around in midair, undecided, and so *drumdik* I nearly went out of my mind. I threw an abstract stone thing, with moving colors in it, at him, and thrust down the nearest recluse switch.

I felt better, though, after throwing something at Hatta.

More my bad-tempered self, I suppose. The pet came crashing in from the gardens and bit me, and I chased it all over the place, trying to land it one with a big furry cushion, and with machines clucking and clicking disapprovingly around us, as they tried to get on with the cleaning. It was quite merry.

Eventually the pet curled up warily on a suspended flying floor, just out of my reach, and went to sleep, keeping one orange eye open and one fang delicately protruding, just to remind me I suppose.

I ate a meal and began to think.

I was tired of being Jang.

2

I took my bubble down Peridot Waterway, with the pet sitting on a passenger couch, staring at me. I'd tried to leave it behind, but hadn't got the bubble side closed in time. It had developed a new game in between starings, trying to swat my bee as it zoomed overhead, always threatening to come down. I noticed that the bee seemed to keep aloft much better with six white paws and a mouthful of teeth careering at it.

I tied up a little way down from the Zeefahr and took a moving street to Second Sector's Committee Hall. The pet bit legs on the street, and things got a trifle noisy, though the Older People seemed to forgive me as I was Jang. Ironical!

We tumbled off, me, my bee, and the pet, and went into the Hall, which is black and imposing. They make it look as antisocial as possible to keep everyone out, but it doesn't seem to work. The place was packed.

I sat down in a free space in one of the gently revolving circles of chairs and pressed the Attention Required light. Everyone seemed to be complaining today. Complaints about picture-vision programs not being erotic enough, and old-established aphrodisiacs and laxatives that didn't seem to work anymore. Moans about fading silk-grass in the parks, falling leaves being heavier than last *vrek,* the starlight being late or dim or something over First Sector last night. People saying they were paying too often for their homes, and thank-you-hysterics who said they weren't paying often enough.

A robot arrived in front of me.

"Request?"

"Age and status change," I said.

There was a sort of hush, and I could feel eyes peering at me and tiny minds thinking: "Whoopee! A freak!"

"Registered," snapped the robot, then couldn't resist adding: "One-A, First-Class Unusual. Do you have medical grounds for this?"

"No."

"Do you have any grounds at all?"

"*I* think so," I said. "You probably wouldn't."

And I glared around at those peering eyes and suddenly noticed the pet was glaring at them too, snarl-hissing nastily. I stroked its pale head and just managed to get my fingers out of its reach in time.

The robot had gone away, but very quickly a messenger flew up to me and signaled me to follow. Everyone else grumbled. I'd jumped to first place, due entirely to original-ity. Probably somebody felt like a good laugh before getting on to the usual boring routine.

I went up the moving spiral after the messenger and was ushered through glassy corridors to a round compact room, with a moving painting on the ceiling and a non-wet water carpet. A quasi-robot official sat in a floating crystallize chair, anchored more or less to one spot by a golden chain. I sat on the other crystallize chair, also anchored but rather lower than his, and, to my surprise and astonished discom-fort, the pet gave a splashing leap and landed firmly on my lap. It sat bolt upright and looked at the Q-R. We both looked.

"Now," said the quasi-robot, gently flicking his mus-tache at me, "what was your request again?"

"Age and status change," I said, undaunted. Well, I pretended I was.

"Hmm," said the quasi-robot. He stared serenely at the spot just above my eyes. My bee fell on my head, the pet jumped and aimed at it, the chair dipped, and we all fell into the water carpet, creating a most ghastly tidal wave.

"Oh *farath—onk*!" I started swearing and hastily toned it down, just in case. You never know with Q-Rs.

The chair followed me and I got back on. The pet landed on me again, unfortunately.

"Yes," said the Q-R, "I see."

We floated gracefully around for about five million *vreks,* and then he added: "You're Jang, of course."

"Yes."

"Hmm."

"And that's the whole trouble," I told him.

"Oh come," chortled the Q-R, just like a maker really, "the prime of life. Total awareness of the eighty senses, the peak of imaginative resource—"

I really detest people quoting that nonsense at me, but I sat very still and listened politely, beaming as though I thought he was the most absolutely *groshing* thing I'd ever floated around a room with. Eventually he shut up. I said:

"You're quite right, of course, but I honestly think I've speeded up in my development somewhere, and I need to go on to the next stage, an Older Person."

"And how long, my dear," and he smiled, "have you been one of the Jang?"

"Ages," I said.

"Hmm."

We floated around again. I looked up at the ceiling picture, and there were these beautiful bodies, with leaves and flowers growing out of them, doing a sort of dimensional dance, so that bits kept disappearing and reappearing somewhere else.

"I've just looked you up in the files," the Q-R told me abruptly. They do it with the telepathy units in their elbows, so Hatta says, but it gives you a fright all the same, to be perfectly frank. The usual mind-blower is: "I've just looked you up in the files, and your new body has not been registered as yet. Thus, you are temporarily dead." I recollect that happened to Hergal once, when I was with him in the Adventure Palace. We both felt pretty funny about it. I think that's why he always stays in Limbo for two or three units now, just in case. Anyway the Q-R went on:

"According to your history records, you have only been Jang for a quarter *rorl*. The usual period is at least half a *rorl*, my dear young lady. Except, of course, in *very* exceptional cases."

"I'm an exceptional case," I cried.

"Oh, I don't really think so, my dear," smarmed the Q-R.

He started to explain, but I didn't understand, and I don't honestly think he did either. So I cut in:

"Can't you test me? Isn't there some sort of guide to find out special cases?"

"Well, er," said the Q-R. He went off into another trance, flicking through memory banks and whatnot. "It is rather an involved business. Mental and physical examinations and so on."

"Right," I said.

I'd actually startled him. *Derisann.*

"What?"

"I'm ready," I said. "When do we start?"

He blinked at me a while.

"Er. Would you wait one moment?" he said, and lowered his chair to the floor. *He went across the water carpet and left me there.* I mean, they never *do* that. It's all part of the superiority thing that they stay in their chairs, and you're the one who has to bob in and out. I'd really confused him. My ears felt hot with excitement and a kind of panic. Was I really ready to go on to the next stage? Was it the answer? Suddenly I felt like bolting out of the door, but I stopped myself. Being Jang was what was getting me down. It must be. Therefore, logically, being non-Jang would help to make me feel better. The door went up and another messenger signaled me to follow.

I went after it, trembling as if I were in the Dimension Palace.

3

We went through a subway under Gold Waterway, a private subway belonging to the Committee Hall, riding in a little sledge bobbing about a foot off the ground on drifts of pretty pink steam. The gold water-light shone through the transparent roof making everything look rather cheerful, except me, I'll bet. I took a serenity pill, and felt gently euphoric and entirely capable of dealing with anything.

The sledge went under archways and ended up in a big hall, full of flying floors. The messenger got me on one, the bee fell on, and the pet ripped and clawed its way after us. Up we all went and arrived in this big, crystallize and steel room, where the bee suddenly found itself magnetized on a rack full of other bees, and the pet was whisked away by robots, grumbling about unhygienic fur and so on.

It reminded me of parts of Limbo, and so did the quasi-robot medicine man in pale attire who waved me ever so graciously to a big soft seat, and sat down opposite—rather higher than me, naturally—hands together, and recording units no doubt whirring away inside.

Then we went through it again. Obvious, I suppose. I

really should hang on another quarter *rorl,* and come back then. Did I know (Interesting Incidental Fact) that quite often people were still predominantly Jang after half a *rorl,* and sometimes went on for a whole one? Wasn't it conversely possible then, I said, for somebody to be out of the Jang stage after a quarter *rorl?* Well, it *had* happened, very occasionally, he admitted (Suave Concession of Point) but their behavior in these cases indicated this and mine, apparently, did not. Anyway, I told him, I'm here now, so you might as well get on with testing me. I suppose I'll have to pay whatever happens. He looked slightly embarrassed, but rode it well. Of course he could, he said, if it would set my mind at rest. (Bland Diplomacy in Dealing with Jang Female Barbarian.)

"Some simple little questions first," he comforted me, and referred to a reading screen which he had turned on in the desk pillar in front of him. "Firstly, do you ever steal?"

Well, all right, I jumped. No good lying either. Anyway, for all I knew, it might be one of the first signs of true anti-Jang.

"Occasionally," I said.

"And what do you steal?"

I had a sudden queasy feeling they were after me for Evasion, so I didn't say a word.

"Let me assure you," he said then, "that anything which is said during these tests will be kept strictly confidential. The only use to which we will put the information is in finding what is best for your future."

Well, robots don't lie, so I answered:

"Different things. It doesn't really matter what, terribly. It's when I'm low, usually, or getting *droad.*"

He nodded, and I thought he looked pleased, which had to be bad, but it was too late now.

"Now, about your sex-life—er, 'having love.' You're predominantly female, but male once in a while, I see. You've devised a very sensible balance, I should think."

Congratulations, me. He was trying to knock my poor little guard down already, was he?

"That's right," I said, "but I've been put on a sixty unit body restriction, for overdoing my changes."

I meant to make him disapproving, but again there was that little smile. Oh . . . *onk!*

"And about how often do you have love?"

"Oh, pretty often, really."

"Could you be a little more precise?"

"It averages about once every six units. Less lately, though."

I'd scored. Non-Jang not to have love practically all the time, and it was true I'd lost interest. . . .

"When was the last time you married?"

"Two units ago."

"I see." Again he was pleased.

"But it didn't work out—" I hastily added, but he glossed over that.

"Do you have a favorite meal or drink?"

I said no. Food didn't do that much for me. He asked if I ate now, what I'd like, so I said nut steak, which was the very first thing that came into my head. I couldn't tell his reactions much after that. He was getting a bit more careful.

It was clothes next.

I'd deliberately come out in the least Jang thing I could get hold of, but it's difficult somehow to get the really *soolka* stuff. This was transparent at the top, but pretty thickly jeweled and embroidered, and the sleeves and skirt were deep gold and almost opaque. No ornaments either, and my hair plain instead of coiled through with flowers and pearls and metal things, with gold bells, probably, on the end of each strand.

"I like deep colors," I said truthfully, "not just glassy metal-silk with a lot of skin showing."

"Yes, I understand. And what do you wear? I see the top of your dress reveals all it should, and most attractive it is too."

Oh, *v . . . n* you!

"It's not what I prefer—" I began.

"Then why are you wearing it, my dear?"

He just went on talking as I frantically tried to explain how Jade Tower and Silver Mountain, and all the other clothes and jewelery centers, drag you off to the Jang counters and stone you with Upper-Ear music, and you just can't seem to get anything in the older range, no matter how you yell and threaten.

"Activities," I heard him purr, when I eventually stopped trying to make him hear *me*. "Do you go to the Dimension Palace?"

"Yes," I said.

"The Adventure Palace?"

"Yes."

"The Dream Rooms?"

"Yes." Anti-Jang? Apparently not.

"Hmm. Do you always program similiar dreams?"

Ah ha, thought I, now you're in for it, *ooma*. My dreams are non-non-non what all the flashes tell us Jang dreams should be.

"More or less similiar," I started, "and—"

"Good," he said. Just: "Good."

"Don't you want to hear what I dream?"

"I don't really think it's relevant."

"Well, *I* think it is." I told him about my last dream, dwelling on the dragon and the lover and the blossoming desert. He just sat and listened. When I stopped, he smiled.

"It sounds very agreeable, if rather energetic," he applauded me.

"But it's weird, isn't it? An abnormal dream?"

"Not at all," he said. "Agreeably normal. For a start, you obviously have your male tendencies nicely coordinated with the female ones. You make yourself both the fighting hero and the swooning maiden. You have a subconscious and refreshing yearning to see the desert waste blossom. And very good color sense, I might add."

"On the flashes," I began heatedly, "the average Jang dream ecstasy is to be a mote of pulsing light, sucked to and fro between fiery suns—"

"The average, my dear, is not always as totally represen-

tative as it might be. You are what is termed an active
dreamer. You like a story. In point of fact, most young people
who attend the Adventure Palace in addition to the Dream
Rooms invent sagas similiar to yours.''

I felt shattered. I think I went pale. No one ever *talked*
about it, having that sort of dream. I suppose I honestly
thought we were queer to have them, and made up tales of
how we'd been light motes afterward, so no one else would
laugh. And I suddenly thought of Hergal telling me he
dreamed of flying.

"But I spend ages on the programming," I tried weakly,
"designing all the costumes and so on."

"That simply means your mind is more productive in
that region than those of your friends who rely on the robot's
judgment. And you are not unique."

There were a few more questions after that which sort of
passed in a daze. Then we went on to pictures.

"That's red," I said as the screen flashed red. "And
that's blue. Pink," I added, "pink with blue edges. Green.
Green and red. Purple." The screen switched from color to
shape, speeding up even faster. "Square. Circle. Cube. Sixth-
dimensional cube. Fourth-dimensional rectangle. Circle. Oc-
tagon." I couldn't work out why all this was going on, but we
rushed away to a succession of buildings and parks and
things. Was he testing my eyesight? Or whether I could talk
that fast? Then the buildings and parks started appearing in
weird mists of color, with dragons kicking them over or sort
of fire clouds going up all around them, and eventually I said,
did he have to, it made me feel funny. I couldn't help it, it
did. And he looked really delighted, the *floop*.

After that we played a kind of game where a picture of a
person or thing appeared, and I could direct objects at it, to
which it responded accordingly. There were sky-boats I could
lose in cloud, and a lovely shot of the Robotics Museum I
floored with an enormous avalanche of syrup and fruit, and I
chased grumpy quasi-robots with mechanical ants, and finally
realized he'd lulled me and I was enjoying myself, that I'd

probably done everything all wrong and proved I ought to go on being Jang for *rorl* upon *rorl* upon *rorl*. There was also some sort of unheard soothe-music about, making me relaxed and gaily irresponsible all over the place, or perhaps I shouldn't have had that pill on the way down. I didn't seem able to put the brake on.

After the pictures, we went on to three-dimensional images, with smell and sound and aura and so on.

I forget all the stuff we waded through. There was one of a snake-thing swallowing itself that kept cropping up, and a woman dressed in flames, dancing to drumbeats that nearly drove me mad wanting to have love with her, or be her having love with someone else, or something. I was getting confused. I honestly thought I was male once. You know, I just knew I was, only I wasn't.

Then we had the last two images. The first was a young male glittering with Jang gear and great big angel's wings, with long copper hair and mustache, and a beautiful male body. Oh, he was *derisann*. Then, next to him appeared this older man, *soolka* and a bit solid-looking. You could imagine him paying for *everything,* and calling you "my dear," like Hatta does but more so. And it was so obvious that, even in my bemused state, I snapped alert, and when the quasi-robot pointed I was ready.

"What do you think of this young male?" he inquired, all smiles, and I steeled myself. I felt I was betraying the gorgeous, lovely, desirable being the Jang male was, condemning myself to a life without love with such as he. But I said coolly:

"Very nice. But those wings are a bore, aren't they?" and that at least was what I usually felt, even though, right now, I fancied him, wings and all.

The quasi-robot didn't waver, however. Still all smiles, he pointed at the other male.

"And how about this?"

"Oh, he's *groshing,* absolutely *derisann!* He drives me *zaradann!* I want him!"

And then—! The two images had swapped clothes, ex-

pressions, wings, everything. I felt utterly bewildered. I knew
dimly this wasn't fair to me somehow. I stared at the copper-
haired young male in the *soolka* clothing and staid expression, and the older male all nudity and chains and gaiety,
with two great silly wings flapping about behind him, and the
quasi-robot said:

"And who do you prefer now?"

And it seemed all right. Really. Logical. The young male
had been made into an Older Person, and the Older Person
was Jang. I'd won. And I'd soon take the pompous look off
that copper-haired *ooma*.

"Him," I said, and I pointed at his now-hidden but beautiful chest.

And the quasi-robot looked pleased.

"Well, that's right, isn't it?" I cried. "He's non-Jang,
isn't he? Absolutely *soolka*, in fact."

"I've noticed," the Q-R remarked, rather gently, "that
you've used Jang-slang predominantly throughout our talk."

"Well," I snapped, "I've heard predominantly nothing
else for a quarter *rorl*. What do you expect? And you haven't
answered my question. The young male is non-Jang now,
isn't he?"

"He is still," the Q-R said, "a *young* male."

And for the life of me I couldn't see it, until the messenger had led me away for the physical examination, and I was
on my back, being internally reviewed by scanners in the
roof.

4

They checked me, thoroughly, making sure nothing had gone amiss with my nerve units or brain likely to create depression or hysteria, and made notes on the way I had designed my latest body. It was a Jang body, of course—not a weirdo body for Essential Experience like Hatta's little efforts, it is true—but Jang nevertheless, at its carefree and most flower-like best. They also went through files on my other recent bodies, and I suppose they were all the same. They tested my reactions to ecstasy and energy, and even put me in a trance-state, in which I thought I was marrying that gorgeous, copper-haired male for the afternoon and then having love with him. I must admit it was *derisann,* but when I woke up again, I knew I'd sunk like a stone.

Even the silver-water cordial they gave me, to lend me strength to face the Committee Hall again, was a sort of test.

I went through the subway on a sledge, alone this time. A robot had apparently taken my bee and the pet on ahead of me to my bubble.

A messenger led me back into the round room with the water carpet, and I sat down in the floating chair again, opposite my original interviewing Q-R.

"Ah yes," he said benevolently. "Not too exhausted, I hope. These tests are rather sapping, I'm afraid."

"Yes," I agreed. "Well?"

He smiled.

"Well." He spread immaculate hands. "I think you know already."

"You refuse to send me on to the next stage?"

"You're not ready, my dear young lady. Your mentality, your tastes, your appetites are still belonging entirely to the Jang. Minor deviations do not count. If, by some error, we had applied for your changing as you suggest, it would have brought you almost immediate distress."

"This is absurd," I said. "I'm distressed now."

"Of course." He looked at me, anxious for my happiness. "I think you will find that the answer to your problem is to throw yourself more wholeheartedly into Jang pursuits. Fill your time. Stop thinking: 'I must be joyous,' and then hating everyone when you fail to achieve joy in this manner. Relax."

"Thank you," I said stiffly. "I suppose I have to pay?"

"That is entirely up to you," the Q-R said blandly. "If you would rather not, there is no need."

So I was spared that at least.

I went out feeling hopeless, in a sort of nightmare. I kept saying over and over to myself: They've done me. It's all a big plot. None of those questions meant anything, just a sort of game to make me think they'd tried.

I got to the bubble and shut the door, and kicked my bee into relative submission. I sat down, and there was the pet in my lap. I looked at the pet, into orange jungles of eyes that had lived somewhere far out near Four BOO, among rock-thrusts and restless desert.

"They're right," I said, "it's no good. I'm still Jang, and I don't want to skip ahead at all. What's wrong then? What is it that's so terribly the matter with me?"

And I put my arms around the pet and my cheek in its fur; it let me stay like that for ten whole splits before it bit me.

5

Hatta signaled yet again, and I was so fed up and bewildered I actually said I'd meet him for eighth meal.

We went to Blue Sky and sat on the see-through floor, with the darkening city moving slowly under us, and tried to eat salad-on-ice without being ill from vertigo.

They had assured me at the Committee Hall that my disgraceful urge to change from being Jang would never leak out, and that my friends, therefore, would never curl up into hooting hysterics at my foolishness—I more or less quote. I kept getting an uncontrollable desire to tell Hatta, though; he always seemed so reliable and stolid. I suppose the ugliness helped. But I didn't. I think the Committee staff had done a good job and I really was ashamed.

As we got on to the confectionery and cactus-pineapple stage, he thrust the marriage proposal at me again, and I again declined.

"I couldn't stand it," I said. "I feel *tosky* enough as it is."

We sat and stared down at the lights lighting up, and I wondered why, if he found the need of me so pressing, he

didn't change into something attractive. I liked Hatta after all,
and in a pretty body he'd be nice. Then I thought, perhaps he
does it deliberately to stop me from ever agreeing. Perhaps
he doesn't really want me at all, and just likes to kid himself
he does. This somehow made me feel as if I'd wilted, and I
said I wanted to go home.

He's very good really. You know he'll probably be
around when you need him, and go away when you want him
to.

I wandered through my lonely glassy palace, looking
vaguely for the pet, who didn't appear.

"You should throw yourself more wholeheartedly into
Jang pursuits," the Q-R had told me. Throw yourself, presumably, anywhere but at the Committee. All right, I would
devise a program of adventures for tomorrow. Thousands of
splits later I lost my mind or something, and went raging
around, totally frustrated at my lack of enthusiasm for anything I could think of. I turned on all the picture visions and
music units, and woke up the kitchen and house cleaners, and
sat there in the middle of absolute chaos, pulling at strands of
my hair.

I took a hypno-croon to bed with me and got it to say to
me, all night long in my sleep:

"I will be constructive, I will be constructive. I will
think of something wonderful to do."

6

And I thought of something. I actually did. I opened my eyes with it nestling in my brain.

I'd work.

Something to involve me, take up my time, something to wake up for. I wasn't quite sure what sort of thing was going in Four BEE. One of my makers had once done a spell with the flashes, and came back home every mid-*vrek* refreshed to an enchanting degree.

I splashed happily in my lagoon bath, dressed as Jangily as I possibly could, just to please them all, and sped away to the Zeefahr in my bubble, thence to the Committee Hall.

I was ushered straight in to my old friend with the water carpet, who looked at me nervously.

"I've decided to take your advice," I declared. "I'm enjoying being a Jang."

"Er, good," he answered.

"Like it?" I pirouetted, displaying all my beads and gold chains and flowers and tinsel and see-through. "And I've eaten the most popular Jang first meal, toasted angel-food, and bought a whole new track of Upper-Ear music—stolen it, actually," I confided, all gay abandon. It was really wild. But my Q-R wasn't taken in. His emotion gauges must have been standing up like quills. He smiled and said:

"And what precisely did you want, young lady?"

Smite him with my fiery wings, I thought.

"Work," I cooed.

"I understand," he said, and we looked at each other.

"I'm afraid," he said a little later, "that we have come back to the original problem."

"Oh yes?" I said, and I must have looked dangerous. His hand strayed to a summoner-button, ready to call in millions of loyal robots to rescue him if I leaped for his mustache or anything.

"You see," he said, eyeing me, "the Committee does not employ the Jang. Your minds should be free to explore recreation and pleasure. Older People, if they wish, may render some sort of voluntary service, certainly, but in the formative years . . ."

"Have you ever asked any Jang whether they'd like to spend a few formative years doing something slightly useful?" I demanded.

"Er—" he said.

" 'New laws for new worlds.' I believe that's one of the Committee's mottoes," I galloped on.

"That is not—" he tried.

"And how do you know this generation of Jang is just like the last generation of Jang? Well? We might all be an emotional breakthrough, and you're just sitting there ignoring it."

He looked flustered, but not by my brilliant, oratorical logic. He looked flustered in the way you look flustered trying to explain to a desert animal that it must pee in the vacuum drift, *not* up the picture-vision. But then he suddenly knocked the breath out of me by asking:

"And what did you have in mind to work at?"

"Well, what is there?" I stuttered.

"Very little," he told me, "particularly just at the moment." He added: "You'll be taking away the chance to work from an Older Person, who's entitled to it," but I ignored that. Who cared? Not him, I bet.

And then he stood up.

"I'll take you," he said, "on a little tour of Four BEE's work centers. That is the usual procedure when someone has a query of this nature."

We rolled out in a little, low-flying Committee Hall sky-boat. The wind kept thrashing my miles of scarlet hair into the Q-R's eyes, but he was very good about it. My bee fell on his head and he was very good about that too.

We swooped into the nets of Second Sector's Flash Center, and the way the Q-R just slammed off the controls and let us go down out of order, nearly missing the nets altogether, reminded me nostalgically of Hergal.

Inside it was bright, plastered with jeweled slogans and reports of particularly brilliant (?) occurrences, such as the latest Jang sabotage, letting in a volcanic cloud-mass over First Sector two nights ago and blotting out the stars (oh, yes, both the Q-R and I remembered that one) or one of Four BOO's desert animals escaping from captivity in Fourth and causing "havoc and destruction." Well, havoc, possibly, I suppose. In the main hall robots came charging in and out, bearing tidings from every corner of the city, and screens relayed pictures from high vantage points complete with in-stant zoom-lens if anything epically frantic, like a moving street jamming for two splits, started to happen. I must say it looked very alert and alive, all of it, that is, except for the Older People, two of them, sitting watching picture-vision and occasionally popping a button or flicking a dial.

"The robots, screens, etc., do the news gathering for the flashes, as you can see. The banks of monitors here receive and sort the Committee reports and essays on social behavior. This computer relays direct from Limbo each day's list of body changes as it is compiled, and this one sends out indi-vidual identifications at the owner's request." The Q-R took me around the room and gave me his little lecture.

"And how about them?" I inquired, pointing at the two oblivious workers.

"Oh," said the Q-R, "they work the buttons which activate each flash."

"So really, without them, the whole place collapses?" I asked.

"Well, not entirely," the Q-R admitted. "Each button pops automatically after half a split."

"I see," I said.

There were one or two other wildly exciting tasks, all of which would happen automatically if forgotten, which was just as well, as you could see the two workers had just about nodded off.

"Thank you," I said. "Where do we go next?"

Pathetic, really. I thought City Planning sounded promising. Actually what happens is this: The Committee does a survey, for instance, and finds how the air traffic going to the Adventure Palace gets in a jam near the Time and Space Monument. So the Committee draws up a report saying this is because of the queue of bird-planes waiting to drop into the Monument nets, and how about making them a special bridge to go and queue on, which will get them out of everyone else's way. This comes through on a computer and is translated by another computer, after which the message is given to the Older Person, officially designated Planner. Swooning at his exhilarating task, he digs up an assortment of suitable machines and programs them to work out the best way the bridge should be built, of what, when, how traffic should be diverted meanwhile, etc. Then, proudly bearing the machines' mathematics, color proposals, artistic balance directions and sign-posting arrangements in paws clammy with enthusiasm, he trundles off to another machine park, gets a robot to feed the instructions into the relevant computer, and palpitatingly watches metal apparatus go to work making the diversion bridge. And they really kid themselves they've made something, this lot.

"That spiral I constructed by the Thought Museum,"

they modestly let drop, keeping one hot eye on the nearest computer all the time, just in case the Committee's found a blockage in Purple Waterway, or anything similarly heart stopping.

I was, by now, prepared for the worst at the Center of Artistic Design.

It's in pastel shades, with gigantic, almost-but-not-really-there water statues outside, and bronze trees dripping bronze foliage over you. I got tangled up and nearly strangled in my hair before the Q-R got me out. He gave me an odd look. Perhaps he thought I was going after a new body again.

And then we were inside, up a couple of flying floors, and I got excited because people were actually *doing* things. I remarked—well, I squawked really—on this fact.

"Ah, yes," my Q-R said kindly, "there is room here for the personal touch."

Then we stopped to look at an elated female bashing bits out of a huge white stone block, and I noticed that (a) she was using a machine with a sharp biting tooth on the end, and (b) that the stone was marked out pretty clearly, and that the marks magnetized the tooth. A bit farther off, the artists had got tired and were letting the machines crank on with it alone, while they had fire-of-wine and biscuits.

My Q-R must have seen me go all pale and mad. He said quickly:

"The actual designing is done by the artists themselves."

"Prove it," I challenged.

We rode up again and found them hard at it, and they really were, only it went something like this:

Artists's question: "If I put a rod in at right angles on the left, will it balance?"
Red light, indicating the thing will fall down.
Artists's question: "If I lift the rod with a second rod, twice its width, and support the two with a skeleton cube entering sideways, will it balance then?"

Yellow light, and a spool of metal paper indicating
  that, yes, that
might do it and (helpful advice) two skeleton cubes
  diametrically
opposed would ensure success.

There was also: "Look here, you robot, I can manage the
eyes if you give me a hand with the cheek bones." And:
"Would your machine mix me that lovely yellow shade the
sky goes at sunset? Mine's gone pink."

I stood there and stared at it all, and went *zaradann*.

"Get me some stone!" I screamed at everyone. It really
bothered them. My Q-R touched my arm and I yelled even
louder: "Stone, and a chisel machine! And paint! Now!"

7

Well, I was an idiot, wasn't I?

It fell to pieces, didn't it?

Not until I'd given it my all, though, of course.

Robots trundled it up and sort of threw it at my feet, this big rough block of impossible-looking stuff. I didn't really know what I was doing, and they were standing around gawping at me. The Q-R sat down in an artistic-looking chair and appeared to be contemplating.

I took aim. There were no easy magnetized markings here, but the rush with which the chisel-tooth started nearly took my arm off. And I found I'd gone right through to the other side. Well, I mean, I'd meant to, hadn't I? Courage! I tried another shot and this time nearly went right through the block after the chisel. I flicked my hair back and had another go, and managed to join the two chasms together with a thin swooping arc. I'd got something.

I hacked and scraped away at the thing for ages, chips flying off into the magnetized pans in the floor, and soon I was crawling about inside the cavities, drilling and bashing. It was very intricate and I liked it, and I'd stopped being conscious of eyes peering.

All at once, someone grabbed me by my hair in an agonizing vice. I swore at them vigorously, until I realized it wasn't a someone after all. My scarlet tresses had got wound up in the stone lace. The Q-R had to come down, ever so patiently, and untie me, and after that he had to come down again and again.

"Oh, use a cutter or something," I snapped, as I finally found myself hanging in a great big oval frame, in a sort of frenzied spider's web of hair, with millions of stone chips buzzing around in it. My hair got shorter and shorter after this and, by the time it was lopped to the backs of my knees, I decided I'd had enough and got out before I went bald.

There were enormous scoops of gloriously colored paint ranged up around my working area, and I dipped in and out of them with gusto. I began to change color too. My hair was now several feet deep in platinum pink, and I had a viridian nose. I played with the color to create illusions, painting the shadowed recesses in luminous, vivid tones, and the prominent planes thunderous crimsons and violets, carrying a motif in an unbroken line across varying angles, and making whirlpools like fire appear and retreat across the stone.

We'd missed endless meals, my audience and I. It was well into the afternoon.

I stood back and wiped my hand across my brow, forgetting. I didn't care anyway. I was proud. I could see it now, high in the Sun Gardens of Fourth Sector, or gracing some glassy walk beside a waterway, reflected softly in the tide. I just hadn't noticed the tiny little cracks where the chisel-tooth had slipped slightly, the small imbalance, the way one side was somewhat heavier than the other.

I went up to it and brought my hand down on the top, a sort of pat on the head for my lovely stone pet. The minute I touched it, it made this ghastly sound and the whole lot, drooling uncemented paint, collapsed slowly and with filthy finality, inward, inward, till it was just a heap of rubble.

They dug me out.

The Q-R smiled.

"It's always as well," he said, "to seek the advice of the computer in these matters."

"V. . . .n the computer!" I said, and, amid shocked silence, he whisked me away.

8

He was pretty nice, really. He didn't tell me not to sit and sulk, as I sat and sulked.

We had a meal injection each, for which he paid, but I don't think it was *that* chivalrous of him. Q-R's always find that sort of thing much easier to do, since the relevant circuits are built into them. After that we fluttered around and saw hundreds of bored people being supervisors of Water-Flow, Air-Traffic control, Food-Planning, etc. All they had to do was pop buttons and turn dials, which popped and turned anyway. It began to get dark, and he said that was about it, apart from the Picture-Vision Devisory Center, and I grabbed him and said I wanted to see it, so we went. I think I only got enthusiastic on a reflex. It was going to be crawling with machinery and computers like everything else, wasn't it?

It's a big dome-y place, with actual picture-vision of simply enormous, gigantic figures galumping around being erotic and so on going on all over it.

Inside we went up and down softly gold-lit corridors, smoky with incense, with big metallic flames writhing around the ceiling, and saw lots of neat little shut-off rooms, with solitary Devisors working away inside them. We weren't allowed to crash in and disturb them, but you could plug in a little pickup and get a complete resumé of what was going on. And what these people were doing was actually coming out of their own minds. They used machinery for reference purposes, like making sure this particular sequence wasn't going to clash with, or be too similar to, the one that had gone out ten splits beforehand. And they were working the controls themselves to make the images do what they wanted on a great big screen in the ceiling.

The ideas were rather monotonous, though, all dancing and twining and having love, full of flowers and floating hair. Gorgeous, but banal. A challenge.

"This is it," I said.

"What?" the Q-R asked.

"The work I want to do," I said. "I mean, they *are* actually *doing* it, aren't they?"

He looked the tiniest bit troubled, but said he would try to arrange a free room for me to try it, if I liked. I liked. He went off down the corridor while I buzzed around outside the neat little offices, peering in and probably frightening people with my paint-smeared hair and green nose, which I'd temporarily forgotten.

A spiral suddenly whirled down beside me and asked me to get on, and up I went, past moving limbs and flowery torsos, into another corridor, where a gaily striped messenger showed me into my own little playground, with my own little control bank and my own little big screen.

I did actually have to ask the reference machine how everything worked, but it was very simple really. And they wanted symbolism, did they, and emotions? All right. I must admit, though, I based it a bit on Sense Distortion, even if I didn't realize it at the time.

I started with this golden-haired girl walking through a sun-splashed forest of moving plants, and after a while the plants sort of became males. Only very slightly at first, but soon you could see for sure. They're beautiful, long-limbed and really *groshing,* but still sort of imprisoned in the trunks of the plants they were, and you come to understand that you're seeing them through the girl's eyes, and she's just imagining them to be males. Then it gets really weird. You see that while she's looking at these plants as men, they're looking at her as another plant, a sort of fantastic, pale-stemmed flower, her arms like long leaves, her hair a sunburst of huge golden petals, not walking anymore, just gently swaying there in the middle of them. Then they start fighting for her, first one at a time, then all at once, thrashing tendrils that become arms, and muscular leg movements that change back into writhing roots. I suppose it was a bit of a liberty, thinking this forest was so sex-starved it would go completely *zaradann* over one fragile-looking little flower, but there you are. Anyhow, this fight comes to an end and there's the victor, a dark plant or a dark male with long black hair. And he moves after the girl-flower, and they go into a sort of running-away from coming-toward each other dance, and finally have love, tangled up in petals and leaves and limbs, which was strange and beautiful more than erotic, but anyway, I was pleased.

I pressed the signal button and a cage came down and took away the recorded track. I sat and waited.

I didn't have to wait long, though.

An intercom signal screeched at me, and the three-dimensional image of some Q-R controller or other appeared a couple of feet away.

"Ah yes," said the controller, "a very reasonable attempt, I must say. We rather enjoyed it."

"Hurrah," I said. I already knew.

"The trouble is, my dear," murmured the controller quite sadly, "that there is too much story and too little eroticism. You must understand," he went on, forestalling any possible outburst on my part, which I felt too tired to make anyway, "that picture-vision is almost entirely watched by the older groups of Four BEE. In addition, most people who watch it simply like to switch on and off when they wish, and if all our entertainments had plots, what confusion there would be, wouldn't there?" Pause for chortle in which I did not join. "However," he finished up, "your color sense and originality are promising. Perhaps we might have another talk about it when you've completed your period as Jang. Your ideas will be mellower then, more conventional, more acceptable, I'm sure. So do come back later on, if you still feel like helping our little company."

I felt like throwing the reference machine at him, but I desisted.

My Q-R met me in the corridor.

"Don't despair," he said. "Have a little rest. See your friends. You were doing so well this morning."

"Toasted angel-food," I said, "makes me sick." And I marched out and left him there, and went home.

PART 3

1

In the night Hergal woke me up crashing on the Zeefahr.

One of my makers signaled me in the morning—I'm not sure which one because he'd changed, still male but another body—and asked me if I was all right.

"Oh yes, thanks. I'm fine."

It was the last I heard of them, actually, but it was a nice thought.

Hatta had got some machine or other to write me a Jang love-poem, and the pet tore up all the silk flowers by the pool and brought them to me proudly, one by one, with a separate sneer in each orange eye.

I signaled the Picture-Vision Devisory Center and asked to have my track as a souvenir, in a bitter sort of voice that they ignored. I got the track, though, and the pet and I watched it run through over and over again, all afternoon, on the wall screen.

Night bloomed over Four BEE, and I went out walking along ancient, non-moving paths, the pet dogging my heels, playing with its shadow and mine, blackly cast from us by the big stars and the jeweled signs sizzling between buildings.

We went fire-riding at the Onyx Playgrounds, at least I did. The pet crouched under the cushions and snarled whenever a particularly bright sweep of flame whooshed by. Other fire-boats, gaudy and gold, leaped past in a spatter of sparks. I noticed two Older People, a male and a female, dressed to match in acid green, sitting in one holding hands and giggling like a couple of Jang. They got me down, somehow, and then they intrigued me, they looked so pleased with themselves. When they pressed their control for down, I followed them. We landed, and I tucked the pet, struggling and obstreperous, under one arm and tracked the couple between the fun booths and the fountains. Jang are always following people around, according to the Committee essays on Jang behavior. I'd never made much of a habit of it, but at least, if they turned around and saw me now, they wouldn't throw a fit or anything.

They were tireless and absolutely boring in what they wanted to do. They kept stopping to catch fire, or crawl down the purple throats of great big furry snakes from Four BAA, and buying the most nauseous playground food you could think of and gobbling away at it.

Eventually they sat down in the middle of some non-wet, rainbow-colored and flower-scented fountains, and started twittering to each other. I'd stationed myself quietly a little way off, but the pet took this opportunity to blow its mind and went crashing over to them, kicking water around with its great big, fluffy, silly feet. I dashed after to catch it before it bit into their sugar thistledown-on-gold wands, or satisfied its bodily functions on their nice green boots or something. But everybody had made a hit somehow.

"What a charming animal," they told me. Oh well, I could see they were prepared to go along with everything tonight.

The pet turned around and tried to bite me, just to show it knew who its friends *really* were.

"What a lovely body, my dear," they congratulated me as I cavorted around, trying to avoid the pet's teeth. "Let's

hope our girl," the female added, "will have such good taste
when she becomes one of the Jang," and they both giggled.

Oh, I got it.

"You're makers?" I asked pityingly, because they were
sitting there quite breathless with wanting me to ask.

"Oh yes. Just," they explained.

"This afternoon," the female said, "Rul gave his half of
the child. We watched the two halves being mated. Oh!" She
patted Rul's matching arm.

"Which of you is going to be the guardian?" I inquired.
Only one maker has to accept legal custody of the child
through its growing years and the time at hypno-school. After
that it becomes Jang and a free agent anyway. These two
disconcerted me, though, by saying:

"We thought we'd both stay together, at least until it
becomes Jang."

"My makers did that," I said. I suddenly felt a sort of
cold hollowness somewhere. "They split up a couple of units
ago." And their faces fell. I was rather ashamed of myself.
"They were both predominantly male though," I said to
cheer them, "that's why." And cheered they were. Well, she
was obviously predominantly female, at any rate. Too predominantly female I should think, to be frank.

I said I must dash off and have ecstasy now, and everybody looked approving, except the *thalldrap* pet, who be-
seeched them with its eyes, seeming to say: "Once we're
alone together, she'll beat me unmercifully." I got its scruff,
dragged it off them, and stalked away across the park.

"You let me down," I accused it. It laughed. Truly, I'm
certain it did. My bee fell on my head in front of a great big
crowd water-skating.

"I wish you could answer me," I snapped at the pet.
"Then we could have a real *dalika,* and make it up afterward
and feel better."

And that was how I first thought of the child. Something
to have a row with. It's a dreadful admission I suppose, but
there you are.

The pet went bounding away to play star-ball with some

pale-haired Jang in the middle distance; I sat on an ornamental stone thing with rubies frozen in it, and the thoughts came creeping up on me.

A child. I, too, would make a child. The male involved was unimportant; he need have nothing further to do with the enterprise beyond providing the other half to mine. *I* would be the guardian. I would watch the flower grow in its crystallize twilight, take it home and tend it, send it out each period to hypno-school and receive it home again each mid-period, glorying in its accomplishments. I could discuss its problems with it. I would stimulate its interests and desires. I would help to make a person, a baby, a Jang, an adult. I throbbed with obscure but passionate love for my yet unmade, unrealized second self.

2

"Iknow exactly what you're going to say," I told my poor old Q-R with the water carpet.

"Indeed."

"Oh yes. You're going to say: 'We have come up against the original problem. You are Jang, and you are too young, and you must go on being Jang and too young for another quarter *rorl*.' However, I've looked it up in the flash records at the History Museum, and it's happened before."

"Perhaps you would tell me what happened before," my Q-R suggested.

"Jang becoming makers."

"I see," said the Q-R. "You want to become a maker."

"Yes," I said.

"And who is the other maker?"

"I haven't decided yet."

"My dear young lady," said the Q-R, "it may not have told you in the flash records, but when members of the Jang have been granted permission to become makers, it has always been when a young male and female have formed a

particularly strong attachment and wish to cement their closeness with a child.''

I was all mental agility this morning, though.

''All right,'' I said, ''I'll admit there's a special male I
have in mind, but he's in Sense Distortion at the moment.
He's had it booked for ages and couldn't break the appoint-
ment, or he'd be here with me now. We've thought about
making a child for a long while,'' I went on, dreamy-eyed.
''A part of ourselves . . .''

''Really?'' asked the Q-R. He wasn't sure, I could tell.
He flicked through circuits and relays, and said, ''Apparently
the ruling is not so strict now, anyway. If you are willing to
undergo the relevant examinations, we will consider your ap-
plication.''

I nearly had a seizure.

''You will?'' I honked.

''Yes,'' said the Q-R. It suddenly struck me that he really
was kind, or really had been programmed to be kind. ''I
know,'' he said, ''how difficult you are finding things at the
moment and, in my judgment, I feel a relationship with a
growing being might well help you. Providing, of course, you
recognize that a certain amount of Committee inspection will
take place during the child's early years.''

I burbled happily. The Committee could inspect what
they liked. I'd trot the child out, singing, ''I love Four BEE
and hypno-school, and I will be Jang beyond Jang,'' if they
wanted. Oh, *derisann* Q-R!

I went by sledge to a pale yellow, soothing sort of room,
where two or three Q-Rs in gold encouraged me to tell them
why I wanted to make a child. When I reeled off all this stuff
about presenting Four BEE with another happy citizen, they
looked quite surprised, but I knew I was saying the right
things. I'd read up on it all, you see. I also said I felt associat-
ing with a child's naivety and innocence would give me a sort
of mental tonic bath, and they went wild at that. I actually
sort of felt it anyway, so I suppose it rang sincere. Apparently
difficult, *tosky,* nuisance Jang like me had been reformed

before by prolonged sexual relationships and the making of children.

Then we got on to another subject: "You realize your chosen male must be another Jang, and where is he?" So I trotted out the Sense Distortion thing again. When you attend Sense Distortion, it can go on for ages, and you can be anonymous while you're at it. It's a sort of safety valve. I suppose, a manner of getting out of it all. So my chosen male, whose name I didn't give, was shut away for the moment and I wasn't quite sure when he'd emerge.

They accepted it blithely; obviously the rules were a bit slacker now or they'd have been routing everyone out of Sense Distortion till they found him.

Then I had to go wait in a room full of bowls of ecstasy pills and love machines, and after a million and one *vreks* a messenger came to take me back, and they said it was going to be all right.

They gave me a little chat next on the responsibilities of makerhood, how I could apply for help and where from, how the Committee would send Q-Rs to inspect my efforts—apparently gaily informal little visits, gurgles at baby and furry toys and so on, but I'm not that *selt*—and warnings about forms I would have to fill out later for hypno-school and the rest. Making children is fairly involved.

I felt terribly overexcited and glowing, with hot cheeks and banging heart. When they sent me on to the medical this enthusiasm registered on the machines, and the Q-Rs looked moist-eyed. I honestly nearly went out of my mind trying not to laugh at them. I had this feeling if I started I might not stop, and they'd mark me as One-A First-Class Hysteric and say no children ever! So I hung on while they took blood groups, brain electricity readings, and chalk measures of bones. Then someone leaned over me and said did I want to make a male or a female.

"Female," I responded, rather aggressively I suspect.

They asked if my chosen mate was in agreement.

Oh yes, of course.

Well, of course he would be, wouldn't he, whoever he was? And it suddenly seemed it had to be someone a bit special, after all.

I suppose they'd corrupted me into feeling that.

3

And the ghastly thing was, the first person I thought of was Hergal.

I tried to reason myself out of it.

Hergal is such a bore, I kept telling myself, and decidedly off-Jang and *zaradann* to boot, and oh, all sorts of things.

But it wasn't any good. I suppose I'll always have a soft spot for the mannerless, vague nonchalance of him, the essence of his life spark, so alien to and yet, in some weird way, so parallel to mine.

He'd still be in Limbo probably, after the last crash—the forty-first, wasn't it?—but that wasn't a problem. As to having him cut out of my circle, I'd since cut myself out as well, so we were sort of outcasts together, so to speak.

Actually he came into the dream. The dream is what they give you while they take the necessary half from you to make the child. The main idea is to get you to dream of being with the child, and it's wildly idyllic, so you're practically weeping with joy in your sleep. I was running with her, my child, across rose fields full of scent and pink sunlight, and both our hair was scarlet, clashing with everything, only we didn't care. There wasn't much to it, just this bursting, sobbing happiness that shakes the heart out of you. And then the child looked up and pointed at something glittering in the sky.

"Maker, what's that?"

And it was silly old Hergal, looking utterly *groshing,* entirely gold and catching the sun, flying around and around in circles on these huge angel's wings that really worked.

So I woke up, and they'd popped my half into crystallize cold-storage; they said to send my male along as soon as he was ready, and they'd get cracking on it. And I thought of Hergal.

I was so happy riding to Limbo on the floating bridge. I kept going off into these crazy euphorics about how wonderful the life spark was, that little, indefinable something which has to be made initially by a male and a female, no matter how many bodies it hops in and out of once it's grown up. It still puzzles everyone, that. The Q-R scientists can't come to terms with it, even now. They sort of go "Er, humph!" whenever anyone mentions it.

"The essential difference between the Quasi-Robot (android) and the living man," the books have it, "lies in the fact that the Quasi-Robot is living flesh motivated by electrodes, metallic plasma, and a steel brain, built into the cells as they grow. Man is pure flesh without electronic or metallic interference, created from female and male cells, containing that ancient element once termed the Soul."

But I was crazy with joy on the bridge, thinking of my half, lying waiting, the tiny spark from my spark, little pale *ooma,* my child, my self. I felt as if I were in ecstasy, but I hadn't touched a pill for ages.

Near Limbo, I realized I hadn't got anything to take Hergal, so I went and stole a robotic serpent with pearl plating, really *insumatt,* then felt mean and went all the way back to pay for it; it wouldn't really be a present, after all, if I'd stolen it, would it?

When I got to Limbo, I had the usual trouble with everyone trying to find Hergal. I hadn't seen the flash about his new body, and wondered what he'd be like this time. I soon found out.

"Oh Hergal!" I practically screamed. "How could you?"

"What's wrong?" Hergal inquired, lazily uncoiling her lithe, silver body from a floating couch and jumping neatly into bounce on the crystallize-rubber floor.

"You're female!" I stated.

"Top marks," she sneered. Her hair was long and twilight mauve, plaited and full of jewelry. She had emeralds pasted on the nipples of her small, delectable breasts, and a groin shield of flowers.

My happiness exploded and was gone. I explained, between the dry sobs of my furious disappointment.

"Well, how was I to know?" Hergal asked me, reasonably enough. She tried to comfort me, but at the touch of her lovely soft arm I rushed out and went home. I'd forgotten to give her the snake, but the pet had fun with it, and for units after I fell and tripped and skidded over dismantled pearl plates. Symbolism again, I suppose, of my dismantled hopes.

4

Hatta signaled.

To torture myself, looking into his four pink eyes, I imagined saying: "Hatta, make a child with me." Ugh! Just to think of it. I didn't suppose the Committee would allow it anyway. The baby would probably grow three or four heads, and hooves or something.

"No," I said to Hatta, not really having listened to what he was saying, but having guessed—correctly too, presumably, judging from his woebegone expression. He went away.

The pet wanted to play and I didn't. We had a one-sided row and it bit me.

Who? That was the question. Who? Who? Who? I couldn't think of anyone I wanted to give their half to my child. Besides, everyone seemed to be being female all over the place. Even Kley.

And then I thought of the sand-ships, one every twelve units, out of Four BEE, across the Burning Desert, etc., into Four BOO and Four BAA. Perhaps some handsome body with a handsome life spark inside it was waiting to be useful there. Oh joy!

"Want to come?" I asked the pet doubtfully.

I knew it would insist on coming, and bite everybody all the time, and go *zaradann* at the worst possible moments. It followed me to the porch, honking softly.

"Come on then." I hefted it and ducked unsuccessfully a bite on the nose which turned out, luckily, to be a kiss instead.

5

It felt really strange, going out of Four BEE.

You had to book your place on a sand-ship, but I was lucky, they said, this was an off-peak traveling time. Actually, it's always off-peak now. The desert and those great black mountains and volcanoes, extinct or otherwise, give people the creeps. When I got aboard I could see my fellow travelers sitting around cringing, waiting to be flung out at the inhospitable bosom of what is, after all, our own planet. There were a few Jang, but obviously a complete circle who didn't want an outsider like me slipping in. They looked pretty female, anyway, even the two males. And they were cringing too, while being superficially ever so young and daring. They'd probably never even sabotaged anything. I must admit the first sabotage I did, with Hergal and Kley, nearly an eighth of a *rorl* ago, I felt really agoraphobic about the great open spaces beyond the lookout post at 6D, though it was sort of wonderful too, to find something your stomach could really churn over at last. The two or three other passengers were Older People, one hugging a pink animal, and I tugged at the pet's scruff worriedly.

"You dare," I said.

The pet, unstained innocence incarnate, licked its shimmering coat.

After we'd been sitting around for a while, a robot came aboard from somewhere or other and checked us, with irritating slowness, against a passenger list in one of the steel pillars.

The robot informed me that my animal was unregistered, and I would have to sign a special document if I wanted it to stay on board. I nearly took the opportunity to have the pet thrown out, but couldn't bring myself to, so I signed. The pet tried to bite the robot. There was a lot of noise. Hey ho, conspicuous again.

There were clankings and the whoopings of sirens, and we started off at a slow gallop. The ejector nets grabbed us with a bit of juddering here and there, and we eased, with a high-pitched whistling sound, out of the electricity wave dome that covers Four BEE. The light changed. There was a soft bang as the dome locks shut. The passengers all glared around at the covered window spaces, looking ghastly with pretended jollity and sangfroid. And then this announcement came on that nearly made me choke with sadistic glee:

"Those of you who wish to avail yourselves of the Transparency Tower in the stern may now do so."

And nobody, of course, stirred. Well, I mean, look at all that *drumdik,* beastly great desert, all those foul natural phenomena, like rain-carved rocks and wind-chiseled screes—I was up before I knew it. All right, I *did* want to avail myself of the Transparency Tower. The robot nearly collapsed, but tottered after me somehow to switch on a guide machine which droned on about natural features. The pet followed me and peered out too, probably remembering its desert home near Four BOO in the good old days, before stupid people dragged it out of its burrow by its long, curling, impossible whiskers, and condemned it to being a pet to some fool like me.

The T.T. was oval, made of glacia-view, resistant to atmospheric pressure, weather, sand, but completely seethroughable. The dome of the roof was also clear, bearing some sort of blurred crest of the old sand-ship fleet. They're a pretty ancient institution. Everyone thought they'd be replaced by body displacing machines until we all found out that they make you vomit. By then everyone was anti-travel, anyway.

"How does it feel to man a relic?" I asked the guide machine, which was trying to bully me into turning into twenty pairs of eyes stuck in a revolving neck. "No, I won't look at that geological fault. No, nor the extinct volcano on my left. I'll do my own looking." And I did. Honestly, the rock spires looked just like fantastic castles from some myth or other. I caught myself imagining they were, and stopped myself. Oh but . . . and the sky was dark, sort of turquoise more than blue, with a ghost of greenness moving through it all the time. Everything else was in tones of black, with the odd pinky-red vein here and there, except the sand, which was just pale and seemed to reflect rainbow. Dust devils shimmered and canyons yawned, and I was just going into a quiet frenzy when suddenly the sides and roof opaqued. I had a moan at the robot about this, but apparently they clear automatically at certain periods of the day and then cloud pretty quickly, in case it proves too much for you and you go *zaradann* all over their ship.

Back below, I found the pet had run off and was having a fight with the pink animal, and everybody else was having hysterics. Couldn't I control my monster, they wanted to know? No, I couldn't; would they care to try? They backed away, and I lunged and somehow got the pet and an armful of teeth as well. The older female grabbed the pink animal and hugged its tattered, snarling body to her bosom. It kicked her.

Then, fortunately, this silvery ringing tone announced the arrival of a meal in the saloon, and we trouped off to gorge. It was pretty *groshing,* really, gold plates and so on, and goblets with patterns and little mauve bubbles blown in the crystallize. We started off with iced fire-tomatoes in red wine, progressed to root steak and forced beans in amber sauce with spices, and ended up with spike-fruits, desert

plums, and lichen cheese with nuts. There were gallons of
fire-and-ice and Joyousness, which contains ecstasy.

I ate alone and fed the pet from my plate, just to get on
everyone's nerves. It wasn't keen, though, and only bright-
ened up when the robot trundled up with its dish of syntho-
meat substitute and cactus cream. I had to pay heavily for
that. They even gave it some wine but what wine precisely
I'm not clear on. It didn't go into ecstasy though, or anything,
thank goodness.

After the meal—apparently they only serve seven meals
on the ships but you could get cold snacks in between; it's
sensible really. Even then, only one man attended every sitting—the Older People went off to watch picture-vision and
the Jang had a swim in the pool-tank, which, I have to admit,
tempted me. Not with them in it, however. I took one of the
large moving-picture magazines from the ship's store and
went to sit in the Transparency Tower, keeping the pet firmly
tucked between my feet.

Quite soon the glacia-view unclouded and I saw a troup
of long-eared things with antennae and ski feet, thumping
across the desert at a great rate. They looked dreadfully purposeful and intense. You could imagine them grabbing you at
parties and telling you all about the Movement. It made me
giggle, then feel odd, as if I'd been cut out of a circle and had
to cry. However, the pet diverted my attention by staring at
them and barking.

"You've never barked before," I admired. "You should
do it more often."

It gave me a withering look.

Several opacities later, I saw that the turquoise sky was
blushing slightly on the horizon, over a tall black funnel of
mountain. There was a dullish boom of earthquake thunder
and the ship sort of shuddered ever so gently. Immediate
signal for cries and screeches from below. In the saloon,
where some of them were having another meal, a solitary
crystallize goblet bounced across the floor. I resigned myself
to the stupid glacia-view clouding over to prevent my incipient, though in fact nonexistent, paranoid hysteria. But it

didn't. It probably presumed I'd have run below, yelling and sweating with the others. So I saw this *derisann* and positively *insumatt* eruption, complete with exploding pink and mauve flowers of smoke, fountains of sparks, and a great whoosh of lava and black ash. What joy! The sand-ship, of course, was suitably programmed to avoid this sort of involuntary cabaret and took off from its air cushions at a steep angle, going to port like anything and soon leaving the panorama behind. Still, I'd actually witnessed a real event. The pet honked.

"All right," I said, "you're always honking. There's nothing so wildly original in *that!*"

I spent a really revolting night, at least to start with. First of all the pet kept jumping on to my anchored float-bed and messing up its soothing, rocking action. Then it kept forcing its way *into* the bed with me. Then there would be a scene, the pet would leave, and two splits later there it would be crashing down on me again. Eventually it wandered off and got rid of its wine ration in the saloon. It was the robot who woke me up this time with the above joyful news. It said I was to be sure to take the pet to the pet vacuum drift, next to the ordinary vacuum drift, as the automatic cleaners should not be got out at this time of night. So I guiltily crawled from bed and forced the pet into performing a pee of insignificant extent in the right place.

Then I really couldn't sleep, despite turning on the bed's cooler-waves, then the heaters, the ecstasy machine, and a lullaby unit that was utterly nauseous and seemed to think I was still at hypno-school.

I got up and tailed off to the T. Tower and, to my great delight, discovered it stayed clear all night, so I swallowed stay-awake pills in case and spent six hours or so with red-flickering, volcanic darkness, low-slung, hard, cold living stars, the quick ignition of animal eyes through rock arches and in strings of gold along the sand. And I actually saw a real dawn. It was less spectacular than in a dome, but they had a sort of ethereal wonder about them, those pale, arrowing green shafts of light that slowly pulled from the dark this round orange sun, which turned brighter and fiercer until I had to look away, my eyes streaming. I saw black spots for ages, and honestly got a bit scared until they finally went off. No one had warned me that you couldn't stare at the real sun like you can stare at that false yellow thing in Four BEE.

6

The Jang passengers appeared fairly soon after. They'd been having some sort of suitable Jang orgy in their single cabin, with ecstasy, Upper-Ear music and, as I gathered the two males were married to the two females, presumably having love all over the place as well. They looked vague as they knocked back their energy pills and ate toasted angel-food.

"*Attlevey*," I gaily cried, to see what would happen. They *attlevey*-ed in return, even more vaguely. Circles seemed to get more and more cliquey every *vrek*.

The pet and I had first meal alone again, and we ate cactus mushrooms and fried root bread. I don't usually eat that early, but the journey had given me an appetite. Trite, wasn't it? The pet snuffled about and decided it liked mushrooms. It toyed with its syntho-meat substitute, but golluped down all the wine with floating cream. I liked the look of that and ordered one. Mine came in a goblet, and very nice it was too, before the pet realized, gave it a good swipe out of my hand, and drank the resultant spilled stuff on the floor. Again the robot came and told me off, and the Older People, who didn't seem terribly Jang-disposed, probably because being surrounded by a lot of explosive volcanoes disturbed them, chat-chatted away about disgraceful lack of training in the pet —all my fault—and disgraceful lack of table manners in me, letting it drink from my goblet. Well! That's one way to put it, I suppose.

I was rather glad when we got to Four BOO. I'd heard the older female with the pink animal tell the robot that I ought to be put out of the ship, and the pet too. Apparently I had priority; the pet was just an afterthought. I didn't think it would happen, though. It's quite illegal unless, of course, I'd turned homicidal, and then they'd have to give me oxygen tablets or hypodermics, maps, drinking water, food, a floating hydro-tent. . . . Still, it makes you feel a bit odd when people want to throw you out that badly. I could just see that woman stunning me with her great big crystallize and gold chronometer, chucking me from the lock-port, and then thrusting the pet down the vacuum drift, through the antiseptic layer, into Nothing. The pet got the last laugh, though.

Just before arrival, I heard this female screaming around, yelling that she'd lost her pink animal. Everyone sort of joined in the search and eventually located these ghastly noises coming from the saloon. There were gasps and grunts and little wounded cries, and a sort of background honking that could only be—

"Oh! You abominable Jang Girl!" screeched the older female. "My poor little Honey-Nut is being massacred by your *thing*." Honey-Nut was presumably the pink animal; the *"thing"* was presumably guess who.

In fear and trembling we all advanced into the saloon, and there they were, Honey-Nut and the pet, and honestly, I think the older female would have been happier if the pet had just torn Honey-Nut's rose pink throat out.

"Aah!" she shrilled. "How *could* you!"

It was a small betrayal.

What the two of them were actually doing was having love. No, really. And apparently it was absolutely *groshing*, judging from the row. The female hopped around, yelping that somebody ought to go and tear them apart, and I think I really upset her when I asked how she'd like being torn apart from her chosen male in the middle of something like that. Anyhow, sense prevailed and we left them alone, watching fascinated until the climax came in a rolling, shrieking ball of flying fur and pistoning paws and thrashing tails. They collapsed exhausted. Well, it must have taken at least thirty splits. I felt ridiculously proud of the pet when it stood up, shook itself, and came strolling over, the epitome of nonchalance. I picked it up and congratulated it, being very careful how I held it. It was probably a little sensitive here and there.

"I'll have the Committee on you!" yowled the older female. "Despoiling my animal! And if she lays an egg . . . !"

I thought she might be going to have a fit, but she didn't, unfortunately. Somehow I got the feeling that Honey-Nut had laid eggs before.

And just then, luckily, the ship announced that we were approaching Four BOO.

7

Well, I really was out of Four
BEE now.

Of course, Four BOO and BAA are pretty much the
same, except for the volcanic pits at BOO and the huge android animal breeding grounds at BAA which produce gorgeous semi-synthetic creatures, like Jade Tower's dragon.
The other thing to remember is that a messenger bee in BAA
becomes a baa, and a boo in BOO. Logical but confusing.

Anyway, naturally the first thing that happened when I
got off the sand-ship was that my boo fell on my head in front
of the Jang, the outraged Older People, a positively glowing
Honey-Nut, and a whole crowd of robots and Q-Rs and general gawpers who'd come to see us arrive. I tried to look
blasé.

I was ever so Jang for disembarkation. I had to attract
Jang males, after all. I wore see-through trousers with little
silver disks on the ankle hems, and a corresponding see-
through tunic with corresponding disks at the hips. Both were
lightly spangled with silver dust. Silver chains clanked
around my groin, and between my breasts big greenish opals
on platinum ropes quivered and bounced. I wore long tur-

quoise earrings reaching to my navel, which also proudly
sported a turquoise to match. My hair was a riot of silk flowers, metal do-dahs, and a big fan comb dribbling pearls.

We were on the Arrival Stretch, a close-shaved area of
feather grass with artistic copper trees with tortured trunks.
Nearby, outside the protective dome, volcanoes roared and
spewed fire, but you'd never have known. They actually re-
duce all that splendor to helping their power station banks,
but that's kind of nice because it makes things cheaper and
sometimes, after a particularly good eruption, everything you
buy is free for the unit.

I stared around and flashed my toe rings, but there wasn't
a Jang male in sight.

We had to give our identities and place of origin at a little
reception desk with glass pillars and a fountain. After that the
others all trundled off into waiting rented bird-planes, bubbles, etc. I made for an old walkway with some rather nice
eighth-dimensional sculptures along it. I wanted to see and be
seen. The pet rushed along behind me, tapping at my silver
ankle disks with heavy white paws.

"Who had love with Honey-Nut?" I felt suddenly
prompted to ask, and we did a little dance together among the
statuary. Astonishing! I felt wildly happy.

This machine thing with tentacles zoomed up soon after
that and began offering me accommodations. They can spot a
tourist in about two splits, the Committees in our cities, and
once they have, they're after you. Still, I suppose it's quite
useful. There were lots of exotic places to "relax and enjoy
myself." I chose the Volcanic Lake Palace; it sounded as
though it would be crawling with Jang males. The tentacled
thing rushed off in hysterical delight and was back in seconds
with a bird-plane in rainbow colors that apparently would be
free of charge. Good. The pet and I got in, and the tentacled
thing gave the robot directions and then slipped tactfully
away, assuring me I would never regret my choice. Well, that
was a real laugh.

I started to feel peculiar the moment we flew over it, this
great big, roiling, heaving lake of lava treacle. Bubbles

popped and exploded in it, and jets of steam hissed and crackled. The Palace was obsidian, of course, and towered up in the middle of the chaos, obviously anchored, but still heaving slightly, along with all the rest. I suppose it was a stunning sight. The dark was coming on, deep blue, and the lake and the massive structure of the Palace glowed like flames. I still felt sick, though.

The bird-plane delivered me at the entrance, a terrace with steam pillars, and I went in. The floor was veined with gold inside, and presently it had other decorations as the pet threw up seventh meal in all directions.

I apologized, did some obligatory paying, and signaled another bird-plane to rescue us.

As we drifted over Four BOO I thought: They can keep their palaces. We'll sleep in a park tonight. Firm ground, and the weather's always perfect, of course, in a dome. And lots of Jang. I'll say I've come here to do some contemplating.

So we went and bought an utterly *insumatt* cube of glass and steel and gold, shot through with wonderful color, containing about fifty possible infinities. It would be worth contemplating this thing, even if nothing else did turn up. Then, in the bird-plane, full of crazy hopes and remembering again with intense joy my half child waiting in Four BEE, the pet and I and the beastly boo floated down in the starlight on a soft park lawn.

I skimmed along, having turned the boo's little evening light on, and chose a grove of diamante trees. I got arranged, had a meal injection, inspected my hair and clothes and everything else in the long mirror in the boo, and then half reclined, graceful and languorous, with the cube anchored to a tree trunk just the right distance away. And I really got lost in it, even with all my crazy hopes and so on. I truly didn't hear their voices till they'd been at it for quite a while.

They were both male, both pretty *groshing,* one white-haired and one dark-haired.

"I'm Sarl," said the dark one promptly, as soon as I'd looked. "This is Lorun."

"How *derisann*," I murmured. The pet snarled, and I tried to land it one surreptitiously.

"Lonely, are you?" asked Sarl. He leered at me. Well, it wasn't going to be him, for a start.

"Oh, I'm not lonely," I said, "just rather hungry. I've been so busy contemplating, you know, I'd forgotten about meals. Is there anywhere . . . ?"

"Come with me," said Sarl.

"No," I said, "I want to go on contemplating. I'm going to have ecstasy soon. Could you bring me something, I wonder?" And Sarl, the *thalldrap*, went marching off to do just that. I looked at my spoils. Mmm.

"And you're Lorun." I smiled.

"That's right," Lorun said. He didn't even sarcastically congratulate me on my remarkable memory.

"This is my pet. I'm afraid it might bite you."

"Oh, I'm used to animals," said Lorun. He came up and sat down, and soon there was the pet rolling on its back, with its six mad paws in the air, going *zaradann* as he tickled its tummy. Well, you couldn't blame the pet. Really, the male had the most arresting body. He was sort of slight but muscular, with long powerful legs and *groshing*, artistic hands. His hair was quite short, only to his shoulders, and he didn't have a beard or mustache, just these somehow frightfully endearing dark eyebrows and lashes, which were crazily *derisann* against his ice-paleness. Good taste.

"I'm sure you *are* lonely," he eventually said, when he'd practically driven the pet and me out of our minds.

"Well, yes," I conceded, "it's possible."

"Stranger to Four BOO, perhaps?"

"Four BEE." I must confess I wasn't even thinking about the child at that particular moment.

"Ah then, as a native, you must let me take you under my wing."

"What a good idea. I'm sure it would be a nice wing to be under."

"How charming you are," said Lorun. "But what about your ecstasy?"

"It can wait," I decided.

But he decided it couldn't. We would have ecstasy together. Just then he spotted Sarl marching back to us across the lawns and terraces, bearing food and wine.

"Come on," said Lorun, "or did you particularly want to eat now? We can wait if you like."

I didn't like, and said no. So we scampered off through the trees like naughty children at hypno-school, our boos dragging along the pet and the contemplation cube, with their lights out.

We had ecstasy in a robot-controlled bird-plane, but Lorun kept messing around with the gears and buttons, and it was like being with Hergal in one of his better moments.

In the middle of the most ghastly nosedive, that any other time would have frightened all the breath out of me, Lorun inquired whether I would care to get married for two or three units.

Even the pet didn't make a fuss about it. I think it was somehow under the impression that it had married him too.

8

Well, I never thought I was cut out for idylls, but apparently I was. We really lived, breathed, ate, slept each other. Lorun also had a present maker who was absent then in Four BAA. Their home was a huge crowd of shut-in domes and spires under a palely golden lake, near the center of the city. It was a pretty select area, with not many other homes down there, under the fawn silk waters. Weird water plants waved around the windows, as we had love and had love and had more love.

And it was all such fun, apart from being so erotically satisfying. We romped and played about with the awful pet, and Lorun really didn't seem to mind it tearing up the creeper curtains and ripping at the air-lock doors. We went swimming and bubble-riding under-lake, visited the under-lake restaurants and playgrounds—also very select and very *groshing* too—talked and laughed and were crazy together. I really thought I was on to something, but I didn't bring up the subject of the child just yet. Somehow there seemed more to this relationship than just a prospective other-self-maker hunt. And then, when the three days were up, Lorun suggested we apply for an extension to the marriage.

We got duly extended and had love to celebrate, nice but not original, and then somebody signaled Lorun and said would he care to help in some Jang sabotage.

"Want to join in?" he inquired.

"Don't you want me to, *ooma?*"

Lorun proved conclusively that he did, so we went together.

I hadn't sabotaged a thing for *vreks* and *vreks,* and felt a bit rusty and *tosky* through the euphoria of being with Lorun. We met the rest of his circle, four weird females with tendrilous hair and one with a single whorled horn growing from her left temple, Sarl and another male. Sarl snarled at me.

"Er, *attlevey,*" I said, feeling decidedly alien. I said circles are getting terribly cliquey and this was a fine example.

"Attlevey," they all droned, looking at me as if I'd just unexpectedly returned up the vacuum drift or something.

"You're Lorun's new marriage, are you?" horny-puss asked nastily. I could just tell her finger-long nails were more than mere Jang decoration.

"Oh, I thought you were still the last one," said another female, with all-blue eyes and eight-fingered hands—even more nail danger. Well, honestly.

"Sorry," I said sweetly, "I'm the new one with the quick temper and the uncontrollable homicidal tendencies."

"Oh really!" they flounced, but still looked a little worried.

Lorun seemed oblivious to it all, Hergal-like, though none of the predominantly female females in my circle—like Thinta and me—were quite as atrocious as this lot.

"Come on then," Sarl said, dismissing me as beneath his contempt. "Let's not muck around."

So we didn't, but lolluped out of this floating park where we'd met, if you could call it that. We went by a succession of float-bridges and moving streets, terribly complicated, meant to be part of the excitement or something. I just got *toskier* and *toskier,* and eventually said they'd have to wait for me a minute. I went out and stole three chains of mother-of-pearl and amber, which I nonchalantly swung around my hips. I felt a bit better then but the circle grumbled about the delay, not realizing about my Neurotic Needs, which was just as well.

Lorun stopped it by just gazing at them and saying, ever so silkily and softly: "Shut up, you double-eyed *thalldraps*."

I felt gratified or something, and then a bit annoyed too, I couldn't quite work out why. Anyway, not long after that we actually had to walk, and we were getting near the outposts of Four BOO. The lookouts here have names as well as alphas. The one we were after was called Dulsa D.

"Here we are!" they announced when we arrived on this flat rock platform at the bottom of millions of flights of non-moving steps. The lookout was a little bluish cube, set near one of the dome locks. We strode up to the ice-glass doors and pushed the call button. I began to feel really nervous, then realized how much I was enjoying being nervous, after which I went deadly calm and stopped enjoying it, which was a shame. Pink lights flashed in Dulsa D. A voice asked us what we wanted.

"Emergency!" we shrilled in panic-stricken voices. Honestly, I thought, you'd think if the Committee worried about these little disasters, they'd program their lookout robots to realize there can never be an emergency, that it's only a lot of stupid Jang trying to get in and mess things up. I suppose that's the answer. The Committee isn't worried. How depressing not to be able to worry someone, anyone, no matter how hard you try.

Naturally, once our screams of terror registered inside, the pink lights changed to red, the usual succession of ten doors opened and shut behind us, and we charged in yelling. Sometimes there are two robots, sometimes only one. This time there were four. Needless to say, we thrilled to this prospect of action.

Lorun and Sarl and the other male grabbed the nearest one and crashed it into the one behind, then sat on the struggling metallic mass and pulled out their dismantling plugs.

Three females rushed another and floored it with swinging ropes of crystallize beads, while horny-puss and I suddenly found ourselves comrades in arms as we jumped the last. I found its dismantling plug while she bashed it in the electricity reflex circuit with her horn.

Glowingly we congratulated each other and headed for the controls. But really, I thought, there's not much you can do except create a very minor shudder in the barrier beams, which allows a bit of real weather or earthquake or something in for about two splits. Still, we'd blind ourselves to that and convince ourselves we were being daring and terrible, upsetting the system. We looked at the scanners and there were these three *ooma* mountains all starting to erupt at once, with lava pouring toward us.

"Now!" Lorun yelled, and everybody smashed around among the buttons and dials with practiced paws.

And the next thing we knew we were on the floor. Four BOO had given a great heave or something. Already the waves would be knitting themselves together again all around, but some of that lava was bound to get through. And then something struck me. This wasn't rain, or ash, or earthshudder that city buildings laugh at. This was painful, deadly, red-hot magma. In Four BEE the volcanoes are fewer and less active. I don't think we could have got lava into BEE if we tried. But to try, to arrange things so lava would be the main course on the menu . . . I felt horrible, cold and sick all of a sudden.

"People will be burned," I said to Lorun, with a surprising total comprehension of what was happening that I could see was beyond the others.

"So?" Lorun said. "It's an Event. We've made something happen. "We've come here before, but never had much luck with the lava. This is *groshing,* my *ooma.* Enjoy it."

"Oh, Lorun," I whispered. And then I noticed something no one else saw: a little green light coming on and off in the wall. I went and looked at it, and it was neatly engraved with the words *Emergency wave shield now operating.* The Committee! I loved the Committee! The wise, wonderful, *groshing* Committee! They knew about Jang sabotage, but they protected the city. All right, let the Jang open up the dome but, with dangerous lava about, have an immediate response mechanism to shield the dome while the waves rescued themselves, and a mechanism you couldn't get at, either.

Our sabotage had been thwarted, and I felt so happy.

I flung my arms around Lorun and kissed him. He looked pleased. He looked less pleased when we ran off afterward and found the city perfect and untouched. The others turned positively filthy. They somehow seemed to think I was responsible for their failure, and if wishing was doing, I suppose I was.

9

After the lava business, I should have been firm with myself over Lorun. But I wasn't. All right, I reasoned, there was something—one item—about him I didn't like, but I was still *insumattly zaradann* over him. I just couldn't say "I'm off now. Get us annulled." I informed myself that I would hold out until the end of our marriage extension, which was in about ten units, and decide then about the maker idea.

Then Lorun said would I care to go to Four BAA in his private bird-plane, and that settled it. Well, I wanted to see Four BAA, for one thing.

"My maker," Lorum said, casual, "is something to do with the breeding farms. We can go and have a look around one, if you like."

The bird-plane was superluxurious and robot-flown. We had love and played rather special Upper-Ear, which made you feel gentle and soothed as well as crazy with delight, and ate sugar plums on gold-ice, and were generally debauched.

The pet came too, and was just as debauched as we were. It gobbled up sugar plums and rubbed against Lorun with positively nauseating love luridly illuminating its wicked orange eyes.

The bird-plane went fast and we reached Four BAA inside a day, just before desert dawn and sunset in the dome. I was sorry to miss another real dawn, but I'd noted sadly that the window spaces in the plane were tastefully opaqued with a gold brocade effect.

We went to Lorun's maker's residence. The maker looked at us vaguely and asked which of us was her child. Apparently Lorun had been in a different body the last time they met. Lorun promptly said it was me, thereby causing tornadoes of embarrassment. We got sorted out eventually and the maker went away with a gorgeous older male with dark red hair, leaving us to our own devices.

We janged around the home, then went out to eat on a blue lake under the stars on a canopied golden raft, attended by jeweled quasi-robot girls with long hair made of non-wet blue water. BAA is the absolute center of all things rich and strange. Dragons with sapphire scales blew fountains out of the lake all around us. A pearl-encrusted serpent came up on the raft to peer at us and I had to grab the pet quickly, in case it thought this was another robot animal like the snake I bought for Hergal. Actually the pet got a bit *tosky* and went burrowing into Lorun's chest, honking.

After eighth meal, we rode through a tunnel of specially grouped stars, very high up, on the back of a wonderful bird with burning silver plumage and a ruby beak; it sang strange love songs in a light, sweet, melancholy voice, the most beautiful and passionately sorrowing I'd ever heard. Practically weeping, Lorun and I lay in each other's arms among the red cushions, and soon he said, "Marry me for *vrek* after the extension ends, or two *vreks*, you *derisann* angel of scarlet light." I think the poetry was contagious, but anyway, I was lost.

"Oh yes," I breathed. "*Ooma, ooma*, oh yes."

But the extension wasn't up yet.

10

We went out to this android animal breeding farm in Lorun's plane.

It sits there, way off from the city, though you can still see the enormous glitter of the dome sides stretching up and up till they're out of sight in the distance.

The farm, the first of seven, only one of which makes actual Q-Rs, is also under a dome, but a small dome with a mere pebble of a sun and sequins of stars, and they're just around to get the animals used to it all. Apparently Lorun's maker is one of the button-popping, dial-turning brigade, but even so you're expected to fraternize with the growing animals, and it seemed really *groshing*, interesting, worthwhile work. I had this sudden vision in which my future gelled, more or less permanently married to Lorun, our child at hypno-school, and me working at the farm with his maker, being ever so companionable and all that. It got to me so much that I turned to him and said:

"Lorun, there was an ulterior motive in my coming to Four BOO. I wanted to find . . ." and then I hesitated, I don't know why, although perhaps I really do know. I felt I just couldn't ask about the child just yet.

"Yes?" he prompted.

"No," I murmured, "after this. I'll tell you later."

He looked a bit irked, but let it pass.

We left the plane and went in and out of pagodas and towers and palaces, stopped by lakes and rode up to cloud masses where birds of fire and perfume were being trained to fly and sing. And after a bit I started to feel depressed out of my mind. I tried to fight it and got high-voiced and over-merry, but it didn't do any good. I think it was the pet's fault, really. It went silent and started to shiver.

"I think the animals here scare it," I said to Lorun, to start with. I mean they were all puffing out flame and scent and waterspouts and goodness knows what, and half of them were phosphorescent or watery, or disappeared at every third step and reappeared at the fourth, or something. And then I began to see that this wasn't what got the pet down. The pet was an animal too, but a real animal, a born animal, primitively conceived and carried, hatched out of a warm, sat-on-by-a-furry-bottom egg, in the desert. These animals were made of the same molecules, by similar primaries and ovaries, but with the Q-Rs' electrically motivated life-spark, and the same subservience to mankind. They're for decoration. They are to be pretty and mythical. And suddenly I recalled my *ooma* dragon in the Jade Tower, and a pain burst in my heart like a great flower. How often had I sat in its harmless mouth, full of pine scent and green fire, that should have been able to champ me into mash? I knew an intense longing to cry but couldn't, and held the pet to my face so that we could share our twin inhibited misery.

Lorun was elegantly, callously, leading me from lawn to pen, from turret to waterway. "Stop!" I wanted to shout. "I can't bear any more." I wanted to set them all free to play in the desert, and then I realized, with even more intense pain, that the real animals would run from them in fear at first, but finally would tear their defenseless bodies to pieces.

Then Lorun suggested we go stare in at the breeding

tanks in their crystallize twilight, and I thought of my real, half-alive child, waiting for its own crystallize twilight, and gasped: "Take me back to the city. Please take me back."

"What?" Lorun was immediately irritated. I became aware how irritable he always was when things went against his own plans.

"I'm sorry," I said, "I feel *tosky*. I can't—it's all those poor unknowing animals. I—"

"Oh, what a fool you are at times," Lorun said almost pleasantly; he thought I was sweetly aggravating.

Misery changed to anger. I suppose I just felt on the defensive.

"Take me back to the city, *v. . . .n* you!"

Lorun's urbanity slipped, but his face said more than words. He came striding over to me and I cowered. All at once the pet turned around from my cheek and snarled at him. It was the first time the pet had ever snarled at Lorun. Lorun at once took time off to propitiate it, to prove to us all how easily he could charm flame from clay. He cajoled and ingratiated and stretched out his hand. The pet possibly thought this was an aggressive move, but was the pet that *selt?* I don't think so.

Growl—snarl—snap! went the pet, and bit Lorun the hardest it had ever bitten anyone, and it had done me a fair amount of damage on the quiet.

Lorun slapped the pet hard, and then he swore. He used words I'd never even heard before; I vaguely recollect trying to remember them for future use, through my sorrow and shock.

"I'll take you back," he said finally, "but not that *floop* beast you're holding so fondly."

"Take both or neither," I snapped.

"Then neither," Lorun said, dripping blood.

"The relief is all mine," I said, ice-cold and feeling as if I was going to be ill underneath the cold. I sounded marvelously final, though. I turned and he came after me.

"All right," he said, "I'm sorry, but the ghastly thing shouldn't have bitten me."

"It had my full approval," I said, but I still wanted to be talked out of it.

"You know you drive me *zaradann*," he said. "Come on. We'll all be friends again." He caressed my hair. "Let's go see the breeding tanks."

I flung him off.

"Haven't you listened to anything I said?" I screamed at him. "I hate it here! I hate the principle of what we do to those animals, what we make them into! I hate this farm, I hate the filthy cities, and I hate every one of the *thalldraps* in them, and that includes you, you precious nothing!"

"I'd better return you to Four BAA," he said, angry and sullen.

It was nightmarish. He took me to the sand-ship base like I asked, and all the way there I kept nearly strangling on my desire to forgive him and beg him to forgive me. But I couldn't. I knew that whichever one of us was right, I could never kid myself we were compatible again. So, no more blind idyll. When we arrived, I said stiffly:

"Thank you for a wonderful time. The marriage will be over in half a unit, anyway, so don't bother about an annulment. Actually, I wanted to ask you to help me make a child, but I see now what a mistake that would have been." I don't know why I bothered to tack that on. It was unfair and unnecessary, and it nearly killed me to say it.

And that was our goodbye. The plane doors shut, and the pet and I were alone again.

11

There was a ship that unit, which was lucky. Well, what's the good of being lucky about unimportant things like that?

I couldn't bear the thought of Four BEE, where my half child waited, so I went back to Four BOO.

I was the only passenger.

I suppose I always am, in a way.

12

When I got to Four BOO I found having the pet around was upsetting me, so I summarily sent it back by robot ship to Four BEE and home.

I hung about alone for ages, in parks and palaces, ignoring any Jang males who spoke to me, or else being violently rude. I was horribly scared that if I took up with one of them the same terrible thing would happen again. It's called disillusionment, I believe.

Then I noticed I was really enjoying chatting to Jang females and registering all their good points.

A body change seemed to be in order, and a sex change as well. I suppose I'd temporarily sated my female side with Lorun and was also rather repelled for the moment by being a female. I didn't see why it should stop my maker-hunting if I changed. I'd probably be better able to size up the *floops* if I were one of them. Of course, my sixty units weren't up in Four BEE yet but, in another city, you have a clean record. Various people who don't like suiciding have trundled off to BOO or BAA to get a body change when they wanted one in a hurry and had been put on ration. Hatta did it once and came back covered in warts, looking utterly *drumdik* beyond belief.

Anyway, I went to Four BOO's Limbo and explained the situation, and how I felt I needed to be male for a while. They said they'd do it willingly—for a price, never forget the price, and there was a dearth of eruptions that unit, so it was damn expensive too—but did I understand that it wouldn't go on the records of Four BEE for five units, as I'd had it done at BOO? This would mean no one would know who I was in BEE for five units, unless I told them, and I wouldn't be able to flash my identity from a call-post until the flash computer registered me.

It all sounded highly unworrying, so I agreed, paid, ordered a soothing dream, and woke up a while later an utterly *insumatt* male. I was thoroughly pleased until I noticed how like Lorun I'd made myself. That did get me down a little, particularly as I now wanted to go punch him on the nose. I went and had a meal injection instead, and ignored all the Jang girls angling to get at me.

My male mind still craved to make a child, even though my way of looking at it was now somewhat different; I also found, as a man, I would have preferred to make a male child. I rationalized that once I changed back I would revert to the original preference, and I was, after all, predominantly female. Nevertheless, I still hadn't solved my maker problem.

I was certainly no better judge. As a male I had even less patience with them, and eventually found a curving and graceful Jang female and married her for the afternoon. It was brief, uncomplicated, and *groshing*. The way it ought to be.

And it was as I was lying back in the twilight feather grass of the park, returning her final wave as she slid deliciously away, that I had the crazy idea. I nearly went hysterical, even though you don't go hysterical the same way when you're a male. Different hormones or something. But I sat bolt upright, called my boo, and stared at my masculine self in the long molecule mirror.

I was going to be the other maker.

13

I tried to look as if I hadn't spoken to the Q-R with the water carpet before, as I explained I was the chosen male. They wouldn't have a record of me in Four BEE, I said, as I'd only just arrived. But, said the Q-R, the young lady had said the chosen male was in Sense Distortion. So he had been, said I, and she'd got fed up waiting and returned to me, one of her past loves from Four BOO. Now *she* was in Sense Distortion.

It was a bit thick, really, but I suppose Q-Rs are programmed to think of Jang as irrational twits, flitting from sensation to sensation and being *tosky* and *zaradann* in between.

Anyhow, after a brief wait, they accepted me.

I had another dream. This time I was with a blonde child who clung to me, all admiring, and I felt protective and strong, ready to guard her against any nonexistent dangers Four BEE might have to offer. It wasn't a field of roses, either, but a fire-ride.

They said would I stay and watch the mating of the two halves, but I felt too emotional and my male impulse was to repress that, so I fled into the night. I was also a bit scared now that they might realize what was going on and refuse to go ahead.

I signaled Thinta.

"*Attlevey* . . . Hergal?" she asked vaguely. Hergal must have crashed on the Zeefahr again.

She looked very attractive, minus her fur now, with clouds of long green hair and a delicate, chiseled-looking pale body, so unlike her rather hysterically stolid personality.

"It's me," I said, and told her who I was.

"Oh! Aren't you *groshing*!" she cried, evidently pleased. She always warms to me more readily when I'm male, I've noticed.

"Come and marry me for a couple of units," I suggested, and she was almost in my lap before I'd switched off.

We went to a floater, and really, to be frank, I did it as much to hide as anything else. It was pretty *derisann*, though. Her current body was awfully lithe at the most ideal moments.

Near dawn, when we were having a brief rest, there was this horrible droning noise outside.

"What is it?" Thinta cried worriedly, clutching me.

We soon found out. Committee messenger bees can barge in anywhere. This one charged right up through the middle of the cloud bed. Thinta shrieked. The messenger indicated me and snapped:

"Come at once to the Committee Hall in Second Sector." Amazing how they could program it to sound so utterly nasty.

"What have you done?" trembled Thinta. "It's nothing to do with me," she hastily assured the messenger.

So they'd found out, had they? Well, it was too late now.

"I'm very disappointed in you," said the Q-R, "and surprised you should resort to such a foolish ruse."

"Well," I said, "it worked."

"Long ago," the Q-R obstinately grumbled on, "this

would have been a punishable crime. Since the notion of crime has been abolished, there is nothing we can do, I'm sorry to say."

I felt hurt in an odd way; he'd been so nice and would-be understanding before.

"But it worked, didn't it?" I persisted.

"Worked? Of course it didn't work."

"What," I demanded. "You mean you found out before you mated the two halves?"

"Indeed, no. I wish we had. We found out *when* we mated them."

"What happened?" I asked.

"My dear young man," said the Q-R, "have you never heard of two negatives making a positive? In this case, unfortunately, the reverse is true. Two halves of the same person make a *decided* negative."

"But one was male and one female," I protested. "I don't understand—"

"We were dealing," said the Q-R, "with a true-life and not an android." Did I detect bitterness? I thought of the farms at Four BAA and began to feel strange. "With a true-life," said the Q-R, "the most important element is the life-spark, and the life-sparks offered both belonged to one being —yourself. The moment they touched they exploded and returned into vacuum. You have killed your child. You will not, of course, be allowed to make another until you are out of Jang, and even then, I'm afraid, you may find it difficult to get permission."

I knew I was going to be sick, and luckily he did too, and turned on an emergency drift for me.

He was quite kind afterward, and stopped me from banging my brains out on the crystallize chairs.

But he needn't have bothered.

I went and drowned in my bubble the first moment I could.

PART 4

1

When I woke up in the Limbo tub, they started straight in at me. I'd gone and got myself a new body in BOO, and then gone and ruined it, and was still exceeding my ration, and I'd have to stop, and the next change—I must have screamed or had a fit or something. Apparently my emotional response wires got all tangled up and something overcharged itself and exploded. I yelled and yelled at them. They said I yelled that I didn't want a new body, but wanted to stay there in the tub forever. They got worried about me and hundreds of Q-Rs fluttered around saying soothing things. They were promising me any body I wanted in the end and telling me that it didn't matter how I kept exceeding my ration, and there, there, and I'd have to leave sometime because other people were waiting. They doubled the number of people waiting every time they mentioned it, and I suppose eventually I got altruistic and agreed to come out.

I chose this terribly ordinary sort of female body. It was thin and fragile, with insignificant breasts and lank straggly hair. I designed it with slow, meticulous, perverted care. I made it too long in the leg and waist, with dark, unvibrant eyes, behind which I could hide and be safe. I was being a weirdo, not as bad as Hatta the compulsive horror visitation, but strange and alien nevertheless, in a world where almost everyone is beautiful. Then I hung around Limbo for ages, and they let me, only hinting every so often that I ought to go home.

Hergal and Hatta came to visit me.

Hergal, a gorgeous male again, stared at my plain sad appearance and looked slightly uneasy. He liked exoticism, after all. Hatta just accepted me with every blink of his four pink eyes.

They were very careful and kind. So careful and kind it was positively tactless and spiteful. Hergal kept making bright remarks and telling me the wonderful things to be seen outside now. Hatta refrained strainingly from repeating his beastly marriage proposition. But I suppose they had some effect on me. I decided to go home after all.

They wouldn't let me go in my bubble. They were ever so diplomatic about it, but firm. They flew me home in a robotically controlled, unmessable-around-with bird-plane in soothing yellow tones.

I went into the porch under the golden flower opening and shutting and wandered through the pristinely clean rooms, where a few machines were still at it, dusting and polishing. I went into the garden and suddenly saw the pet by the pool having a thorough and very involved sort of wash.

"Oh pet!" I cried. I remembered sending it away from me, home alone, so callously, just because it reminded me of my time with Lorun. I realized how long I'd left it alone and not thought of it, and was stricken with aching remorse. I rushed forward, arms open, and it gave a screaming, honking, hysterical sort of snarl and fled away across the gardens, hooting.

I felt awful about it, shocked and weak. It was a final blow. I sat there by the pool, hugging my refused arms, racked by pain and guilt, and suddenly woke up to what was the matter. I could have laughed it was so simple. It wasn't bitterness the pet had just displayed, but genuine, bewildered fright. I'd changed. I was no longer the known Jang girl with long scarlet hair, willowy waist and exotic bosom, all beauty and physical grace. I was this lank, thin, paste-faced twig of life. It didn't know me. *Farathoom!* I probably even had a different smell!

So I leaped into my bubble, rushed over to Limbo, and burst in. They looked quite peculiar when they saw me. I explained and they backed off, saying, "Oh no, er, no, no, er, certainly not . . ." and so on, after which I remembered how I'd unintentionally won their sympathy before, and went into these feigned hysterics, screaming about the awful things I was going to do, like jumping into the tub as I was. They gave me a spray of something that made me go limp, and then discussed me flurriedly and agreed they'd better humor me. So I made them get out my records and ordered an exact copy of what I'd been before, scarlet hair and all.

I walked out to the pool, jingling chains of gold anemones and purple shells, singing a Jang ditty. I was unprepared for what happened. This white furry comet hurled itself out of the glass-grass and leaped into my arms, covering my face with soaking wet kisses.

"Oh, what fools we are." I almost wept as we chased each other around the pool and got tangled up together in the resustated silk flowers.

The pet gave me a sudden long, telling, orange stare. It seemed to be saying, "Do you know, there was some stupid female here earlier, trying to pass herself off as you?"

2

Things didn't seem so bad after that. I married Hergal for three units, and we had a *groshing* time. The pet got to like him, but Hergal was always a bit *tosky* about the pet, looking around nervously to make sure it wasn't creeping up on him for the kill or anything. Everybody thought I was terribly original going back to an earlier body, and lots of people started doing the same. It was fun. You could actually recognize someone occasionally. Then Hergal and Kley got married and went off to BOO for a while, Kley female and being a real bully and screaming at everyone, because for some reason she's always so aggressive when she's female. As for Danor, she—still a girl—was the center of vast attention because she'd stopped having love with anyone at all; of course everyone was running after her—even Jang from other circles—and it'd become quite a fashion in Four BEE to be "yearning for a *vrek* in her arms." But Danor and I still shared a sort of cold shadow and never spoke of it.

Hatta came around, and I found he too had reverted to an old body, the three yellow-eyed one, with spots. Still, there was only one head to cope with, at least.

"I didn't ask you at Limbo," Hatta began, "but I still wish you'd marry me for a little, just a morning if you like."

"I've told you," I told him.

He sighed, looked mournful, though you could barely see it through all that ugliness.

"You don't understand," he said.

"No, I suppose not."

"Can't you see," Hatta said, pathetic, "the body I'm in doesn't matter that much? I'm still me."

"Well, be you in a *groshing* body and I'll marry you immediately," I said wildly. "That's a promise."

"No, no," wailed Hatta." Oh, look, think, *ooma.* I want you—I want *you.* You've been a hundred different bodies; I've wanted you as you are now, as you were with all that silver hair and the antennae, as you were all those *vreks* ago with soft-blue tinted skin and golden eyes. I've wanted you as a male. I've wanted you as you were last, pale and thin, a little nothing girl. Can't you do the same? It's not the body that matters; the physical side is a joke in Four BEE and BAA and BOO. It's irrelevant. It's like wanting someone because they're wearing red toe-rings. Oh, *ooma,* can't you understand?"

And I almost did. I really almost did. But I couldn't stand the thought of having love with him as he was now.

"Go away, Hatta," I snapped.

And away he went.

3

And that evening Four BEE was shocked, stunned, stultified, nonplussed, and staggered by the news of the Great Archaeological Expedition.

Flashes came sizzling across the city. A "sympton of the times," they called it, a "general desire to get out and at it!" Well, I knew the feeling all right.

Apparently this man, an older male from BEE, had spotted what looked to him like possible ancient ruins out in the desert between BEE and BOO, but well off the sand-ship route. It was quite likely, since nobody ever went into the desert now except to rush through to another city, preferably without looking at anything. But this male—eccentric and exciting he sounded—actually went out there in his special private bird-plane, with *clear windows!* He'd been making some sort of study of ancient pre-city history, wars and sagas and whatnot, and then the civilizations that grew out of them like obstreperous phoenixes, nomadic and desert-roaming and so on.

I was fascinated as these flashes continued at great length. They ended up by saying this supermale wanted vol-

unteers. I nearly went *zaradann*. I signaled the Flash Center
and asked where I could get hold of him. I just didn't stop to
think. I felt wildly excited again. My poor battered old brain
was closing up to all the recent bad bits and fastening its
frenzied tentacles on the Expedition.

The Flash Center robots were very helpful. They put me
through direct to this man, in his weird all-long pillars and
false-hair carpet villa. He was known as *Glar* Assule, the *glar*
presumably self-designated. He was handsome but in a most
odd way. He'd chosen a body that looked somewhat aged. I
mean he had lines, wrinkles, and the jet black hair receded
from a big domed forehead. He'd honestly made himself look
just like a real *glar* from all those aeons ago. He wore a black
robe and a single steel ornament on a chain. I gathered that
the ornament was based on some design he claimed to have
found in the desert on one of his earlier trips.

"Good evening, *Glar*." I dug in at once, radiating enthusiasm, but he didn't respond. He frowned at me.

"How may I help you?" he asked, looking as if the
thought of helping me made him go ice cold from the feet up.

"Well," I murmured, respectful, "I've just heard about
your *grosh*—marvelous expedition, and how you wanted volunteers."

"Indeed," he said.

We sat and looked at each other's three-dimensional images.

"Well," I said eventually, "I want to be a volunteer."

"I see."

Oh *floopy farathoom*, it was just like chatting to a Q-R.

"Look," I said then, after this long beastly pause, "if
you want volunteers, you're just going about the best way to
get them, I don't think."

"Actually," said *Glar* Assule grandly, "the sort of volunteer I had hoped for would not be one of the Jang."

I laughed. No, really I did. It just rushed out of me like
something with wings. I really detested him. He was literally
chucking all the failures of the past *vrek* back in my face by
saying that.

"You don't want Jang," I barked at him. He jumped. I can be pretty nerve-racking when I try. "Why not?"

"I don't think I have to explain," he said.

"Oh but you do. Common politeness, or have you never heard of it?"

He went stiff and pompous, then droned out:

"Jang are too irresponsible, I'm afraid, for the serious study I have in mind."

"Well," I said, "Jang are probably all you'll get. We're all pretty *droad*"—I didn't care about using the slang on him now, he deserved it—"and have this *groshing* youthful enthusiasm apparently, which is being wasted. I personally can think of nothing nicer than studying an ancient ruin, in the middle of those *derisann* black mountains, but if you told my makers about it, they'd probably laugh till they puked all over you." Whereupon I made a very nasty Jang-slang sign at him and bashed the recluse switch.

Well, he'd never take me on anyway, so there was no harm done, I reasoned, as soon as the glow wore off and I began to reproach myself.

But I got a real surprise. Ages afterward, when I was deciding whether or not to signal Thinta and go drown my sorrows with her somewhere, experimenting as to whether the pet would go around my neck, which it wouldn't, the signal light came on and there was *Glar* Assule again, very edgy and pink looking.

"I think," he waded in, "that your youthful rudeness points to possible spirit, and I might consider giving you a place on the team after all."

But I was feeling sadistic.

"Oh yes," I crooned, "and just how big is the team?"

He hummed and hahhed, but we got there eventually. There were three others. Apparently he'd been sending out personal flashes for ages, with no luck, and the official flash had brought in these three droopy-sounding persons who were just doing it, I noted later, out of misguided notions of culture. They weren't actually Jang, but they were useless. Twitty old *Glar* had realized I might be really interested to sit around and listen to him expounding theories and so on, and to poke about among the rumbling dark mountains of our lost forgotten world.

He still had to be a nuisance though. He'd take me, he said, providing I apologized.

"I apologize," I said at once. It didn't matter to me. I couldn't resist, though, once his image was gone, making that sign again and hissing:

"No I don't. I meant every syllable."

Childish, but slightly satisfying.

4

Thinta told me I was *zara-dann* to go, Kley laughed raucously, Hatta just looked repulsively sad. I wished he looked handsome and sad, and then I could gratify my impulse to cuddle him and say "Oh, *ooma,* don't!" without being sick immediately afterward. He didn't, though, so I didn't and wasn't.

I was amazed when Danor came to see me. There were about eleven males and even a couple of females hanging around her, with a glittery, predatory look of waiting in their sequined eyes.

"They have a running bet," said Danor, drawing me aside, "to see which one I'll succumb to first."

I was startled by Danor; once so dashing, now she seemed . . . serene?

"That sounds pretty *drumdik,*" I said. "Have you tried changing to male to shake them off?"

"Yes, actually I did," whispered Danor. "They all promptly suicided and came back as girls." She gave a giggle and I saw a ghostly, sad little hint of mischief in her eyes. "Anyway, *ooma,*" Danor said, "have fun in the ruins." And she kissed me so sweetly I made an abrupt mental note that, next time I was male and Danor female, it might be an idea to try the floaters again and see if we could do any better that way. As for the hangers-on, they went every shade of green and puce, wondering if I'd beaten them all to it.

Glar Assule signaled me again and said the team was going to meet in five units outside—guess!—the Robotics Museum.

"How *derisann!*" I glowed, and he gave me a dirty look.

He said he had some urgent things to attend to for the next three or four units, hence the delay, but I think he was just procrastinating, hoping a few more people would call him and ask to go. No one did, though, and five units later there we were, feeling beastly and conspicuous, with this rotten little robot bee buzzing around us, getting snippets of information for the flashes. I told it to something off, and everyone looked disapproving.

The three other volunteers were an absolute catastrophe. They weren't even pro-Jang either, at least not here. They thought I should be having love or ecstasy, etc., well out of their range of reception. They insisted on calling me "dear" all the time too, with a sort of undertone that showed they'd really like to call me lots of other things, like Scruff-Bag, and Intolerable-Pest-for-Coming-and-Spoiling-Our-Chance-to-Get-at-the-*Glar*. They were all female.

He turned up late and bloated with himself; he took us to a private sand-ship he'd hired specially and had reprogrammed to get to the right place. It was full of his equipment, his robots, and his idea of how to furnish a sand-ship—which meant orange hairy drapes and blinding bronze—and him. The females twit-twittered around him. "Yes, *Glar*," and "No, *Glar*," they smarmed. And was the *Glar* comfortable? And could they tell the robot to get the *Glar* anything? I was so glad I'd brought the pet. They cringed whenever it went near them, which it didn't actually, if it could avoid them. *Glar* Assule wasn't too bad, though. He looked as if he was repressing a seizure, patted the pet's head and nearly got bitten, and said he was glad I'd taken an interest in the desert wildlife. I agreed the pet was pretty wild.

Anyway, we eventually got started and—joy and delight!—there was this Transparency Tower, clear all the time. We went to sit in it, but pretty soon the three females got uneasy; they went off to rustle up some desert orange on ice, or play with their light-crochet machines.

The pet and I and the *Glar* stayed on, and he looked quite impressed by the way the desert mesmerized me. Once I saw a troop of purple animals with long, long fur, burrowing around some dunes, and he was actually able to tell me what they were.

I began to feel lighthearted. Don't ever do that; it tempts some dark and evil force abroad in the universe.

In the night, I gather, the three females had a fight as to which one was going to have love with dear old Assule, and then, when they'd practically killed each other and the victor staggered along to his cabin with torn plumage and smeared eyelids, it turned out he was stoned with sleep and threw her out when she protested. It really made a din, all this, but the pet and I got a good laugh out of it.

Dawn came and we were there. The females were very upset because they'd arranged this elaborate first meal for the *Glar* and he refused to take time to eat it.

He was very good at getting us organized, though. I suppose his domineering streak helped. We had hot wine and four oxygen tablets each.

"When you get there," he said, "remember to breathe normally and not strain to get extra air; you won't need it. And it's *not* like swimming under water, when you don't breathe at all," he added to me. I shrugged. All right, so all Jang swim under water. So. Then the robots got our equipment and went out through the small air lock, and we went out afterward, and oh—

It's all *real* out there.

It's all beautiful and real, and throbbing and singing and alive!

I staggered; he grabbed me and snapped: "I told you you had to breathe, didn't I? Why don't you pay attention?"

But I had breathed. I'd more or less gasped my lungs inside out.

It was all so—

And so—

I shook as I stood there.

It was dawn and red this time from some *ooma* mountain bursting flames, and greener near the top of the sky, and velvet dark above that, with a last sugar-sprinkle of stars. All around, the tall shapes—not buildings but mountains—craned up and up as if to see us, or possibly to avoid seeing us and just stare into all that clear sky. And the sky was so enormous. It made me giddy.

"Here we are," said the *Glar,* as grandly as if he'd invented it. "Come along." And we trooped after him across the blood-soaked-by-light dawn sand.

He pointed to a rock platform and some rock terraces leading up to it, and up again from it.

"There's the site," he announced.

"And here's the sun," I breathed.

The pet suddenly lost its mind, or found its mind or something, and rushed from my side to roll and spray everyone with the crazy sand.

"Oh, stop it! Stop the nasty thing!" chirruped the females.

The *Glar* never even noticed.

He was striding on ahead, the robots and machinery trundling after him, making big runnels in the sand for us to walk in.

The site was supposedly something to do with those nomads and things, a primitive rock citadel where they stopped off once in a while, and these were the foundations. Assule reckoned they'd been covered with sand for ages and then some pre-rain storm had blown it all off. It would rain soon, he said, and then we'd have to scramble back to the ship and take cover. They were very wet rains, apparently.

The third female kept going swoony and having to lean on Assule because she hadn't mastered the breathing technique. The others were furious they hadn't thought of that one first.

We had first meal up on the site, sitting on heavy rugs. Assule went on and on about the civilization that had been here first. It could have been very interesting if he hadn't managed to make it so boring. I don't know how he did it, actually. Some latent talent for sending everyone *droad,* I suppose.

After this, he went stamping around the site, disappearing and reappearing from behind rock spires, with about six robots to give him a hand. The rest of us sat on the rugs and the world became turquoise all around us.

Eventually he came back.

I sat up straight and waited for him to give me an ancient swing-pick or something, but he didn't. He said:

"I think I'll start machines six and eight over there." And my heart fell down the stairway of my ribs into my stomach and lay there like solid storm. Here we were again: Always consult the computer. . . . The machine knows best. . . . Oh, they pop automatically in half a split, anyway. . . .

"But *Glar,*" I burst out, "aren't we going to do anything ourselves?"

"What?" He was scandalized. "Of course not."

"But can't I even brush the sand off the relics as they come up?" I pleaded, being pretty optimistic too about those relics, I must say.

"Certainly not," he said, "you might damage something."

The three females fluttered agreeingly and looked at me as if I was obscene even to think of going near anything so precious with my clumsy Jang hands. So all he truly wanted us for was just as an audience to his boring old voice.

And all through that *derisann* desert unit, I traipsed around behind those machines, with the pet at my heels. They drilled and sawed and nothing was found. They clipped and buzzed and inched up the terraces, and drew a complete blank.

"It's definitely a foundation," he muttered all over us, till I felt quite sorry for his embarrassment.

It went on and on, unit after unit. A bird-plane with covered-in window spaces flew out to us from Four BEE bringing supplies. The females cogitated sullenly. He was proving unobtainable, and they were pretty bored with his ideas by now.

And then, one evening, just as he was going practically *zaradann* with frustration, one of the machines gave a great hoot and a heave, and the rock floor gave way, and smash, crash, boom, down it fell into a vast underground chamber underneath. When the sand and gravel cleared, we pounded up and found we'd discovered a storeroom or something. At least Assule said that's what it was, though I don't really think he knew, but was just guessing.

The machines lowered other machines into the cavity to send us up pictures of what it was like, and very uninspiring it was too. The search lasted for ages, and eventually they unearthed this one shard of ancient pottery stuff that was actually, according to the *Glar*, breakable. So he wouldn't let us go anywhere remotely near it, and the robots took it back to the ship to investigate it.

It was quite late when Assule came howling into the saloon, screaming about an inscription.

"It's an old desert proverb," he croaked, holding on to one of the females for support. She smirked. "Yes, yes, it is. You can just make it out. Look at this three-dimensional re-production machine number nine has made."

"What's it mean?" we asked. It was unintelligible and blurred, and in another language, though one or two words sort of looked a little familiar, here and there.

"Ah," said the *Glar*. He sat down and gave us another lecture on the nomadic peoples before he told us. What the inscription actually said was:

DO NOT BITE THE SUN, TRAVELER,
YOU WILL BURN YOUR MOUTH.

According to Assule, this was their way of saying be sure you stay in the shade where you can and wear your *oosha*—which is a sort of desert man's sun hat thing—and carry enough water. In other words, the sun is a dangerous enemy; don't take risks or you'll get hurt.

But somehow there was another significance in the words for me. They haunted me all night, and I didn't sleep. I went to sit in the T. Tower, and they haunted me there too.

Don't bite the sun, don't bite the sun—my mouth burned me.

6

Next morning Assule was much better, or worse, depending on how you looked at it. His confidence had been restored. He strutted and preened himself all over the place, and even allowed himself to have a half-interest in one of the three females. It was rather engaging, watching her trying to coax him off to some cave or other, when all he wanted to do was tell her about this terribly old tribe who used to eat each other, ceremoniously, of course, when the *ponka* herds got low.

"Now that we've made a start," he deigned to say to me as we ate third meal, "we'll find all sorts of levels under the site, I've no doubt. Weapon rooms, for example."

Oh, it really could have been interesting.

Well, it could.

I mean, I've got this thing about ruins and citadels and weapons and dragons and exotic intrigues and so on. But Assule soon made it seem as though we were listening to him reprogramming one of his floating floors or something.

Anyhow, the machines went on digging and churning and crashing, and found absolutely nothing at all. Once there was this boom, and we rushed off to see what it was, but it was just some power charge or other exploding.

I began to feel claustrophobic about the site and wanted to rush out into the desert and roll around like the pet kept doing, but I felt a bit agoraphobic too, so didn't. I actually thought the pet might run off and leave me for its native element, but it always came back. I got used to seeing it scampering across the rock fells and dunes, mottled with loose grains, sneezing and honking happily and then leaping into my arms and scattering sand in every direction.

Things were tense now. It wasn't our silly insignificant tenseness, either, it was sand tenseness and mountain-and-sky tenseness. Assule informed us that it was the desert waiting for the rain. He felt it too, you see, but the females didn't. They looked blank and I could see the thought: Oh, well, you have to put up with these terribly attractive males who go batty now and then.

Another plane came out with supplies, and one of the females actually gave in and elected to go home on it. The other two glared at each other to see who would be next. A little later one of them, the more typical of the two, took me aside among the rocks.

"You know, dear," she tweeted, "I really can't understand what a little Jang girl like you sees out here to make her stay."

"Oh, it's Assule," I said.

"Assule?" she queried, shocked.

"Oh yes." I smiled. "I know he couldn't go on without me."

"Well!" she started.

"Oh, it may sound vain, I know," I said, sweet and sorrowing, "but when you've known him as long as I have . . ."

"Known him as long as—?"

"Shared his ups and downs . . ."

"Ups and downs—?"

"Been his support and comforter in times of stress . . ."

"Comforter—?"

"You realize that he needs you, really needs you, just for the odd word of encouragement, you know, just the occasional warm embrace," I finished up, watching her control her impending hysteria.

"He's your maker," she suddenly accused, seeking a reasonable explanation and a way around what I'd said.

I looked affronted.

"Certainly not," I snapped.

Poor woman. She went white around the nose and her eyes gave off sparks as I strolled away.

It was a bit of a nuisance, though. I had been toying with the idea of going home and now I'd have to stick it out to the bitter end. Couldn't have *Glar* Assule prancing around, all happiness and joy, without his little support and comforter, could I?

But the desert was making me feel really strange. I kept on having dreams about being a desert woman, in an *oosha* and long dark veil, trucking across the wastes, by burning day and black night, the odd volcano my scarlet lamp. Sometimes I had this child with me, pale-faced and anxious.

"Maker," it kept saying, "where's the next watering place?" And I knew it would die on me if we didn't get to one quickly, and I didn't know where the watering place was or even how to recognize it. And then the dream would sort of slip and we'd both be lying there flat out, our faces in the sand, with this huge orange fire ringing around the sky above us and a voice pounding and pounding out:

"Don't bite the sun. Don't bite the sun."

And then the site was invaded.

Oh, it could have been a laugh, really, if any of us had had a shred of humor left that morning.

There we were at first meal on the rock, Assule, the two females, who now studiously avoided me, myself, and the pet. I looked up from a plate of fried root-bread and honey, and what should I see, ho-ho, but this tawny, furry face staring at me from around a rock. The pet barked. Yes, it was one of those again, the long-eared purposeful ones with ski-feet. It flipped these ears around, twitched its antennae, and sort of went "Fpmf" down its nose.

"Assule, what's that?" I started to ask, when suddenly they were on us. I suppose it was the smell of cooked food that brought them. They'd probably been traveling for units across the sand, following their furry noses. The females screamed as great elongated feet came down splat in the root-bread and tawny paws flailed among the opal-wine.

"Are they dangerous?" I tried to ask Assule, while I attempted not to be trampled into the honey.

"Come on!" Assule yelled, and we rushed out of it and back to the sand-ship, leaving the rugs, the meal, the machines, everything, at the mercy of those great feet and ridiculous ears.

We staggered into the T. Tower, turned on Zoom Scanners, and stared. We had a perfect view of the citadel foundations positively dripping furry bodies. They were devouring the food, slurping up the wine, and going "Fpmf!" all over the place. Pretty soon they began to eat the rugs, spreading honey on them first, I might add.

"I just hope they don't get at the machines," Assule just hoped, but they did.

They were really very intelligent, in a *zaradann* sort of way. They had a lovely time finding out how everything worked, then dismantling it. They rode machine number eight down the terraces, clinging on all over it and bomping the sides with their feet; they rolled clear when it finally pitched over and smashed to bits in the sand.

Assule had, by this time, set up a background music of steady wailing. I kept trying to find out what the animals were, and he seemed to think I was awful for still wanting to know. I suppose it was too much, really.

About noon some of the wild activity quieted. They lay around the site, sleeping it off.

"I just hope they don't spot the sand-ship," Assule started off again, and sure enough it was the signal for furry paw pointing, "fmpf"-ing, and a general pound in our direction.

"Oh! Oh!" screamed the two females.

"Please be calm," snapped Assule, suddenly deciding to be calm himself for a change. "We're quite safe. I'll activate the shock wall."

He played around with some red dials and things marked: For purposes of defense only. Unauthorized use punishable by fine—which was a pretty obsolete injunction, since no one gets fined for anything anymore, though the Committee probably wishes they would. Apparently it worked. There was a sort of shimmer in the air around the ship suddenly, and as soon as the ski-feet made furry contact, they jumped about five yards high and keeled over, looking utterly blissful.

"It won't kill them, will it?" I implored.

Assule didn't throttle me, surprisingly.

"No," he said, "something smaller would be killed, yes, but they are simply stunned. I don't believe in damaging these interesting species unnecessarily."

I felt relieved, and really, they looked ever so happy as they reeled off the shock wall. They kept on trying for about three splits; I think some of them only did it to have an Essential Experience. You could see them inspecting their fallen comrades' ecstatic faces first and almost weighing things up, thinking, well, it looks like fun, and then rushing into the wall, ears and fur flying. In the end, though, they went off and had a "fpmf" talk about the situation, came back and carefully towed the casualties (?) out of shock range, then picked them up over their backs and went leaping away across the sands.

The females started going swoony, saw Assule wasn't taking any notice, and gave up.

We waited about twenty splits to be on the safe side, deactivated the wall, and wandered out to the site. According to Assule, there was no chance of their coming back. Apparently they never return to the scene of one of their raids; in fact they'll go miles out of their way to avoid it, once their extraordinarily strong smell-powers tell them they're getting near. It seemed to point to a sort of guilt complex, as far as I could see, but Assule more or less told me not to be a *floop* when I said so.

And the site was *drumdik*. Oh, the utter, unqualified abandoned mess of it all. For once the females and I joined forces in trying to stop Assule from going completely *zaradann*. It wasn't much good, though. He went roaring around the rock turrets, dabbing at honey and chewed rugs on the machines, cradling broken robots, and screaming at intact robots to mend everything. Actually, once he stopped getting in their way, the robots from the ship made a very good job of it. Machine number eight was the only failure, and they had to scrap it.

"In order to prevent any further calamities, I'm going to get the robots to rig up a shock wall all around the site," Assule told me, over the row of banging and repairing, "around the site and the ship. A radius of about—" And he quoted some vast area or other. I was barely listening.

"Look, Assule," I said, "now's our chance to prove we're better than the machines."

"What?"

"No, listen," I persisted, ignoring his horrified indignation, "while they're out of action at least let's try to find something ourselves."

"Certainly not," said Assule. "I've told you, machinery is best."

"Well," I said, "they don't seem to have found much so far."

"Please don't forget the pottery shard with the inscription. Of course, no doubt you think that very little in your untutored Jang fashion."

"Look," I said, "I'm just as interested as you are, honestly, but really that machine fell right down into your storeroom, or whatever it is. It could have smashed and buried all sorts of valuable relics, if there'd been any more than the one we found."

"I find your attitude offensive," Assule glowered. It was just like talking to a lump of rock.

"Talking to you is just like talking to a lump of rock," I said.

Assule went pompous.

"You will apologize," Assule told me.

"Oh, for goodness sake," I snapped, "I'm not going to apologize for stating a fact. And while we're at it, I unapologize for the other time."

And then I really got mad at him and made that Jang sign again.

Without waiting to watch him go into automatic combustion, I turned around, leaving even my bee, and stalked off.

Right off the site.

Away from the sand-ship.

Into the desert.

7

I'd heard of people doing that, walking off in fury and not realizing where they were going. Thinta told me I once made her so angry with my stealing habits that she walked right into the pool without taking any oxygen, and nearly ended up in Limbo.

When I realized, I found I didn't know where I was or anything. There was no sign of the site or the ship, nor a sound of all that noisy repair work that had still been going on when I left. There was just sand and more sand, glittering, and a horizon of black crags and impending sunset. I had this moment of absolute, icy panic. I was lost. Then I had this second moment of absolute, icy panic. Oxygen! I'd had my usual four tablets this morning, which would last me till tomorrow, but after that, what then? Oh, I really got in a state.

Then I had a thought. Turn around and follow my own footsteps back through the sand, that's what I'd do. Which is what I did, and I was really getting elated when they suddenly stopped in a fresh drift. There are always little sand winds eddying around, and this one had really made a nice job of losing me. I climbed a rock spire and looked around in every direction, but saw nothing but rainbow glitter on the smooth and unmarked dunes.

And then I did see something, and this thing was moving. Oh no, I gasp-thought, the ski-feet are after me. I wondered what ghastly furry death they would condemn me to. Then I saw that this thing was a solitary thing, and much much smaller than a ski-foot, and it was streaking toward me over the faceless desert. The pet! Wonderful! It must have followed me, leaving its own track of six fresh paw marks, which we would now follow back to the ship. Calling and honking, we bounded to meet each other. The pet leaped into my arms and kissed me passionately on the nose and ears.

"Oh, *ooma*," I gasped, "clever, *derisann ooma*!"

And holding it nestled close, furry and comforting, I started back along its track.

And then, of course, this sand storm had to start, didn't it?

I was so scared. You couldn't see or breathe or anything. I got my transparent tunic off and wrapped it around my face. I could glimpse things that way through the embroidery and the sand, and I could just breathe slightly too, and with the oxygen tablets it was enough. I tried to protect the pet, but it burrowed into my skin and seemed all right. I suppose it had weathered storms before. Its fur fluffed up around it too, in added protection. There was no point in going on and, besides, my bare parts were being nastily stung, so I got us into the lee of the nearest bit of rock and cowered down into the sand there and waited.

I'll never forget the sound of that sand wind. I think I'll hear it all my life.

Visibility cleared eventually and I dug us out; we stood there and stared around us. Well, if I was lost before, I was *really* lost now. I redonned my tunic and began aimlessly walking. Every so often I'd sort of choke out to the pet: "It's no use, why bother?" and slump down. And then I'd get fierce with myself and say, "But I'll never find it if I sit here, and I might if I walk on." And on I'd go until the next choke and slump.

It was very dark and still. The stars were out. And there was this colossal feeling of waiting. The pet kept lifting up its head and sniffing.

Then this roaring started, somehow near yet far away all at once. I wondered in vague hysterics if there were still dragons in these parts, or if the ski-feet developed new and particularly awful personalities at night. But it was only thunder, in fact. And soon there were blinding green flashes of lightning to go with it.

"The rain," I said to the pet, my sunken heart going down to about my kneecaps, but the pet just looked thrilled and wriggled until I let it go. It dashed about and rolled in the sand.

"Well, I'm glad you're pleased," I said.

In its good old desert units I imagined the rain was a big event; even though I didn't know anything about it, I'd worked out it only happened every three *vreks,* from what Assule said.

And then there was this sound. A kind of soft, soft, pat-pat noise, like tiny paws clapping. I was just thinking how pretty it was, crazy and disorientated as I'd become, when the heavens opened and the desert was under water. The rain rustled and thundered to the earth, but over it all I could hear a chorus of excited twittering and wailing and squeaking all around me from millions of small furry throats in sand burrows and rock holes, celebrating the rain-rite. You couldn't see eye gleams through the deluge, but I knew they were there. The pet got one of my ankle chains in its mouth and gently but firmly tugged me to some sort of shelter in the rocks. A bit late, though. I was soaked. I'm sure Four BEE could produce a rain-resistant fabric, but who needs it in Four BEE? The only rain there had been a couple of widely spaced drops after a minor Jang sabotage.

The pet honked and honked.

"You're right," I said, trying to dry my wet face on my wet hands, "it *is* beautiful."

And it was really: solid silver wetness, the song of the desert drinking and drinking all around me. And from the burrows and holes, the song of life.

I never thought I'd sleep through the discomfort and the noise, but I did. I dreamed that I was a desert woman with a child, and we had found, at last, a watering place.

Dawn, like a pale green note of music in the mountains, woke me, and I sat up, damp, cold, and alone.

Now I'll die, I thought, out here with no nice robots to carry me to Limbo. I'll die of cold and hunger and oxygen deficiency, and loneliness. The pet had gone. "The rain's stopped, anyway," I congratulated it, as I crawled out of the rock and began to see.

And then I nearly did die, but not because of anything I'd thought of. It was what was out there that did it.

I'd never seen such unexpected, unlooked-for beauty. That the dunes, starved of water for so much of their life, could return a vote of thanks like this for what to them must have seemed a mere half-cup, was beyond me. I groveled mentally before the wonder of it all.

The desert had blossomed.

I thought the rocks were on fire again, but it was the flame of sudden flowers, the sparks of erupted gorse. Cacti had leaped high in the night, bursting as they went into showers of green orchids. Pools lay between the rock sweeps, perhaps draining even now, but crowded with quick fern, starred with petals grown in seconds by rain, knocked free by rain in ten splits. And in the sand grass was waving. I looked and far off, in every direction, I saw the purple and the green, the gold, the peridot of blowing stems, not silk or glass or satin-of-steel, but living feathers, greenness that breathed. And I breathed, deeply, slowly, because the growing things had saved my life, had given me, in a night of miracle and silver, all the oxygen my lungs would ever crave.

I went forward, nervous at first, afraid to tread on this carpet of life, but all around the little animals were rushing, bouncing and orgying in the growth. I saw a tribe of ski-feet in the distance, dancing together in a weird, almost awful, dance of strange and primitive joy. Suddenly I was part of it. I, with my brand of mankind, my Jangness, my cityness. I tore off the ridiculous chains and see-through, the earrings, the ornaments. I could have put real flowers in my hair, but could not be so sacrilegious as to pick them. Besides, my hair was scarlet fur, and I danced and ran and laughed and sang with the mad small animals among the glory of the woken green; it was so hot now, I was dry as a bone.

Then I found the pet.

It burst at me from the grasses like a pure, pale blossom.

I can hardly remember the laughing and the running now, and the playing and the dancing, but I remember the happiness, the happiness like a wound, that bleeds the life-spark.

Oh, we ran, side by side, the pet and I, and never have I known such closeness with any of my race, my mankind, as I knew with that white animal I stole, in casual and neurotic need, from a store in Four BEE.

Once, when we lay in the grass, I said to it:

"You must have a name; no, no, you must. You are a personality, the same as I, a being, a life." And I called the pet Thunder-Flower, because of the flowers all around us, that grew from rain and flaring light and thunder, and then we ran on.

And how simple it would have been if we had never found our way back to the sand-ship. But we did. I hardly noticed the slight familiarity of the landscape. The rock ter-races were bright with flowers now in the redness of twilight.

We rushed on side by side. Sometimes I was a little ahead, knee-deep in the dune grass, sometimes it was the pet, its head barely cresting the green, its fur pink in the sunset's aftermath. And then it was ahead of me and I saw it leap high, clear of all the grasses, and drop back, and not appear again. Then I saw the shimmer in the air.

"Oh no!" I called out to the desert and the sky. "Oh no,

oh no, oh no, oh no!'' And I ran on and flung myself against the shock wall that Assule had erected to prevent calamities.

Yes, it's a strange sensation, an absolute tremble of fiery ecstasy all over, like the near-climax of a love machine, but I was barely dazed when the robots came and picked me up.

The pet, of course, was dead.

8

Assule kept telling me what a fool I was.

"I told you about the shock wall," he shouted. "You might have been hurt far more than you were."

He didn't mention the pet. He did mention that any accident I'd suffered was really my own fault for rushing off so rudely. I just lay there in my cabin, looking at him, and said "Shut up" every once in a while. The females hung together in the doorway and said how disgraceful it was I'd been found quite nude, and where were all my chains and seethrough?

Once they'd drawn off a bit, I made one of the robots bring me the pet's limp, furry, white body. I stared at its glazed orange eyes. It looked so full of bliss in death.

"I want a plane back to the city," I told the *Glar*. "Now."

Well, he was only too pleased to see the back of me, so he got one, and I got in and rode home, staring at the covered-in window spaces, the pet in my lap. There was nothing left to see, anyway. The desert's blossoming cannot be sustained for more than a single unit. The glory I had run through had been dying already.

At Four BEE I went straight to Limbo.

"This is my pet," I told them, "it's very important to me. I want you to give it a new body."

But they wouldn't, and I'd known they wouldn't. They tried to explain how ethical they were being.

"We cannot do this for an animal," they said. "Besides, it has been left too long." But this was only an excuse. Oh, please, make it have been an excuse.

So I went home alone. And I was alone there too.

And I dreamed all night of the desert and the sun I must not bite, and at last I knew the significance that the proverb held for me. I was so tired I could admit it now. I had tried so often and so hard, and it had been no good.

The sun. Oh, yes. The sun. A little bit of breakable clay had suddenly defeated me, from its nest in a desert of rainbow and erupted fire. I knew what the sun was; perhaps those records meant it the same way, I'm not sure. The sun was the Ordained Way of living. In my case it was the Ordained Way of going to hypno-school, of being Jang, graduating to an Older Person, one's entire life mapped out irrevocably, even death not allowed, but merely a new body, or a long rest in a mind-darkening twilight, after which the cycle begins again, with all past memories wiped clean. So irrevocable, so unavoidable, so terrible, so dull, so doomed to a tragedy that was even too small, too dull, too doomed to be a tragedy at all. Don't bite the sun, you'll burn your mouth. I'd bitten ceaselessly, hopelessly, and I was burned, I was burned. I was a cinder.

I knew what was happening to me, and repeated aloud:

"The pet has officially cut me out of its circle." After which I knew I had obeyed the rules and was free to weep.

PART 5

1

I lay around home for almost a tenth of a *vrek*, in a kind of stupor. I must have cried most of the time. When I started to come out of it, the first thing I noticed was how sore my nose and eyes were, and how inflamed my cheeks were where the tears had gone on and on streaming down. So I had a soothing face-salve pack, and soothing eye-lotion pads, and in about twenty splits I looked normal again, at least. Then this pop-pop came from the porch signal, and I switched on the image, and there was this *derisann* male, with long honey-colored hair and mustache, and a lovely, tawny, athletically slim body.

"Hergal?" I asked.

"It's me, dear," said this beautifully modulated voice, and that "dear" told me it couldn't be anyone else but Hatta.

"H-Hatta?"

"Yes, dear," said beautiful, *groshing* Hatta. "I heard all about it. I'm so sorry. Can I come in?"

And I activated the door and went down to meet him. We met in a goldish sort of hall, and he looked so *derisann* and sad for me that I just grabbed him and started howling my eyes out again. He was so good. He's always so sweet really, Hatta is, I think he's compulsively kind.

He put me on a couch and turned on the lullaby rhythm and the most soothing upper-tonal music he could find, and then he sat and rocked me gently in his lovely arms.

When I got a bit better, he mopped me up. I just sat and stared at him as he poured me fire-and-ice, and fed me small sugar grapes.

"You're so wonderful, Hatta," I said, and his hands trembled. "Oh Hatta," I said, "let's get married. Now."

But he made me lie down for forty splits before he'd even let me say it again. Then he said, very softly:

"Are you sure, *ooma?* Are you?"

"Oh, Hatta," I said, "don't be silly. How could I possibly object?"

He kind of shook his head, but he sat and waited quite patiently as I had another face pack and got ready, and then we went out to his rented bird-plane, and shot off to the Ivory Dome. We promised to have love exclusively for the afternoon, and to come back and pay afterward as well, as you have to if you're inside the annulment period.

Then we went to one of the underwater caves, green and shells and stuff, and had the most glorious love. I think when you're shaky and recovering from something, you receive better. Anyway, it was *groshing.*

"Oh, Hatta," I sighed afterward.

But he turned away.

"Oh Hatta, what's wrong?" I asked. I got up and went around to the other side of the synthetic seaweed couch, and he was lying there, his eyes shut, great tears rolling down *his* face now. "Hatta, Hatta," I implored, "*ooma,* what is it?"

"Can't you see," he asked softly, "how useless it all is?"

"What?" I said. "I thought you wanted me to marry you. I don't understand."

"No," he said, "you don't, do you?"

"But I loved every minute," I said. "Didn't you?"

"Oh, yes," he said, "I loved having you, my *ooma,* and

you loved having my body, my new, unreal joke of a body. I loved *you,* and you loved the shell of me."

"Oh Hatta," I said.

We were silent for a long while.

"I love you," he said then.

"I know," I said.

"And you love my body," he said.

"Yes," I said "and, Hatta, I think you're so terribly nice and *derisann* and—"

"And you don't love me, do you? Just the outside."

"Yes," I said.

And he wept silently.

And I got *tosky* again.

"Hatta!" I screamed at him. "Look, I just can't stand this on top of everything else. I'm in such a chaos, I can't cope with your chaos as well. Really, I'm sorry, but if you don't stop I'll go *zaradann*."

He apologized, got up, said he'd pay the other half of the marriage-fee, and went away, leaving me the bird-plane.

And when I saw him next, he had four arms and scales. Poor, poor Hatta. If only he could learn to hate.

2

I booked Sense Distortion after the episode with Hatta. I think word of my unusually hysterical state had been passed on to the Committee, because I didn't have to wait long. They even sent a little blue-and-pink sky-ship for me, all merry and gay and so on, and they played merry and gay and so on music to go with it.

"Ah yes," they said when they saw me, and led me away by the hand.

So I lay down in the soft furry cubicle and waited to become a flower, and my last thought, I recollect, was, Where did this fur come from, a desert animal? And I vowed to dismantle the fur room at home.

And then I was in this still, morning forest with a pale sky, and I was a tall plant, gently waving and growing, my mind full of plant thoughts, receiving sunshine and feeling my molecules transmute it into green cells. This was very soothing. I was a flower for ages, and it should have done me good. After being a flower, I became a mountain, which was rather grand. I think I felt a bit like Assule, actually. Certainly I thought the sort of thoughts I bet he did. I am ancient and enduring, I am a god-thing, I am eternity. I ignored the winds and the sand chipping me, the rain eroding me, the hot sun drying me up. Later, I was a lake, blue and rippling, miles of me, and it's wonderful to be so long and wide, and aware of every inch and eddy of yourself. I kept giving gentle little twitches, flinching the sun off my skin, encouraging my water plants to grow.

I came to and was surprised at first to find I had two arms and legs and hair, and all the boring rest of it. I had this impulse, which apparently is quite common after S.D., to dash off to Limbo and say "I want a long, blue, rippling body." But they sidetracked me. They came buzzing along and gave me a meal injection, and encouraged me to write poetry on a machine about my experiences.

Thinta came to meet me—I have this feeling they suggested she should, and of course, Thinta, being loyal and painfully duty-bound, came haring over in her safe pink birdplane. Oh, yes, she was being very safe today. You'd never think she crashed on the Zeefahr too, not so long ago, just like habit-ridden Hergal.

"Let's make water dresses," twittered Thinta.

We went and got the stuff and the instructions, and wandered for ages along galleries of clacking light-crochet machines, steel-knitters, and picture wool on which you can paint with electric rays, landscapes and things to bewilder yourself and your friends with. I wanted to see what Thinta would do, and fairly obviously stole some fire-needles; she just looked a bit uneasy and pretended she hadn't seen. Well, I really *was* being humored. Wild possibilities of how I could drive everyone *zaradann* flitted through my brain, but I felt too basically fed up to pursue any of them.

We ate fifth meal at the Fire-Pit, then went and made our dresses in the deadly perfect sunshine of the Ilex Park, with a lot of jade leaves bashing us. In the middle of it all, the jade reminded me of the dragon in Jade Tower and all the other animals in Four BAA, and then of Lorun, and I started crying again. The tears got muddled in with the water dress and ruined it.

"Oh," Thinta kept imploring, "oh, do stop, *ooma.*" I only managed it because I could see how upset she was getting. I'm not sure if it was sympathy that was disturbing her or embarrassment. Probably both.

We had sixth meal and Thinta enthusiastically paid for it, and then gave me a gentle fluttering sort of little talking to, on the sky-ship where we were eating it.

"You know," she started, "everybody has silly times."

"Do they?" I inquired unhelpfully.

"You know they do, *ooma,*" Thinta said. "Look at me and that business about wanting to be a cat thing, and the fur and the purring reflex that, thank goodness, the Committee was wise enough not to give me. Now I can see how ridiculous I was being and laugh at it. Ha, ha!" Did her laugh sound a bit strained?

"I don't think you really laugh at it," I told her callously. "I think you pretend to laugh, when really you're furious you can't sit and purr at me."

"Oh, really," said Thinta, looking as annoyed as Thinta can look, which means she just looks puzzled. The only time I'd ever seen her really angry was over the refused purring mechanism. "Anyway," she said, "what I'm trying to say is, anyone can get over anything."

"I see," I said.

"Oh yes, really they can, *ooma.*"

"Perhaps they can," I said, "but perhaps they shouldn't."

She couldn't answer me. She tried but she couldn't. Well, I couldn't answer myself, could I?

I really did try, though, to get back into life as I'd known it, but it was like a tunic the wrong size; it didn't fit me anymore. If it ever had. I shopped and stole, bubble-rode and fire-rode, went and cursed the Robotics Museum, and married Hergal again, though I could feel he didn't enjoy our afternoon very much. He was too worried I'd start crying or something all over him, though I very considerately didn't. I went to the Dimension Palace and didn't even get properly frightened, just thoroughly *tosky,* though I suppose it was the best result I'd got so far.

Finally I thought of the Dream Rooms.

I went to Fourth Sector's version, which has purple clouds and floating cubicles, and took about eighty splits programming the robot to make sure I got a perfectly *groshing* fantasy. I didn't even have any guilt feelings this time—my Q-R with the water carpet had indirectly done that for me, at least.

And there I was, this fantastically erotic and famous dancer of an ancient desert tribe. We'd been captured by another more powerful tribe and taken in chains out into the desert with them as slaves. We lay by night under the cold desert stars, glaring at their big, dark blue tents, and the biggest tent of all, which belonged to their chieftain. I'd never seen the chieftain, but apparently he'd seen me and heard of my reputation in the dancing line; now, at the beginning of my dream, he'd requested my presence before him in his huge tent, and sent me this *groshing* costume to wear. I got into it and admired myself in the mirror his servants held up for me. It was scarlet, embroidered with seed pearls and silver disks and bled-red tassels. I had thick black hair, oceans of it, and green eyes, and I looked *insumatt.* Then this old wise-woman of our tribe came clanking up in her chains, poor old thing, and drew me aside.

"You must kill him," she said, not messing around or anything.

"How?" I said. I wasn't overly bothered. I mean, we were all bred hard fierce, and brave (as usual) out in this desert.

"With your knife," said the wise-woman. "Here, I saved it for you when we were raided."

And there it was, this bone-handled deadly blade, given me by my maker in my infancy or something. I caressed it, and promised to slay the terrible chieftain—the signal for my people to break loose and conquer the bewildered, leaderless enemy—or perish in the attempt. I was going to fall madly in love with him, of course, and not be able to do it, and he with me and not be able to punish me, and then our tribes were going to unite on equal terms, and everything was going to be *derisann.* Only things started going wrong.

It was all right to begin with. I stepped out, having concealed my knife in my scarlet sash, and strode between the campfires toward his imperious tent, positively glowing with pride and beauty. Slaves held the door flaps for me and in I went to this blue incense gloom and the rusty murk of torches. And there he sat, dark-skinned and black-haired and marvelous, and the drums started, and these thin pipe things, and cymbals, and dried seeds shaken around in clay pots, and I poised myself and started a slow and sensuous dance, guaranteed to hypnotize the place. The music got faster and faster, and I whirled and spun, and then whipped out my knife and leaped at him. And I stopped short. I was meant to, but not for the reason I had. I was meant to halt because of his beauty, but actually I halted because there, on his cushioned chair, sat a great big furry ski-foot, gently flapping its ears.

I yelled and dropped my knife.

"Have some cactus-pineapple," offered the ski-foot, indicating a silver dish. "Now, now, don't be silly," coaxed the ski-foot as I backed away. "I do so hate shyness."

I looked around wildly and found the whole tent-full had changed into the most ridiculous things with fur and feathers, long ears and trailing whiskers, little twitchy noses and long twitchy noses, horns and antennae and various tails, and they were all quacking and clucking and grunting away at me encouragingly. I only sat down because my knees went weak.

"That's much more cozy," said the ski-foot. "Now, do tell me, why are you trying to kill me? Was it because of our raid?"

"You enslaved us," I tried to choke out all my prearranged dialogue but really, it looked so earnest and furry and concerned. I giggled hysterically.

"Dear me, she's hysterical," observed a large plumed dragon on my left.

"Have some wine," said the ski-foot, "you'll feel better," and it reached toward a side table. But the table had ideas of its own. It unfolded four furry legs and walked calmly out of the tent, the wine and stuff bouncing around on top of it.

"Stop it," cried the ski-foot, and the assembled company gave chase, squawking and booming and falling over each other's tails and apologizing. "Come along," added my host. "I think they'll need some help." So it and I added ourselves to the chaos, and we all pounded after the table, through the coals of the campfires. The table broke into a run and we never seemed likely to catch it, though our pace didn't slacken. We pounded over the dunes, under the white stars, whooping and hooting, and the ski-foot grabbed my hand in a large capable paw.

"Must keep together, you know," it panted. The poor thing was quite out of breath already. It probably only wanted to hold hands so it didn't get left behind.

Every so often something would fall off the table with a crash and we were soon rushing through thousands of silver dishes and goblets and crushed fruit.

"It's no use," the ski-foot suddenly said and sat down in the sand, pulling me with it. Everyone else stopped and gathered around. The table gave a great kick of its furry heels and disappeared behind a rock.

"That's the seventh we've lost in ten units," said the ski-foot, and tears gushed from its eyes. "We can never catch them."

Everybody started crying, and I started crying too.

And I woke up crying.

Oh, I *complained*. There was a terrible row at the Dream Rooms. Q-Rs rushed out and said I mustn't upset everyone else. Eventually I was taken to this purple plush room full of robots, and this chief Q-R, also in purple, asked me to give them a full account of just what was wrong with my dream.

"Well, everything," I cried. "I mean, it was a dream, an unprogrammed dream. And it really made me unhappy."

They said they saw that and, oh dear, they just couldn't

understand it, it had never happened before, would I object to submitting to a mind reading? I said yes, I would object. They said the trouble was probably that I was thinking too hard about other things. I gave up eventually.

"I refuse to pay, though!" I added belligerently.

Of course, under the circumstances, they would not dream of charging me.

I went home.

Well, it was something to make history, I supposed.

I started to cry again, remembering those forlorn, *zaradann* animals, weeping over their lost table; then I saw the funny side as well, and started laughing at the same time.

Kley signaled me, looked frightened when she saw me, and hastily went away again and left me alone.

I wished I could leave me alone too.

3

I decided I could leave me alone, after all.

I'd been in this body a long while, even if it was two bodies, really, one a duplicate. I looked irritably at my scarlet hair. Gold would be nice for a change. I carefully never admitted that I knew no one would be bothered that I'd changed, no one would run away honking and hide its white fur and orange eyes among the silk grass, thinking I was someone else.

I knew Limbo would make a fuss if I asked for a change again. Humoring me was one thing, but I was a bit quieter now, and they might not be so anxious to help. I went and looked at the bubble, but I was bored by now with that way of dying. All right, I thought, I'll admit it for once, I'm just as bad as Hergal. I kill myself to get a change, not just because I'm *tosky* or depressed. But I'm not going to admit it too often. I daren't.

I signaled him.

"*Attlevey,* Hergal," I said. "What, still blue-haired? I think we both need a change. How about the Zeefahr?"

He was amenable for once.

We rode out there in his plane and poised a while among the clouds, watching the tiny speck that was the Zeefahr's dome down below.

"Ready?" Hergal asked.

"Quite," I said. I determined to enjoy it, but I didn't.

He arranged the controls with practiced hands and leaned back, casual and nonchalant. Everything began rushing up at us at a ghastly rate. The dome grew bulbous, shining, terrible.

"Hergal!" I screamed. "Stop us!"

"Can't," was the last thing I heard him say before the impact blotted everything out.

And the first thing I said to him, as we woke up in the Limbo tub was, "Hergal, why do you always do it like that? It *hurts.*"

"Pain is a reality," Hergal said, and turned out his communication light.

4

The circle got together at the end of the *vrek* and had this typically Jang party. I married Hergal, and Kley, male now, married Thinta, and Danor—having temporarily sloughed her following—just came and looked beautiful, and Hatta was just going to come and look ugly, and then didn't come after all.

We used the floaters, drank fire-and-ice and snow-in-gold, had ecstasy and love machines, a lot of noise, having love, and messing about. Hergal and I had both got these angel's wings. They were strong, actually, and we found, by sticking to it, that we could sort of fly very clumsily, short distances—inside the clouds, of course. We'd both had an official warning from the Committee about our body changes. If we didn't wait thirty units, they'd put us into cold storage for thirty units after the next suicide. It's pretty uncomfortable, Hergal tells me; it's happened to him before. And they did take away Hergal's license on the bird-plane.

My bee crashed on my head in the middle of it all.

"I don't know," Thinta said through Kley's hair, "why you don't reprogram that thing."

"I suppose I must like it falling on me," I said. "I suppose it's different." I don't often admit that either. I must have been pretty ecstatic.

We abandoned the floaters about dawn and ran through Four BEE singing and semi-flying, all the way to the Robotics Museum.

"Oh, don't hurt it," Thinta implored us. I think she must be approaching adulthood or something. I've suspected it for a long time. We floored robot caretakers and bashed about disconnecting things, feeling wildly happy and quite *zaradann*. Jang are always doing it, actually, but we kidded ourselves we were original. Then we stood around in the chaos, idly kicking at broken things with our gold-sandalled feet.

Four BEE's yellow sun was just coming up over the rim of the transparent roof, bringing another unit of perfect, monontonous sunshine and joy.

I felt this singing noise in my ears, and the room darkened, though it should have been getting brighter.

"Oh God," I said, "I'm absolutely *droad*."

I think Hergal must have caught me, or perhaps it was a catch net. Anyway, I never felt myself hit the floor.

5

They were really worried about me in Limbo. Apparently I'd actually "fainted," something nobody's done for aeons. They popped me back in the Limbo tub and gave me a compulsory new body, in case there was something wrong with the old one, even though they couldn't find anything. I had Thinta worried too. She came to visit me when they made me stay in for observation for four units.

"I've brought you some ecstasy pills," she said, "and a moving picture magazine on fashion."

"Thank you," I said. I tried to look interested.

"Er, *ooma*," she quavered then, "I didn't tell anybody, but do you remember that funny word you said, just before, er, just before . . ."

"I fainted?" I asked. I was quite brave about my freakiness by now. "No."

"You said . . ." Thinta paused. "You said you were *droad,* and you said, just before you said you were *droad,* you, er . . ."

"Look, Thinta," I began.

"No. All right, I'm sorry. You said 'Oh . . . God'?"

"Did I?" I inquired.

"Well, yes, you see, you did, actually."

"Are you sure it wasn't just a groan or something?" I queried.

"No," said Thinta.

"Well," I said, "what does it mean?"

"I don't know," Thinta said. "I looked it up in the history records and they sort of mentioned it here and there. It sounded like a kind of very large, special computer."

"Doesn't seem very likely to me," I said.

"No," Thinta said, "it's just—it worried me somehow."

Well, all right, so now I'm worried too. Thank you, Thinta *ooma*.

I worry sometimes now. I wake up in the night from all my weird dreams of the desert and think, God? *God?* But there doesn't seem to be an answer.

I'm very calm now, anyway. Serene. Like Danor, perhaps. I don't usually get excited or angry the way I used to. I suppose I've come to accept the sun, and given up biting at it.

Hatta signaled me again the other unit, all lumps and bumps and tentacles, and it seemed such a shame really, but I just can't stand him like that. I know he needs this proof of love, I can understand; he's trying to hide it from himself now and just keeps on again about how important it is to be ugly sometimes, and how going away with him as he is would be an Essential Experience. Perhaps it would and I ought to. Perhaps sometime I will.

And not long ago, as I rode in my bubble, I suddenly thought how wonderful it would be if there was somewhere in the city where you could die without the robots ever finding you. Of course there's the desert, but it would be a kind of dirtiness to die deliberately in the desert in all my cityness, like using it as a huge vacuum drift. I made them bury the pet out there—yes, I can actually say it now—but that was different. It had to go back into the sands that hatched it. I belong in this twilight that hatched me. Or do I?

Or do I?

DRINKING SAPPHIRE WINE

PART 1

1

"Hergal," I said, "if you say that one more time I am personally going to knock you straight through that wall."

Hergal looked at me in grave wonderment.

"All right," he complied, and said it. He didn't look surprised, either, when I got up and did exactly what I'd promised I'd do. Maybe he was only humoring me. As he lay there on the other side of the wall, surrounded by bits of shattered silk-of-crystal, I added:

"I suppose you're too much of a damned ignoramus to know what comes next?"

"Absolutely," said Hergal, removing glittering chips from his long orange hair and wringing spilled orange wine from his sleeves.

"Swords at dawn," I said, "or pistols. Take your pick. My challenge, so it's your choice."

"You *have* been at the History Records again," remarked Hergal, "and as I observed prior to our little *dalika* just now, being a male half the time is getting you all tangled up, old *ooma*. You're predominantly female, so why don't you—" No chance to finish. I laid him flat on his back again.

He stared up at me woefully.

"Swords?" I inquired. "Or pistols?"

"*Graks,*" said Hergal. "If you want to play ancient grandeur, do it in the Adventure Palace like everyone else."

And thus, rising to our gold-shod feet, we glared momentarily eye to eye, after which he strode out into the morning, whistling one of the current Jang favorites: "I only want to have love with you, for you are so *derisann.*"

About twenty robots and Q-Rs, of various descriptions but unanimously unfriendly, were bearing down on me, so I also strode out of the little restaurant on Crystal Terrace and made off along Crystal Walkway in the opposite direction to my friend, mate, and crony, Hergal the Turd.

To be quite frank, what really tied me up in a knot was the pure logic of Hergal's deductions. True, I had been at the History Records—again. True, I, predominantly female as I was, had been male with no break for almost three *vreks.* There had, of course, been a variety of assorted bodies, but they were all much the same.

There were many like Zirk, who, when a male, tended to rangy heroic types with shoulders the width of Committee Hall doors, rippling bronze musculature, and a loud persona—for which Zirk made up, when female, by being about three feet tall, delicate as porcelain, and timid as a Four BOO sand-rabbit. Then there were the ones like Kley, who, when male, was a quiet, well-mannered nonentity, and became a raging bully when in girl-shape. I, however, remained much the same either way. Always inclined to violence, chivalry, and general moodiness, the size of my breasts, or any alternative apparatus I happened to have about me, didn't really color the situation to any vast degree—at least, I don't think so. But my particular circle, which had enlarged itself, as most Jang circles do, over the last twelve *vreks,* had got sensitive about my "eternal maleness"—as Hergal was pleased to call it. I had come to the conclusion that Hergal, himself predominantly male, resented my intrusion on his preserves. He and I got on well enough when I was female and he male.

But I had noticed, as time slithered by, that when we were
both of one ilk, the fur flew. Another thing that troubled male
Hergal in the male me was perhaps my superior success with
the female portion of the group.

Thinta, in fact, was becoming a bit of a pain.

"You need looking after," she would say. "Someone to
keep an eye on you. You remember that business before. I
haven't forgotten. Neither has the Committee, you can be
sure of that." And then, glowing her cat's eyes at me, "We'll
get married for mid-*vrek*, and you can come and live at home
with me, and everything will be *groshing*."

Thinta's home was another of the ubiquitous palaces of
Four BEE, with seven emerald towers, each one packed floor
to roof with pale-green cats. Thinta had always had a cat
fixation, which, unit by unit, seemed to be getting worse.
Open a door in her place and a cat fell out; lie down on a
couch in her place and a cat jumped on you. Having love
there with Thinta could be an ordeal. The first time, I thought
it was Thinta wailing and making those long, white-hot,
silver-wire runnels down my back. But it wasn't Thinta, it
was three of Thinta's cats.

"No thanks, Thinta," I said. "We can marry for a unit,
yes. But we'll go to the floaters."

But Thinta still liked to keep an eye on me. She would
signal me in the center of night, and wake me out of deep
slumber, and ask:

"How are you?"

She would arrive in her safe pink bird-plane at all the
least convenient hours of sunlight, and say:

"Are you *sure*?"

Meanwhile, Zirk, when a sand-rabbit, timorously appeared at the tables of restaurants where I was eating, or on
the surface of water-skating pools, and whispered flutter-
ingly:

"Why, *attlevey, ooma. Fancy* meeting *you*!"

And Mirri, Hergal's last love, the one he added to our
circle personally, and with whom he spent so many secret
hours, now pursued me up and down the movi-rails, walk-

ways, and sky-lanes of Four BEE, her hair flapping like a rainbow flag, and her face alight with predatory instincts. Even Hergal I vaguely recall arriving at midnight in female form, and saying in a fascinated calculating fashion:

"You know, I think I begin to understand you at last."

The scene with Hergal, however, in Crystal Air, had come about because we'd heard Danor was moving back from Four BAA.

Danor and I. That was distant history.

Danor and I and that silly chilly sequence those many *vreks* before, when she told me—he then, I she—that he couldn't have love and like it. Danor jumping from a window in the floater clouds, and falling hundreds of feet into the city—pointless action, since the robots would be on him and have him removed to a new body inside the hour—yet just as if he *meant* it. . . . To me, now, that event was somehow the beginning of what happened to me, all those things that happened to me back there, twelve *vreks* in my own past. My fight against the world, the biting and snapping of a wild animal at the sun. Look over my shoulder, and I'd see, in the wreckage, the struggle to find a challenge, the wild attempt to make a child and the fatal mistake that killed that child in its crystallize twilight; the nutty relationship—the only relationship that held anything for me—my love and my rapport with that pet I never named until it was too late. My pet who died. Death, death everywhere, death in this society where no one *dies*. . . .

"I wonder what sex Danor is going to be for the homecoming," said Hergal, looking at me obliquely through his apricot lashes.

"Female," I said.

"Yes, she did stick at that for quite a while," said Hergal.

Maybe he'd guessed why—because she said it was easier to pretend to passion that way. Lucky she never read the History Records as I had done, and found, among their other little horrors, the ironic essay on frigidity, some ten *rorls* old.

"Still," said Hergal, "she's been in BAA long enough

to get over her perpetual girlhood. That'll leave just you and Hatta as the circle freaks.''

I resented, I'll admit, being classed with Hatta, whom we'd just seen bundle by outside, looking like a scarlet balloon on three legs that had been struck simultaneously by lightning and plague. Hatta had also thrown knives in my heart, but that was way back with the rest. Now he seemed to go about his compulsive ugliness in a spirit of inventive venom that was almost engaging. Each body was worse than the last, which should have been impossible. Maybe he hoped that we'd both throw up fourth meal at the sight of him when he leered in at the crystal window.

"Seen Mirri lately?" I asked Hergal casually. I, too, had an armament.

"With you, I saw her," said Hergal, "but don't reckon on making Danor. Danor cracked up when you cracked up, and got out of BEE to get away from you. That's why this is the first time she's been back since."

"How flattering," I said, "to have such a profound effect."

"Listen," said Hergal, "you sit up there on your tail in the History Tower, in the dust with a couple of rusty robots that don't know what *rorl* it is. You read about things that don't exist anymore and won't ever exist anymore. Adventures, wars, illness, obsolete social behavior patterns—*poets.*" This last was a knock at my appearance, modeled by me from a sort of amalgam of the romantic pale young men who, with masses of loosely curling dark hair, slight and graceful build, aquilinity of feature, and large shadow-smudged blue opals for eyes, were conjured three-dimensionally on the history walls from long-ago drawings of a vanished intellectual world. All these beings traditionally died young—of ancient, unheard-of diseases of the lungs, at sea, in battles, in burning planes and unexpected accidents. It seemed required of them, and I won't say I never laughed in their pretty and tragic faces. Death of that kind was a hard thing to realize, even for me, in this place where death never permanently threatened human life. Imagine those poets' expressions, rescued by the robots of Four BEE, and emerging newly clothed in flesh from the Limbo Tub. "Do you mean I have to write more verses of my bloody poem after all? How utterly *drumdik*."

"Listen," reiterated Hergal slyly, "you haven't had a body change for ages. Go to Limbo and have one, and I'll meet you. Do you remember that body of yours with the cinnamon skin and the lemon hair? That was really *insumatt*."

"You mean the female body?"

"Oh, yes," said Hergal. "Why not get them to look it up and order it again? Then you and I can make a couple of units of it."

"So you know for certain," I said, "that Danor is coming back female." Hergal looked at me. I added: "Danor and I have a longstanding agreement. I shouldn't like to let her down. Perhaps you could persuade Mirri. I'll tell her I've got something else on."

"You only get them," said Hergal, "because you're still seven-eighths one of them. It's cannibalism."

"What erudition," I said. "Can it be you've been to the History Tower too? With so much time on your hands these days . . ."

"You're a misfit," said Hergal. "You always were. You don't go to the Dream Rooms because you can't even get through a dream anymore without messing it up. You're trying to live eighty *rorls* back in the past because you can't come to terms with things as they are."

"You can," I said. "You've stopped crashing onto the Zeefahr Monument, and last mid-*vrek* you hanged yourself in Ilex Park off a jade tree, where all the kids from hypno-school could see you. How well-adjusted."

"At least," said Hergal, "when I get out of Jang I'll be able to make a little kid to *go* to hypno-school, since I didn't manage to annihilate the last one."

Definitely he had been snuffling about in the History Tower. The words were archaic, as half of mine were now.

But no matter. This was the moment when I swatted him right through the wall, and we presently parted company.

I'd known, however, despite my challenge, that he was a safe dead loss for a duel, even if he had read about them. Picture Hergal firing from the shoulder at ten paces in the dawn. Yawning would spoil his aim.

2

"*A**ttlevey*," said a sharp metallic voice. I detected who it was before I looked round.

"Well, if it isn't Kley," I said.

Kley was female right now, which meant watch out, but, when I glanced about, in a new body. Dazzling. Hair like lava, eyes like raw gold, skin like polished brass, and dressed to kill in see-through patterned with gold daggers, and with a brazen skull—of all antique masterpieces—grinning on her groin shield.

"I must say," she said, "you're looking pale."

"That's the idea, Kley. My body's designed to look pale."

"Oh, yes. You're being a consummated poet, aren't you?"

"Consumptive, *ooma*, consumptive," I said.

"Filthy," she said. "Your ideas are absolutely sick."

"Sick as anything," I agreed. "Sick as three Jang in an angelfood factory."

"And your vocabulary!" she bawled. "Those *words! Factory?* What's *that*?"

"A place where they make audio plugs," I said.

We were on the old, non-moving walkway that trails up from behind Third Sector Committee Hall, and leads eventually to the History Tower. It was a remote route, not much favored, for the Tower itself was rarely visited, and so Kley's arrival on my heels was as unexpected as it was unwelcome.

"You ought to pull yourself together," she now bellowed, her voice striking and bouncing back off the steel statues lining the walk. "It's all over the city about your *dalika* with Hergal. Even the flashes reported it."

"Whoopee," I said. I had turned and was walking on, but she kept after me and even grasped my arm firmly with a gold-gloved hand.

"Danor's coming back on the sky-boat at sunset."

"Yes, I know."

"And you're going to meet her?"

"Kley," I said, "right now I'm on my way to the History Tower."

"Oh no," she said, "you're coming with me. I've been reading the latest Jang love manual, the *Purple Summit.* You're going to marry me for the afternoon and we're going to do everything it says together, including the Trapezium with the red-hot Star-Whip, and—"

"Kley," I said, "look at me. Do I look strong enough to go through anything like that?"

"Of course you don't," she snapped. "That's how you had the body made, isn't it? But if I know you—"

"Kley," I said, "you don't."

Unlike the bright and burnished History Museum— where a couple of *rorls* worth of Flash Records and similar junk were kept—the History Tower, Harbinger of the Arcane, was suitably black, old, grim, and uninviting.

And the facade worked pretty well. How many people went there? Twice, when I was pouring over some vis-plates, I heard the distant puttering of somebody else in another part of the building, the hiss of a flying floor going up and down. And once an Older Person, female and disapproving, came marching in to look up the origins of some committee motto for a treatise she was writing—or said she was. I wasn't in my poetic body then, and she scowled at me as I slouched there robustly. I heard her later mutter something to one of the elderly robots that clanked about the Tower that Jang should not be allowed in.

And when did I first enter those portals? About twenty units after I got out of Limbo that time, twelve *vreks* gone, when I made history myself by passing out cold, and was compulsorily refitted with flesh. Thinta had visited me, oh yes, I well recall. Thinta, clothed by innuendo: "Do you remember that funny word . . ." I had uttered it, apparently, on my way down. The funny word had turned out to be "God." Thinta said she'd looked it up in the History Records. She said it sounded like a kind of very large special computer. She said it worried her, so she'd come along and worried me with it so she could feel better. In the end I arrived at the Tower to investigate for myself. I never really unraveled the mystery. The farther back you went, the more fragmentary the Records—and it was something to do, I believe, with the days when uncertainty was everywhere. However, I began to like the privacy of the Tower, and I began to delve into the Records, fragmentary or not, for their own sake. The things they teach you at hypno-school are barely a scratch on the surface.

It was a substitute, too, let's face it, for the activities I'd given up, like the Dream Rooms, since even the most meticulously programmed dreams—awash with swords, dragons, and so on—invariably turned into nightmares of the unprogrammed sort. The very last time I went I woke up screaming, and created history once again in Four BEE. I'd dreamed I was fighting a great monster of fire that burned flesh from bone, and it wouldn't die however often I severed its head or pierced its heart. That was a dream I'd grown used to since, but at least I didn't pay a Dream Room any more to saddle me with it.

In the Tower, a crotchety robot came wheezing up. It

looked quite pleased to see me, and its lights did a little display. The rooms smelled of metal and dust and a sort of incense smell, too, from some of the very ancient books which were kept in special vacuum containers and turned over by air jets rather than machine, to keep them from crumbling into bits.

Actually I didn't delve much on this particular visit. I sat in my alcove with some old (about ten *rorls*) music playing at me, and began to entertain rather romantic thoughts about Danor. Of course, she might be the disappointment of the *vrek*. Or she might have turned into a Hatta-horror, though it seemed unlikely. Poor frigid Danor. My reading up here had given me a few ideas. Looked at calmly, Danor was in the nature of a scientific experiment, but dress yourself in a poet's skin and you find you've reached for a machine, and started to compose poetry to go with it. A Jang love poem for Danor, as elegant, charming, and empty as an unfilled room.

She must have left Four BEE about the same moment I emerged from Limbo, carrying a cask of metal tape under my arm—that depressing saga of events I'd authored there. Possibly Hergal's mouthings were true; she'd fled in fear of me, since our individual descents into misery occurred about jointly. But why come back?

Finally I switched off the music and abandoned the alcove. Beyond the transparalyzed windows, the Four BEE sun was trudging down the sky.

And there, on a steel bench, lolled Kley, smoking a hilarious golden cigar.

"Paler than ever," she remarked acidly. She flipped open an armband and offered me an energy pill, which I declined. "Going to faint at Danor's feet, are you?"

Yes, someone would always dig that up.

"That shouldn't be necessary," I said.

"Well, come on," she vociferated. Her finger-long nails flashed in the sunset. "The whole circle's going to the lock to welcome her in. Probably a few other circles, too, recollecting that old thing she had about playing hard to get."

"Go on, Kley," I said. "Strain yourself; play hard to get."

She nearly got me with a sideswipe of those nails, and five robots came over and hustled us out with disapproving creaks.

3

Bells rang. A soft explosion marked the closing of the dome locks, and Danor's sky-boat sailed down out of Four BEE's turgidly perfect sunset like a large silver bird.

You could tell the boat came from BAA, city of the fabulous. Rubies flashed on the covered window spaces, which protected the passengers, as ever, from glimpses of the wild desert that reigns and rampages about beyond the domes. And when the exit ports opened, they spilled a crowd in trailing cloaks of noncombustible fire and similar finery, and with alarming android pet animals and crates of extraordinary luggage, not to mention a flock of baas, now bees. No longer did I use a bee. I carried things about on my person when I bothered to carry anything. The old bee, which always fell on me, more than partly with my own connivance, now lay among that heap of forgotten detritus that cluttered the upper rooms of home.

Hergal was loitering at the edge of the Arrival Stretch with Zirk-as-hero. Both gave me sidelong apprehensive looks, and Zirk flexed a bicep or two in obvious warning. Of Hatta there was, fortunately, no sign, and Mirri had not come either. Thinta, however, materializing in a mild frenzy, darted up and glared at Kley with one of those unique Thinta-glares that convey as much menace as a lollipop.

"Attlevey," said Kley, poking me in the ribs by way of a comma. "She here yet? Or do I finally say *'he'*?"

"Are you all right?" Thinta asked me. "You look so washed-*out*. (Danor? No, at least, we don't know.) Did you remember to have a meal injection?"

Nobody knew what body Danor was going to be in. Zirk was having a bet with a Jang male from some other circle that it was that nice little thing in pink, and the Jang male—Doval, by name—was saying he thought it was the other, nicer little thing in red.

"Yes, Thinta," I said.

"But are you sure?" Thinta persisted. "Because I've brought some nutrition pills with me in case."

Just then I saw Danor. It was quite easy to spot her—yes, her. The dashing quality and the poignancy were still there, and you could see them clearly, shining up like light through colored glass. If you really looked. The others were still jostling and haggling and waving at the four points of the compass. And Kley suddenly yelled out that maybe Danor had graduated to Older Person status, and slapped on the back a dignified woman, who promptly began to complain about it to the nearest robot. Amid the confusion I slipped my guards—Kley, Thinta—strolled across to the reception area, and reached it at the very split Danor came away.

Hair like a blue raincloud, and a BAA dress of transparent lightnings. She was leading by a chain of sapphires a sort of swan animal, elegantly stepping on very stiff legs, its plumage just the shade of her own lavender eyes.

"Hallo, Danor."

She glanced up and at me, quizzically.

"You know me? How *derisann*. And you?"

I told her.

"Oh—" she said, as if she were going on to say something else, and then hesitated. But her eyes, those lavender eyes, were open as two doors on a sort of turmoil—alarm, pleasure, cowardice, memory. She'd gone right back to the time she/he jumped off the floater, I could tell, right back to the Secret. No one else knew, surely? No one but me.

"You sealed my lips with a kiss, remember?" I said.

"Did I? Oh, yes," she said. Then a troubled frown. She had apparently progressed beyond that kiss now, beyond the Archaeological Expedition, to the part when I, uttering incomprehensible moans about God and boredom, fell prone upon the floor of the Robotics Museum. Returning afterward from Limbo, I had found her gone, or would have had I been thinking of Danor then. "Are you happy?" she said to me, blatantly, gently.

"I'm noted for it," I said. She looked away. "And you? How was BAA all these *vreks*?"

"Insumatt," she said, "of course."

Her swan meanwhile had lifted one stiff immaculate leg and was peeing up the side of a reception pillar, a thing which surprised me, since the android animals of BAA are generally without bodily functions. Two Q-Rs were spraying disinfectant over all of us except, maybe, missing the swan. Zirk had come bounding up too, and was staring nonplussed at the scene, his Herculean face going magenta with explosive emotion. Finally he got out:

"You must be Danor!"

"Danor?" I said. "This isn't Danor. Danor is the nice little thing in pink."

Danor remained silent.

Zirk floundered and his pectorals deflated uncertainly.

"Well, I did reckon the one in pink was . . . But then, who's this?"

"Does it matter?" I said. "You look after your interests and I'll take care of mine." I craned to his ear. "After all, I gave up the Danor idea when I saw you and Hergal getting to work. I should watch Hergal," I added.

Zirk spun round, registered Hergal's position, and then galloped boatward to envelop the pink girl with Four BEE gallantry. How surprised she was going to be. Kley and

Thinta were gawping at me, and Kley's golden eyes had a leopardine gleam.

"Danor," I said, "there is a robot bird-plane for hire about ten paces to our left. You didn't protest a moment ago, so I assume you won't now." And I took her hand, and she, I, and the swan ran for the plane and leaped inside. The swan landed on the dashboard, its beak making a merry rattling sound and its wings smiting left and right. I depressed the "PAY ON LANDING" button, closed the ignition switch, and we were sailing into the velvet upper air of the city. The swan also erupted into flight and whizzed about our heads.

Danor giggled, hauling on the sapphire chain. The swan settled abruptly and the bird-plane plunged to port.

"How silly," said Danor. "Be calm," she murmured to the swan, and to me: "It was a genetic mistake. The flashes in BAA reported it. It came out of the tank wrong and they were going to dismantle it. But I asked Kam if I couldn't have it, and he said yes and arranged it."

"How splendid of Kam," I said.

"Kam was an Older Person," said Danor. She folded her hands in her lap on top of the swan. Very serenely she said: "We lived together for eight *vreks*. Yes, *ooma*, a Jang girl with an older male. Watch the buttons," she said softly as I inadvertently spun us into a Hergal-type dive—the old Hergal. "The Committee finally got around to suggesting we part company. They told us, very kindly, that it was not done, not good for us, not healthy. They told Kam that he was ruining my life, so he made me go."

The swan began to sing in a high-pitched inappropriate voice:

"I only want to have love with you, for you are so *derisann*."

We changed to a bubble, and got along Peridot Waterway and so home. I didn't pay for the bird-plane—I seldom did when I could avoid it—but I felt I had to for the bubble, since the swan, obviously a creature of irregular habits, crapped lethargically all over it. Danor did not apologize for the swan, for which I admired her.

At home, we went into the suite of rooms I still occasionally used. An immediate machine came crawling out of the wall and sidled up to Danor, imploring her to let it get her some topaz meringue or crushed fire-apple. Danor declined, which intrigued me; once she had adored food at any hour of night or day. She inquired instead if the swan could have some syntho fruit juice. I acquiesced with mixed feelings.

We sat together in the garden by the pool under the huge artificial stars of Four BEE—Danor, the swan, and I.

"Can it swim at all?" I asked.

"Oh, no," said Danor. The swan was apparently a total failure, which was why she loved it.

We had said no more about Kam. At least, I had asked nothing and Danor had volunteered no more. But now, reflectively, she began to talk again. I could tell from her voice, so level and unbitter, that the story caused her great pain, but it was a pain she had mastered. She was informing me, not because she needed to, but out of a sense of fairness. Because to her, as to me, the brief weird trouble between us in the past had achieved importance over the *vreks* which followed. Danor and I had never been close. In those days Hergal was nearer to me, even Thinta, in her irritating way. But now, under the monotonous starlight, we might have been the offspring of the same makers, brother and sister.

"When I went to BAA," she said, "I was male again for a little while. A couple of other-circle Jang had followed me; I did it to shake them off, and it worked. One unit I met this older male in the Weather Gardens—you know the place in BAA where they have special weather effects, thunderstorms and snow and everything. I was with a crowd watching an avalanche—they only lay it on twice a unit and it was rather impressive. Then this male came up to me, and he said reproachfully: 'If you were going to be here, why didn't you signal me?' I said I didn't know what he meant. Then he stared very hard, and he blushed. How often do people blush? It was sort of unusual and rather attractive. He'd designed himself very handsomely, and he didn't have that pompous, anti-Jang look either. He said: 'I am sorry. I thought you were my child. He's predominantly male, and his last body did look very like yours. But how stupid of me. What must you think.' I said I thought it was quite natural, and I didn't mind, and was he the guardian? He gave a little smile, the sort of smile that isn't really a smile. 'No, the other maker is his guardian. I don't often see either of them.' By this time the avalanche was finished. When he had looked at it, his eyes were really far away, unfocused. He didn't seem happy or enthusiastic. Have you noticed, *ooma,* I expect you have, how nearly everyone is always happy and enthusiastic, and rushing about, and laughing and screaming? He was very restful, and I suppose he thought I was restful, because we were both very silent and sad-eyed. Presently he said he was called Kam, and would I care for a glass of opal wine or some Joyousness or something. Just then I think he wanted to make believe I was his child and I'd come to visit him. It eased out, bit by bit, how he and the other maker didn't get along well now, and the other maker, predominantly female, had insisted she be guardian to the child, and it rather seemed she might have turned him against Kam. Kam didn't actually say this. He was trying to be impartial, simply because he felt angry about it, and knew he might not be. I liked him. I said I wished he were *my* maker, I hadn't seen my two since hypno-school ended.

"That was the start of it. We began to go about on a maker-child basis. I was still male then. He was so very nice to me. He paid for everything, and he took me to see the sights—things I hadn't even heard of. And he introduced me to his friends, though most of them were fairly anti as usual, and even had me meet a Jang circle or two, the children of his contemporaries. One day there were these two gorgeous Jang girls in his palace. They'd seen me and liked me, apparently, and Kam had encouraged them. He came in, being jolly and maker-ish. He expected I'd want to get married to one of them for the unit, but of course I didn't. And it wasn't just the old thing—the having love thing—either. It made me realize.

When I didn't bite, the two girls eventually flounced out. I
told Kam I was predominantly female, and due for a change.
He looked slightly taken aback. He looked something else,
too—nervous, and not only that, somehow glad. I knew then,
and I think he did. I went to Limbo that night. He didn't go
with me. This was the body I came out with. I wouldn't
change it now, and if I had to, I'd replicate—fortunately
that's a successful fashion that you started, *ooma*. I ordered it
in these soft colors because I'd seen he liked them. His home
was all blues and mauves like evening skies. Am I making
him sound *floopy, ooma*? He wasn't. But he was very kind. I
came back at dawn, and I wondered if he was still asleep. But
he'd been up the whole night. He was walking about on the
roof, and he saw me and came down. To begin with, I felt
scared, he seemed so flabbergasted. He just stared at me. And
then he apologized and mumbled something about you never
knew with Jang, I might have turned up the shade of a fire-
ball, with a knife on each hip. I simply took his hand. I didn't
know what I wanted, really. I wasn't analyzing or being rational, and I wasn't afraid. I didn't even remember the idea
that Jang never have liaisons with older people. I mean, they
never do, do they? I suppose, maybe, it must have happened
once or twice, but only for a unit, and all hushed up and
hidden afterward, with everyone ashamed and rushing off to
suicide or something.

   "He said, 'Darling, I'm at least half a *rorl* older than
you, and you know I can't follow Jang custom and marry
you—there's no provision for older people to marry. You do
realize that?'' I said, 'Doesn't matter.' He looked troubled,
for me, because I was a Jang and breaking the unwritten
law—though probably it *is* written, too. So I kissed him. I
hadn't planned to. I'd resigned myself anyway, ages before,
that having love, for me, was a nonevent and always would
be. You see, I hadn't imagined it would be any different with
him. I just wanted to make him happy, because he was so
special to me. I was ready to play and pretend anything.''
Danor's eyes sparkled. Sublimely, majestically, she made a

particularly unequivocal Jang sexual gesture. "Well, well, *wasn't* I due for a surprise?"

"Yes," I said, "I'd had a couple of ideas about that too."

I tried not to sound sullen. Kam had stolen my thunder, but never mind, at least her story was original.

"All that marrying business," Danor said, glinting. "All that delay. Part of me always knew I'm spontaneous. He taught me that. Oh, *ooma*," she said suddenly, the light fading from her face, "I loved him. Do you understand what I mean?"

"Yes, I know about love," I said. "Like God, it doesn't seem to function anymore."

"They won't let it function. Do you know what happened? One night his child arrived—how ironical. He was a sort of amber male with cold eyes. He took one look at me and ran off to his guardian, and about three splits later there was a messenger baa in the house from the Committee. They spoke to both of us, together and individually. They were very kind, that was what made it so silly. They explained that the age and experience difference simply wouldn't work. That Kam was a maker-figure for me and I was a child-figure for him. I said, what did it matter if we were happy? But they convinced Kam, and that unit he said I must go. He was very firm. He ordered me out, and his eyes were full of tears."

I glanced at her. She was still calm, wholly in command of herself. She looked very beautiful, very desirable in the cool starlight, which, despite its artificial idiocy, is effective. But what can you do with a friend who sits grieving stoically by your pool for a lost lover that isn't you?

Just then, the swan tottered—probably drunk on its syntho-juice—to the water's edge, and tumbled in.

I had a moment's wild hope it would regain a lost instinct and begin to swim, but it sank like a stone, only its beak protruding for an instant, honking out a snatch of song—"You are the wonderful sun of my sky!"—which was presumably the only way it could cry for help.

I suspect the swan had reminded me somewhat of the

pet, though the pet's intelligence had been razor-sharp, for all its *zaradannity,* while the swan was manifestly a mental deficient.

Not stopping to calculate, I plunged straight into the pool after the bloody thing, and swiftly emerged with its struggling, wet-feather body, which I deposited on the bank, against great opposition from the swan itself. It promptly puked the water it had swallowed into half the silk-flowers and then sat down on the other half with a look of mild self-congratulation.

I rose from the pool, my poet's gear of black cactus-velvet plastered to my skin, and my loosely curling hair matted to a consistency guaranteed to shred my skull when next I came to brush it.

Danor had begun to cry, almost unobtrusively.

"Poor swan," she whispered, but I knew who she meant.

I knelt by her and, regardless of my saturated condition, she clung to me. I was familiar with this scene, had acted in it with myself as Danor. I held her close, and presently picked her up and carried her inside. At the door I paused to tie up the swan and send some house machines with towels and things to look after it. Danor thanked me between her sobs.

I set her on the larger, goldwork couch.

"We haven't married," she said flatly. "Jang tradition."

"*Vixaxn* Jang tradition," I said quietly, and her mouth was tearfully laughing as I found it.

4

Danor lay sleeping like an azure dream, but outside in the sunny garden the swan, having snapped its leash, was plodding about and sneezing like a vivacious klaxon. Though it was the pop-pop of the porch signal which had waked me.

I switched on the signal image.

There stood a three-dimensional of Zirk, flexing and un-flexing his deltoids grimly, and almost purple in the face.

"*Attlevey*, Zirk," I cheerfully greeted him.

"*Attlevey!*" roared Zirk. "*Attlevey!* You lying, double-crossing, maladjusted *thalldrap!* You regurgitated, *tosky*, maker-making *promok!* You—"

"*Attlevey* again, Zirk. Let's start all over, shall we? What do you want?"

"You've got Danor," Zirk accused.

"Danor's here, yes."

"So it *was* a filthy trick, deliberately perpetrated. The whole circle standing there like fools, howling at the wrong female 'Welcome, Danor!' And you'd dragged her off. And she's been here the entire night, and you never married. Lis-

ten," he growled, "Jang get cut out of circles for doing half
of what you've done."

"Piss off, Zirk," I cordially invited him, and flipped the
recluse switch.

Outside, the swan had sneezed down a couple of miniature copper arbors, and seemed set for the pool again. I went
out and got it and brought it in. A machine bustled from
under the bed and tied up the swan, and gave it a plate of
something, who knows what, but it tucked into it with enthusiasm. Danor had woken. She looked as though she might
have heard my chat with Zirk, but she only said:

"Do you think we should signal anyone, Hergal or Kley?
Or Thinta?"

"I have a feeling we won't need to," I said.

However, it was Hatta who communicated next, though
not from the porch.

Danor and I were in the bathing unit, not precisely bathing. Some houseproud machine or other, trying to anticipate
my needs, had deactivated the recluse switch. Heralded only
by the signal light, scarlet, balloonlike Hatta materialized in
our midst.

"Er," said Hatta. Maybe he flushed, no one could tell.
The image winked out, but around thirty splits later, at a
more appropriate moment, he reappeared.

"Sorry," said Hatta. He cleared his throat and said,
"Hello, Danor."

"*Attlevey*, Hatta," said Danor. "How are you?"

"Oh, mustn't grumble," said Hatta.

"Why not?" I demanded. "Looking as you do, I'd say
you have every right."

He peered at me sorrowfully.

"You haven't been very ethical," he said, "and to involve Danor—"

"I involved myself," said Danor.

"They want you out of the circle."

"Splendid," I said. "And don't expect any tears."

"Zirk's been going to the History Tower," said Hatta
carefully to me. "Did you know? He's been there all night.

You recall that foolish joke you had with Hergal—about a dwull.''

"A what? A *duel*?"

"Duel, then. Yes. Well. I think Zirk's been looking them up.''

Close by, the swan sneezed. Hatta blinked uneasily.

"Don't say that," he warned. "It's no laughing matter."

I met Zirk outside Silver Mountain two units later. Danor was inside, buying some pet vitamins for the swan, and a pet-maintenance Q-R was giving it an injection to stop it sneezing. Zirk came up behind me, tapped me on the shoulder, and, when I turned around, knocked me about six blocks down the street. I don't really remember it particularly. I woke up flat on my back, or nearly, since some unknown Jang girl had cradled my head on her lap. The sky was full of robot planes in midswoop, thinking someone had suicided as people were always doing every second of the day. A small crowd had gathered, as usual when anything vaguely out of the ordinary occurs, and Zirk stood, arms akimbo, grinning his great white teeth.

"OK," he announced, "I've challenged you. Are you going to accept?"

The Jang girl gazed down at me over her glamorous breasts, and stroked my brow.

"There, there," she soothed.

I smiled at her, but Zirk shouted:

"Don't you waste a split on him. He's going to be cut up and cut out in that order. He's had love with half the circle without marrying them."

The Jang girl looked shocked. So did the crowd, and the robots milling from the planes. I got up and my head rang, and I staggered, but no one helped me this time.

"Well, do you accept?"

I'd cottoned on to the general idea by then.

"All right, loudmouth, I accept."

Zirk beamed. I might have known the History Records

would have a worse effect on him than on me. He was all thick-brained swashbuckle and teeth.

"I'll mince you," he promised. "Do you accept swords?"

People round about, mostly the Older Ones, asked each other what "swords" were. Some of the Jang knew from their Dream Room fantasies and the Adventure Palace.

"Been practicing?" I inquired.

"Do you accept swords?" he grated.

"If it will shut you up."

Zirk looked about at the crowd, and flexed everything he had.

"Since my body is a good foot taller than yours," he said, "I'm willing to permit you to get a new one on a larger scale."

"Gosh, *thanks*," I drooled.

"The time is tomorrow at dawn, Ilex Park, west corner."

I could see the crowd making a mental note. We should attract quite an audience.

Just then Danor and the swan came out of Silver Mountain. The swan had stopped sneezing but, judging from the disinfectant aroma, it had done a few other things instead.

Danor halted when she saw the gathering.

Zirk bowed to her, bulging.

"Everybody understands," he said penetratingly, "that none of this was your fault. I've no quarrel with *you*, Danor. In fact . . ." He coyly winked, then spun on his heel and rolled off.

The unneeded robot planes were scurrying skyward, but a couple of Flash Center bees were homing in, so I took Danor's hand and began to walk her and the swan quickly away.

"It's happened at last," she said, very low.

"It certainly did. I bet the flashes will be blazing with it tonight."

"Have a body change," she said. "Come back a female. Then he won't have the gall to fight you."

"What does it matter?" I said. "It's my fault for starting

it off with Hergal. And in any case, if he shoves his crackpot pseudo-steel fencing foil right through me, the Limbo Tub will have me back on my feet in no time, right?''

"But, *ooma*," she began, "don't you see—"

"Yes," I said.

I saw. If Zirk really meant what he said, and melodramatically stabbed me to the heart, it would be the first intended murder committed on our planet for over sixty *rorls*.

5

Somewhere about then, I made a decision. I decided that if Zirk and I were really going to that sort of limit—a killing—he was going to have to kill *me*. The decision was rational, which was rather a joke, since I have always been an emotional and impulsive character. I can think in straight lines, but, when it comes to the point, I find myself running about in circles, as usual. However, the thing with Zirk was that if anyone received the label "murderer," it wasn't going to be me. Zirk had, after all, so far led a fairly blameless Jang career—an excess of suicides and body changes, a measure of dome sabotage, and a nervous breakdown or two—but these were all perfectly normal as far as the Committee was concerned. I, on the other hand . . . Oh no, I wasn't taking any chances.

Yet there was something working against me, something I'd never have reckoned on.

I'd forgotten that, ever since that last compulsory body change twelve *vreks* before which followed the historic swooning, I hadn't suicided once. In itself this was fairly untypical, particularly since formerly I'd been one of the worst offenders, constantly drowning in order to acquire a new exterior. But suicide had become unappealing to me after that traumatic time; now I waited the prescribed thirty units between each change, and anyway, hardly ever did change. What was this? Could it be that I, even in the safe cities, had acquired an antique and obsolete fear of death? Or was it rather, perhaps, that somehow, somewhere along the stony path of my pathetic Janghood, I had evolved, despite everything, a *life*-wish?

And for the record also, for about a *vrek* I had been indulging in fencing practice, off and on, at the Adventure Palace. Presumably Zirk had taken a course, too, but really, built as he was, a power axe was far better suited to his style than a poetic slender sword, weapon of emaciated princes and dreamers.

Dawn takes place always at the same split each day, prophesied always by the same streamers of rose and ember, and the identical singing of mechanical, light-reactive birds, dumped here and there in the parks and gardens. Imported real birds from BOO ignore dome-dawn with lofty disdain, and, having witnessed an authentic desert sunrise or two, I don't blame them.

The jade leaves of the jade-trees of Ilex Park glowed and flashed under the pink sky. Long, black-green shadows were creeping down the slopes, and a little artificial ground mist—most artistic—was smoking about in the grottoes and groves.

As I approached the west corner, however, I began to hear the hubbub.

I won't say my heart sank. It had been fairly sunk for hours, what with the depression that had set in at the thought of letting that moron Zirk impale me. But a cryogenic sensation idled up my guts like a cold snake out for a walk. Of course, odds on there would be a crowd, after Zirk's public fashion of announcing our plans. This, though, sounded as if half the city had crammed itself into the park, and I wasn't in the mood for making a spectacle of myself in front of forty million sensation-seeking *thalldraps*.

Just then I came to the carefully sculptured avenue that

leads down to the west, the sun behind me. And out of the trees nipped Doval, Zirk's out-circle Jang friend, afire with enthusiasm and importance.

"Attlevey," he drawled. "Got your svork?"

"Sword. Yes, I do."

"And your seconds?"

I looked at him sourly. Zirk really had been reading things up.

"No."

"Well, you ought to have seconds," said Doval. "Zirk has."

"Let me guess," I guessed. "You and Hergal."

"Kley and Hergal," Doval announced loftily.

"Female seconds aren't generally allowed," I said, "not if Zirk wants to follow the old customs accurately. Or has Kley changed?"

"No," said Doval. "She's just slavering to see you gutted."

"How sweet of her," I said.

We walked down the avenue together, Doval eyeing my fine-honed silver-of-steel sword with contempt inadequately masking his interest. The house robots, which can be quite versatile with a bit of re-programming here and there, had made the sword yesterday. They had been making my clothes and other gear for two *vreks*.

"Danor not with you?" inquired Doval.

"Something wrong with your eyes, Doval?"

Danor had been tense and pale, so last night I'd slipped a minor soporific in her snow-in-gold, and left her sleeping. The swan was firmly anchored to the bed, its beak stuffed three inches deep in a plate of swan-food.

The noise of the crowd was impressive now, and as we emerged from the trees into the clearing Zirk had elected for our duel, most of my fears were realized.

The bulk of the onlookers were Jang. Glittering and giggling, shoving, pushing, and gulping their pills, an enchanting picture they made. The air was full of their bees, bringing them mirrors and scent and cigars and wine and meals and pets. And every so often the bees would ram each other, and Joyousness and bright-blue kicking animals would rain upon the press below. Zirk, Hergal, Doval, and Kley between them had recruited their own bees to erect a temporary fence to hold the crowd back from the clearing. Some terraces went up on the north and east sides, so they would all get quite a decent view, damn them.

Zirk himself was sitting on a big platinum chair, stripped to the waist. Somewhere in his reading he had been led astray, for he was wearing a rather peculiar helmet, brazen greaves and so on. Need I say he looked magnificent? Because he did, and also a complete idiot. Kley, in spiky gold with gilt dragon heads pasted over her nipples, was honing Zirk's sword personally, and sparks were flying. Hergal lounged in the shade, handsomely bored. I could see he was regretting the inconvenience already—was I worth all this trouble? The rest of the circle were there too. Thinta in pale-green see-through with a cat or two hooked on; Mirri, a male for once, being very obviously married to Thinta and making sure I noticed it. I even detected Hatta by a blunder of scarlet among the glass shrubbery.

Doval strutted up to Zirk and said something. Zirk grinned, Hergal yawned. The circle clustered together and looked at me out of their cozy togetherness. Then Mirri detached himself and came over.

"I've said I'll be your second, since you haven't got one, you *thalldrap*."

Hatta, tripoddling up behind on his three legs, said:

"Me, too. You may need us."

"May I?"

"Zirk will rip you in shreds," said Mirri, twisting his mustache playfully. "So you're going to have a painful time till you get to Limbo."

Everyone seemed so certain Zirk was going to finish me that I suppose I might have relaxed with a happy sigh and just let events take their course. However, I've never been a lover of pain—I'm a whimpering coward, in fact—and I could just see me, bleeding slowly and agonizingly away in the silk-grass while Kley or somebody misled the robot rescue planes just long enough to make sure I got the most out of it. Naturally, you couldn't really fool them, and they'd save me in the end; they always do. But for someone who flies to the medicinal-salve-dispenser for a hangnail, the prospect was unpleasing.

"Aren't you pale?" said Mirri. "Scared?"

"Shut up," said Hatta. "If you're his second, you're supposed to be on his side."

I won't say Hatta's loyalty touched me, but his stolid sense of fairness certainly brought a note of humor to the *drumdik* scene.

The Jang crowd, meanwhile, were setting up a hooting howl for us to begin. Zirk stood up and cracked his muscles loudly. Doval, primed in the formalities, came over and offered me wine, which I refused. Zirk swilled his mouth and spat, all brutal, on the quartz flowers. Then he marched into the clearing's center and Kley brought him the sword. It was a sort of cleaver, notched here and there to suggest previous (nonexistent) fights. Zirk had certainly caught the spirit of the thing.

I, modest sword in hand, joined him.

"Right," said Zirk. "To the death. Agreed?"

He really was about twice the size of me, and, for a couple of splits, I wished I'd done as he suggested, and got Limbo to fit me up with a new heroic body. His sword was definitely nasty, and bloodlust gleamed in his eye. And there stood my lovable circle, hoping for, and anticipating, my demise. My vitals turned over and icy sweat threatened my brow. But I nodded and smiled in true histrionic fashion.

"Ready when you are, *floop*."

And sword clanged on sword, as they say. Sword also clanged on air and tree bole—Zirk's sword, that is. I'd temporarily forgotten how much more agile slight, poetic me was than this musclebound freak. Besides, I had the art of it somewhat, while he obviously believed he only had to swing at me heartily and presently he'd cleave me from crown to crotch. Which, left to himself, he probably would have done eventually. But he wasn't left to himself, not quite. Two things had happened. Some of the skill I'd learned over my *vreks* of practice-fencing asserted itself automatically. I found myself parrying and riposting very adequately in all directions on a pure reflex. Additionally, my peerless cowardice had turned into a bright-red anger, which mounted and blazed the longer I fought him. It wasn't like any of those noble fighting dreams I'd ever programmed for myself. I was just shaking and snarling with fury at the mean-mindedness of them, the way they'd ejected their stupid little poison-sacs at me. Maybe, too, there was something of the old rage on me, the rage against our whole way of living, our mores and our superficial codes.

It was quite warm by now, and I could just hear the squealing and yelping of the Jang crowd beyond the barrier—experiencing our battle secondhand, as we all did most events—but everything seemed to be coming from miles off.

Just then the edge of Zirk's cleaver slashed diagonally over my chest. It bit through velvet and satin-of-steel shirt, and through me.

There was no pain for a moment, as if my body didn't realize what had happened to it. Then the pain did come, a white zinging pain from shoulder to ribs. It felt as if he had laid bare tissue and bone, but there was no chance to look, luckily. Blood, my blood, was running exuberantly from the wound, as if it had been waiting for ages only for a chance to get free of the skin envelope, and now, burbling to itself, fled like the kids at hypno-school at midperiod.

I knew enough to guess that the more I bled, the less chance I had of getting Zirk. Which was splendid, wasn't it? Just what I wanted?

Then I saw Zirk's face.

It had tightened, knotted up. It had a look of alarm, even of fright. He was a mirror. I saw what I had become by looking at him. And I understood then that I was going to kill him. Strive as I might, I couldn't stop myself.

I don't know how long it took. Not long, I suppose. From the moment I admitted my desires, I seemed to open up and

catch fire. I didn't feel any danger from him. I found after
that he'd nicked me again once or twice, but nothing like the
first time. At this stage I was driving him back, the way you
drive a reluctant house machine back into the wall, back and
back.

Suddenly he collided with a tree. His arms went wide, he
aimed a mad blow at me and missed me, and I went in under
his arm, catching him hard in the thigh. He screamed in agony, a deep bellowing scream, connected with his bulk. It
was like a cry out of prehistory indeed. It seemed to silence
the whole city, let alone the crowd in Ilex Park.

I could have left him like that, to pump out his life there,
as I thought he'd have left me. But instinct, which had possessed me, was too thorough, too clean. As he was falling,
eyes rolling, mouth stretched over his teeth, I struck at his
heart. He made no other sound, merely crashed like a colossus in the silk-grass, his weight tearing the sword from my
hand. I could never have come near his heart unless he'd been
on the way down; he was too tall.

6

They flew at me in unison, and at once.

"What a fight!" said Mirri, squeezing my arm, and I could see his male eyes already looking forward to the next female session he planned with me. *"What a fight!"*

Thinta and her cats meowed in my ears, which were beginning to din thickly:

"Ooma, are you all right?"

"He's excellent," said Kley. "That hulking dope didn't stand a chance."

Even Doval was smirking: *"Ever* so good."

Only Hergal wasn't there—looking green, he'd gone behind a tree. I could conjecture how he felt. There was no triumph now, only a grizzly, clammy horror, heightened by the extraordinary attitude of my friends, not to mention the crowd, most of whom were dissolving into hysterics of nausea or delight. The blood loss was telling also, and any split I was going to repeat my famous action of twelve *vreks* ago, and faint dead at their spangled feet.

Above, dimly heard by me, the wailing of robot sirens as the rescue squad homed in on Zirk. The sirens seemed to fill

my lungs and push them out of my temples. Then a solid bulk
inserted itself between me and the black pit I was about to
fall backward into. Some kind of strong hand got hold of me,
and I became aware, through the swarming black stars that
were invading my eyes, of a scarlet presence on my left.

"Hang on to me," said Hatta in a voice so full of con-
spiracy that a feeble laugh reverberated my shattered frame.
"Or do you fancy being carted to Limbo too, along with
Zirk's last body?"

"No thanks. Hatta, you're amazing."

Hatta got me around, and we began to make it toward the
avenue and away from the clearing. Not even Thinta, apparently, tried to stop us; maybe they were fascinated with the
approaching Limbo team—I was too far gone to see or care.

Hatta, three-legged monster that he was, managed me
reasonably well, but somewhere on the avenue I imagine I
dropped in my tracks, for the next thing I knew I was hanging
over his unrestful balloon shoulder, and we were jogging
along at a cracking pace.

"Hatta," I mumbled, "do you have to run so fast? Two
legs would be bad enough."

"Clearly," said Hatta, "you don't know what you've
done, do you?"

"I think so."

"Then if you know, you'll know why I'm going fast."

My head swam with the motion of our career. I could no
longer feel the wound of Zirk's sword. I must have said so,
for Hatta panted:

"I put stuff on it, of course. Now quiet."

Quiet came, black as the mountains of the desert, soft as
Danor's hair.

7

I woke to find the swan seated on my belly, dulcetly singing: "You are the wonderful sun of my sky." I took this initially as a sentimental gesture of concern for me on the swan's part, and was quite moved, until I recollected that this particular ditty seemed to be its method of calling for help. I struggled up and discovered, sure enough, that it had got its leash—snapped again—tangled around the bed legs, and was slowly strangling. I released it with some difficulty, and it strode out in search of Danor or food, or both.

The windows had been clouded. I cleared them. Outside it was night, the sky glowing with stars and flash signs.

I felt almost normal, and the sword slash had healed completely in response to Hatta's quick-cure salve. It could only have been a flesh wound after all, though a bad one.

Hatta had apparently brought me home, also. A noble gesture, or maybe he was just nosy and/or after Danor.

There was no sign of either of them, but, following a split or two during which I warded off urgent robot plates with viands and noticed that the recluse switch was firmly depressed, I picked up the sound of their voices in the garden.

For some reason, or perhaps it was obvious, I guessed they were talking about me, so I sneaked toward the door and leaned there.

It was a strange sight, an azure angel in conversation with a red balloon, and, midway between them, the swan staring up at the dome-sky in a bemused yet creative fashion, as if trying to fathom the secrets of the universe.

"It's all so silly," Danor was saying vehemently. "So stupid, so silly, like everything else."

"It may be," said Hatta, "but the fact remains that it's a Committee order."

"It must have happened before," said Danor, "sometime."

"Never, they say. At least, not on city record. The notion of crime has been abolished for *rorls,* so they don't know what to do. That means they'll invent things, and that means a superlative screwup."

Stunned by Hatta's perception, rancor, and colourful choice of words, I emerged on the marble terrace, and Danor jumped guiltily.

"What Committee order?" I inquired.

But they burst out, Danor:

"How could you leave me behind like that?"

And Hatta:

"How long have you been there?"

I said:

"You were involved enough, Danor. About one split, Hatta. I repeat—what Committee order?"

"A Committee messenger bee came while you were sleeping," said Danor. "They want you and each of us at the Committee Hall in Second Sector tomorrow, first thing."

"Surprise, surprise," I said. It sounded but too familiar. "And how's Zirk?"

"They've kept him in Limbo for observation," said Danor.

"Nice for them."

"You ought to take this seriously," said Hatta.

"How will that help?"

We sat and stared at the pool.

The swan teetered to the edge, but Hatta flapped it away again with his bizarre arms.

"You, er, you know I'll stick by you," said Hatta.

"Please," I said, "I've got enough problems without that."

"Oh, *ooma*—" said Danor.

"Oh *ooma* nothing. If he 'sticks by me' at the Hall looking like that, they'll slap an I.A. First-Class Maladjusted label on him from the start, and what good will that be to me, might I ask?"

"You are a bastard," said Hatta, unnerving me again slightly, for strong language, even when obsolete, was not generally his province.

"No such thing, Hatta, not anymore. Been in the History Tower too?"

"I've been just about everywhere you've been, and you know why," said Hatta.

Yes, I knew why. Hatta loved me, and once, when I had been broken in pieces by everything and he arrived on my porch with hair the color of honey and a body fair as morning . . . I'd only got to dig up my metal-tape saga from twelve *vreks* ago to find that dismal story.

"Get going, Hatta," I said. And Hatta, as ever, got.

"You're very unkind to him," said Danor.

"I suppose Kam would have acted differently?"

She looked at me.

"Yes, Kam would."

"But Kam wasn't Jang," I said. "Jang—Jang—bloody Jang."

We sat silently in the garden for some while, and the swan careered about in the flowers, occasionally falling down or singing: "The wild white magic of your hair, the warm mauve magic of your eyes, both drive me *zaradann*."

I wondered if I'd see my old Q-R of the water carpet, the poor sod who'd formerly nursed me through my successive ambitions—the anti-Jang change, the work search, and my last scheme to make a child, which ended in such horror and wretchedness. However, there was neither sight nor sign of him. Maybe he'd had to be dismantled after his dealings with me—the strain must have been considerable. Or possibly he was just keeping out of my way—ditto.

Danor came with me, which I could have done without. I anticipated a grim sequence ahead.

We went through the usual Committee Hall routine of tunnel-rides, flying floors, waiting areas, and finally emerged in a circular cold-cream room with seats in tiers, mostly empty, and a central dais, mostly full. Q-Rs with miserably stern faces were packed onto it, their memory units and what-have-you no doubt clacking and clonking away in their joints. The people back on the tiers were all Older, and obviously had some vague status—doubtless merely titular—in the running of the city Committee affairs. Along the edges of the dais, like a garish flower bed, sat just about every Jang I had a nodding acquaintance with in Four BEE. Not to mention my circle. Kley, female; Mirri, female—fast work, she must have overdosed her meal injections again; Thinta, female of course, but no cats—probably forcibly torn from her at the entrance; even Hergal, male, and neurotic at being here and covering by slumping in attitudes of defiant nonchalance; and, at the very end, a tiny, delicate, perky little creature, tinkling crystals, with pale-pink satin lotus buds in her hair the exact exquisite tint of her mammalian tips, *Zirk!*

I burst into raucous laughter at that, overwrought as I was, and had to be restrained. Danor tugged at my arm, bees zoomed, Q-Rs flapped, and Older People muttered disparagingly. A male Jang appeared at my side.

"Get a grip on yourself," he said.

"Get a grip on your *graks*," I suggested. He was nothing special, gray and gross, an unimaginative haphazard body choice, but at least no duplicate limbs or heads, and no scarlet: it was Hatta come back to be my Tower of Strength.

"It's Hatta," said Danor.

"I know. Who else could it be? How'd you change so fast, Hatta? Your thirty units weren't up."

"Never mind that," said Hatta, embarrassed by his self-less act—he detested suiciding. "I took your point last night."

We had reached the dais, and were now separated. I found myself right in the middle of everything—room, Q-Rs, Jang, the lot. An unenviable position.

I tried to relax, but it was difficult. Muscles tensed and the skin twitched under my shadowy poet's eyes.

Everyone was fluttering and whispering. Nobody actually came out with a direct sentence. I looked around at them and beamed beneficently. "Well, isn't this fun?" I said in a loud voice.

It brought the Q-Rs to attention, as I'd suspected it might. One in the center, an important-looking being in gold, rapped on the little table in front of him.

"You will kindly not display levity. This is a very dreadful situation," he said.

"Oh, *awful*," I agreed. "Poor Zirk cut down in his prime, and back five splits later looking like a refrigerated silk flower."

Zirk jumped up and began to squeak malevolently at me, with crystalline tears welling from her dusky eyes. Other Jang joined in, and the gold Q-R rapped and rapped until a gong went off somewhere, and everybody stopped shouting in surprise.

"This inquiry will be conducted with propriety," thundered the Q-R, rather optimistically. He turned to me. "You will now give us an account of what precisely led up to this unfortunate event, whose significance, clearly, few of you comprehend."

"All right," I said. "One day when I was standing outside Silver Mountain, Zirk—male, and about the size of a small museum—knocked me flying and challenged me to a duel. That is—"

"Yes," said the Q-R. "We have looked up dueling in the files and we know."

"I agreed to the duel, and we met in Ilex Park, where, due to superior skill and more practice, I won. Zirk is now

happily installed in a new body, and everything, I should have
thought, is *insumattly derisann*.''

There were some laughs at this, which the Q-R ignored.

"It is not," he said. "Neither is that a full account."

"Oh, well, I do apologize. I thought it was. Of course, I
omitted to say that Ilex Park at the time was its usual unin-
spired jade-green and the dome sun was rising in its usual
damn silly way and the dry ice was puffing about nicely all
over us. Is that better?''

"You will be silent," said the Q-R.

"Don't bank on it.''

"You will be silent," went on the Q-R, "or you will be
silenced by hypno-spray. Which?''

"I'll be silent," I agreed.

"Jang Zirk," said the Q-R, "perhaps you'd give us your
version.''

Zirk got up again, balancing precariously on her weeny
silver-slippered feet. She dabbed her eyes and said, huskily
now: "I see it was ever so *selt*—er—foolish of me. But I, um,
lost my temper.'' She tittered like a peal of bells. Just think of
Zirk loosing her temper, ooh! How quaint of her.

"Permission to speak," I said. They looked at me. "If
Zirk continues like this, I'm going to be ill all over your
lovely white room.''

I shouldn't have risked it, but I was past reason. Giggles
filled the air, Zirk stamped and nearly fell down. Next second
a cool rain dropped on me from an overhead bee, and I was
rendered duly limp and speechless, only my ears and eyes and
brain left ticking, which I could have foregone.

And Zirk *was* continuing.

"It was just the way he lied to us all and carried Danor
off. I mean, we were all so *frightfully* anxious to meet her!
And then, not marrying! So shocking to avoid a Jang custom
like that. Well, I just got ever so angry''—eyelashes flittered,
mouth pouted—"and when I *met* him, I just couldn't control
myself. Oh dear. And we've been such sweethearts in the
past, he and I. I couldn't *tell* you the times we've married and

had love. Oh, there I go, digressing. Well, I only meant it to be a sort of friendly bout. But he went *zaradann—zaradann*, I tell you. I've *never seen* such a thing." Zirk clasped her pink-nailed hands and sighed with terror. "He cut me down without mercy."

8

After Zirk, everyone had a say.

Thinta said I'd always been unstable, but it was my temperament, and I meant well. She hoped the Committee realized that she'd been a good influence on me, and had always tried to keep me out of trouble.

Kley said I ought to be whipped, and volunteered to do it.

Mirri said Zirk had wounded me and I'd played quite fairly. She said I was mad but she didn't mind. She said Danor had forced me into acting ignorantly and thoughtlessly, and the Committee ought to ship her back to BAA.

Hergal said I'd killed Zirk deliberately (he was the first to use the word "kill"). He added that Zirk asked for it and would have got me if he'd been able. The Committee then asked Hergal about my earlier challenge to himself, and Hergal told them, in detail. He said I was predominantly female and needed a sex change back and that was all that was wrong with me and could he go now because he was fed up with being there. The Committee said no.

Danor looked as pale as I'd designed myself to be, and

gorgeous. She said calmly that it had been a mutual decision for us to go away alone together and to have love without marrying. We hadn't meant to upset anybody. The Committee said hadn't she spent a lot of time with an Older Person in BAA without marrying, and hadn't the Committee there advised them to part? I could see her hands trembling when she answered yes, that was so, looking at them straight on and not lowering her voice. The Jang gasped and exclaimed at her daring and obscenity and were gonged into quiet. The Committee said that her actions were curious and showed unusually antisocial tendencies. Danor did not answer, but when she sat down again she shut her eyes as if she were very tired.

Hatta said my first challenge to Hergal had been a joke, and Zirk was a fool. He said Zirk had meant to kill me (other Jang later supported this, recalling Zirk's threats to me outside Silver Mountain). Hatta said I hadn't meant to kill Zirk, only incapacitate him, but Zirk fell on my sword. There was an outcry at this.

Doval said I was terrific with a sworge and I'd known exactly what I was doing when I went for Zirk. Doval said he hoped the Committee would make dueling a regular pastime in the parks, and a roar of delight drowned even the gong.

Several out-circle Jang girls said I was wonderful, and several out-circle Jang males said I used to be all right when I was female. One male said if I ever came near his circle he'd meet me in Ilex Park and do better than Zirk did.

Altogether, everyone more or less said different things, and nobody really fully agreed with anyone else, either about me or what I had done.

About nine thousand mealtimes had gone by, and the Jang were noisily pleading for food. Even the pompous Older People looked uncomfortable.

At length the gold Q-R announced that if we went next door, we should discover sustenance, but we should come back in an hour when we heard the gong. To begin with I thought I would be left in my hypno-sprayed condition, alone and foodless, but a bee came over and shot me full of something, and I got to my feet all faculties restored.

I took Danor's hand as the crowd went milling ahead.

"I can't tell you how sorry I am," I said.

"Then don't tell me," she answered, softly, smiling, still Danor.

Gray Hatta came up.

"You should have done what they said," he predictably told me.

We went through into a merry yellow room where the Jang were falling on nut-steak, wine-cakes, and rock-cherries with shrill cries. The Older People had gone off somewhere more peaceful to stuff themselves.

"What would you like, Danor?" asked Hatta politely.

"Oh, nothing, thank you."

"Nor me," I said.

"You must eat," instructed Hatta.

Zirk came floating up then, a couple of males trailing her interestedly. Both bore a distinct resemblance to Zirk's male bodies, a strange phenomenon I had noted before here and there. Maybe everyone only wants to have love with themselves really.

"Attlevey," said Zirk to me, lowering her pastel lids. "I do so hope you didn't mean those *drumdik* things you said about me, *ooma*. When this nasty business is over, possibly we could meet and have a talk about everything, um, do you think?"

"Zirk," I said, "you may be steeped in scent and prisms, with a waist the width of my wrist, but if you don't beat it, I'm going to tip the nearest jug of silver-cordial right down your cleavage."

"Here now," boomed Zirk's escort in bass voices. They were waving their ten-ton fists aloft when Mirri thrust between them.

"You!" she yelled at Zirk, "you're worse than *her!"* indicating Danor. "I think you've got an absolutely *farathooming* nerve." And she slung a bowl of rock-cherries in Zirk's powdered face and began to pull out her curled flaxen hair in handfuls while Zirk screamed pitifully.

Zirk's two champions tried to rescue her, and someone

who fancied Mirri came haring across to rescue *her*. Presently, chaos reigned.

Danor, Hatta, and I, for once in agreement, shrank to the side as an incredible Jang fight broke out in every direction. Some were siding with Mirri, some with Zirk. Some were just enjoying themselves. Nuts, cakes, and bubbling liquor flew through the air, and shrieks and crashes resounded.

Suddenly a siren tore across the uproar. An amplified Q-R voice bellowed: "Cease fighting at once or you will be sprayed."

Violence faltered and petered out. Jang stood staring about, their clothes in ribbons and their faces daubed with bruises and crushed-orange.

"You will return in orderly fashion to the Inquiry Hall. Take your seats, and remain silent."

It was just like hypno-school. Which, considering the recent antics, was not to be wondered at.

Everybody filed docilely through and sat, surreptitiously brushing off their see-throughs and getting cake out of their jewelry. The Q-Rs were still on the dais, but a look of abject horror had settled on their faces. They were well and truly scared—not for themselves for their programming doesn't really allow them that, but for us, for what we might do to each other.

When everything was quiet enough to hear the dust-absorbers at work in the ceiling, the gold Q-R rose to his feet and focused on me.

"We have come to a decision," he said.

Up till that instant, despite my earlier—disregarded—caution, I hadn't credited the situation with too much importance. It was harrowing only because of its stuffiness. Cities run by robots and androids specifically geared to serve the community didn't intimidate anyone that much. I hadn't expected them to take any vital action, beyond another inconvenient black mark against me and some sort of piddling little reprimand, and perhaps a restriction, like putting the parks off limits to me for fifty units or something. Punishments were never used and fines were extinct. The only powers ever exercised were always, however exacerbating, supposed to be for your own good in the end.

But something in the Q-R's somber tone sent white-hot sparks through my innards.

"We want everyone to understand this," said the Q-R, glancing about at the Jang witnesses. "The notion of crime was abolished long since, so it has not been easy for us to determine what we should do. We have comprehended that the Jang Zirk was the aggressor in this particular instance, and that, had the circumstances been reversed, he would be sitting now where the Accused is sitting." A murmur at that "Accused." The Q-R continued: "Nevertheless, as under the ancient laws which preceded our present data, it is the actual Killer who is to pay the penalty."

No murmur at that second word. It struck too deep, like the very blade I'd used. Killer. I have killed, therefore I am a—

"Also, by reference to certain zoom-scan pictures recorded in the Flash Center, we have observed the face of the Accused during the combat. Unmistakably, the intent to kill was present." The Q-R turned again to me. "It is a rare occurrence. Or it was. Since death no longer exists, the desire to kill—founded as it was on the idea of being rid of something—has mainly atrophied. Where it has not, the Dream Rooms and Adventure Palaces have diverted the emotion along harmless channels. Now, however, one of you *has* killed—not himself, which is his right, but another against his will, and the fancy may well take root in many minds. Look at the violence already unleashed, look at yourselves. Although anyone murdered in the city can be reclaimed immediately at Limbo as with a suicide, this does not detract from the frightfulness of the act of Murder itself, and it is on this premise that we have passed sentence. You had better remain sitting," he added to me, quite compassionately, so I guess I'd attempted some stab at getting up, but my legs had gone to jelly and I hadn't made it. "There is a choice," he said. "Please consider carefully. You will have three units in which to do so. Firstly, you may go to Limbo and experience Personality Dissolution. As you know, this means your consciousness will be darkened and your memory wiped clean. As is usual, you will re-emerge three *rorls* from now and resume life in the cities, unhampered by past guilt, or by these antisocial drives which have grown up in you (this last merely the culmination of many suspect misdemeanors, one of which, we remind you, concerned the destruction of your unborn baby due to sheer folly on your part). When you leave PD yours will be an entirely changed ego. You will commence again at the child stage, as is general, with a suitable Q-R guardian, knowing only that you are returning, but recalling nothing, either of this current era, or of your present personality. Normally PD is performed for those who have lived many *rorls* and feel the urge to slough the mental accumulations of time. In your case, it is considered a cardinal condition, if you are to remain as a citizen of the Fours.''

No noise in the great circular room. I couldn't even hear my heart beating. If it was.

The Q-R narrowed his eyes as if what he told me hurt him.

''The alternative to loosing your identity and your individuality so soon is this: that you leave the dome four units from today, and exist thereafter in the desert, in exile, denied access to Four BEE, Four BAA, and Four BOO for the indefinite period of your natural human span—which might possibly continue anything up to a *rorl*. You will be supplied, of course, with every life support and commodity you may ask for, within reason. Also you will be permitted, before your departure, one final body choice, so that you can design a body best suited to your needs and your situation. Additionally, your location will be monitored, and, should you require medical or other functional aid, it will be sent you. Otherwise no contact with any city or citizen will be granted you. The disadvantages of this alternative are several, as you can perceive. Loneliness and fear are hazards. And, as your body grows older, it will age, an unpleasant process, not recommended. In the end, provided you do not suicide before, a natural death will terminate your life, after which the city will reclaim you, and PD will be carried out in any case, in order that finally you may be returned into the social structure of Four BEE.''

He folded his hands.

''In either circumstance, every one of your present relationships, intimate or otherwise, is over forever. On your reemergence, three *rorls*—or more—from today, your contemporaries may have passed themselves voluntarily into Personality Dissolution, and even if they have not, you will never remember them nor they you in your reawakened form. Not one here with you at this moment will you be likely to call lover or friend again in the future.''

Abruptly the heavy quiet was broken. Some Jang girl was wailing that they couldn't do it to me, it was ghastly, unspeakable. I think I'd only married her for a unit once, about a *vrek* before.

''This choice,'' our instructor cut in and silenced her, ''is the only one you are offered. There is no other way. You must resign yourself, and decide. *Rorls* in the past, you yourself would have met death—actual and total death. Obliteration—as the punishment for your crime. We have tried to act in your ultimate best interests as well as those of the community at large, and it has cost us a great deal of energy and time. You have three units, no more, no less. Sort out your affairs and consider your plans carefully. As for the rest of the Jang in this room, we hope you will take the warning to heart. Please now, go home.''

They hurried by me as though I had plague.

I had.

Thinta and Mirri were crying, even Kley was crying. Hergal looked as sick as he had in the park. Zirk too. No doubt she was thinking that but for my fencer's skill, this choice would have been hers to make, not mine.

The Q-Rs also stole away, and the Older People. Eventually I was left with only Hatta and Danor.

I wondered dully if Hatta would say, ''I told you so.'' He didn't. He stood staring into nothing. I'd forgotten he loved me, or thought he did. It was in some ways almost as shattering a blow for him, for he was going to lose me forever and a unit.

Danor put her face against mine. There were no tears on her cheek, yet the sorrow hung on her like a sad smoky perfume.

"Danor," I said, "hold me. Don't let me go."

9

You bet I had a party. It was the inevitable thing to do. The extreme reaction which extremity forces you into.

Besides, everyone predicted I'd give a party. They also predicted that at the height of the festivity and abandon, I'd leap from a roof or dive into a pool without an oxygen injection and not swimming, or maybe, if their luck was really in, douse myself with Joyousness and strike an igniter in my ear. That was the only way to behave, after all. For there was only one answer to my choice of alternatives—die and let Limbo destroy my soul, or at any rate, wash it spotless and characterless. Three *rorls* of oblivion, followed by a repeat childhood and permanent amnesia, were a dire fate for a Jang, a crushing blow none of them spoke of, but which you could tell they were considering from the way the color fled their cheeks. But the other thing, exile and despair among the dunes, companionless till the end of my days, growing dry as the sand, creaky and wizened as the cacti, and agoraphobia everywhere—never, never! If, by some master stroke of insanity, I had accepted that, I would put paid to myself inside a quarter *vrek* anyway. So, glorious, tumultuous suicide *now* it would have to be. Go out with a bang, *show* everyone what I was made of . . .

They were so interested in what I'd do, so fascinated by the notion of my macabre farewell feast, they forgot or mislaid their revulsion at my contaminating doom, and flocked around me from sunrise to sunrise.

I wondered if one or both of my makers—last seen many moons ago—might signal me, to say goodbye, or something. Anything. But they didn't. Probably they were both in Boo or Baa, and didn't get to hear of it or even realize it was me, their child, until it was too late.

Under sentence, I felt hollow, pithless. The first and second units of the time they'd allowed me, I woke with a feeling of blind clawing terror. The second unit I wept, and Danor wept with me.

She asked me if she should go, but I said stay. I needed her, or thought I needed her, I don't know why, because it didn't really help, though she was steady and tender. The swan wandered about peeing on things and falling on things. The swan saved us a little, but only a little. I made an arrangement for Danor to have my home after I was . . . no longer in residence.

One excellent fact: Everything I bought was free, including the extra novelties for the party. I suppose the Committee understood I was incapable, in the circumstances, of groveling out thank-yous in a pay booth.

Nearly all Four BEE's Jang must have come to that party, or it seemed like it.

It was my last night in the world, and I'd taken enough ecstasy to launch a small rocket into space. I was absolutely numb with it, couldn't feel a thing; even the prospect before me seemed unimportant, bearable almost. So what were three *rorls?* There'd be other Danors. Hypno-school was OK, mainly you didn't know about it anyhow, and I was going to make an utter *promok* out of my Q-R guardian. My ego would strike back through the brainwashing and consciousness-darkening, somehow it would. I was incorrigible, wasn't I? So drink up and swallow the pretty pills, and goodbye

Danor, how I'll miss your beautiful—better forget about that, my friend, if you're going to be a kiddy all over again in three *rorls'* time.

The whole riot took place in the Moon Gardens in Second Sector. Blue and green fireballs of non-hot flame lit the groves of filigree trees. The fountains ran with blue wine, and a dragon or two from BAA glittered here and there, and BAA android females sang in sweet voices, plants growing from their heads and bursting into blossom. The sky was full of Jang riding starry birds, and rainbows, and golden-scented rain.

We also sang at the long tables, most of the vomitous Jang hit songs, delivering them with passion and sincerity. I was toying with the idea of slashing my wrists in an antique style of suiciding princes at feasts, but concluded I was too hazy with ecstasy to get it right, and abandoned the fancy. Then came the Masque of Death—a small entertainment I'd dreamed up that evening to give them all colic.

I designed it via a thought-receptive screen, the sort of effort the Dream Rooms and the Picture-Vision places use. The resulting montage was thrown three-dimensionally out into the Moon Gardens, and grim and grand it was.

Six pairs of dancers, three male and three female, in emerald and scarlet velvet with golden-tassel hair. They danced and they embraced, they offered each other gifts and smiled into each other's eyes. Then came death—the Ego-Death of Limbo's PD. It was a black-enameled worm and its head was a white skull. It thrust between them and they were smitten in its coils. They lay on the grass like broken flowers and the worm laughed, and sang a brief song of my composing, telling how Ego-Death was best for them and the community. I must already have been fairly ecstatic when I invented that song. It was silly, garbled, and amazingly bitter and terrible, and you could see the Jang blanching at a distance of fifty paces. Then bells rang and the fallen dancers rose. They bowed to the worm, and went on bowing until they shrank down to the size of children. They didn't know who they were or who the others were, their friends and lovers, but ran off after the worm, kissing its oily tail, with blindfolds obscuring their eyes.

"That's it," Hergal said to me. He and Mirri were consoling each other. "That's absolutely it, old *ooma*. Blindfolds and *thalldrapping* worms."

Thinta lay in a fountain of Joyousness, meowing, and Kley had come as a male, pathetic and inhibited, his eyes red. Hatta kept pouring me wine, wine the color of sapphires. "Drink up," he said whenever I flagged. "Take another pill."

If Zirk was there, I never saw him, or her.

Suddenly it was very late, about two hours before dawn, and I'd disappointed the Jang by not suiciding, which dismally cheered me.

"Danor," I said, "let's go back home. For the last time."

So we went. Up Periot Waterway in an open boat, up the bright staircase, under the anemone opening and shutting on the porch. For the last time.

I was so drink-and-drug-sodden I didn't know if I could actually do anything, but some of Four BEE's pills are wonderful things, and paleness had touched the sky when we lay stilled and silent in each other's arms. And I recalled that night so long ago when impotence had ravaged us, and it had *mattered* and meant so *much*.

Danor said quietly:

"I loved this time we've had. After Kam, it's meant a lot to me. I'm only sorry, so sorry—"

"Don't talk about it," I said. "It's nearly here."

And then I fell asleep, abruptly, as if I could escape that way from what came closer with every split.

I was standing by the pet's grave. My pet from all the *vreks* before. My pet who died on the shock wall the day after the great rains, when the desert blossomed. City robots from Limbo had buried it, at my request, out in the sands beyond the dome, because I couldn't let them incinerate its white body, like a fall of snow, in some neat, hygienic pet cremator.

I'd never known the site of the grave; I hadn't gone with
them. Yet here I was.

All around was desert and the dust wind softly blowing,
but I scarcely noticed it yet. For on the grave sat the pet itself,
washing with an infuriatingly thorough concentration. Then it
looked up at me, a couple of its six white legs still hooked at
amazing angles around its head, looked out of its orange
eyes.

"You're dead," I said to the pet. "True death. Obliteration."

"Certainly my body's dead," said the pet casually, "but
whoever told you that everything else dies with it? What
about that thing they use at Limbo, the thing the androids
don't have, the life spark, the soul? My, my, have *you* been
led by the nose."

Of course, the pet had never been able to talk—one of its
virtues, maybe. It didn't even seem to be talking now, yet
somehow I heard the words, and imagined they came from it.

"Why am I here?" I asked.

"Why indeed? Obviously, you'd much rather stay in the
city and get washed out, or whatever it is."

"Oh, you're wrong. I'm afraid to wake up, because then
I have to go and let them do it."

"Why do you? They're only a bunch of dopey quasi-
robots trying to work out all the answers, and getting tied up
in their rewire circuits. As for you, have you forgotten *everything*?"

"How else could I get by, without making myself forget?" I said, and didn't at first know what I meant.

"Finally you can only get by by letting yourself remember. Look."

And we were up in a bird-plane, but it was open all
around so you could see every way at once, and feel the
scratchy wind and smell the sand and rock smell, and the
smell of the wide sky.

Dark sky, even at noon, sky of an indigo greenness, sky
with a blinding, scorching sun, a sun in space, not a mechanism revolving in a dome roof like a child's toy. Below, the

land, the pale dunes, the black mountains shaped like spears, like towers, like fortresses. On the horizon one volcano pouring its crimson plume into the air, fierce, uncompromising, and real. A wild land, a cruel land, a land to catch you out, bury you in sandstorm, broil you under the sun, freeze you under the stars, dehydrate and suffocate you in the heat with its low oxygen count. A land to thrill and humble you in that single unit after the rains, when all the barren sand is bright with green, and ferns spring toward the mountains and cover their flanks like a rolling ancient sea.

"Here I am!" shouted the desert, loud with life, for life there still was in it, waiting, stored, like seed. "Here I am. Did you forget me? Forget me despite your dreams of me, your dreams of the sun and the rain and the antique tribes who roamed me once with their herds and their weird ways? You, who moaned and whined, covering metal-tape with cries and yearning, you, you effete *thalldrap?* Now's your chance to prove you can do more than sit on your tail complaining and drinking sapphire wine with your tears of self-pity. Come on, come and do battle with me, come and fight me. I'm more than a match for you. I'll devour you if I can, but I'll do it cleanly and openly, not with words and dark little tanks in Limbo. Don't be afraid of human death and human age. I've seen it all, and I know it. It's just dust blown over the rocks. Look at me, how dead and old I seem, and yet, watch me grow, watch me live. Come on. Come and find me. I'm waiting."

"Pet," I said, "I've forgotten your name."

"Names," said the pet. "Is that the only thing you care about?"

And it bit me hard, so hard I woke up with a shout.

10

I went into the foyer of the Committee Hall in Second Sector, and quite a big silent crowd was standing there, gawping. There were messenger bees too, and zoom-scanners zooming in from the nearest Flash Center, since I and my fate were exciting news, the first bit of drama for sixty *rorls* or whatever it was.

"Please follow me," said a tactful Q-R. "I'm sure you'd prefer to do this in private."

"No, thanks," I said. "I'll give my decision publicly, out here. After all, everybody's so enthralled."

It was a grandiose and gloomy occasion. The Q-R slowly went away, and presently the others from the Inquiry came shoveling out, led by the spokesman in gold.

I won't say I wasn't shaking all over, and I won't, in fact, say any more about the state of my mind and my nerves, because they were fairly serious. But somewhere in me was a rod of steel to which I clung. I'd had a vision, as good as any vision given to any poet, sage, or prophet in the past. I wasn't elated, I wasn't confident even, but somehow, I *knew,* and with the end of doubt had come the death of despair.

"Fine," I said, when I saw their depressed, executioners' faces. "I hope everybody can hear me, and I hope the Flash Center is getting it too, because what I want to say is important, and it's just about time someone did say it. I'm only embarrassed it took this pseudo-trial to push me into making a move."

The Q-Rs began to look bothered. Was I going to create yet another disturbance? I went on fast, before they could start ordering sprays. "My decision is this: I'm heading into the desert."

There was an interruption at this point. The crowd set up a lot of noise, even the Q-Rs seemed to be buzzing, in the region of their necks. Then everyone was saying shut up, shut up, to each other, since they could see I hadn't finished. So I bowed, and continued:

"You think I've gone mad, and that's probably a logical assumption on your part. I'm scared, I'll admit, at what I'm going to do. But I tell you, we live here like a lot of embryos in a breeding tank. Every need is catered for. The Committee wipes our noses for us and picks us up when we fall down. Outside the domes we have a planet which actually belongs to us, and which half of us have never seen and would rather not see. I have seen it, and I like what I saw better than the sort of style and judgment you can see in Four BEE." I looked at the Q-Rs. "So I've got the list of my requirements drawn up, and, brace yourselves, it's a long one. And I'm ready, when you Q-R gentlemen are ready, to get down to it."

The gold Q-R said extremely clearly, as if explaining to an imbecile: "We hope you have not been hasty. This is serious."

"Don't I know it. I told you, I've made my choice. If you think you have some damn right to give me an alternative like the alternative you gave me, I think I have a right to pick which course I accept. I'll take the desert, and you can take Limbo PD and shove it right up your electronic valves."

I felt I was unfair to those Q-Rs, who were blindly serving the community, or attempting to, as their programming ensured they must. But then, how could anyone ask me to be

otherwise? Nobody expects the condemned to embrace the
axe.

But nobody expected either, at least I don't think they
did (certainly I didn't), the cheer that went belting up from
the crowd in the Hall. Even the people cheering seemed unnerved. They were cheering me. Not so much for my speech
but for that very thing which so appalled them normally.
Because I had defied the System, bitten again at the burning
sun.

The cheers faded. A self-conscious void followed. Into
the void, I spoke.

"Come on, then. Here's my list, a whole boxload of it.
Let's not *grak* about."

PART 2

1

I got a sand-ship off them, and it wasn't easy.

If they exiled you to the desert, they reckoned they'd put up for you a nice little palace with every mod. con., and there you'd sit, *vrek* by *vrek*, staring up at the glassy ceiling, or down the vacuum drift or something, till boredom got the better of you, you selected a tasteful high window, and jumped out of it. I won't say they definitely encouraged you to suicide and get everything over with quickly (and so back into PD in civilized fashion), but the idea that survival might be wrested from the situation, purpose even, was clearly indigestible to them.

What did I want a sand-ship *for?* To be mobile, to move about in? Well, yes. But—I reasoned—it would save them a bird-plane trip for me going from the dome, and it would also save them time, energy, and building materials. A sand-ship came ready-fitted, of necessity, with all life-support systems—oxygen pump, provision dispenser, water mixer, freezer storage, heat and cooler units, stabilizers (essential since about two-thirds of the desert is earthquake zone), defense mechanisms, even service and maintenance robots. And there must be surplus ships. How often did they run? And even when they did, they mostly ran passengerless, citizens who traveled preferring planes and sky-boats, which, they felt, kept them at a safer distance from the agoraphobic waste. Think, I kept saying, of the bother it would save the Committee if they just gave me a sand-ship. And, at last, they reluctantly responded.

Of course, I was acting on impulse merely. I'd been in a sand-ship before, twice, and seen what they had to offer, but their mobility did head *my* list of favorables. I had some mad notion of fizzing along the desert by day and night, the Outcast, a dangerous hazard to authorized traffic, shouting embittered songs at the sun and stars. My future seemed bleak, so I had clothed it in colorful hysteria; that way it was almost tolerable.

By the end of the fourth unit, I had to be out of the city. I hadn't seen any "friends" since the party, nor Danor since our parting at dawn, when I had woken from the dream and wildly chittered my intentions in her ears. I was terrified she'd start trying to dissuade me—maybe succeed—but she only nodded. "Yes," she said. "I think you're right. Yes, yes. Go and tell them, *ooma*." The last embrace was hurtful, and better undescribed. I wanted no one to see me off. So, from the moment I left home, I was entirely isolated, already exiled, though, what with the cheering crowd, and the Committee Hall and Limbo swirling with Q-Rs, I scarcely felt it. Then came the last journey across Four BEE to the dome lock.

I was female again by then, which, hormone-wise, no doubt made everything much worse. But I'd had to opt for a sex change—Hergal probably vibrated with glee when he heard. This was the final body I'd ever be allowed until my "natural death," all of a *rorl* perhaps away. I was predominantly female, and I didn't dare risk that fact catching up with me out alone in the wild when I could no longer alter things. Besides, I'd had a generous portion of masculinity, and should have sated that side for some while. I didn't feel comfortable, though, being a girl again when really, under ordinary circumstances, I wasn't ready to be. I kept forgetting my physiognomy was different, which was embarrassing enough, and, seeing myself in mirrors, was startled and demoralized, despite the beauty I'd ordered in Limbo as my right.

And I was very beautiful. It was the most beautiful body I'd ever designed. I was going to have to live with it, literally, and watch it, too, decaying. It was, therefore, the sort of loveliness which is not perfect, but draws its charm from a measure of imbalance, which can accommodate flaws and make little of them, for a while at least. A slim, agile body for traversing harsh regions, excellent muscle tone, long legs, long fingers, breasts not too large—able to resist the sag that would come with *vreks* of gravity. Good bone structure in a face light and versatile, to hold that smooth flesh taut to the bitter (how bitter?) end. Oh, yes, I'd thought of everything, hadn't I? For, reading in the History Tower, I had learned fully of the myth of Old Age and the roads whereby it traveled.

My skin was tawny-tan to complement and survive the lashes of the sun, my hair one shade fairer than my skin, straight and bright as a tan flame. The poet's eyes I kept, the large blue opals with their shadowy rims. At least I could recognize their glances in the ambushing mirrors of the city I was leaving forever.

The bird-plane was anonymous. Two Q-Rs rode with me, innocuous guards.

I had never felt much for Four BEE beyond a kind of contemptuous familiarity. Now it didn't look dear to me, or precious, yet so known and so secure. Never again will I ride on Peridot Waterway, never again watch the tragic dragon spray its green fire before Jade Tower, never again wander the movi-rails beneath the artificial stars, or drink snow-in-gold at Blue Sky, or lie with some lover in the plastic-cloud floaters, or . . .

The poet's eyes were weeping down my girl-stranger's face, and with my unknown tawny slender hands I made obscure crushing gestures, as if it were my emotion I tried to crush.

At the lock, somehow, there was no crowd. Obviously secrecy and intrigue had been perpetrated to mislead the populace.

The sand-ship stood waiting there. I stared at it with icy fear, as if it threatened me, this thing which was to be my home.

Every scrap of my belligerence and my defiance had gone. The dream was insubstantial as smoke. I wanted to beg them to let me stay, but I knew they never would, so somehow kept my mouth shut.

They escorted me into the ship, my two Q-Rs. The robots were already busy here and there; the automatic motors were humming to be off. I didn't have to drive or navigate myself, of course. It would do everything itself, to my specifications. It wasn't a big ship, but pretty big for me. The Q-Rs showed me the monitor beam they'd put in, the thing I could use to signal the city for extra supplies or medical help. It would relay through a computer, naturally, and be very efficient, and that meant that, even in this way, I couldn't communicate with another human being. While I was myself, I would never hear a real human voice again. And, though I might see the bird-planes pass over, or distant sister ships go gliding by along the horizon of the dunes, never again would I see a real human face.

"All right," I said to the Q-Rs. "I understand where everything is." I hadn't had to pay for anything; I wouldn't ever have to pay from here on. One advantage of exile. I wiped the tears from my cheeks and glared my escort out. "Now, get off my ship."

They went immediately, and once the doors had shut, I flipped the switch for automatic drive.

The window-spaces were covered, but shortly there came the bang of the dome locks, closing behind me for the ultimate time.

I sat very still and very stiff upon the velvet seat, feeling the unseen desert clasp me round.

Alone at last.

2

How many times in the city I had longed for privacy, sought and won privacy, and sighed with relief. Privacy is a pleasant thing when crowds surge below and friends hammer, unheard, at the porch signal.

I got up eventually, and went about the ship. It thought for itself, and had no need of my supervision. Steady on its air cushions, it would swoop to port or starboard to avoid rocks or faults or exploding volcanoes. Clever ship. I could foretell I might begin to talk to it sooner or later, call it by a pet name; talk to the robots too, probably, program them to carry out inane tape-voice calls and motions of recognition when they saw me. No doubt I should murmur endearments to the love machine, pretend it was Danor, Lorun, Hergal . . . Oh, I could see everything before me, like pictures painted on my mind.

I chose a sleeping place, one of the several cabins the ship possessed. It was done up in cream and blue.

At least there'd be Picture-Vision, human bodies on perma-celluloid for me to watch. Song tracks to play and moving-picture magazines too, in the ship's store. And after all, ecstasy in abundance. If I planned it carefully, I could stay ecstatic for ten units at a time before I had to give it a rest. Because, even then, I knew I wasn't going to suicide. Oh no. However bad it got (and it was going to get bad, wasn't it?) I wouldn't give them the satisfaction.

I sat an hour or so in the pale-gold saloon under the chandelier, before a delicious untasted repast the robots had served. I'd already inspected the automatic food and water machines, marveling aloud, until I caught myself, on their intricate, self-maintaining activities.

The ship was still running, north, east, west, south—or in a circle—what did it matter? Solar battery by day, friction circuits by night, or during recharging. You could hear the systems change over, one to the other, if you listened hard.

I took a robot into one of the game rooms, and we played star-ball for a while, but I missed the bad language and the sulking or spiteful victory noises of a human opponent. Even when the ball went smack into the robot's faceplate, never a word. Just imagine Hergal—no, don't do that. Don't imagine anyone.

All this while, there had been one small part of me I had managed to keep hidden. The part which was thinking of the desert everywhere around. On my first sand-ship journey, I had run to the Transparency Tower in the stern to observe the landscape, and gone into euphorics over it. Now I wouldn't go there. I was afraid. Afraid to see and afraid to confront my reaction to seeing. As soon as I understood this, the evasion began to prey on me.

Nibble, nibble. Cowardice becomes you, *ooma*.

Go on, go on, get up and look.

'Fraid to face the nasty-wasty waste.

Nag, nag, nag.

At length I rose, girded my loins, so to speak, and skulked down the corridor.

On the sand-ship runs, the glacia-view of the towers clouds and clears in spasms, to lessen the shock. Most passengers go crazy and foam at the mouth when they see the desert: I never had, and my hauteur had known no bounds. But this time I'd been hoping, I think, that the glacia-view would be opaque. However, it was night outside, and the towers stay clear nocturnally, presumably judging everyone a-bed.

Desert night. Yes, I'd forgotten.

Pale sand hills, seas of sand under the stars, black crags supporting black sky. To the west, one of the ubiquitous eruptions going on, but so distant as to be only an enlarged sequin on the dark. And yes, it was powerful, beautiful, but it was unfriendly, cruel, vast, limitless. And I was afraid. It wasn't like the dream.

Nowhere to run now, but to this inhospitable land.

Go to the sand and say: Help me. Go to the rock and ask it for love and kindness.

The stars stare down, the bones of the planet stare up, and I am caught between as if on the points of two daggers.

The tower, clear on every side and above, seemed swimming around me in a blur of black and paleness. I clutched at objects in panic, as if to prevent myself from falling from a great height, and accidentally activated a siren which went whooping off in the ceiling. This saved me, by a hair's breadth, from something I had no name for, pure insanity, maybe. I bashed at buttons, and the siren relapsed into silence. Then, I fled from the tower and into my safe cabin with its window-spaces of solid blue brocade.

I lay among the gauzes of the anchored float-bed, crying soundlessly. For, having come to fight the desert, I couldn't even face it now, I, who had danced, so long ago with my pet, among its rain-green dunes.

Three units and three nights we ran, the ship and I. I lay on my bed and the machinery rocked me, and fed me pills to make me sleep, and injected me with meals, and wiped away my tears with anodyne sponges.

"How kind of you," I sniveled to it, forgetting I had set the switches for this care, and wanting to forget.

The third night I dreamed I was in a great hall. Outside

the hall stood people, not from the cities but from the desert, ghosts of the nomads that had wandered about there eons back. The hall had many tall windows, each of which was thickly curtained. But the curtains kept drawing themselves open, and then the nomads would intently gaze in at me. I went from curtain to curtain, closing them again, but as soon as I pulled one pair together, another pair would part.

At the hall's center stood a table with a flagon on it, and in the flagon, bright-blue wine. I knew if I could get to the table and swallow the sapphire liquor everything would be all right. But somehow, I wasn't permitted to drink while the people outside were watching. And the curtains opened and opened.

Finally my eyes opened, and I was awake.

A crystallize chronometer had been set going in the wall by one of the robots, part of normal sand-ship-run procedure. It wasn't on city time, but desert time, and it told me that among the geography outside, dawn had come.

I swung off the bed and stamped into the bathing unit. I splashed and brutalized myself under freezing jets, was dried and almost accidentally creamed, powdered, and perfumed by wild machines that leaped on me from the walls. In my cabin, a meal-injection, and four oxygen tablets downed in a pint or so of fire-and-ice.

I strode toward the forward end of the ship. Coming to the bank of switches, I almost wavered, but the dream had infuriated me. There was, after all, no sapphire wine of forgetfulness here. With a flailing hand I spun a dial, and thereby indicated to the ship that it must stop.

An immediate sighing among the motors. A soft shuddering. Presently, stillness, broken only by quiet settling noises. I stood there, as if waiting for the crack of doom.

Come on, doom's not in here.

Suppose, I thought, suppose I've stopped us right on top of an erupting volcano. But, of course, the ship would automatically have adjusted such an error, overridden my order, and dashed to a safer spot. No good trying to get out of it that way.

The doors slid back with a subtle hiss, as if trying to
catch my attention.

No need, I was hooked already.

I looked out, and my legs turned to water, but I gripped
the doorway and went on staring.

"Come on, *ooma,*" I was burbling to myself, "you
weren't scared before, you liked it before. How *derisann,* you
said. Merely observe the majesty of the mountains, all black
and jagged on the turquoise sky. Concentrate on the horizon,
the color of those special rose sweets Thinta used to eat. And
the sand. Go down and touch the sand. How *groshing* it is,
isn't it? Come on, you bitch."

I tottered down the ramp and half fell, strengthless, on
my knees. The sand felt dry and brittle, each grain separate
and individual, pressed into my skin. The atmosphere also
was dry and brittle, already hot from the risen furnace of the
sun, and the rocks were blistering.

"No, don't look at the sun. Remember, you can't, not
like a dome sun. Now, a bit at a time. Just start with the
sand."

Air whistled around me. The planet appeared to spin in
slow arcs that I could actually see and experience. When I
lifted my watering, barely focused eyes to the horizons, the
mountains seemed to tilt, about to collapse on me. The sand
sifted through my fingers. The rocky ground beneath me, at
least, felt almost stable.

Breathe shallow, remember, don't strain to get extra
lungfuls: the tablets will take care of the oxygen. No, the
mountains aren't falling, nor is the sky. I won't be beaten. No
I *won't.*

Then I raised my head slowly again to face the land, and
I screamed.

It was standing there, eight-legged, on a rock. Hardly a
petrifying sight, obviously scared half out of its own probably
limited wits. About the height of my kneecap, pale lemon in
color, its fur standing out from its body like a brush in fright
or surprise. Two gray eyes of incredible innocence and a
chocolate ruff completed the enchanting picture.

My heart swelled. I'd forgotten the animal population of the desert. At BOO they trap desert beasts, attempt to train and tame them, and sell them in the Fours as pets. My pet had been such a one. More interesting and more trouble than an android creature, pets frequently run amok in the streets of the cities, biting all and sundry.

"*Attlevey,* beastie," said I, in the voice of a saccharine *floop.* I was trembling at the contact, at the live presence so near to me, when I thought I should never see or touch anything live again. How I ached to grab that ludicrous furry real body. "Are you hungry, beastie? Fancy a little snack? Wait there, pretty beastie. Don't go 'way."

Making the most absurd gestures of patience and supplication, I crawled backward, scrambled up the ramp and into the ship, and flew madly for the provision dispenser.

What would it like? Nut paté? Salad-on-ice?

I loaded a platter with messy, hastily prepared delicacies, and stole back to the doors. Would it have run off?

At first I couldn't see it, and desolate tears burned my lids. Then I spotted its lemon form, lying backward on a nearby rock, sunning its stomach, and looking at me upside down with pop eyes.

"Here, pretty, pretty. Come and try the nice first meal maker's brought you."

I recall, with nauseated shame, my antics. How I crept about on the sand, hoping to approach. How it bounced upright, eight legs set for retreat. How I fell back, apologizing.

I finally deposited the plate about ten paces from the ship, and removed my obviously leprous and unwanted presence to the doorway. Where I sat, motionless, watching.

Lemon-furred Gray-Eyes remained upright about half an hour, pointed nose pointedly in the air. Eventually, with a proud and aloof demeanor, Gray-Eyes pattered up to the food and began to eat. Pausing only once, when I ventured to congratulate it, to direct at me a look of disdainful warning: Shut up, or I go.

Witnessing Gray-Eyes golluping made me hungry, but I

didn't dare leave the doors in case it was gone when I returned.

Soon the food platter was empty, and Gray-Eyes, having licked it pristine and turned it over to make sure there wasn't some other tasty bit of something on the reverse side, sat down and began to wash. A fascinating sight, particularly since none of the eight legs seemed terribly well coordinated with the others. Perhaps Gray-Eyes was very young, or perhaps it just didn't care.

When it rolled over for the ninth time, I laughed, which wasn't the thing to do.

Gray-Eyes drew itself to its full height—two feet?— made some sort of blood-freezing threat-display—bared gums, daft ears back, ruff bristling—and bravely ran for its life.

My loss at its flight was mingled with hilarity. I shouldn't have laughed, I knew it. But oh, the relief of laughter.

It wasn't till I had gone down to get the plate (charming with saliva, and slightly chewed) that I realized the desert had stopped rotating and the mountains tilting. I looked right up at the sky, beautiful arch of heaven high above. Agoraphobia had perished, along with the cactus-cream, in Gray-Eyes' silly little teeth.

There was something I wanted to say to someone. I couldn't think quite what, or to whom. Maybe one of those ancient rituals . . . prayers? But going in, stubbing my toe on a rock, it was other things I actually said.

3

So my love affair with Gray-Eyes began, and a stormy and tempestuous affair it was to be.

I'd only meant to stop to do battle with my phobia, and the place I'd picked was random, chosen blind and angry by the spin of a dial. Odd to consider how important the most haphazard and trivial of decisions can turn out.

Naturally, once I'd made contact with my visitor, I reckoned on staying put a while longer. I planned to win the little *thalldrap*'s interest and affection by stuffing food down its gullet until it was too fat to waddle off again to the Hard Life. Failing that, I was prepared for kidnap. To such doleful measures are the lonely reduced.

All that first unit I prowled the adjustable veranda I'd forced into constructing itself along the "porch" side of the ship, or wallowed on the pillowy couch I'd installed there just by the doors. A robot, programmed to bring me Gray-Eyes-tempting trays from the saloon, scurried back and forth. Absorbed in my scheme, and probably more than half *zaradann,* I gobbled things myself off the trays, watched magazines, and frequently cajoled the desert: "Come on, aren't you hungry yet?"

It never occurred to me, though it should have, with my previous experience on the archaeological site in the past, that something other than the expected guest might materialize, having sniffed the odor of victuals on the breeze. Luckily nothing did, for in the condition I was in I might well have accorded it equally friendly treatment, and got divided, devoured, and digested along with the meal as a reward.

I hadn't really looked at the terrain much: getting over my fear of its openness had been enough. In the desert, initially, everywhere is like everywhere else—sky, sand, mountains. So far, this was the extent of what I'd seen in my involuntary roost. Then the day began to ebb, the world turned to topaz and gold, and the color of the sky seemed to sink away into the disc of the sun. I found I really could touch the beauty of it then, as I had touched its beauty so long ago when I was free to travel where I wished, and the city still owned me. Now, tinged with my sorrow, the loveliness was bittersweet, but strong as wine.

The ship perched on highish rocky ground, which in turn fell quickly away into a valley of dunes edged east, north, and south by the fabulous, many-shaped crags. None of these looked particularly violent, and the lava traces I was still able to detect, more or less at a glance, were absent from their lean, gnarled thighs.

The scent of the desert changes at sunfall, as it changes at dawn. This I'd forgotten, maybe only because I couldn't bear to remember in sterilized Four BEE. At early evening it's a smoky voluptuous scent, like a candle of incense burning down, but this alters, as the air darkens and the stars emerge, to a hollow, almost spiritual smell of emptiness. After the rains, the perfume of green oxygen fills the spaces, and inebriates.

I'd got up from the veranda, and wandered down and out into the dunes, a damn silly thing to do, as are most of the things I do, let us admit. Suppose something were to pounce—

Something did.

Gray-Eyes.

"Gray-Eyes!" I shrieked, and God, how that high female voice got on my nerves after three *vreks* of baritone alternating with silver tenor. Apparently it got on Gray-Eyes' nerves as well, for, leaving the steaming dish I had laid out for it but ten splits before, it fled.

I tore my hair and rushed for the veranda, yowling at the robots to fetch more food. It was too awful to have lost the wretched animal when I'd been waiting the entire day. However, I needn't have had such a fit. For no sooner had I collapsed upon my pillowy couch than Gray-Eyes reappeared, virtually out of nowhere, thumped up to the dish, and resumed work. Nevertheless, its rear end was noticeably tense. "I'm doing you a favor," that rear end said. "I mean, I don't really *like* this muck, but one doesn't want to be rude. Still, watch your step. It won't take much for me to bolt."

I cringed, quietly, eating up Gray-Eyes with my glance. Every twitch and burp was dear to me. I longed to cradle it in my arms. Let's face it, *ooma,* I thought, it's the only child-substitute you'll ever get, some poor little animal you've seduced out of the dunes with your filthy synthesized nutmeat.

One of my reasons for remaining a male so long had been that child thing.

I'd killed my child, too, hadn't I? Due, as the Q-Rs said, to sheer folly. They'd never, never have let me make another child, even when I was out of Jang. They didn't trust me, despite the fact that after my one mistake I'd hardly have fooled about in that area again. (That was the stupidity of their assessments, wasn't it? They could act on deeds, but not on psychology, the knowledge that you might have *learned.*) As a male, my paternal urge was around ten percent, very low. But when female, though only at certain intervals, the yearning came strong.

So here I was in the waste, female and childless and yearning. So watch out yourself, tiny lemon-fur, I'll make a pet out of you yet. And this time there'll be no shock wall, and no death for you. I'll wrap you in cloud cotton if I have to, I'll defend you with my good right arm.

4

Several units I courted Gray-Eyes by putting out sumptuous feasts. Dawn, noon, and sunset came to be the set times for feeding—Gray-Eyes, naturally, determined these times. Having fed, Gray-Eyes would wash thoroughly, presumably in order to scent itself with the aftertaste of syntho steak-jelly and liver-root. During these ablutions I was careful to observe a respectful silence. At last, the guest would lie down on the rocky slope just below the ship, eight paws pointing heavenward, belly distended, and looking at me upside down.

Always then I made the fatal mistake of trying to approach. Sometimes Gray-Eyes would let me get within arm's length before scooting away across the dunes—or into them, for I would soon lose sight of it.

Through the daytime, only too aware of filling in the hours, I went for brief trudges here and there about the sand valley. A modicum of caution had returned, and I didn't wander too far from the ship, never out of sight of it, and always I took a robot with me. I wasn't sure, in an emergency, quite what it would be able to do, for they carry no armament, of course. Still, perhaps, I could get it to sock any

ravening monster on the jaw. My knowledge of local fauna
was more or less nil. My most dangerous encounter formerly, I had to admit, had been with the ski-feet, whose
worst fault might only have been that they'd trample you
underpaw in order to sample your earrings.

The robots weren't meant for the outdoor life, though;
they tended to get dust and rainbowy sand in their valves,
and would suddenly stop in the middle of nowhere to service
themselves with reproachful, martyred clatterings. Fortunately nothing attacked. In truth, apart from Gray-Eyes, and
maybe other gray-eyeses, the valley appeared uninhabited beyond the odd pale furry snake, humping morosely from dune
to dune. The watercourses in the desert were sunk deep, and
rare, and none seemed present hereabouts, which probably
accounted for the depopulation.

Nevertheless, I enjoyed my walks—falling down sand-
slides, over rocks, into small faults. The air hummed with
heat, and a few miniature hard-shelled insects, which dived
about on tinsel wings, made strange faint whispery noises.
They seemed indigenous, for I couldn't remember seeing
such entities elsewhere. But then, how much *had* I seen before?

At night, the cool came. The sky was black, but outlined
against the mountains, oddly phosphorescent. Stars dazzled.
I'd already got a couple of landmarks—a northern crag that
reminded me of a fire-apple (round and pitty, with a sort of
stalk); another to the east like an enormous cup, its sides
eaten inward by wind, sun, and rains, its summit widening
into a large smooth overhang, which one unit, no doubt,
would come crashing off and frighten me into a paroxysm—
if I were still in the vicinity.

Then—about three hours after sunset, almost to the
split—the Sisters would go off like two great guns to the
south.

I hadn't been able to resist calling them that. Sisters and
brothers were figments of the past, ancient history. In the
cities, nobody was permitted to make more than one child
per Ego-Life—that is, between PD sessions—so conse-

quently nobody ever got a sister or a brother. The supposition of related flesh from one's own makers had intrigued me when I read about it in the History Tower.

By day, the Sisters were very far off, blue and vague with distance, like two pillars of almost-blown-away smoke, about half a mile apart, and apparently identical. In the dark, lit with their own red glare, as they puffed up steam and the odd fountain of molten pumice, they had a suggestion of slender aggressive villainesses from antique romance, tossing their ruby hair. Lucky for me they were too remote to wreck the valley. At any rate, their nightly performance only lasted about ten splits.

Tonight I'm going to get you, Gray-Eyes.

The sky was turning cinnamon and green as I lurked on the veranda, dish of goodies in hand.

"Here, Gray-Eyes," I yodeled. "Come and have your lovely seventh meal!"

Gray-Eyes, you bet, was intending to do just that, and came racing from the rosy dusk. However, no platter lay in the sand. *I* had the platter, I, Gray-Eyes' wicked step-maker.

Emitting encouraging noises, I held the plate in Gray-Eyes' direction. Probably the rotten little *floop* would take to its heels. But no.

Gray-Eyes stole toward me with a sidling, anxious motion. "I know you'll slay me," its tragic gazes said. "But I've no choice since the skin is sticking to my ribs." Some ribs. It was already so fat it could hardly walk. I would have to diet the poor thing later or it would go off bang. Maybe the provision machine could rustle up some starch-reduced kidney-rissoles?

Now Gray-Eyes was on the veranda.

I backed, very slowly, into the ship, and set the plate down on the floor of the open general area beyond, between the steel pillars. Then I sat stealthily on a velvet seat, my hand on the switch which would shut the doors.

Gray-Eyes entered the ship with a look of unconcern and indifference. Obviously, Gray-Eyes fought dragons and conquered citadels in its spare moments, *I* was the only thing which gave it nightmares.

Gray-Eyes reached the plate and fell to.

Then conscience smote me. With the ultimate power of capture in my grasp, I felt a positive slime-crawler, and took my hand off the switch. Oh, let the animal go free. I pictured it, a prisoner, sodden with fear, huddled pathetically under a table in the saloon, refusing to eat, refusing to move, pining away. My, my, was I in for a lesson.

Presently, seventh meal decimated, Gray-Eyes stationed itself, legs straddled on the mosaic, and began its washing procedure. However, the rite seemed rather shorter than usual, and was soon concluded. Next, Gray-Eyes rose, and glanced about for the first time.

Its eyes frequently goggled, thus it was hard to be sure if it were as genuinely madly interested as it now looked. But, after a brief sniff about, still goggling, it turned and headed for the interior of the ship, and my mood jumped a notch or so. Being very slow and careful, so as not to cause panic, I crept after.

Then Gray-Eyes reached the saloon.

And then it started.

A robot was laying seventh meal for me at the center table, and very nice it looked. Jeweled plates, crystal goblets. The glitter perhaps attracted Gray-Eyes, or the possibility of further refreshment. Whatever it was, Gray-Eyes proved an opportunist.

The plates went one way, goblets the other, and the silver placemats discus-ed in four directions. One cought the robot in the thorax region, and presumably activated some metaphysical theory that if there was trouble, the robot was going to deal with it. It lunged about, registered the position of Gray-Eyes—currently unsuccessfully champing a fork on the rugs—and made a grab. Gray-Eyes spat out the fork, which shot into the table leg, and went into its threat-display, naturally to no avail. So it bounded for the wall drapes and ripped its way up them, and onto the latticework ceiling, and inevitably reached the large, decorative chandelier, which depended, glowing with chemical fire, above us.

"No, Gray-Eyes," I cried. "Naughty."

I'd always liked the chandeliers on the ships, but not now that this one was swaying in vast donging arcs, fortunately non-hot flames hailing on the robot and me and everything else, Gray-Eyes slithering and scrabbling at the center.

"Come down, Gray-Eyes," I entreated.

I pushed the robot to a spot where it could catch the flailing lemon bundle, but Gray-Eyes studiously avoided us, and toppled instead, frantically clawing, down a fresh lot of draperies, landing at the archway where the robot-kitchen lies, tastefully hidden behind crystallize automatic doors.

"No!" I yelled.

Even the robot made a noise—involuntarily, I think, some overstrained joint protesting.

But it was no good. Trailing clawfuls of shredded curtain and faintly shining with droplets of chemical fire, Gray-Eyes sped with hurricane force at the doors, which obligingly automatically opened, and vanished into the metallic jungle beyond. After which the doors *jammed*.

Some of the vandalized satin-of-gold had got caught between them, no doubt, hence the difficulty, but the reasons for the fault were my last worry. I shouted useless orders at the meal-robot and at the other robot that had come thudding in to help. They were trying to bash the doors down, unaccustomed to such catastrophes, and over their racket I could hear the sound of metal racks going over and ball-bearings or something rolling, and something else rolling, which was probably Gray-Eyes, and then a most terrifying silence.

Just at that split the doors unjammed abruptly and both robots fell through into the kitchen. I didn't stop to pick them up as they lay there threshing feebly among the steaming debris of Gray-Eyes' passage. Gray-Eyes itself stood precariously poised, with noncommittal lethargy, upon the brink of the chute which passes down into the bowels of the provision-dispenser.

I took the kitchen in one leap, but wasn't quick enough. With a nonchalant yawn, Gray-Eyes slithered from sight.

Down in there a whirlpool of—what? I didn't know, but my mind's eye supplied an amalgam of steel cleavers, pulverizers, mincers, pestles and mortars. Wailing, I flung myself upon the machinery. There was a little button, I'd seen it before, a little black button with an enormous red message printed over it:

TO HALT MECHANISM, DEPRESS ONCE.
WARNING! USE ONLY IN EXTREME EMERGENCY.

I stabbed at the button with both hands, and next instant the world went mad.

First off, the machine regurgitated Gray-Eyes at about eighty knots and covered with this evening's proposed menu—cactus-pineapple, cheesecake, the lot. This object, propelled through the kitchen doors, which had jammed open now, thonked to earth out of sight, and made its departure, stickily and fast (as I later deduced from pineapply pawmarks on the rock outside).

Post Gray-Eyes, there erupted from the provision dispenser about a hundred miles of leather-of-steel moving belt, plus a gallon or two of cold soup which promptly flooded the kitchen area and washed through into the saloon and beyond with liberated gurglings. This, however, was a mere divertissement compared to what followed.

Scarcely had I time to curse than an explosion cursed louder, from the guts of the ship where the lower tubing of the dispenser shared bow-storage space with the tanks of the water mixer. The whole ship, taking umbrage, bucked and writhed and seemed about to turn turtle.

Things previously undamaged rained about my ears; worse than earthquake, the floor wriggled queasily. Rugs, robots, furnishings, and I floundered among the heaving soup.

Then nemesis. A great whoosh, a wave of heat and a wave of cold, the ominous grumble of some force restrained —followed by the splintering roar of restraint collapsing.

Last, a bang to end all bangs as part of the roof of the sand-ship ejected into the night, oxygen compression whistled away, and a jet of combined semi-synthesized food and ready-mixed water arrowed northward at the stars, missed them, and crashed spent upon the recumbent desert.

5

"Help!" I screamed into the monitor beam. "Help! Help!"

Far off in Four BEE sleeping circuits presumably engaged, and the link awoke. A crisp sizzling on the frequency, followed by the cool, stern voice of the computer, interrogating me across the miles.

"What is it that you need?"

It was no good trying to be prosaic, up to my knees in soup with half the ship gone and half the alarms of the ship going off all about me, quite pointlessly, I might add.

"Need? Need? Can't you hear?"

"I can hear perfectly. What is it that you need?"

"Help. I told you."

"Help of what kind?"

"A couple of crates of roofing, a new provision dispenser, and—oh, dammit—a deaf-aid if this bloody row keeps up."

Clicks and whirrs greeted my gospel.

"I am afraid we are not quite clear as to the nature of your request."

"Listen, fool," I raged, "turn your recorder tapes on and record this. A desert animal fell down the chute of the provision dispenser and when I turned it off—the dispenser—something went *zaradann* and it's blown a hole in the bow of the ship. The oxygen is still pumping, but the concentration is none, since it's all leaking out of the roof—the hole I mentioned. And I've got a thirty-foot water-and-food spout from the explosion, which I assume means both the provision dispenser and the water mixer are totally *grakked*. And, as they're in the bow, that may also mean the drive motors are *grakked* up too. Thus, if you don't offer a friendly hand fairly quick I'm going to perish of starvation, dehydration, and oxygen deficiency. While static. What have you got to say to that?"

"Where is the desert animal?" asked the monitor computer.

That surprised me. Maybe it had my files in its little brain-cupboard, or perhaps curiosity had overcome its reflexes.

"The desert animal has fled to its burrow covered in cheesecake," I said.

The computer ticked and tocked away. Reasonably, it inquired: "Your other option is still open. Do you wish to suicide and return to PD?"

"And save you the trouble of rescuing me? No, I don't. Just you tell those Q-Rs to keep their side of the bargain and get off their—"

"Here is an emergency robot-activator. Are your robots standing by?"

My three robots were actually still splashing around on the floor, but I thought they'd pick it up, so I said yes, and the code came through, all squeaks, howls, and honkings, which, coupled with the sirens and buzzers and warning bells, nearly reduced me to a permanent audiophobe.

However, it worked. About ten splits later the robots, reprogrammed to operate at maximum efficiency and with specialized orders to deal with the disaster, were pounding from stem to stern of the ship, setting everything to rights.

Even the alarms were gradually turned off, and the soup began to withdraw its hold, leaving only a stray lentil, artistically draped.

"We have located your position, and an automatic high-speed repair bird-plane should reach you in one unit's time. You are advised to be alert for it. Till then, the robots have received instructions in the matter of food and water rationing and the temporary sealing of the ship. Defense and other mechanisms should work as per normal." There was then the slightest pause, after which the computer added: "We trust such an event will not be repeated. Desert animals should not be allowed aboard your ship."

"Balls."

6

An entrancing night.

An extra oxygen pill to be taken, which I was sure I didn't need, but it was robot's orders, and a temperature stabilizer installed in my cabin which hummed jauntily to itself. The pill made me lively even though I felt enervated, so I couldn't sleep. The stabilizer noise didn't help either, or the robots thudding and bonking about on the roof. They'd managed to stop the water jet, after a couple of hours.

The soup smell was evaporating, but not fast enough for the cleaning machines, which burst from the walls at irregular intervals and sprayed the ship with scented deodorant, and stuffed rags and itty disinfected brooms into every crevice. I began to prefer the smell of soup. At least it was quiet.

Finally I took refuge in the Transparency Tower, which, temperature unstabilized, was now freezing. But it was as far from the din as I could get. I glared out at the desert, wondering where Gray-Eyes was now. Probably licking itself silly getting off the cheesecake, maybe with a few friends in to help, telling them about the ogress in the funny moving house who had chucked our hero (heroine?) in a mincer,

from whence it had only escaped by means of its cunning
and gallantry. Doubtless it would be back anon with a hungry look, and then I was going to get a stacked plate of
something and throw it right in its face.

Frankly, I thought the sand-ship the Committee had so
generously given me had gone a bit to seed, for I'm sure
others have had occasion to stop provision dispensers now
and then, without such dire results. So, if they'd palmed me
off with shoddy goods, serve them right that they'd have to
send me succour all across the burning waste.

In the end I feel asleep in the chair in the tower, and had
some exhausting overoxygenated dreams. In one, the sky was
raining robot planes, each of which landed with a shattering
bang. In another, a beautiful male emerged from the desert, a
male from one of the old tribes, bronze skin and midnight
hair, and swooned away at my feet with a piteous cry for
water. And I, a calculating gleam in my eye, ran to get the
aforesaid water, and of course the water mixer had exploded
and there wasn't any. I was trying to force anti-dehydration
pills between the unfortunate devil's tightly clenched and
scowling teeth when the desert sun came up and woke me.
And two seconds after the light touched my face, the Transparency Tower frantically opaqued, so I shouldn't see the
frightening dawn. Though it was still there, outside; waiting
for me? Well, at least there is always that, I reasoned senti-
mentally.

Fair dawn, always fair, so red, so emerald, so golden,
bathing the sky behind the jagged silhouettes of the eastern
mountains, and the peak I called the Cup looking just like a
cup with pink Joyousness-type bubbly-clouds swimming over
it.

So, without stopping to tidy up or go and inspect what
the robots had achieved, for their dramatic hammering had
ceased, I plodded to the outer doors, opened them, and went
out to greet the morning.

The sun was already shining on my porch; below the
rocks the unbroken sand looked like a carpet of pale jewels,
except, I hazarded, bow-wards on the other side of the ship,

where the spout of part-food, part-liquid had fallen yesterday.

The revolting fountain had angled northwest, and I couldn't see the disaster area from my southeastern veranda, for which I was thankful. I was staring up into the flaring sky, wondering if the super-fast robot plane might be early, when the revelation came to me.

It came coiling about the side of the ship, born on the dawn wind. It came like a rope of silver on the air. Green-silver. For a second I was dumbfounded, trying to place that unique and magic scent. Then I knew.

I tore around the ship, narrowly avoiding collision with a placidly ambling robot still intent on repairs. Tore round, and pulled up too fast and fell prone. Which was quite appropriate, for among the extinct nomadic tribes the prone position was the one in which they worshipped their gods.

The deluge of mixed water and semi-made food had covered about half a square mile of dunes. It hadn't lasted very long, maybe three hours all told. The rains, of course, which come only once in every three hundred days, and not even then necessarily, do at least last a whole glorious diluvian night. After the rains you could understand, even if you marveled at it, the extraordinary reply of the desert. But this.

Green shoots blowing like fine green hair before that morning wind. Green shoots thickly massed over half a square mile, like slender soldiery in some fable. And the scent of them, the smell of their sap, and the oxygen they expired. Some in bloom—little flowers or buds that might turn out to be anything, except that there wouldn't be time. The generating life of the sands, dormant, brought to fruit prematurely and by accident. And in an hour or so the sun would be draining the soul from them. By sunset they would be black and withered in this waterless place. By dawn tomorrow you could safely offer a prize to anyone able to detect their ruined dust among the other dusts of the land.

I stood and swore. I felt I had betrayed those shoots, dragged them up here on false pretenses without even a night of rain to sustain them, sold them out to the cruel sun. Dawn, *farathooming* dawn.

As I snarled there, along came a conscientious robot with a tray, and on the tray one meal injection (large), one draught of silver-cordial (small), six anti-dehydration tablets, four oxygen pills, and a lot of space.

"How *groshing*," I remarked, knocking things back, and shooting things into myself ferociously. I balked only at the oxygen. "Look at that field out there; I'm not going to need these things. At least, not all of them." The robot whirred worriedly, and went into a tape-monologue-dehumanized voice stressing rather than alleviating solitude—about how I must take *all* the pills, *all* the pills. So I had to reprogram it quickly in the interests of peace.

When it had gone, I sat on the already hot rock, digesting my horrible first meal, and staring at the greenery. The idea arrived presently and was perfectly simple. No doubt anyone else would have thought of it eighty *vreks* before I did.

"Hallo there, it's me again," I informed the monitor computer jollily.

Quite probably it blew a steel gasket. It sounded like it.

"Wait. Wait," it chuntered out, and a wild rattling broke loose for a whole split before it had calmed itself down, or been calmed. Then: "There is no need to panic," it said. "The repair bird-plane is on its way, and will reach you at—click—click—computed time of desert sunset."

"Who's panicking?" I gravely asked, hoping it would get the point that of the two of us, *it* was. "I opened the link because I have another request."

"No other requests are acceptable until the first request has been granted."

"Nonsense," I said. "Suppose I'd broken a femur?"

"They are extinct," said the computer, either mishearing or, lacking certain vocabulary, making an uneducated guess.

"Listen, you," I said. "I'm an exile. Very well. But I'm

positive that while I opt to stay alive, the Committee *has* to keep me that way. So if I say I need something *urgently,* you have to send it to me.''

''We cannot send you any femurs,'' moaned the computer.

''I don't want a *drumdiking* femur, for God's sake.''

It probably thought it was a femur that had fallen down the provision dispenser, but now something worse had slipped out.

''Godgodgod,'' it asked itself, searching frantically the stockpiled labyrinth of its brain. ''Godgod? Godgod? Godgod?''

''Shut up. Cancel. Be quiet,'' I cried. ''Forget about God. It's a sensation, a belief, I don't know—forget it. Forget about femurs, too. They're *not* animals, I've got a couple anyhow, and believe me, if I *do* ever break one, you'll hear me screaming quite clearly in the city without recourse to a monitor beam. What I want is this: one extra water mixer, on rather a large scale, about the size of the ship, say, and rigged for adaption, and some housing for it, and, obviously, self-servicing equipment tied in. And you'd better use a displacement machine, because I'll need it by noon at the latest.''

There really was a sort of overcharge then. But the computer surmounted it.

''Why do you request this?''

''Because, my perma-steel friend, I'm going to make the desert waste blossom!''

The silence which followed was predictable and far from pleasing. But I stuck it out, knowing they had to listen, couldn't just leave me there; I'd got the Q-R Committee by their service-to-humanity-programming curlies. Though a menace, I was human, and I had a need, so—

The displacement machine had been an inspiration. It was a body displacer, of course, meant for people use, but since hardly anyone does use them because of the violent nausea that generally results, they are sometimes recruited for sending intercity hardware about. (Dematerialize on Angel Walk in BAA, rematerialize smack in Peridot Waterway, BEE, but that sort of mistake doesn't happen often, only when some Employed Older Person pops the wrong button.) If I could make them agree to my demands, BEE could shoot that water mixer out into my valley inside half an hour, and since water mixers are the stuff of life everywhere, it shouldn't be so hard to find one—or make one—by noon. Then, oh then—a nourishing rain could fall, and my garden—yes, I really thought of it already as My Garden—could go on growing, and, what is more, go *on* and *on*. If the desert yielded so verdantly after one night of rain, what *couldn't* happen here?

I was fired, ablaze with enthusiasm.

I beat the computer down—and the Q-Rs clustered by it now, I should imagine.

"I can't see a friend, can't even talk to a friend," I histrionically bawled. "Alone in the sands, and all I want to do is water a bit of *real* garden." (Boo-hoo)

There came at length a long long silence. From that silence, I knew I'd won. The computer spoke:

"For this item there will be a charge. You will have to pay."

I was het up enough at that moment they probably realized they'd get a mass of utilitarian energy from me, even on tape.

"Yes. Plug me in and I'll pay."

And I did. I gave them their water mixer's worth, and double. I sobbed and laughed and blessed them, and called down upon the city the joys of the firmament. It was worth it, and I didn't even know then how worth it it was going to be.

7

The paid-for water mixer arrived in the afternoon, with a low thud of displaced air. They'd aimed it at a spot about halfway along My Garden and just enough to the south of it to avoid crushing or smashing any of the growing stuff. The positioning was so perfect, I thought they must have made a mistake. They'd probably have liked to materialize the water mixer smack in the middle of everything, including me.

It was a big machine, too, everything I'd hoped for, and stylishly housed under an elegant ice-white cupola with pillars and steel-glass all about below, and doors that were set to open only to me or my robots. We wouldn't have any dear little desert animals barging in here, at least. The adaptors were excellent, too, and took my instructions like a miracle.

For an hour then, distant hummings and skitterings within the cupola, after which it finally happened. Vents swung wide in the dome, mother-of-pearl nozzles emerged like questing trunks, and fine, wide-spread jets of ready-mixed water began to fall, not only on My Garden but also on the dry, southwestern side of the water mixer, so perhaps

I should be seeing another My Garden come up there as well, sooner or later.

I didn't know how much moisture would be needed, but the best method seemed to be, since it was intended as a long-term policy, little and often, with a rest by night for the machine to fix a fresh supply. (Water mixers synthesize their components from any rubbish to hand, and refine and inter-mingle them dextrously in the old water formula known even to the ancients. Anything can be made in this way, and it's a pity no one realized this fact before they'd completely drained the seas and the soil.)

Pride was not in it as I paraded the rocks around the ship, watching the "Rain."

See, *ooma* Garden, it wasn't a betrayal after all.

It was going to be about a mile west to north now, in addition to stretching half a mile from the ship.

Then the grand ideas started to come. Why not more? Why not My Gardens on every side, why not a valley of My Gardens? I might be able to get further water mixers from the city, if I confused the computer enough, or, failing that, get this one mobile, and wheel it about, doing shifts—two hours on the western land, two hours east, two hours south, etc.

Perhaps nothing would grow after all. The dunes couldn't all be so fertile. (Don't kid yourself, remember the rains—green everywhere.) And the valley was how big? An oval roughly, about ten miles maybe north to south, eight miles west to east. A tight schedule for one water mixer. But if it *were* all fertile in the end, all green . . .

Interruption to reverie was sudden and unexpected, though it shouldn't have been.

It was a laughable and terrifying sight.

Chugging along from the area obscured behind the ship, and making quite obviously for My Garden and the water-mixer housing, came what must be described as a tribe of Gray-Eyeses.

There were about twenty of them, all physically alike,

except for grotesquely varying sizes—several were as small as a Jang girl's hand, two or three as large as a double float-bed. Demeanor seemed to accord with girth. The small ones tumbled and bounced and sometimes paused for boxing matches with each other till some adult (?) superintended them back into line. The big ones had a look of solemnity, even menace. The ones in between broke into fits of either mood, now stern, now downright balmy, clocking each other around the jowls, then striding on with a regal air, noses aloft.

Had they come to get me? What had Gray-Eyes Mark I been telling them?

However, they ignored me, though they knew I was there. (You couldn't miss the pointed way they sniffed upwind; it made me feel like dashing back in the bath unit.) What they were interested in, as I had first feared, was the rising of green.

Now what? Run into the Transparency Tower and activate a defense mechanism, something like the shock wall that had killed the pet? See their lemon bodies drop in ecstatic death, before they could tear up the precious shoots? No, I couldn't do that. Couldn't, couldn't and wouldn't.

Feeling stupendously brave in my cowardly way, I bounded down the rocks toward the procession, waving my arms and shouting: "Shoo! *Grak* off! Get out of it!" To which there was a thoroughly stunning response of complete uninterest.

I was almost on top of the Gray-Eyeses now, and dementedly picked up handfuls of sand which I flung over them. There *was* a reaction to this. A few of the smaller—younger?—Gray-Eyeses ran up and began to turn somersaults about my feet, which, despite everything, nearly undid my resolve to be fierce and adamant. And then a large one looked back, registered the action, and returned doggedly toward me. Now he/she would assume that I was massacring his/her offspring, or whatever they were, and floor me with one enormous paw.

"Help?" I asked experimentally. There were no robots

in sight, naturally. "Look," I said tremulously to the advancing foe, "I think your family is *derisann,* but keep your feet off my blossoming waste, will you? And whatever you think I did, I didn't."

It reached me. I could gauge its size accurately now. It was exactly a head taller than me and rather more wide. Its eyes of deeply aqueous gray stared into mine, and it set its two front paws—compensating efficiently on the other six—upon my shoulders. Numb with fright, I stood my ground. They were quite light, those paws. At least it wasn't giving a threat display.

"Er," I said, "I only meant—"

Its mouth opened and a pale-pink tongue emerged, healthy and wholesome as a flower. It licked me.

Was it embracing me, or just using me as a balancing post? Why was it licking me so thoroughly? Its tongue was very nice, but I didn't really want my face washed with it. Was it getting the taste?

"So kind—*groshing*—thank you," I gabbled in a nauseating attempt to ingratiate myself.

Presently the licking stopped. I opened my screwed-up eyes and it patted me gently. Its paws left my shoulders. With one admonishing backward glance, scooping the little ones before it, the large Gray-Eyes went after its mates.

Feeling shaky with alarm, and laughter, I sat down in my tracks.

It was hopeless anyhow, they'd reached My Garden, and all was lost. Perhaps they wouldn't damage *everything*—

"Idiot," I said then. "Fool." Admittedly I'd seen what they were at. But I should have guessed long before.

They would never wantonly harm anything growing, except the really stable fixtures of the desert, which they used for food and then only sparingly. They had a respect for vegetable growth, it was bred into them, and not surprising. After the rains, they hadn't touched a thing, only danced in the lushest spots, had an orgy or two, played. And that was what they were going to do now, hold a post-rain rite. Be-

cause they thought it *had* rained, and somehow they'd
missed it.

My Garden was going to be the scene of a celebration.

They wouldn't make a lot of mess, probably add a bit of
home-grown fertilizer here and there. Would they be able to
adjust? What would happen when they realized the "rains"
and the plant growth were going on and on? Had I wrecked
their ecological thingammy?

Ah well. Too late now.

A few more came in through the unit, Gray-Eyeses, and
some insects, and a couple of snakes. It gave me a lump in
my throat the size of a small mountain.

It was the robot rescue bird-plane, swooping in and
breaking the sound barriers, that ended the ritual.

Gray-Eyeses and friends, sped, wriggled, and flew in all
directions, and vanished like sorcery in the dunes.

A door opened in the plane and a machine rolled forth,
robot voice-box patronizingly announcing: "Help is at
hand," or something.

I tried not to glare as it began to fix my ship.

What can I say? How can I record the dream as it
evolved everywhere about me, record it, and yet keep the
dream intact? I could state every event as it occurred, every
tiny and wondrous event.

The first bud opening, the first great ferns stretching for
the sky, black-green on blue-green. Me bubbling like a *thalldrap* to one of my overtaxed, constantly reprogrammed robots: "I think this one's going to be a *tree,* a *real* tree."

Or there was the morning the sandstorm came, first like
a golden gauze across the distant mountains, with Dopey
staring admiringly at it, "My, that's pretty," until presently
it smashed into us, wham, and flayed everything to within an
inch of its life. Robots and me, swathed in bits of see-
through to protect our eyes/optic circuits and lungs/chest
valves, scurrying along between the slender irrigation canals
we'd only just finished digging. (Brilliant notion gleaned

from remembered antique manuscripts in the History Tower, these channels take water to the farthest reach of a plantation. They're meant to come from rivers, I believe, but we had to keep them filled from the water mixer. They were backbreaking to dig: I ached for ten units in muscles I never knew I had. The robots got stiff and fed-up, too, and needed oiling.) For about an hour we plunged around, tying things down and draping things over things, and six or seven times I trotted into the ship and shrieked down the monitor beam for a wave-net protector, which performance met with neither applause nor success. Luckily the plants, or most of them, nourished on so much liquid, withstood the storm.

Shall I mention the units I simply sat, watching the swaying green, or wandered through it, sometimes trailing the perambulating "Rain"? The water mixer plus housing had now been adapted for mobility, and followed its allotted course, looking most curious and spectacular, and from the distance, perfectly like some fabulous monster. A great gleaming white cupola, stalking transparent steel-glass legs, mother-of-pearl nozzles waving from its crown, spraying delicate mists of water, stopping at the newer areas for more prolonged sprays, then making inexorably onward. At night it returned to rest beside the ship, humming to itself as it made fresh tankfuls. It, too, was overworked. It could, in fact, despite my plans, patrol and moisten only a short distance from its daily supply north, west, east, and south from the ship, a round tour of about four miles. I'd need eight or nine more water mixers to realize a decent job of watering the arid wastes, and hadn't I just tried to get them?

"Your request cannot be granted," said the monitor computer, and said it again. And again. And . . .

"Found out what a femur is yet, dumb-cluff?" I infuriatingly asked it, and heard the poor thing go rattling off to itself. The routine never varied and I never got the water mixers. I once tried pretending the first had met with an accident—fallen down a fault or off a mountain, I forget—but they checked us via the monitor system, and discovered it merrily stumping about on the eastern perimeter of My Garden spraying efficiently, so that didn't work either.

Even those few miles, however, the sight and scent of them. Everywhere the water fell vegetation grew. A young forest was coming up to the east, and, starting just below the ship and spreading a quarter of a mile, tall, tall, slim trees, many-ridged trunks the color of dark jade and leaves thin as whips, strung like strips of green glass over the sky, making incredible patterns as they crossed and recrossed each other in the breeze. Flowers, too, every shade and hue, as the old books used to say. Some were climbing the veranda struts, and soon I wouldn't be able to move the sand-ship even if I decided to.

About thirteen units after the robot rescue plane had rehabilitated my vessel-home, a small avalanche took place over on the eastern slopes of the mountains, and the faintest of tremors disturbed the ground. Off went the alarms in the ship, and everything tried to dive for safety and found it couldn't, since I'd switched out the automatic drive.

When I'd quietened the sirens, I had to face a fact or two about the earthquake-prone terrain. I could stabilize the ship, mobile or static, but what about the Garden out there?

We'd begun to get quite handy and capable, the three robots and I. (I'd given them names by then, as I'd known I would, *and* programmed them to respond to them, *and* I chatted away at them, too, just as I'd feared. Still, it was eccentricity rather than desperation, and it had practical uses, for they came now at a name-shout, and if I told one to fix supper I could specify, and the other two—who might be hoeing with me outside or something—wouldn't fling down tools and charge off as well. They were known as Jaska, Borss, and Yay, the tags of three ancient chieftains Assule had once spoken of during the Archaeological Expedition. Assule had been a bore, but somehow the names stuck, maybe only because it was so boring: so Jaska this, and Borss that, and Yay the other. I think they were related or buried together, I can't recall.) Anyway, Jaska, Borss, Yay, and I, along with machinery borrowed from the ship, began to try to manufacture stabilizers of our own out of materials got from Four BEE under false pretenses.

I told the monitor beam how sad and *droad* I was. I said I was going to design a charming little tower as a hobby. Could they let me have some steel of something and silk of something else? Oh, and some weeny components, nothing much. I'd worked out that, so long as they thought I was up to something deadly, piffling, and useless, they'd let me do it, and I was proved right, for piece by piece, out came great crates of stuff for my "tower." I supposed they'd concluded that when I got purposeful about things, I also got violent, and upheaval followed, and I supposed probably they had a point. However, Jaska, Borss, Yay, and I got to work on the load, using one of the ship's stabilizers taken apart as a model, and, some units later, we began to dig holes and put down our first efforts. Only when disaster struck would I know if we'd got the formula correctly, but it *looked* right. I even wondered if we could build the extra water mixers ourselves, but it would mean stretching the tower-myth out rather thin, and also dismantling the existing mixer for a blueprint, and if any of us messed it up, we'd have no mixer at all. So, for the time being, a four-mile circumference of greenery it was going to have to remain. Anyway, that was fairly tiring.

Most days I went out with J, B, and Y and we turned over the soil—it really was starting to look like soil, too— and inspected growth, and tied weaker things to steel sticks, and made a note of where looked the most parched so the water mixer could give it an additional blast. Though the oxygen was invigorating even under the adolescent, burgeoning shade, it got very hot, and after a morning of it I would stagger off someplace and swoon away for an hour. Sometimes I would find a recumbent Gray-Eyes swooning there before me. I never knew if I met the original Gray-Eyes Mark I; it hadn't come to the ship again, certainly, which was, no doubt, as well. I was too busy to mourn or be glad at its absence, too involved in the project to be lonely.

My beautiful body got more tanned. I was the essence of

dark honey now, and my fair hair bleached to milky amber with fiery streaks in it like decorative silver chains. The poet's eyes were two iridescent, almost colorless blue pools in that dark face. Mirrors made me jump even more, though a couple of exhausted evenings I lay on my veranda staring in one through the fading red charcoal of dusk. Sexuality hadn't been much of a problem yet. I was too worn out. The love machine had cobwebs on it, or would have if the ship's cleaners didn't burnish everything nearly skinless. Still, the reflection of the beautiful girl with the eyes of the beautiful young man I had formerly been induced in me a kind of sinuous excitement I was going to have to beware of.

Thriving on water, every day the growing green rose higher and stood more strongly. Forest leaves tapped on my cabin windows, which faced out now, for I'd replaced the brocade with glacia-view. My window gazed southeast, like the veranda. I could see the dawn come up like rubies and limes behind the serpentine trees. And, if I had gone to my couch, the Sisters generally woke me with their sullen guns and villainous red hairdos so far across the valley.

What can I say? Maybe not all that.

This is a kind of retaliation, isn't it, to that other screed of mine, composed in Limbo twelve *vreks* before in distress and query? That—the question. This—the answer. Or part of the answer, for all my life will be a reply, to myself and to my world.

Maybe, though, I should only say that a *vrek* passed by across my valley, a hundred units. And that one day I went out of the ship, and I saw everything with a kind of unexpected clarity, as if I hadn't seen it before, hadn't watched it grow, or helped it.

The sun was blazing down already, that cruel unbiteable sun. Black mountains cradled the valley, and a rim of glistening sand. Within that, My Garden, like a green smoke drawing nearer, and, as it neared, seeming a vegetable city with domes and towers, avenues and arcades, palaces and porticos, and a couple of Gray-Eyeses were running about in them, being careful not to tread on anything.

I was totally ready to cry, being, as I said, sentimental and a *floop*. Just then the monitor beam signaled me, a rare occurrence, so I packed away my emotion and went to investigate.

I had corrupted the computer too, so much was obvious.

It said only two words, but with such triumph, almost obscenely:

"*Thigh* bones."

8

First unit of my second *vrek* in the valley.

Me on the veranda eating melon pancakes, thinking lazily of the work we were going to do today, Jaska, Borss, Yay, and I.

Water mixer on the prowl, dimly visible through an early haze, now and again hidden by trees, ferns, shrubs. A confused snake courting itself in the grass about nine feet off. Nose to tail: "Come on, give us a kiss." The tail coyly refusing.

Then a familiar-unfamiliar sound in the sky, the snake going stiff as a ramrod, and I walking out and staring up.

Sometimes bird-planes had passed over, actually far to the west. Rarely did you catch their noise. Purely at random, I had established my haven well off the sand-ship and plane routes. This abomination, however, was directly overhead and presently swooping earthward.

Farathoom, and similar oaths. Watch out for the purple trees! (I had a name for everything—generally analogous. This saved muddle. Sometimes.) No, the purple trees had escaped barbering. The thing was going to land right in the cactus roses. It did.

Pancake still in hand, I thudded from the porch and ran to the plane. Very garish it was, and drizzling colored neons, but I didn't bother with that.

"Get the Infinity off my flowers, blast you! Look what you've done."

The anticipated robot voice came melodiously from the opening door:

"No need for alarm."

"I'm not alarmed. But you're going to be if you don't move that tin can of yours."

Just then the visitor emerged, a roly-poly machine, somehow conveying broad smiles, wires waving, lights popping on and off. It had Flash Center written all over it.

"Don't tell me," I said. "Some soup-brained *promok* spotted a fern in the desert, and mentioned it to some other Older *promok* at a Flash Center, and now they've sent a reporting machine to collect some pulchritudinous flashes to be pulchritudinously flashed all over Four *flooping* BEE. Yes?"

"Oh, *yes,*" chortled the flash machine, programmed by some incorrigible moron to sound like the worst type of human jolly. They probably thought the distraught Outcast would be glad to chirrup away to something human-sounding, however obnoxious.

"Well, old *ooma,* you can just hop back on your plane and go," I said, "before I turn the water mixer on you."

The flash machine looked uneasy somehow. Maybe it wasn't rustproofed.

"Oh, but please. Everyone's ever so interested. There's even going to be a special interruption to Picture-Vision, and a perma-film of all this put on for five whole splits."

That rocked me. The last time that had happened had been when—when—well, when? Ever? Surely the Committee hadn't thought this up? Perhaps people *were* interested, or some people. Perhaps Danor might want to know how I was making out. Or Hergal. Yes, I could just see Hergal, reclining somewhere, semi-ecstatic, with golden limber limbs elegantly stretched like one of Thinta's cats. He might even get romantic over me for half a split now I was in noncombatant female form. Thinta, on the other hand, liked me less that way. Possibly she would mutter something like: "I *tried* and TRIED with her. I did all I could. But she *wouldn't* listen." It hurt to think of them, but it was a pain I'd have to get used to. I couldn't always just shut off whenever some image of the city stole up on me. Sometime I'd have to face it. But part of me had warmed. I looked at the flash machine differently.

"Well," I said, "if you'll shift that plane over a bit, and let me do the talking."

"Of *course*!"

"And could you readjust slightly, and speak more in the frigid supercilious vein I've become used to with machines? Oh, and I'll need half an hour to get ready."

Vanity.

Oh, well, the first chance I'd had to be vain for over a *vrek*. Could be the last chance, too.

A good machine can rustle up clothing in fifteen splits if you know how to inspire it. I'd long since got out of wearing traditional Jang see-through in BEE, so I'd had lots of practice in the art. The ship clothing machine, left in the wall till now, nearly went *zaradann,* and threw off a gown of synthosilk the color of fresh snow and embroidered with zircons. The cosmetics chute had fun, too, and tossed jeweled bottles of this and that at me with a disarming, childish delight. My feminine side had reestablished itself with a vengeance.

I emerged back into the outdoors, looking unbelievably glamorous and confident, eyelids enameled, earlobes spangled, and even the calluses rinsed off my ringed hands with medicinal salve. This was how Danor and Hergal and the rest were going to see me, if see me they did. Prosperous, fortunate, desirable, happy. And out of reach.

"You have been three half-hours instead of one," stated the flash machine.

"Oh, good. You've reprogrammed to sound unpleasant. That's a relief."

"No I have not, but my batteries will go flat if—"

"If we waste any more time, so let's get going."

Full tour. Everything. They'd cut it later, anyway. Five splits! What could they show in five splits? Just enough, maybe.

Trees in a stasis of showering green, irrigation canals sparkling like crystal, the monstrous water mixer lifting on its legs and striding off, a solitary Gray-Eyes caught napping in the fern. Me, pampered and relaxed. Jaska and Borss digging Yay out of a subsidence. ("You'd better cut that." Bet they wouldn't.) Fruit ripening—no, I didn't know what it was, but as it had grown here on the north side where the original water-and-provision spout had erupted, possibly some of the semi-constructed food had taken root or whatever it did. I'd be testing soon to see if it was edible.

Eventually the flash machine asked for a speech. I considered "*Vixaxn* the Committee," succinct and sincere, but decided if I really wanted any old friends to see this reel I'd better think of something else.

So: "I just want to thank the Committee," I said, dewy-eyed, "for being so considerate. I made a terrible mistake, as everyone knows, but, despite exiling me, the Committee has been the soul of good will and consideration."

"How about loneliness," the machine asked, abruptly brutal, "and impending age?"

"You can be lonely in a crowd," I said, "worse than out here. And age is something the ancients used to cope with, so I can cope with it, too, can't I? Besides, I've got a good half *rorl* or more before I need start worrying about that. I'm built to last."

When the flash machine had gone, it was rather quiet for a bit.

I tidied up the cactus roses, but they were tough, and their scarlet heads were soon raised high again. So was my sun-bleached one.

Finally I got on the monitoring beam and asked the computer if they would relay the flash film to me on my own Picture-Vision unit. After a pause the computer said yes, and then:

"Currently, bones are reinforced while the child is growing in the crystallize tank," said the computer. "So are teeth and nails. They no longer break."

"That's a relief," I said. "Are you going to drop this femur business now?"

The computer rumbled.

"What is God?"

"I can't tell you. Don't ask again."

"This word does not fit into my vocabulary."

"Nor mine. Don't worry about it. Get them to wipe off the tape or something."

Rattle, pattle, ping.

The film wasn't bad. I didn't understand then (how could I? Maybe I could have, should have) how un-bad it was.

The Garden looked wonderful. Unbelievable. What effect would that produce after the silk-of-glass flowers and jade ilexes of the city? And I, well, I looked as I'd wanted to: radiant. My speech was in, even the hint of diabolic irony I hadn't noticed had slipped through on the "good will and consideration" bit. Still, probably the citizens would just scream: "Ooh, nasty real rough trees with creepy-crawlies up them, and horrid Jang exile murderer much too brown, and never trust people who give themselves pale eyes, ugh!" And rush for the vacuum drift.

Peace be with you.

9

Ten days went by after the day of the flash-film. I had no reason to count them then. I went on hoeing and patrolling and inspecting, lying, as if dead, on the veranda in the cool of the evening, oiling J, B, and Y, and watching the stars budding in the night darkness and the shadows lying blue and purple along the spaces of the forest. The trees had continued to grow and were now about twenty feet in height.

The sun fell on the eleventh day, as usual, and twilight hollowed the sky, and the water mixer came swaggering home, folded its legs, and settled.

"Look at that *sky*," I said to Yay, squirting oil into him and feeling rather embarrassed by the intimate gesture. (Heaven preserve me from getting a crush on a robot in my solitary state. I called them all "he" already.)

Looking at the sky, however, I saw a cluster of footloose stars, and heard again that tiresome sound which could only be a bird-plane. Off course, presumably. Over it went, flying south, and very low. Then, quite suddenly, it landed just beyond the perimeter of the Garden, about half a mile away.

I jumped up, half troubled, half elated. More Flash Cen-

ter film to be shot? Or had those surplus food supplies come
in early? I was very impressed they hadn't sat down on the
greenery. A glacia lamp of mauve chemical fire burned over
the porch. I hooked it off and, attracted by diversion, began
to walk in the direction of my mechanical visitor.

Not a long walk, following the useful little steel paths J,
B, and Y had put down here and there. But I was to be met
halfway.

A grove of ten-foot feather ferns rustled and parted.
Shadows slid and dappled. Hard to ascertain form, even with
the stars and my lamp. I ordered:

"Don't come on for a split, robot, particularly with a
heavy load. Let me guide you, or else you'll go crashing into
an irrigation canal like last time."

"Attlevey," someone said, soft as if the ferns had said it.

I nearly left my skin. The lamp fell on the path and
bounced wildly like a lilac dune-frog into some bushes.

So I couldn't see her, even though I knew it was Danor.

PART 3

1

"I'm sorry, *ooma,*" Danor said, "I didn't mean to shock you. But I wasn't sure what else I could do."

I tried to say something, but my teeth were chattering too much.

"I remembered you aren't male anymore," Danor continued soothingly. "And we—I won't impose on you."

"D-D-D—" I tried feverishly. Oh, God, get a grip on yourself. "Danor," I grimaced.

"Yes?"

"Danor, you shouldn't be—what are you doing here? Isn't there some sort of Committee bar on anyone visiting me?"

"Oh, yes," she said, so quietly only the greater quietness of the desert made her audible. "According to their records, no human must visit an outcast. If they do, they forfeit their right to return to the cities. They gave everyone a talking-to after you left."

"My dangerous tendencies, rubbing off on you, contagious, like a sickness . . . forfeit rights to return . . . what do you mean? Do you mean—?"

"I mean," said Danor, "of our own volition, we've made contact with you. Because we don't intend to go back to the cities." Very feminine and not at all coarsely she added: "They can stuff them right up."

I wasn't sure if the feeling in my chest and throat was nausea, tears, or nervous asthma.

"Oh, Danor, what an idiot. Get on your plane and get going. It's all very well, I've got some sort of ambition out here. But it's still rackingly lonely. Oh, get on your plane. Say it malfunctioned and you never meant to land. Say you spat in my face—horrid, antisocial freak that I am."

"Don't be silly, *ooma,*" said Danor. "I wouldn't dream of saying it. Neither would—" she broke off, and through my panicky emotion I became aware that she'd broken off here and there before, and that some of the related actions had been plural.

"Neither would whom? You're not by yourself."

"No," she said. "He has a private bird-plane. We can live in that if we have to. We don't want to crowd you, or make you feel any obligation. It's our own decision to come out here. We can move off over the mountains, if you'd rather."

"You still didn't say who," I said.

"Kam," she said. "Who else?"

She spoke his name, not in the way I'd heard her use it before, as if she had lost him forever and learned to exist with the fact. She spoke his name with a sort of exultation, not possessively, but rather as I had said, only half an hour before, "Look at that *sky.*"

And then, despite the unprecedented situation, and the amount that hung palpitatingly upon it, despite the fact that, as a female, I felt nothing sexual or even romantic for Danor, a pang of scorching jealousy went through me. A compound of many things, no doubt, recollected male pride in my love-making with the specter of Kam, who held her before me, hovering in the air; the fact, too, that no chosen male had followed *me* into the waste, no one had been near and dear enough to consider it or be considered.

"Shall we walk on, to the plane?" she asked. "Will you come and meet him? I came alone to try to lessen the fright I'd give you. How are you, *ooma*?"

"Simply *derisann*," I grated. "*Groshingly, insumattly marvelous.*"

She lowered her eyes—lavender eyes, designed expressly to please Kam.

"I'm sorry," she said again. "You must think us terrible. We *did* see the flash-film. I think everyone saw it. But truly, *ooma*, I'd thought of this before. And we won't stay if you don't want us to. Even though you've made this place so lovely."

An impulse in me told me to reiterate my warning to go, not merely from concern now, but from irrational malice. But, shaking to my soul, confronted even by two people to be jealous of—two *people*—I said hoarsely:

"Yes, all right. I'll meet him."

The whispery insects indigenous to the valley had long since made a home deep among the green, and by night their dry rustling filled the avenues of the Garden. Starlight flecked the paths and faceted unreal tourmalines to spark among the leaves. Once Danor's eyes suddenly flooded with tears—something beautiful she'd glimpsed, you could tell. She said nothing more, afraid I should censure her cowardice in not risking everything till she saw what could be done with the dunes.

Parked on the southern perimeter, lights beaming, the bird-plane was blue and modest.

Danor went up the ramp before me. She called out nothing to him, simply stood there, then turned and smiled at me. That smile. It would have looked silly and sugary on anyone but Danor, but she gave it a sort of genuine gleamingness, or perhaps her authentic passions did.

The plane, though smaller, was rather like that of Lorun, my sometime lover from Four BOO, everything laid on in miniature as it were, float-bed, bath unit, little provision dispenser. Of course, I was peering about at it, avoiding looking into the shadowy area of the control panel where Danor's Older Male was sitting.

"This is Kam," Danor said, introducing us politely. So I did look at him then. I felt disproportionately disagreeable, as I mentioned. The whole thing had thrown me flat on my nose.

"*Attlevey,* Kam," I said, making a big thing of the Jang slang—Danor and me sweet young Jang, him elderly decrepit gentleman.

He wasn't, naturally. He looked scarcely older than either of us, since bodies are all made youthful unless otherwise requested by the Older Person in question. Only in the eyes and the way he moved his face—his expressions—could you see the extra years, the Experience of Life. And he was a handsome bastard, in true style, smoke-dark hair, smoke-blue eyes, tanned like a beautifully varnished smoky bronze. Which made everything much worse. He was the first male I'd seen for one hundred and something days, and he belonged—every square inch, you couldn't miss it—to my friend Danor.

So now I was jealous of both of them.

Yippee.

"Saw the film then, did you?" I inquired. He'd said nothing yet. He smiled too—what a smile that was, maybe he couldn't help designing himself to be so attractive, but he could try and tone it down a bit for my sake.

"Yes. We saw the film together."

"Oh, together. Surprised you made the time to see films."

He laughed. Not at me, with me. Showing me I'd cracked a joke, and if I'd only get off my arrogance kick I'd be simply *super* company. I frowned unbecomingly.

"After you left Four BEE," Danor interpolated, "we disintegrated rather."

"Poor things. It must have been absolutely awful for everyone, stuck there in the dome, and me out here in the middle of nothing and nowhere with nothing and no one—" I

stopped just before the self-pity, creeping up under a cloak
of fury, got me by the ears.

"Yes, we were selfish," Danor said, "and very, very
frightened. Up until you actually left, everyone kept going
by being angry and fulsome, and having a mad time—like
the party. But on the fifth unit . . ." She stopped and her
face was pale, so pale it took me back into that Committee
room when she had stood there, palely answering the Q-R's
rotten probings about Kam and her, her hands trembling. She
hadn't wanted to be there and answer them, but she
hadn't had much choice after I'd done over Zirk in the park.
After all, it had been my own fault, hadn't it, throwing
around challenges, getting violent, blaming everybody but
myself.

I sat down on one of the rather pleasing midnight-blue
seats.

Danor didn't resume talking. I could feel Kam looking at
her, her looking at Kam, and great mutual gusts of sympathy
for me passing between them.

Let's face it, he hadn't jumped down *my* throat for
screwing his lover the moment his back was compulsorily
turned by BAA Committee. And he had more rights than me,
sniveling little predominantly female fool.

"Er, would you like anything?" he quietly asked.

"Don't be kind," I said, "or I shall smother the upholstery with tears. Maybe Danor could go on with what she was
saying, and I'll try to keep my ill-natured trap shut."

"Oh, *ooma*—" said Danor, but Kam must have shaken
his head, telepathically advising her to do what I said. They
really were a pair, just like lovers in old books—one mind,
one heart and so on. They'd have made you puke if there
hadn't been that sense of something shining and rock-hard at
the spine of their idyll.

Danor went on in a light matter-of-fact voice.

"First of all, Hergal went and crashed on the Zeefahr
again. We thought he'd given that up, quite a surprise. She—
Hergal—came back a girl, and rushed off in a dreadful state

with some other-circle Jang male to BAA. The male resembled your last body, *ooma*. It was sort of funny and sad. Thinta just shut herself in her green palace with swarms of cats. Mirri and Kley looked frightful. Mirri finally booked into Sense Distortion. As for Zirk, she got cut out of the circle. She was going around and around the city, female, with about six enormous other-circle males, and half the time saying she was someone else. So the Committee are on to her for Evasion, since paying for home and various other things in another name doesn't count, apparently. And Hatta looked unbelievable the last time we met."

"Utterly *drumdik*," I managed. "I can imagine. Eight black eyes, four yellow ears, and a tail."

"No," said Danor, "that's just it. Female, and beautiful."

Even in my arrested state, this registered. Hatta—only once had I known him to be beautiful, and never female.

I'd looked up by now, and shown some signs of incipient animation. Kam had popped a button somewhere and cool glasses of a non-Jang white alcohol had appeared. I drank, cautious at the shared, unknown but tasty liquor. Was I going to forgive them their naive and unkind arrival, all glittering with their love?

"Yes," said Danor, "Hatta as a girl is riveting. I don't know what she felt; she never spoke of it. But obviously she was making up for lost time. She was marrying male after male—generally two or three a unit."

"Oh well," I said, feeling dreary again in my mateless condition, "good for Hatta. And what about you?"

"I sat in your palace," she said. "I kept thinking about you. I know how stupid and useless and selfish I was. *I* hadn't been exiled, you had. But, *ooma,* I couldn't help it. People said you'd suicide and come right back to PD, but I knew you wouldn't, not after what you'd told me—that dream. The desert was—*part* of you? I'd known that somehow from the very beginning. Do you remember the Archaeological Expedition? I thought it then. I thought you'd find some wonderful buried fortress or something, and stay in the dunes, oh, *vreks*. When you spoke about it, the sand was blowing there, behind your eyes."

"She won't believe you if you put it like that," said Kam.

He might have read my thoughts, too—though I hadn't balked at the words as much as I would if someone else had offered them. Danor wasn't artificial. If she said she'd seen sand blowing behind my eyes, she meant it. And really, I knew what she meant, too. It stirred me, scared me, made me want to run out and start up the hoeing or dig another irrigation ditch.

"I believe her," I said. "No doubt you understand why I believe *her*."

He nodded, a little embarrassed suddenly, becoming aware probably of how they paraded their feelings without meaning to or being able to do anything else.

"But then," Danor said, "Kam signaled me."

"Ah ha," I said, "just like in an old romance. I might have guessed."

They both blinked, but, having got them both off balance, I didn't feel spiteful anymore, rather protective, really. Though they hardly needed my protection.

"I gather," Kam said, "you know about the earlier business."

"I think we both know about each other's business in respect to Danor."

"Ah. Well. Maybe."

"To recap," I said, "the Committee in BAA fed you a whole lot of indigestible rubbish about you being bad for each other."

His eyes abruptly glinted.

"Don't be tactful," he said, "or I'll smother the upholstery with tears." Danor giggled. I found I had too. Oh, well. "The Committee actually said I was messing *Danor* up, so I cleared my unhealthy carcass from her path."

"And then, despite many experimental love scenes with

groshing older ladies, the nagging pain continued in your heart," I said. They gazed at me. "Meanwhile, back in Four BEE, Danor wandered pale beside my pool in the deserted palace. And then. Hark! A signal popping and winking. Danor sadly switches on the image, and there, or here, is her lover. With screams of joy they greet. Well," I added slyly, "you did tell me not to be tactful."

"That's all right," said Kam generously. "You're not far out. The screams from my end were somewhat deeper. Otherwise . . . I asked her to meet me in BEE; my boat was due in four units."

"When we met," Danor said, "we just went back to where we'd been before, only rather furtively. Kam really did pretend to be my maker half the time. I think Hergal guessed. Just before she fled with her new marriage partner, she kept on about you when you were a male. I think Hergal was more distressed than any of us. Isn't that odd?"

"Peculiar," I agreed.

It transpired that finally the idea had come to Danor—ignore the Committees and fly the cities, and live for love in the wild. They'd just come around to the notion when my film was flashed out. It made a sensation—which it hadn't been meant to, at least not in the way it did. Possibly the Committee had allowed the film in the hopes that I, emaciated and dolorous with despair, would provide a nice extra example of what unsocial tendencies got you. Or possibly even, if I looked fairly healthy and jolly, people might stop worrying and debating about me, and get on with the *droad* city round. But—

"Half the Jang went running about on the mono-rails immediately after," said Danor, "screaming and shouting. There were sixty-eight sabotages of the dome that night, and sand and volcanic ash and a couple of earthquakes got through. About forty Older People went crazy as well, and got roaring drunk in your honor, and drove the Q-Rs mad at Ivory Dome saying they wanted to get married to each other."

"A historic evening," said Kam. "In the morning the Committee signaled Danor, informed her that she and I had been registered as together once again, and must part for our own sakes."

"So we said we were leaving," said Danor.

"At which the Committee," said Kam, "accused us, in a most extraordinary tone, of planning to join you in dangerous, out-dome, anti-city activities, and that, if we left, it would be assumed we also wished for permanent exile. Like you, we could expect aid and supplies, and like you, we could expect to remain outcast until natural death placed us at the Committee's mercy for PD."

"God," I said.

Kam looked at me.

"That's a very old concept."

"So is the concept of androids working *against* people. But it sounds to me as if the Committee is boiling all over its electronic brain casings."

"Quite," said Kam.

"So why ever did you come?" I asked, breathless (breathless and girlish beneath these charming eyes I would have to accept as paternal or fraternal). "Knowing—what would happen."

"I said they could be damned," he told me, "and Danor said much the same, with a few colorful Jang adjectives thrown in. Because I want her with me, and she wants me, and if the only way we can have each other is by leading what, after all, used to be a perfectly normal life, then that's the way it's going to be. If you'll befriend us, you've got a willing pair of hands for your greenery out there, two pairs, in fact. If not, and we realize you might rather not, we'll go and try to get something started elsewhere, the way you have. The growth rate of vegetation in the desert is phenomenal, which has always been known, and accepted, and entirely ignored by everybody but yourself." He was really getting going. I loved watching him. Better to have a crush on Danor's Kam than on a *flooping* robot. "I admire the way you've organized this," he said to me, and I glowed, choosing to forget the fact that almost everything had occurred as a result of accident, mismanagement, and idiocy on my part. "I'd like to help, and Danor would. And I'll tell you something else. Four BEE blew to the skies the night they showed the film. There are going to be others coming out here, too. Plenty of them."

2

Naturally, I told them to go. Go on, I said, who wants the company of sweet-natured girls and delectable males, both of whom praise me, and offer help for hearth and land, and promise further comrades to come, and who make me laugh and want to hug them sick? Well, obviously, I didn't do any such *zaradann* thing.

We sat a long while over our white alcohol in Kam's bird-plane. We got a little drunk and made drunken plans. I said they must come and live on the ship, for now at any rate. Plenty of cabins, I said. All colors of the rainbow—yellow, scarlet, apricot—but maybe they'd better have the violet one, it would tone with Danor nicely. And they'd be able to insist to Four BEE that they have a water mixer. Two, even. One for the home, one to make shrubbery. The Committee, if they hadn't denied it to the Outcast Killer, surely couldn't deny *them?* Naturally, they'd have to move out of my vicinity temporarily, in case the Committee monitored their position. (A beam had been installed compulsorily on the plane, so they could call for aid, etc.—or was it to spy on their activities?) While we were in proximity with each other, the Q-Rs would tell us to share my water mixers, but if Danor and Kam were over the mountains at the time, the city must deliver. Then, once the goods had arrived, my guests could return, plus water mixers, and we'd have three lots of "Rain" for the Garden. This seemed very logically worked out, and rather sharp. Kam congratulated me again on being devious.

It got latish, and suddenly the Sisters went off with their usual thump and the unopaqued windows pulsed with distant red. I'd been impressed by the windows and the arrivals' lack of phobia. Love had sustained them? They didn't jump much, even now. However, reaction to the Sisters expressed itself from another quarter. From somewhere aloft exploded Danor's swan.

I'd forgotten the swan, and so had they, it seemed. Perhaps they'd slipped it something to keep it quiet on the journey out. Currently awake, it raced gawkily for the exit, and fled from the plane. Once outside, it burst into klaxon sneezes. Probably it had a pollen allergy.

Danor was concerned, and Kam practically helpless with laughter; I somewhere between. It looked as if the swan might well be a child substitute, too, for Danor, since she and Kam could never become makers in the city. Recalling my pet, and the horrendous adventure with the devil of the provision dispenser, I eventually sympathetically followed Danor down the ramp, out into the night.

Danor called to the swan across the dark, intermittently volcano-lit spaces of the whispering Garden. In reply, from odd nooks, eyes sparked gray (Gray-Eyeses, obviously) or gold (snakes). The swan meanwhile could be heard faintly klaxoning to the left and plodding stolidly over everything growing at ground level from the sound of it. I recalled that old fear of mine—that real desert animals might attack an android version, outraged at it for its weird similarities and differences.

"Danor," I said, "I'll get it; I know the paths," and shot into the undergrowth.

I was going quite fast, despite Kam's alcohol, when the

klaxon ejections abruptly ceased, but right then I spotted the swan.

It was lying full length, swan-fashion, on the earth, and, for a second, I thought it was dead, and nearly let out a screech of primeval woe, as once before, so long before, yet clear as yesterday. More clear. The pet lying dead, and I—

But no, the swan wasn't dead. It was lifting its brainless, elegant head, rubbing its neck on the stem of a tall flowering cactus—thankfully not of the prickly variety. And now the swan was rolling on the cool, water-mixer-moistened soil. Its plumage was filthy already and it had petals stuck all over its beak. But unmistakably it looked glad, in the throes of genuine haphazard pleasure.

I hefted it under one arm with difficulty, and took it back to Danor.

One hour later she and I had it in the bathing unit, flapping and flailing, as we rinsed our future from its lavender quills.

3

The bird-plane took off in the morning. Watching it go, even knowing they would be back, something shivered in me. But I put my stale fright aside. I wasn't going to be alone anymore. Danor and Kam, and others, plenty of others, so Kam had said. My head was ringing with elation.

They planned to put down just on the other side of the nearest ridge eastward, signal BEE on their monitor-beam, and let fly with all the jargon we'd thought up for the water mixers. Then Kam was going to adapt it—or them—as I had done, merely a matter of reprogramming them.

After that the bird-plane would return, followed at length by one (or two) water mixers, striding like terrifying beasts from a myth across the mountains into the valley. If Kam could inveigle the computer, as I had done, into using a displacement machine for delivery, the whole thing could be over and done by sunset tonight.

Tonight I would dress for company. So I spent about an hour during second meal with the clothing machine, arranging for smoke-amber satin-of-glass with amethyst fringes.

Most becoming. The cosmetic machine could do my hair too, curls and coils and pearls and things.

The swan had gone with Danor, blessings on it. Last night it had rolled right over some fresh young flowering shoots, which had somehow survived. Yay and I did our usual tour in the tracks of the water mixer. We wound up on the northwest side, examining the curious earth fruits, which were now ready to be picked and tested by the food equipment for edibility. Of course, they might be poisonous or nontoxic but foul. Still, they looked nice, succulent red and yellow, and some little green crispy leaves in huddles, a sort of sand-lettuce, not to mention the bizarre, gold-freckled, dark tubers swelling in the shade. Borss and Jaska staggered into the ship with armfuls of stuff to set the testing in progress.

The sun was high and hot by now, the sky the hard deep turquoise of noon. The mountains were like carvings from night left behind at dawn, the edgings of sand like powdered silver. And here light was raining in dapples of golden green through the tall trees. The trees were rising in avenues; there were glades and beds of flowers, as if the Garden had actually been designed, as if someone had left the seeds ready, buried in the dunes, formally laid out, each held in a dry time-pod until there should be enough prolonged water to break the spell and wake them. What an idea. Had someone? Some ancient, eccentric, brilliant ancestor of the cities, long before even the nomads violently trudged the waste?

Cogitating, up to my eyes in soil from the fruit picking, I suddenly heard the thrumming of a bird-plane, and looked heavenward. Danor and Kam back so soon?

No. This one was coming from the west. Coming roughly, perhaps, from the direction of Four BEE.

Off course, or playing air games. It would pass over.

A black speck in the burning green-blue sky, it resolved itself swiftly, showing its underside, dropping by hectic degrees. Someone was fiddling with the controls. Or, nervous, had screwed up the robot programming.

The plane swiveled slightly, and all at once dived. Instinctively I ducked, without real cause, as the vessel sliced the atmosphere above the trees. Was it going to crash? And on my prickly-fire bushes?

At the last possible split, the plane righted itself and flopped into an offhand landing in the grove of purple trees, about a hundred yards eastward.

I had been leaning on one of the metal things the robots rustled up to serve as hoes. Now, hoe in hand, soil on face and in hair, and combined interest, alarm, and ferocity in my glance, I made toward the belly-flopped plane.

They'd brought down some of the boughs, I furiously noticed, furious as a maker whose child has been bopped on the nose. Don't tell me, the *Garden* is now a child substitute. The plane, however, appeared intact, its door stood open, and a wild din was emerging, a din you couldn't actually hear.

Upper ear. Jang high-tonal-music tapes.

I reeled, swamped with giddy delight, scowling, and burst up the ramp into the plane, looking neither left nor right. I found the tape control instantly and, with the practice of *vreks,* smashed the button for silence. The mind-blowing horror receded. Shaking myself like a Gray-Eyes which has accidentally rolled in some cactus, I glared about.

"*Attlevey,*" voices murmured, silkily, joyfully.

The tiny plane, built to carry two, or three at the most, was crammed with five Jang. Their hair was shades of yellow, hyacinth, viridian, pink-orchid; the two females had long, long nails, the males' nails were even longer. They wore see-through, chains, rings, bracelets, anklets. They were smoking incense through tubes from a weeny glass bubble fixed in the ceiling, their eyes were dark with ecstasy, and full flagons of Joyousness were clasped in their pretty paws. They smiled up at me from their semi-recumbent positions on the couches or each other, and their sequined faces were full of visions and mysteries, and shone with the pure radiance which only total imbecility can bring.

Oh. Beautiful.

"*Attlevey,*" they reiterated. A male with flowing dark-green locks waved his hand.

"I'm Naz. This is Felainnillaloxiandphy."

"Oh yes," I said.

"We know who *you* are," he said.

"You do."

"Oh, *ooma-kasma,* we do."

I shrank. Effusive turd.

"Well, *ooma-kasma,*" I said, "I really think you actually don't, or you wouldn't be here." A cold anger, not untinged by blind panic, had welled in my reinforced bones. "Just tell me, have you informed the Committee you were coming here?"

"*Ooma-kasma,*" drawled Naz, popping an extra pill down his gullet, "we went right in the Committee Hall, and oh infinity, did we like anything tell them. Listen, you *thall-draps,*" went on Naz, demonstrating, "you can all jump in the vacuum drift. We're off to where everything is for *real.* You bet."

"So they know you're here. What did they say?"

"They said: If you go you can't come back—oh—if you go you can't come back—oh—" Naz discovered he had broken into an involuntary but apparently Naz-pleasing song, so went on. The other four, Felainnillaloxiandphy, joined in.

So there they were, a parcel of useless Jang idiots, entirely enmeshed in Jang mores and habits, intent on molesting my desert. Did they really realize what they'd done? That they *had* been exiled? "For real. You bet."

"Do you have any link with the city?"

"Four BEE? Oh, yah, yah, *ooma,* my *ooma.* They put in a monitor beam in case we need any more ecstasy or incense," Naz broke off his singing to reassure me. "Say, *ooma,* have a pill?"

"No. Get on your beam link and tell the computer you didn't mean it. You want to come back."

Naz broke off again. Something had penetrated.

"But we *do* mean it, *ooma-kasma.* And we *don't* want to go back."

"Yes you do. Have you looked out yet?" Their windows were as opaque as their brains. Maybe they'd get agoraphobiafied and throw up all over the grove, but at least they'd leave afterward. How could the Committee refuse them reentry? After all, they seemed model citizens to me.

Inspired by the suggestion, they were scrambling about, agile and luminous, and nearly trod me under their sparkling feet as they dashed into the great outdoors.

It was worse, much worse, than I'd thought.

Not a trace of insecurity or fear.

They were wandering from tree to tree, flower to flower. "Oh, *ooma-kasma*," they were extolling each other, "just look at this, and this. Infinity, it's all so *groshing*," as they squashed flat the buds and picked the newborn blossoms to stuff in their abysmal hair.

Maybe the Gray-Eyeses would get them.

Maybe the snakes would strangle them.

Maybe the food tests would prove the fruits were poisonous, and I could feed them to the Jang: "Computer? I'm afraid I have five Jang here, suicided, ready for PD."

They were swaying and swerving in the direction of the sand-ship, holding hands and pulling off leaves so they could admire them better.

"Ooma-kasma-maa!" they warbled back to me.

"Coming," I grimly answered.

4

They but *loved* the ship. They'd never been in one before. They dived into the cabins and out of them. They flung open the doors to the pool-tank and dived into that and came out soaking wet. Two of them, the two females—Felainnilla—got hold of Yay and tried to dismantle him, with yipping recollections of previous city dome sabotage. Having stopped this, I found the other two males—Loxiandphy—had programmed a machine for some sort of bright mauve paint, and were painting with it all along the tasteful walls of the corridors things like THE DESERT WASTE IS COSMIC, *OOMA* or CACTUS COME AND EAT MY SOUL. They weren't too hard to deflect, being smashed to the very small back rooms of their tiny minds.

At last they flaked out in their entirety in the saloon, and I got clearing-up operations under way. I glanced in on the food tests, hopefully, but the poison analysis wasn't complete and, in any case, looked as if it might be negative. Perhaps I could grate some syntho-something in their fifth meal.

For they'd ordered fifth meal from Borss, and it had come. Tucking in with good appetite, they bawled away about how wonderful it was to rough it in the wild, so clean, uncluttered, and fresh, *ooma-kasma*. Then a male with hyacinth tresses (Loxi) and the female of the pineapple curls (Felain) went rootling by on their way to clash nastily with the scarlet cabin. I just knew they'd very carefully married before they left BEE. Unable to resist having love in these bucolic surroundings, the dust-pink Nilla girl and Phy, a grim, macabre cobalt creature with jewelry to match, thudded out to the yellow cabin. Naz lay among the debris of nut-steak-on-fire and smiled in laconic fashion.

"Well, *ooma-kasma*. I know you don't believe marriage is necessary first, so what about it?"

I still had the steel hoe in my hand; I showed it to him.

"I've been male enough times to know just where to aim so that it hurts," I said. "Until I can get you off my patch, I realize I'm stuck with you, but don't push your luck."

Even I was not that desperate.

"Ooma, ooma," sirened Naz, as if I'd injured his inmost id, "what a disappointment you are to me. You, the shining star of Four BEE's Jang, and in such a becoming body."

"Listen," I said, "I know our teeth are reinforced, but unless you shut up, I'm definitely willing to try and knock yours right down your throat."

I got the monitor beam going, but the computer took a while in coming on.

"There's been a mistake," I informed it. "Five Jang have arrived here that didn't mean to—a bird-plane malfunction. Can you send someone to take them back? I don't think they'll make it on their own."

The computer rattled, then:

"Once they have made contact with you, they are to be considered as exiles."

Its metallic voice-tape sounded altered somehow, even less approachable than before.

"God!" I shouted at it, to see what would happen.

"God is a primitive and untenable invention," it promptly replied. Somebody had reprogrammed it. No longer was it a fascinated adversary, it was a cold, cold enemy who wouldn't play games. From here on, its answer would, in every sense, be no.

"OK," I said, "you're being unfair and clunk-headed, but I expected nothing else. Go fry in your storage batteries."

It never even twitched.

Thus, what? Here was I stranded with five awfuls, who would ruin my dream by sheer lack of personality. Yet they *were* outcast. And if I slew them (murderer, killer, why else were you cast from home and dome?) it was PD for them. And maybe even *their* barren little egos were dear to them.

If only Kam were here, Kam and Danor.

But they weren't, and wouldn't be till sunset at the earliest, and I had no means to signal them. I must cope solo.

There was a slender chance.

I went back into the saloon, where Naz lay stretched in midair on a float-cushion he'd got one of the robots to blow up for him.

"Changed your *derisann* mind, *ooma-kasma*?"

"Naz," I said, "I think we ought to talk. I can tell you're the mainstay of your circle. The others look up to you, don't they? It was your decision to leave the city?"

I'd hit the target, fair and square. He smiled indulgently. Ecstasy had presumably faded from him a little, since he actually heard some of what I said.

"You know, *ooma-kasma,* you know. Well, they've got to have someone. I'm stronger—you think so?—than Phy— he's the other predom male. Loxi's just everywhere and on the moons. Nilla's a girl, never anything but. Ultra-female, you know? Scratchy. Felain, she's predom tangled-up. She suicided every day for a whole vrek, got so bad even the Q-Rs thought she'd done it mistakenly. Then they stuffed her in cold store for thirty units. Now she really only wants to go with Nilla, and Nilla won't be a male, and Felain doesn't want to be a male, and it's a real live *floop*-show, *ooma*."

I sat down. As he'd let all this out, a little streak of intelligent, bewildered compassion had shown on his face.

"It sounds bad," I said.

"Oh, yes," he said. "Did I tell you Loxi starved himself to death in BAA? Took ninety units. And Phy gets melancholia in the dark. When it's night, he'll cry."

"That will be something to look forward to," I said; but my heart was rending me with its claws.

"As for me," he said, "I don't have problems. Life is just one gray-rose nebula from dawn to *grakking* dawn."

And before I could stop him, he'd shoveled handfuls of ecstasy down his throat and was soon floating in every direction, singing: "Oh, it's great, *ooma-kasma*. The ceiling is full of little chandeliers—one, two, three, one, two, three . . ."

After this, any attempt to get through to him was a pointless exercise. It was only as I'd caught him on the down-surge of ecstasy that I'd got such a wild repercussion to my mild, would-be clever query.

But I could see their whole circle was in a right mess; not model citizens, just the normal kind, jollity and delight for the skin, neurasthenia in the joints.

Makerish again? *Five* child-substitutes?

Along the corridor, outside the apartments, shouts.

Beyond the closed yellow door, a groaning male voice entreating: "Nilla, Nilla, do it again." By the closed yellow door, pineapple-curled Felain clenching her fists and yelling, and Loxi saying: "Oh, er, look, *ooma,* for my sake—"

Now ecstasy was wearing thin, their true human traits were showing, their foibles, bad nerves, and wretchedness. Felain was poorly insulated electric fire, Loxi, unideal partner, a tepid, nonquenching puddle.

I put back on the storm I'd lost with Naz.

"You two," I raged, "if you want to live on my land and in my ship, you can just get used to taking orders from me."

"Squiggle off," said Felain, so I spun her around with one hand and smacked her in her delicate puss. I don't like hitting people. They may hit you back. Besides, I didn't want to damage her looks when she was now stuck with this body, and the healing salve was the sum total of what we had till a robot-rescue arrived to set her nose, or whatever.

A welt appeared on her damascene cheek, and having

noted she wasn't going to biff me, I felt shame ooze in my spine. But too late for shame, and it wasn't too bad; would pale to nothing in half an hour.

"Now listen, and take this in. You poured off your plane, you trampled through the bushes, you picked the leaves and the flowers. So now you're going to come with me and do some chores out there to make up for the damage. You, Loxi, minus your chains and bells, and you, Felain, in something the briars won't rip off your back in three splits."

Felain lowered her lashes and gave me an unmistakable look through them, so for a moment I felt I was almost back in my male poet's body.

"Yes, *ooma*," she said demurely.

"So. See to your clothes and get outside," I gruffly added, resenting the muddle she was making of my hormones. Loxi flew to obey, and Felain slunk, provocatively.

Within, cries and moans reached a crescendo and dwindled.

"You two," I said through the door, "are to be out on the veranda in twelve splits, dressed for hard work."

"You're kidding," muttered Phy. "I've worked hard enough."

But the crawler's whine was in his voice.

Nilla, the dusky-pink delicacy, who obviously dominated both Phy and Felain, called sweetly:

"Twelve splits is too soon, *ooma-kasma*. Come in and we'll show you why."

So I opened the door and went in, demonstrating that I wasn't to be intimidated.

Quite instructive it was, too, to one of my relatively modest tastes.

"Very artistic," I said, "but you can still make the deadline. If you don't, my robots, which I have programmed to take instructions only from me, will come and bring you out as you are, accessories and all."

I hadn't actually reprogrammed the robots and, having masterfully stridden forth, I rushed to do so. I put in an override order, too, in case anyone tried to block *my* block. Yay, Borss, and Jaska bore it with softly ticking forbearance.

After twenty-five splits. Felainnillaloxiandphy stood uneasily giggling and jostling in the porch, Naz having ecstasied into unconsciousness in the saloon.

I was going to have to teach them to garden, since there was nothing else I could do with them. At least they jumped when I spoke. Even Nilla was being cautious.

Felain sidled by, but I'd calmed myself. Poet no longer. Confront the facts, as a female, it was Hergal I wanted, wormwood truth I would now admit. Never mind. I'd got the upper hand with this lot, for a while anyhow.

And in about two hours the sun would set, and my friends would be coming home to save me from complete collapse.

5

The sun dropped like a jewel below the western horizon. There the mountains seem to sink back into the sands, leaving open that way to the cities from which, half crazy and running, I had come. A western horizon of tall dunes mounted on low rock, taller dunes since the sandstorm, maybe bare stone after the next.

Amber afterglow. Jang strewn along the veranda wailing about bones torn from sockets, muscles liquidized, sunburn. Luckily their skins—not one seemed to have designed a really desert-suited body—had not reacted too badly. Nilla, least burned of everyone, mewed that she was the worst burned. Felain rubbed salve into her, dreamily.

They'd worked very hard. Too hard for themselves, harder than they'd meant to.

Only Nilla still picked flowers. I'd seen her. Just like a child from hypno-school nicking a goody from under a Q-R's nose. Nilla might be a handicap. I was fairly sure she'd done this predominantly female thing only in order to throw her circle off balance, in particular hapless Felain. Still, they were stuck with Nilla as a girl now, Nilla included.

Even Naz had loitered out onto the veranda. He lay on
the pillowy couch, humming.

I'd had to warn them not to stare at the sun.

And now the sun had sunk.

I'd been so sure Danor and Kam would be back at this
time that I'd been listening and looking around for several
splits for their plane. Once I thought I heard it, but was mis-
taken. I'd been banking on their help in dealing with this
mob, most of whom, I had the feeling, hadn't been Jang for
very long. Danor was about my age in Janghood, Kam, of
course, older.

But the plane didn't come. And didn't come.

The sky emptied out into palest indigo. Stars burned
through. The Jang, forgetting to grumble, stared at these phenomena silently, not taking ecstasy or howling about "This is
where it's at, *ooma-kasma*," or anything. Even Naz was filling his drug-shadowed eyes.

"There's no moon," complained Nilla.

"So go up and make one," Phy told her. He wasn't
crying with melancholia either. If he ever had.

Presently it was a mealtime, and they vaguely went off to
eat it, like good children. I'd told them, attempting to intimidate them with numbers, that Danor and Kam would be here
later, but they'd forgotten.

I stayed outside, watching, waiting.

The sky darkened. There was a silken rustle of subsiding
sand about a mile away, the sound of it trickling easily across
those spaces of quiet. The day had tired me out.

The Sisters woke me, punctual as ever. They woke the
Jang, too, who had collapsed in comas of exhaustion in the
saloon. They came hopping out to see the volcanic fireworks,
half-scared, half-admiring.

"Your friends are late," said Naz. "Got any ecstasy? I
took all mine and the machines won't dispense; say you programmed the robots to program them not to."

"That's it," I said. "You can forego the ecstasy, or
you'll be unfit for work tomorrow."

Naz, lethargically cursing me, meandered off.

No Danor, no Kam.

My guts had turned cold. Irrational. Anything could have delayed them. Most probably trouble with the newly set monitor computer. And yet, and yet.

"Ooh-weeh!" screeched Nilla at the Sisters, more or less in my ear.

I got up. I was going to check with the blasted computer, even if it did mean giving the water-mixer game away.

"I'm inquiring about some fellow exiles of mine," I said. "Danor, female body from BEE, Kam, older male, BAA. They've put down over the mountains from me, eastward, I'm not precisely sure where. Have they been in contact with you on their monitor beam?"

Rattle. (Even the rattle sounded more efficient, more resolute.)

"They have."

"When?"

Click.

"Computed time of desert noon."

"Noon?"

"Noon."

I wasn't obviously going to get anything for free, so I sold us out.

"What did they want?"

"Two water mixers."

"Oh—ah—how odd!" I, falsely amazed.

"The request was refused," said the computer. "Their plane was given your coordinates and they were told to join you and share your water mixer."

"Did they argue?"

"For approximately one hour."

Good for Kam. I could imagine.

"Didn't work, though, did it?"

"It did not," said the computer, without even a metallic hint of satisfaction.

Heavy chill dark was thick around me, not entirely due to the night beyond the windows.

"So, if they were coming here, I could expect them pretty soon."

Click, click. No answer.

"Well, shouldn't I? Or earlier? About seven hours ago, in fact."

"Unless they have decided to abide by Committee suggestion and order a home built where they are presently located, without growing things."

"Don't try and fool me. You know and I know it was a plot to get a water mixer for us here in the valley. And you know they should be back here now. Did they link with you again?"

"No." Rattle, rattle. "Perhaps they have realized the enormity of what they have done, and elected for suicide and Personality Dissolution."

A white wave broke over me. I cut out the beam link, and stood, holding my breath with tension. Suicide? Not them. So what had happened?

There was a noise on the veranda, shouts, excited thumpings. The Jang had apparently spotted something. Could it be the plane?

I sped veranda-wards, and emerged among an applauding, pointing mêlée of Felainnillaloxiandphy. Something had come over the eastern mountains and plummeted into the greenery about ten feet from the porch.

"Oh, look, it's a desert bird," they were inanely squawking.

"Out of the way, *floops,* it's an android, and I know it."

It was Danor's swan.

I knelt by the swan, which, exhausted but apparently whole, was recovering in the grass.

"Oh God, swan, what's happened?"

And the swan fluted: "You are the wonderful sun of my sky!" which sent the Jang morons into raptures. But not me. It was the warning song, the song which pleaded for aid.

When they saw my face, the Jang row ebbed.

"Naz," I said, noting him full length on the pillowy couch.

"Sure, I'm awake," said Naz. "Are you going to give me some ecstasy, *ooma,* my *ooma,* or your own nut-brown self?"

"Naz," I said, "I think you've lived longer than the rest of your circle, and I think under your sprawling hide there lurks a spark of intelligence. You and your crowd foisted yourselves on me and I'm stuck with you and you're stuck with me. Just over those mountains there, those low ones, a couple of friends of mine are in trouble. I don't know what kind, but it must be bad. And their monitor beam is probably out so they can't call for city help, all they can hope for is mine. Now, listen. I'm going to take Yay—the robot—and your bird-plane, and I'm going over east to look for my friends. While I'm gone, Naz, you'll have charge of your circle. And if I come back and find you've ruined my ship or my Garden, I'll tear you limb from limb and stuff the bits down a sandhole. Is that clear?"

"I'm not clear quite how you'd manage it," drawled Naz.

"I don't think you're entitled to our bird-plane," said Nilla.

"Entitled!" I squalled. "When you think you're entitled to my home and my land and to pick my bloody plants to bloody pieces. Every moment I waste on you, two people out there may be in agony, or *dead* without benefit of Limbo."

That sobered them. Nilla looked down. Naz said:

"Go on then. I'll take charge. How about some ecstasy before you go?"

But I was running, Yay clacketing on my heels, for the plane in the grove of purple trees, so no doubt he didn't catch my obscene answer.

Yay took forever at the controls before we lifted. I'd told him to check them out, remembering the wild Jang landing, and sure enough there was something wrong that he had to correct before we could get airborne.

We made it eventually, up into a black-marble sky veined with faint cloud.

I didn't know exactly where Kam had aimed for—it had been pot-luck, anywhere over the ridge, just so a few miles and rocks stood between their place and mine.

I know that I was thinking even then that they'd crashed, and it seemed so illogical for a plane to malfunction that the computer's words came back and back to me. Maybe the desert had suddenly swelled up around them, huge and terrifying, a delayed phobia, robbing them of courage, sense, even of love. Maybe suicide, or panic, had caused Kam's blue plane to dive into oblivion. But no, I couldn't believe it. Wouldn't.

There were a good four hours of darkness left as we searched along the eastern ridges, scouring them with the plane's underlights. Twice we went over the Cup, and I could look down past its rim into a vast, extinct volcanic crater; truly it was a cup, even inside, and once that bowl had brimmed with fire.

Near dawn we landed to recharge the friction batteries, which were crackling fretfully, then, after half an hour, went up again.

First pallid intimations of sun-arrival on the sky far below.

With daylight, it should be easy to spot . . . anything, not of the desert.

I saw the wreckage one hour after sunrise.

It lay along a sandy shelf, smoking dustily. Shadow and night had hidden it, for we'd passed this area before. From the positioning they'd been on their way back to the sandship, coming from the dunes beyond the eastern mountain slopes.

I shut my eyes and each of my senses when I saw. I felt no grief, no sickness, and no anger, only a great blank of nothing.

But I made Yay land our plane. I had to be certain they were dead, and then I had to get back and contact Limbo. Ego-death was better than absolute death, or so we all believed. Danor and Kam would be Danor and Kam no longer,

but, *rorls* in the future, they'd come back from PD at least
living.

I wasn't relishing the thought of what I'd find—stray
human parts, blood . . . The plane made a perfect touch-
down on the rocks. I opened up and got out.

Then I heard the new noise, the thrub-thrub of motors in
the sky I had just vacated.

I stared up. A tiny black dot circling westward. Limbo—
it looked like Limbo even from this distance. Limbo robots
zooming in to save the life sparks of Danor and Kam.

Yes, circling nearer, I could see now it was a Limbo
craft. Circling nearer, near enough to check, with its beamers,
life or death below; circling, but not landing. Not *landing*.
Then—

I looked again, past the wreck to where the rock shelved
up into a hollow arching, hiding its cavelike depth from the
sky above. And I saw Danor standing there gazing back at
me, and Kam about a yard in front of her.

I ran, and they ran, panting in the thin air. The three of us
ran together and more or less collided. We clung to each other
on the rock, muttering things that made no sense, and overhead the dark city messenger droned away.

"They've only got Joyousness laid on in their stupid
Jang plane," I said, "but if you don't mind a bit of ecstasy,
it's not bad."

"After yesterday," said Kam, "ecstasy would be a
pleasant change."

So we drank Joyousness and ate toasted angelfood,
which was the only thing their first-meal-dispenser button
would give us (typical).

And then a tale was unfolded. Kam's account and Danor's. I'd like to write it in the old way, with ink and pen,
frame it in gold, and set it up in the ship's saloon for everyone to see.

Having asked Four BEE for the water mixer, argued, and
got nowhere, they set the controls for my ship and up they
went. Presently there came a clucking in the panel. Kam

checked and got the panel to check itself. The panel told him it had malfunctioned, and it was too late to right itself since something had snapped somewhere and poured off oil into the batteries. About two splits later the batteries cut out.

Danor said she stood there, wan and useless, just expecting to take his hand and say goodbye. But Kam pulled all the guts from the float-bed and they baled out on them. It was brilliant and chancy, but it was the only chance they had. Luck and the float-gas held, and they escaped with minor abrasions, falling on the rocks about fifty feet below the spot where the plane itself crashed, and slowly climbing up to it, no easy task without oxygen tablets.

The monitor beam had had it, but they reasoned that this fault would duly have registered in Four BEE, and a rescue plane would come to see what sort of situation they were in, salve their cuts, and probably dump them back in my valley.

Around sunset they heard the throb of motors, left the overhang where they'd sheltered from the sun, and waved clothing and arms about. Sure enough the plane came closer and closer. Soon it was close enough to see it was a Limbo item. Certainly it saw them. In the gathering gloom they made out the flash of its beams, registering them.

But it didn't land. Just circled there. After about ten splits it went away.

It gets cold in the desert at night, particularly up in the mountains; the stars hammer on the rock and strike frost. Kam raided the plane wreck, and managed to coerce some warmth out of a dying battery or two. It got them through the night, with no margin.

Just before dawn the Limbo plane came over again. It's a wonder I didn't bang right into it, but I and it must have sidled by each other in the darkness somewhere, and the sound of my own motors camouflaged it. It circled them once more and went away. They knew by then.

There used to be a certain bird in the desert, but I think it is extinct by now. It lived off carrion and, noting a dying animal from on high, it would circle there, watching, till the last spark of life went out. Then swoop and devour the corpse.

The plane from Limbo had been watching. It was waiting for Kam and Danor to die. They had a vast choice of deaths. The natural ones of exposure—too much sun, or too much cold—or starvation, dehydration, or oxygen deficiency. Or they could hurl themselves from the rocks, or find a handy bit of metal in the wreck and slash a vein. Once dead, the Limbo plane would swoop and carry them safe to PD in the city.

I suppose with me, the first exile, the one the Committee had outcast themselves, they'd felt obliged to observe the rules. But with voluntary exiles, PD was obviously the best place for them, and the quicker they got there the better. So the Committee was kind enough to help them make their decision.

It was horrifying. It was true fear with a naked face.

Could they still, those compassionate Q-Rs programmed so long ago to serve humankind, be kidding themselves that they were acting in humanity's best interests, protecting us from ourselves? Or had the old grievance at last asserted itself, the grievance that twelve *vreks* before had suggested itself to my instincts? Even in the tanks, you can't breed a human without the relevant cells from two other humans; however, given these cells, the child comes alive and grows on its own. But the Q-R, bred from selected metals and flesh—man outside, machine inside—is born from a blueprint on the great farm at BAA, and brought to life by the force of an electronic charge. They have no actual life *spark*, no "soul" as the ancients termed it. Could it be that they'd come to resent the lack? Or had the blueprint itself somewhere gone wrong?

When they bailed out, Kam had taken the swan, but the floater wouldn't tolerate the combined weight or the swan's kicking, so he had to push it off, trusting to the memory that it had flown before—one of the few things it could do. And, after dropping like a stone for a couple of feet, the swan opened its wings and saved itself very efficiently. Once they were all down, the swan had stamped about the terrain dis-

contentedly, obviously under the impression that Danor had
organized the crash on purpose, for some incomprehensible
reason. Finally it vanished, and neither of them could find it.
In the circumstances, confronted with doom as they were,
they thought it possibly for the best that the swan had deserted them. Perhaps it would make out in the desert, even get
back to the valley. They had considered that possibility, too,
but, inadequately clothed, with no oxygen or water, they
wouldn't have lasted an hour on those treacherous slopes.

Danor was bowled over by the swan's display of concern
and intelligence on reaching me. I mentioned the Jang only
briefly. It would be bad enough to have them in our laps on
our return, and we had no dearth of problems.

The oxygen pump in the Jang plane was doing wonders
for Kam and Danor. So were the Joyousness and angelfood,
surprisingly enough. They were both tanned almost black, of
course, but otherwise seemed OK. Only their eyes retained
the darkness, the knowledge of that fate the Committee had
intended for them. Beyond the bare facts, we hadn't spoken
of it too much.

At length I tapped Yay, and the plane, overcrowded
again, lifted up into the sky and headed homeward.

It was a beautiful morning.

6

The moment we were in sight of the valley, I could tell there was trouble. Don't know why, unless it was that thick black column of smoke wending up into the ether.

My first thought was that the Jang had razed my sandship to the ground and half the Garden with it.

But then I made out that the smoke arose from a point just beyond the western perimeter of the Garden, and my plot and home were untouched.

We landed in the grove of purple trees—why not? The grass had been flattened by the first arrival, and Yay, more careful than the Jang, did no further damage to the boughs. I got out first and at once they were on me—Nillaloxiandphy.

"*Ooma, ooma,*" they bellowed. "Three more, three more fellow exiles!"

"*Derisann,*" I said. They hadn't bothered to ask if my friends were found, safe or dead.

Nilla added:

"That swan thing pecked me." Never a cloud without a silver lining.

Naz came strolling up. He lounged against a tree.

"Like it's all happening," said Naz. "Did you see the smoke? Their plane went out of control, but they got clear before it blew up. And guess what, *ooma-kasma,* they're Older People. Did you get your circle together over the mountains?"

"Yes, thanks. But Kam and Danor aren't my circle. Circles ceased to exist the moment you left the city. Where are these three arrivals?"

They were on the veranda, sipping Joyousness quite unworriedly.

A male, two females. They all had garnet hair, attractive, healthy tan bodies, and smiles. I had time to notice Felain seated by one of the women, looking fascinated and fascinating, the swan comfortably asleep in her lap, when the male jumped up, advanced on me, and grabbed me in a sort of passionately platonic embrace.

"My dear!" he cried. "We are overwhelmed by your achievements. We have been saying for two *rorls* that the young have the perfect kind of uncluttered, headstrong wilfulness that was needed to give the Fours a smart kick in the pants. I hope you'll forgive our intrusion. We aren't planning to live on your doorstep, so to speak, but near at hand, if you'll permit."

"They won't give you a water mixer," I found myself saying.

I was confused and overtired, and these three looked so alike.

"Then we'll build our own," said the older male.

"Your own what?"

"Water mixer, my dear. I have wasted several very boring *vreks* among the army of Committee-employed Older Persons, bungling about with a lot of buttons that would go off on their own anyway, but it has taught me, unintentionally, the odd bit of mechanical know-how. I see you laugh, and rightly so. What is this silly old fool rambling on about? Good for you. Never respect years, only deeds."

"But I wasn't laughing at you. It's just that I've seen a few Older Persons employed, and I agree, but I never realized they realized—" I stopped, having tied myself in a knot, but he got the gist. His eyes were awfully bright and rather mad, but he looked—refreshing somehow. The left-hand female was stroking Felain's pineapple hair with a gentle open friendly sensuality that surprised and encouraged my liking.

"Ah, yes," said the mad male, "let me but explain. We three were part of a great Jang circle in our youth, *rorls* back. We're very ancient, you see, and never had PD. As Older People we have fermented rather than matured. We hung out in BAA, but this looks much more like it. We've often tripped off into the desert for mid-*vrek*. Ever met that idiot Assule—calls himself a *Glar?* Good, good. Then you'll know what a pest he is. Spent eighty units with him on some ruin he'd dug up, and him pissing himself at the idea of grubbing about in the dirt instead of a robot. Got a whole vase out myself, with my bare hands. Had a picture of a galloping ponka herd painted round the sides. Till the damned bugger came creeping up and screamed in my ear: 'Ah! You *touched* it!' Dropped the bloody thing, of course."

I nearly laughed myself sick. The mad male looked gratified.

"I'm Moddik," he said. "The ladies are Talsi, and Glis with the pretty pineapple girl. Now, about this water mixer—"

"Wait, wait," I cried. Everything was going too fast. "My two friends back there have been stranded on a mountain all night, and I'm nearly off my feet. Would you forgive us if we called it quits till this evening? I think we ought to have some sort of meeting, all of us, to try to sort everything out. We'll need to pool our knowledge and so on, and I'm too woolly-headed right now."

'Nonsense," said Moddik, "I don't believe it. However, we'll be quite perfect till later, exploring the potential of your splendid valley. Did you know you have *binnimasts*?"

Nervously I glanced at myself, thinking I'd broken out into some rare skin disease.

"Er, no . . ."

"Yes, you do. A whole colony of them. Look, there's one now!"

I turned and saw a lemon object rolling in the sunlight.

"Oh, they're *binnimasts,* are they? I called them Gray-Eyeses."

"Did you? Much better too. *Graks* to *binnimasts.* Gray-Eyeses it is."

7

I sank into sleep and dreamed of Moddik the mad male with a long white beard, and looking quite ancient though very sprightly, for his young body had been well and truly belied by his tones. He was jumping about over the archaeological site with an inexhaustible supply of pitchers of sapphire wine, one of which, every so often, he would drop with a thudding crash. From a nearby pillar hung the flayed skin of *Glar* Assule, a fact which filled me with delight rather than apprehension. Elevated on a cloud sat a Q-R Committee. They aimed lightning bolts at Moddik, which he effortlessly dodged. Where they hit the ground, they turned into the wreckage of bird-planes, and out of each lot of wreckage emerged beautiful joyful people, laughing. "You won't get us that way, you steel-arsed bastards," warbled Moddik. And apparently they didn't.

Danor woke me, gently, just before sunset.

She had a rough message to make up for it.

The Nillaloxiandphy brigade had the Picture-Vision on, and there had been a flash broadcast—just like when they flashed out the film of Me in the Waste. I'd missed it, being asleep, but Kam, hearing the row the others made, went in and caught the end. Moddik and Talsi were out in the Garden, Glis and Felain in one of the cabins, apparently, and didn't respond, so they missed it too.

Once so rare, flash interruptions to Picture-Vision seemed on the increase indeed. Neither were they normally relayed out-dome. It rather looked as though the Committee had made sure we got this one on our wall, in addition to the citizens of Four BEE. And they said they were going to repeat the flash. The hour they gave corresponded chronologically to desert sunset.

I flew about, demented, and grabbed the nearest article of clothing, which turned out to be my party outfit, meant for yesterday. Looking incongruously glamorous in amber with amethyst scintilla, and a nervy frown, I arrived in the P-V room just in time. Not a large area, it was now packed with the Jang and the three older outcasts. Danor's swan had sat in a seat and wouldn't be moved—it had pecked Nilla again when she tried. Danor and I perched by the wall with Kam.

Presently the flowery orgies faded off the screen, and a solemn Q-R appeared. The Jang promptly made crude noises and shushed each other. The Q-R produced a second or so of guff about not alarming anybody, and how unhappy he—the Q-R—was about the situation and the action that had to be taken. Then he gave a brief résumé of the events which led up to my exiling—accurate, I had to admit, if biased—my departure, and the film they'd shown of me. Several misguided citizens had since followed me. Of course, they were the lunatic fringe, and perhaps safer in exile. However, the valley was now a hotbed of unbalanced, anti-city activity. In order to discourage further of these misguided citizens from leaving the dome in order to join the misanthropic band, the Committee wished it to be known that in the future, aid and supplies to the exiles would be limited to the barest minimum. They could expect oxygen, vitamins, the basics of food materials, but no luxuries (a kind of protein porridge would be all we'd be able to coax from the provision dispenser, once our current supply of syntho ran out, and no drinks, ecstasy, energy, or similar). Water mixers we had, and must make them go around, rationing in emergency, but we might ask for painkilling drugs and medicinal salve should we require them. Anything more drastic and we could forget it. (Thank God, I thought, thank God Danor and Kam hadn't sustained serious injury.) Building materials would be sent to us on request, but in specific form, nothing left for us to shape to our own ends. In fact we'd get nothing at all they thought we might be dangerously creative with. We were on our own. And we were to be left on our own. No one else was going to join us. No sand-ships, bird-planes, or other vehicles would be given to those known to be sympathetic to us. Those with their own planes would have their licenses withdrawn. Private flights outside the domes were prohibited forthwith and until further notice, and general intercity traffic would be restricted. Citizens were asked to bear with us this inconvenience in the interest of communal harmony.

Lastly, the Q-R said, staring out at us from the wall, his face without malice or pretension, only sad—self-convinced, at least—"The unhealthy craze which has swept the cities will shortly evaporate. The exiles will be left to their own devices. Having defied order and the laws of order, they can hardly expect the Committee to keep them in dome-fashion, free of charge. Their plight is sorry and pathetic, and will presently be resolved in mutual suicide and PD, which is still open to them, and will always be open to them until they are ready to return to it."

The image faded, and roses fell down the wall. The flash was over. We switched off and sat in silence. Then Kam said quietly:

"They added a line or two this time. And they were using upper-tonal to emit a depressing atmosphere."

I hadn't got that, and was relieved, for depression had swamped me and I'd thought it was me. The Jang, obviously relieved too, booed and blared militantly.

Suddenly Moddik was on his feet.

"Load of rubbish," he said vehemently. "Silly nonhuman fools." He shot a glance at me. "You look as if you agree. Splendid. Just give their basic food elements to me when they come in, and I'll fiddle about with them a bit. The meals ought to be even better than they are now. Besides which, half the stuff can simply be reprogrammed from its own leftovers. All you need is an infinitesimal atom of fire-apple and you can process for fire-apple till the sun falls. Food machines don't need great shovelsful of the muck to do an analysis. Our precious androids are just trying to flummox us and everyone else, and it won't work. As for their building specifics, I'd like to see them foist a prefabricated utility-palace off on *me*. And I know a way to get a blueprint for water mixers and just about everything else, simply by wiring one of your robots into the original model for a couple of hours."

We gawped at him with mingled hope and disbelief.

"Come on. Get your jaws off the mosaic," he said. And to me: "Where's the meeting you spoke of earlier, and when?"

"The saloon," I said. "Now."

Not a very orderly meeting.

First of all, Loxi fingering the fringe on my dress and "Oh, *ooma,* I had one like this once, when I was a girl—in BAA—all flames it was . . ." Naz moaning about ecstasy, and Phy suddenly breaking down in floods of tears, his dark-ness-melancholia finally catching up, or just plain fear at our plight. Talsi, the non-Felain-fancying older woman, com-forted him in a makerish—no, be precise—*maternal* way, very touching to behold. Danor and Kam sat close to each other, calm as could be, secure in their bond. I didn't feel jealous anymore, but a sort of hollow place had come in my heart, and notices stood on the bare sand of it which read: "Vacant, and never now to be filled."

"Very well," I said, when things had settled a little, "we each know adequately who everyone is, and what our own and each other's problems are likely to be, so maybe we don't need to go into that right at this split. Our total numbers are eleven, not enormous, and our sexual leanings, despite our current bodies, seem fairly fluid, so I'm not sticking any labels on anyone. We're going to have to cope with that as best we can, since we won't have a chance of changing for the rest of our lives.'' The slight murmuring that had started up fell off again at this doomful clarion call. ''However,'' I tritely said, ''situations have a habit of altering unexpectedly. Who knows what tomorrow may bring?''

''Sand fleas?'' volunteered Nilla.

''From here on,'' I said pointedly, ''we have to work together where possible, and try not to drive each other *zaradann*. For this purpose I suggest splitting up, and not living altogether in a bunch here on the ship. If Moddik can do what he says in the way of adapting—''

''I can do more than I say,'' interposed Moddik flatly.

''Yah, yah,'' said Naz. ''Has yet to be seen, my *soolka* old *ooma*.''

''Good,'' said Moddik. ''Healthy opposition. I may clip you around the chops, young man, but don't let that stop you. How many water mixers were you wanting?'' His bright glance flashed at me like a couple of steel animals up on their hind legs, ready for havoc.

''About nine,'' I said, to gauge his reaction. ''But that's for the valley. We'll need more for the extra homes if we're going to have them.''

Moddik nodded, got up, and went out.

I thought we'd offended him or something, but Glis smiled at me and said:

''He really is entirely brilliant. He's going to wire up your third robot—Borss, is it?—for the blueprint to the watermixer outside. He'll also use the monitor beam to request building materials. When they arrive, he'll start reconstructing. You simply have to understand the principle of reprocessing, and then you can alter any substance eventually to fit your needs.''

''And Moddik does,'' I said.

''Oh, yes.''

''It sounds impossible to me.''

''Oh, no. After all, most of the machines can do it, and

once you grasp the fundamentals of the mechanical brain, which Moddik has, it's easy."

"Oh yes?"

"When we were at hypno-school, two *rorls* back," put in Talsi, rocking the now smiling Phy upon her walnut satin bosom, "they sometimes gave awards for signs of genius. In those units it was even possible to make some sort of career for yourself if you wished to and were clever enough. Modik won all the awards. Glis was a little boy when she was a child, and also very talented. I'm the stupid one. But I have a strong makerish streak, as you see, tied into my sex drive, so I shall be quite useful." She beamed about, managing to catch Naz's eye, Loxi's eye, and even mine. Phy's she didn't need to catch.

Right then Moddik strode back in, and he'd done as Glis had said.

"I'm very glad you got through to the computer," I said, "I wasn't sure the link would still operate." And with only this for introduction, I told them what had happened to Kam and Danor, after which Kam and Danor were madly questioned by hysterical Jang and briefly and sanely questioned by mad Moddik. Having established the facts to everyone's horror, I thought I'd better add the final grim epilogue—or prologue? "Something has gradually become clear to me, one rather gruesome truth. Which is that, of all the three bird-planes that came out here, not one was without a malfunction. Moddik, Glis, and Talsi's plane was out of control on landing and went up like a rocket just after. Danor and Kam's plane got here OK, but on the second flight spilled oil into the batteries and nosedived. The Jang plane made a rotten touch-down so I got my robot Yay to check and correct it, and if I hadn't I imagine my body would now be tastefully bedecking the mountains in various stages of incompleteness. This coincidence seems rather odd, to me. Even my sand-ship wasn't of the best, and the provision dispenser exploded at the first possible opportunity." There was silence thick as velvet in the saloon. You could hear the desert night wind furling round the ship. "How often do planes malfunction in the

city? Ever? Perhaps once every *rorl*. Now, I'm not saying the
Committee has done anything positive, but I do think that
maybe they've let their robots get deliberately careless, forgotten to service the servicing machines, something like that.
I don't quite know how they managed, since they're supposed
to be permanently programmed to protect human life. Possibly they've got around it by recollecting that even when we
die we don't actually *die,* and what's mere Ego-Death to an
android? Our life spark goes on, they see to that. I don't
know. My theories are embryonic and the whole thing scares
me. But I know this. By one means or another, subtly, uncon-
sciously even, they are out to get us. They want the desert
clear of us and our anti-city-system ideas. They fear that
we'll overthrow the harmonic rule of law and order, bring
civil collapse, anarchy, and destruction in our wake—God
knows how, but that's the core of the matter. So we'd better
watch out from here on. Every supply the city sends us we'll
machine-check, just in case someone's omitted something
and the next prefabricated building block goes into automatic
combustion and blows us all to PD." I paused, about long
enough to take a breath. "I might add that food has been
growing here on the northwest side, and the toxicity check
has proved negative. For my eighth meal tonight I'm going to
sample homegrown produce. If it's pleasing, we can extend
the venture. Self-sufficiency isn't a bad thing to aim for, particularly placed as we are."

Everybody stared at me. Even the shock of Q-R treach-
ery had been slightly muffled by surprise at the food announcement.

"*I'm* not eating it," said Nilla predictably. "I bet it's
absolutely *drumdiky*."

"No one's asking you to," I said. "I've explained that
I'll do it."

"Splendid heroic attitude," said Moddik. "It's probably
delicious. But one point. The city syntho-food contains certain additives. Introduce additive-free substances into yourself and your body chemistry may change."

"Yes, I realize that," I said, "but I think I'll acclimatize. If I don't, no one else will try, that's all."

Felain and Loxi were looking at me worshipfully. Danor looked faintly troubled. Kam said:

"I'd like to volunteer to do it myself. You're the founder of this enterprise. It shouldn't fall to you."

"It's the very reason why it *should,*" I said.

I felt quite glad of their admiration or concern. Actually I had total faith in my ability to survive a few rosy fruits and a slice or so of tuber, or I'd never have done it. After all, it was city food to begin with, if unmixed and now intermingled with the properties of the wild. Somehow, having gone through so many traumas with the desert and survived, I'd come to feel there was nothing further to fear from it. An adversary to respect, to battle with, but not a mean one, not underhand. If it came at you, it came head-on, with a storm or an eruption or a tribe of marauding ski-feet. Not slyly, with a juicy fruit whose pips, germinating in some inner tract, would turn my skin green and scaly or my voice into a bark. Besides which, the negative tests showed that any effects that did crop up would be minor and easily reversed.

You don't get a coward like me being a heroine with a *real* dragon about. I hang my sword on the wall, and get under the float-bed, *ooma.*

8

What a night.

No one went to sleep. I think Nilla kept up to see if I'd go into a fit after my eighth meal of grown food. I could just visualize her standing interestedly over my spasming wracked body, saying: "How frantically *drumdik, ooma-kasma*. What a *floopy* thing."

Actually, the only symptom the food produced in me was a desire for more. It was marvelous—fruits like nectar, tubers tart and succulent. The assembled company watched me eating, and followed me uneasily about afterward, patently expecting me to drop dead, despite the toxicity tests. Even Kam asked a couple of times if I was OK. The two-*rorl* older people were less bothered, and about Sister-blasting time, I caught Moddik in the saloon, nibbling a fruit.

"I thought we agreed," I said.

"Couldn't resist," said Moddik. "We can compare dermatoses later. It's not, my young friend, that I don't entirely defer to your leadership."

"I'm not the leader here," I said, slightly unnerved.

"Are you not? Just wait till the next crisis and we shall all be there, bleating about your feet for directions."

"Then I absolutely abdicate."

"You won't, you know. Like most loners," said Moddik, "you carry the seeds of violent authority. Loners need to be bossy. They quickly learn it's the only method they have of shoving people off their backs."

This conversation stuck in my craw, mainly because it had the doleful ring of logic.

Moddik next informed me, as we gazed from the veranda at the nightly dual eruption in the south, that he'd noticed a few additional edible items growing here and there westward. Somehow he seemed to know what everything was for—sun-peaches, fat green roots, a nut tree which wouldn't bear, he said, for about a *vrek*, and might need extra water, even vines from which we could make our own purely fruit-based wine.

"Moddik," I said, "you've been here before, haven't you? I mean, done something like this?"

He chuckled like a wicked little old man in a book, his young tan face crinkling like the dunes themselves with almost harmless vitriol.

"Not quite. I piddled around somewhat with a hydroponics garden in my youth."

"You're going to be a great asset, Moddik," I said. "Thank goodness you came. Why ever did you?"

"And why did you?" said Moddik.

Not long after he went charging off and came charging triumphantly back with Borss, ghastly with exposed wires and plates unscrewed. Apparently we had the water-mixer blueprint. Presently everybody had to get chemical-fire lamps and follow our magician off to the west, where his plane had exploded, and here, under the whip of his instructions, we poked and probed about in the sand and smoke for bits of scorched metal, plasti-ware, and glacia-view.

"You'd be surprised what use I can put this to," said he.

"*I* shouldn't," spat Nilla.

Moddik roared with laughter, and then he went over and lifted Nilla up in the air, looking strong as a robot and mad as mad. Nilla struggled faintly and seemed scared and pleased.

"So, little predominantly-female-who-isn't, you think

the nasty old Moddik gets his thrills that way, do you? I much prefer beating the weak and helpless to a pulp.''

Following this exchange, Nilla regarded him with a smoldering resentful interest.

Eventually he herded us back to the ship, and I was astonished to see that Yay and Jaska had put up a sort of shelter place for him over in a clearing near the grove of purple trees. I remembered I'd reset the robots to take orders only from me, but naturally, in Moddik's clever case, this had meant nothing.

"My workshop," said Moddik, and went inside with Borss of the trailing wires. Shortly, a frightening sound of bangs, thuds, and drilling burst upon the fragrant air.

The sun leaped up behind the eastern peaks as I sat alone on the veranda in my now somewhat stained and tattered finery. The Jang had finally retired in odd order—Felain and Glis, Loxiandphy both with smiling, voluptuous Talsi, Nilla petulantly alone (ha!), Naz euphorically with handfuls of ecstasy Moddik had indulgently conjured for him, after I'd said oh, all right, all right, to his never-ending lament. Danor and Kam, arm in arm, close as leaf on leaf in our Garden, closer than ever since their night on the mountain when death was closer still: close as the world itself. I, who rescued them, had approached the outskirts of their citadel, but no more. How could it be more?

It was a little like one of those ancient plays, which Moddik said were still put on in his youth, when all the characters leave the stage but one. Now for my soliloquy.

Not quite alone, however. The swan, adventurously, had flown up onto the ship's roof and made a nest or something over the cooler vents, which would probably get blocked with its feathers. And from the strange shelter where Moddik still lurked came a pale busy humming.

The water mixer—did it know it had been blueprinted, was no longer unique of its kind?—arose on its tall legs and marched away, tender-pink nozzles spraying.

Sunlight stirred the avenues of the forest to an incredible

scalding green. Beyond the Gardens, the desert painted rainbows.

A sort of happy sadness enveloped me. So beautiful, the dawn, and hope like the oxygen bright in the air, and I alone. Yes, the swan was noiseless on the roof, Moddik's shelter humming grew faint as the whispering of the insects waking in the bushes.

Now I should close my eyes. And become the princess on the gate of her silver tower, waiting for her lover to ride, the somber warrior on his starry beast, across the glistening acres of the sand.

I had shut my eyes. Self-disgust made me open them.

And something was sparkling out there. Look down through the forest, beyond the slope of the Garden, way out to the dunes beneath the black upthrust backdrop of the eastern mountains. Something.

But what? No ships or planes would be taking this road, not for many a *vrek*, if ever. A rogue machine on the rampage? But from where?

Maybe there was a simple explanation: e.g., I was going nuts.

"Moddik!" I shouted. "Moddik! Hey! Help!"

He came out into the clearing, his hands full of bolts, rivets, and panes of ice-glass I didn't know we possessed.

"Sorry to break up your genius activities, but would you step up here and tell me if I'm hallucinating?"

He stepped up and looked out. Then, from a bejeweled pouch in his tunic he produced a lens, and looked through that.

"Ah!" said Moddik. "Might have guessed. Can't keep everyone in line, not even in the Fours." He handed me the lens, and I, too, looked through its telescopic sight.

There wasn't an excess of detail, the distance was still too great, but just enough to make me shiver, and glance around to be sure it *wasn't* a silver tower gate I was mooning away on. The figure out there was a dark silhouette in the sun, but male he was, riding on a starry beast. A real starry beast—a dragon of diamonds with eyes of gold, and striding a good twelve feet from the ground on huge prismatic paws.

"I believe it's an android animal from BAA," said Moddik admiringly. "Lad must have stolen it. Enterprising young devil. I guessed that Q-R rubbish wouldn't stop them coming out, not the really determined ones."

My legs were shaking and I wasn't quite certain why, or wouldn't let myself be.

"Thanks, Moddik," I said. "I'd better go and meet him." Moddik grinned and I added lamely: "Before that dragon thing stamps down half the Garden."

9

Even the shadows were green in the Garden. I'd felt tired before; I was wide awake now. Just because I was going out to collect some dope of a Jang male off the dunes, probably tossing ecstasy down his throat, and howling. "*Attlevey, ooma-kasma,* it's *insumattly derisann,* believe me, and I'm all up on the stars, you bet."

Garden's End was still about half a mile off, though the perimeter seemed to be widening itself a little, small dry grasses seeding, pastel-yellow thistle flowers clutching the sand. Coming from the shade, the sun strikes like a blow on the skull. I thought, collecting it for the three-thousandth time, I ought to get the machines to make me one of those old tribal sun-hat things, an *oopsa* or *oosha* or whichever. But I was brooding on down-to-earth practical details in order to stop my fantasies racing up my spine into my brain like an invading horde.

The beast was striding on toward the sand-ship, and me, only a few hundred yards off now over the dunes.

It was almost like a return of my agoraphobia, those few splits I was crossing the open sand. I was half scared to look

up, even when the ink-black shadow of the gemstone animal
fell thankfully around me. However, shading my eyes with an
arm from the elbow of which amethyst trimmings still
dripped, I raised my eyes, and stared aloft at the dragon's
rider.

"Nice weather," he flippantly remarked. "Bit warm. But
nice."

A lot of things hit me at once. I wasn't ready for any of
them.

"Who are you?" I demanded, gritting my teeth with a
sensation of white-hot lava crowding me from my flesh.

"My name's Esten," he said. "*Derisann* to meet you."

"Damn you, you've got a *farathooming* bloody cheek.
What are you up to, you bastard? What's the *grakking* game,
you—"

"Esten," he supplied graciously, as if I'd forgotten, and
was only filling in with insults to cover the lapse.

"Balls, Esten," I said. "How'd you get it? Where'd you
get it? Why'd you come here in it?"

"Oh, *this?* You mean the body, do you?"

"What else, you God-forgotten *floop* of a Jang *thalldrap*?"

"Oh, well," he said, and just waved his hand ever so
vaguely, and smiled. It was a long-fingered artistic hand and
a charming unexpected smile, the smile of a poet for an attractive girl, the bittersweet greeting of one who is a lover of
life despite the tragic death that is slowly, inevitably, devouring him. I knew it pretty well, and not surprising.

He was in my body. The last one, the poet's, slight and
graceful build, aquilinity of feature, mane of loosely curling
dark hair and large shadow-smudged blue opal eyes and all.

He hadn't missed a trick. Not a *farathooming* one.

Even the gestures were mine.

Only the tan was different, designed to take the sun. Dying of consumption the poet might be, but he didn't fancy
sunburn on top of it.

"Well," I said, "I'm waiting."

"And very lovely you look doing it," he said, gallantly. I

must have looked, actually, like an electric circuit about to blow its valves out. I tried to calm down.

"Either you tell me," said I, in a measured, steely voice, if a bit heat-melted at the edges, "why you chose to arrive like that, or you can turn your—your whatever-it-is around, and prance off back to BAA."

"I can't do that," he said. "You know it."

"Then explain your conduct. Quickly."

He gave the BAA dragon a little tap and it gracefully knelt. He gracefully slid off and leaned there on its side, immaculately fragile. Oh, I knew that stance. He must have seen the pot boiling over again, because he held up one of those poet-swordfighters's hands and said:

"It's quite simple and perfectly mundane. You'll be sick if I tell you."

"You'll be sicker if you don't."

"Very well, my lady of Jang. I saw the magic film, the film of the enchantress in the waste with her green garden. And I lost mind, soul, and heart. To you."

"Crap," I politely replied.

"Possibly. I told you you'd be nauseated. But you insisted on knowing my reasons, so it's your own fault. There is something about your unique brand of boorish, arrogant stupidity that ties me up in a bow. So adventurous, so cynical, such a funny combination of valor and cowardice, idiocy and intelligence. Your dear little face being all lick-arse to the Committee while obscene signs shone from your eyes like neons. I knew at once I'd never fancy another female as long as I lived. So. I traveled to BAA in the legitimate last public sand-ship running, intrigued my way into the android-animal breeding-tank domes outside the city, persuaded some *floop* of an Older woman to let me try a quick dash over the sandy waste on a dragon, and never bothered to go back."

"What about oxygen?" I said.

"They keep supplies on the out-city farms in case they need to leave the farm-domes in a hurry. Oxygen, anti-dehydration tablets, meal injections, the lot. I nicked what I required when the Older lady was resting, after our little—er —chat.''

"Fascinating," I said. "You still haven't mentioned my—your—body."

"Obsessed with you as I was, what else could I do the moment I reached BAA, than order a replicate? It seemed also an excellent way to instant seduction. You've heard the theory, I suppose, that most of us only want to make love to ourselves? Here's your chance, *ooma*. A never-to-be-repeated offer."

He didn't make a move, however, just went on looking at me.

I knew the theory fine. Another thing he'd stolen from me. Something in it, too, if my reactions were anything to go by. My heart was slamming about in my throat, and the other responses—those denied hormones pining so long—were leaping and prancing like things possessed. So, of course, I resented it. His cunning plot, my physical inebriation. And I didn't trust him, he was too clever.

"You're too clever," I said. "I don't trust you. I'm not sure I believe you, either."

"My oxygen ran out last night," he said. "This slightly asthmatic wheeze isn't part of the act, it's real. If I collapse at your feet, will you take me in?"

"Forget it," I said. "One point you overlooked. I know the line; I should, I invented it. Get back on your animal and follow me. I suppose I'm stuck with you the way I'm stuck with all the rest of them."

"Won't you join me on the dragon?"

"No, thanks *awfully*."

So he swung back up, and the beast rose, and they paddled behind me over the last stretch of sand, along the steel paths of the Garden, to the ship.

It wasn't a pleasure to watch him. I think a small part of me was emerald with envy. After all, I'd hopped it from that excellently designed skin before I was really ready. Now, here he was, poetically swooning all over my veranda, with a reemerged Nilla scurrying to bring him food, drink, and cushions, and even Felain and Glis out and about, Glis getting medical machines to take his pulse and Felain cooing in his ears.

I stood at the other end of the veranda and sulked, glaring around with an air of rabid interest in the state of the climbing plants, the sky, the day. When Felain kissed his hand, I got off the veranda and went stalking toward Moddik's workshop.

The dragon had nodded off enormously in the grass at the forest's edge. It was a full android, with no need for food or water. Little curls of scented smoke came from its nostrils. Rather nice it was really, but, unfairly tarred with his brush, I hadn't gone for it much before. What would the Gray-Eyeses (*binnimasts*) think of it? And the swan? That was better, I was cooling down a little.

I knocked on Moddik's weird-shelter door. A strange clattering ensued. Then the door opened to reveal Moddik among a confused undergrowth of wires, steel frames, and transparent webbing. I began to believe what they'd said, he and Glis, about his knowing how to get anything from anything, as a machine does. In Moddik's case, the *rorls* had obviously been put to good use. Everywhere actual machines were clicking and spatting, and Borss had been propped like a demoralized drunk in the corner.

"Is the arrival pleasing?" asked Moddik, tactfully blunt. "Is our young leader glad?"

"No, our young leader isn't glad. The arrival's Jang, and he's had the abysmal gall to turn up here in my last male body—or a replicate."

"Ah!" said Moddik. "I said he was enterprising, did I not? An acquaintance of yours, perhaps, from Four BEE?"

"You know, that never occurred to me. He says his name's Esten, and I never met an Esten that I recall. He doesn't behave like anyone I knew. Or even misbehave like them."

"His manner may be assumed, carefully worked out be-

forehand in order to mislead. His name could also be false,
since, out-dome, it hardly matters.''

I sat down to muse on this and hastily got up again with a
yell. Moddik removed the six or seven pointed rods from the
chair, and began to stuff them in an extraordinary apparatus
that appeared to be growing into a gray jelly at the center of
the room.

"I could ask Danor," I said. "She was in my circle. But
then, he may not have been in my circle." As I said this, the
pulse in my throat slammed me so hard I had to swallow to
get rid of it. "He, oh, he said he got the body at BAA, via
BEE. I suppose he reckoned that way, even if BEE got suspi-
cious, they'd never catch up to him in time."

"Bright lad," said Moddik. "I shall look forward to
meeting him. My prefab horror should be arriving, courtesy
of the Committee, about noon," he added. "I gave them
directions, so it won't land on the fire-root or anything. Then
I'll want that extra machine I mentioned from the ship—and,
with any luck, by sunset tonight, the first water mixer will be
serviceable. Not as beauteous as our friend out there, just
ropy old steel nozzles and an ice-glass dome, but it'll water
the land, and that's the idea, isn't it?''

"What can I say?" I asked him. "I'm overwhelmed."

"Then go and investigate your double and leave me in
peace, you wretch of a Jang girl," roared Moddik, flapping
sleeves and steel tubing and an unseen, nonexistent, ancient
sorcerer's white beard.

"Hallo, *ooma,* may I join in?" Danor asked, gliding into
the saloon from which Yay and Jaska were clearing the messy
remains of the Jang's dawn meal. I was eating the home-
grown sun-peaches for mine. I handed her the dish, with
slight misgiving.

"They're lovely, and they seem OK, but are you sure
you want to? I may start an indiscriminate hair growth or
something."

"Might be pretty," said Danor. "Long flamy gold-
brown hair growing out, um, everywhere."

We giggled secretively in the way of females who have shared many and varying experiences together. Having been in the same circle did count for something, despite my constant propaganda to the contrary.

"Oh, well, anyhow, that smashing nut Moddik was in here last night gobbling those pink things, so I reckon we might all just as well get boils together."

We gnawed in silence awhile. Presently, pouring us fire-and-ice, I told her about the advent of Esten, what he had said, what Moddik had said, quite a lot about my own feelings on the subject.

Danor looked taken aback. I hadn't, selfish and feeble-minded that I am, thought of the implications for her confonted by another me-as-male, a duplicate of the one with whom she had whiled away the hours without Kam. But, in point of fact, this scarcely seemed to trouble her, and she received my awkward mutterings calmly.

"No, *ooma*," she said, "I was just considering what Moddik said, how it might be someone you know. I haven't met him yet, but—do you remember what I told you about our circle when I got here?"

"Yes," I said, and elegantly held up my hand (his gesture—my gesture—I'd caught it back off him). "Honestly, I did think of that. But, how would he ever dare?"

"Oh, I don't think daring it would be the problem," said Danor.

Hergal, female, with a male like my previous body, going off to BAA . . . I looked into my wine and didn't say it. I truly didn't know what I should say, or think. Or do.

Not, of course, that really I could do anything.

10

The unit passed, though "passed" is hardly the word for it.

It seemed to me the whole organized (?) structure of the community was going to pot. Or, at any rate, there were now only Yay and me out there hoeing, tying things up, earmarking things for extra water, and also—food task—pruning the vines and fruit trees and getting quick-growing fern to go south, south, dammit, and get off the tubers. Borss meanwhile had somehow become Moddik's assistant in the workshop, which I could hardly resent (I told myself resentfully) since they were water-mixer making, a deed due to be for the general good.

However, other members of the general good . . .

Danor and Kam were over in the western area of the Garden. Moddik had said he thought he'd seen some *gerkalli* fruits, or something equally unlikely-sounding, coming up there. We'd gone to look, and sure enough *gerkalli* fruits they were, apparently. Kam had offered to stay and weed them out—desert weed is very nice, and can be directed into a grand display at the edges of the irrigation canals and thereby off the crops, since luckily it prefers hanging over water to strangling things. Kam and Danor also planned to extend one of the canals to join up with another, so I gave them Jaska and my blessing, thinking how worthwhile they were for helping and working so spontaneously. Back on my own with Yay, though, I had to keep pushing stupid "I-am-solitary-and-fed-up" thoughts from my mind. My cursing was a pleasure to hear. If any one had.

Naz lay on the veranda in permanent ecstasy, smiling at the green branches above. The swan lay in the green branches, smiling down at Naz. Esten's dragon, which was going to be a drag, had been tethered at the edge of a clearing after it had torn up a young tree and bitten it in pieces with innocent cries of delight.

Nilla was making Her Own Garden. Moddik had suggested it, presumably to occupy her nonexistent mind. She was appropriating flowers and replanting them in Her Own Garden, where fortunately they took philosophical root. They were, without exception, pink flowers, like Nilla, with her magnolia skin and dusky strawberry hair, and she was making, for a centerpiece, a Jang abstract sculpture out of bits of Moddik's leftover ice-glass. Which was all going to be, of course, astoundingly useful.

Moddik's expected materials arrived at noon, as he'd said. He'd somehow persuaded the Q-R set-up to use the displacer to get them through quickly. Crates of atrocious, incomprehensible metal objects and plastic slabs therefore exploded into being in the clearing, and scared Esten's dragon into ripping up another tree. Moddik checked them himself to save me the trouble.

The rest of the party were located thus: Glis and Felain in secret in the yellow cabin. Passing the door once, there seemed to be some sort of poetry and music recital going on rather than what one would have expected. Talsi, meanwhile, was being brazenly wanton out among the groves with Phy and Loxi. From their direction—roughly due south—climactic screams came with monotonous regularity.

As for Esten, he had been invited into Talsi's grove and

graciously declined; he had been invited into Glis and Felain's cabin and had declined even more graciously. Nilla had
tried to lure him into Her Own Garden, but he had sensibly
said he felt exhausted and was going to sleep for ten hours.
I'd tried to keep out of his way, mostly because I'd rather
have plonked myself right next to him.

"Take the green cabin," I said. "It's the last one free,
and you may have to share with Naz, if he ever comes around
enough to get there."

Before Esten vanished to slumber, however, I'd seen him
in conversation with Moddik at the workshop door. Very earnest they both looked. Was Moddik explaining the inter-
valvular pump circuits or something?

I stamped about in the greenery in a furious state of
complete irrationality, and uncovered, during the course of
the afternoon, four sets of Gray-Eyeses having it off, a snake
making a hole and digging up one of the anti-earth-tremor
stabilizers I'd so laboriously put down, and a new mauve
animal swimming in an irrigation canal, which took one look
at me and fled wailing into the undergrowth. Gradually many
new types of this and that were wandering in. A sand-rabbit
or two bounced through the fern, and dune-frogs croaked
messages to each other through the desert nights. The insects
were acquiring most *derisann* extra colors on their tinsel
wings, and very *groshing* they looked. I passed from wonder
to annoyance and back twenty times, and it was sunset, all at
once, before I was ready.

Moddik showed us the water mixer at sunset, his eyes
brilliantly alert as the shiny little wheels that spun in the
mixer's dome.

It wasn't lovely to look at, as he'd predicted it wouldn't
be. Rather shorter than the original striding giant of whipped
cream and mother-of-pearl, its semi-opaque ice-glass dome
looked slightly indecent. Its squat body, mounted on tall yet
somehow squat metal legs, had a freakish demoniac appearance. But when he touched the activator, the water misted
from it like a sweet dream.

It went bumbling off purposefully, just as the original stalking colossus returned. They passed each other, stepping imperiously over the smaller trees, and looking like a beautiful maker and her ugly child who, differences unresolvable, refused to speak to each other.

I thanked Moddik lavishly. The Jang were impressed.

Nilla said, "How *drumdiky* it looks. Not decorative at all. Makes me positively *tosky*," trying to inspire Moddik to maul her. She was wearing her most unembroidered see-through and had been picking the flowers again to adorn her hair. Moddik patted her on the head with a wicked look of senile indulgence, and Nilla fumed.

We were going off to sixth or seventh meal, but Moddik said he'd had a meal injection and wouldn't bother.

"And I can easily get through the night on some stay-awake pills, my dear young leader, and present you with eight or nine undecorative but useful water mixers come the dawn. Now I have the mold, it's just a production line in here."

"Stay-awake pills," I said. "Meal injections."

"You mustn't think Jang have the monopoly on misuse of the body," he reproved me. "Never fear, I shall snore the whole unit away tomorrow."

"How disappointing for Nilla."

The Jang were riotous in the saloon. Why not?

Danor and Kam, tired by honest toil, as I was, talked quietly with me. Naz floated above our heads on a float-cushion. Where was he getting so much ecstasy from? Moddik must have given it to him to keep him quiet. Loxi sidled over and invited me to the never-ending Talsi orgy, and I said something vile enough to send the entire menage hurrying off to their float-beds.

I went along the corridor with soil-burned feet and a spiteful mien.

Yellow cabin: Felain and Glis, no music now.

Apricot cabin: Loxiandphy, plus Talsi. It sounded like battle in there, what on earth—? Oh, *graks* to it.

Violet cabin: Danor and Kam. Controlling of foul thoughts. Sleep well, or whatever you're up to, nice people.

Scarlet cabin: Nilla, who else? Pink Nilla on scarlet bed, pink hair spread on scarlet pillow. Nilla constructing a plan of action—how to get Moddik. Rotten dreams, *ooma,* and if you pick any more of those flowers I'll bury you up to your neck in Gray-Eyeses' natural fertilizer.

Green cabin: Esten stretched out for ten hours' sleep. Estenmyself.

The poet's body, slender steel in a marble glove. Limber and strong as whipcord, didn't I just know? Shadowy eyes, shut, lashes like black fringes of needles. White plains, dark valleys, hair line curling fern . . . Damn, damn, and damn.

Well? Why not go in? So you lost mind, soul, and heart to me, eh? Here I am. Show me.

Hergal, I said, almost aloud. Just the kind of mean, tantalizing game you'd play on me. Give me so much on a plate you know I'd never take it, then leave it all up to me to come crawling back.

Yet, so clever to make yourself me, to sound even rather like me, certainly not really like you, Hergal, my friend, my lover, whom I knocked right through that wall in Four BEE, thereby beginning the end.

I'd gone past. I'd reached my own cabin, the blue one.

I went through the open door alone, and shut it.

11

The subtle muted cabin lights didn't come on. Some other mess-up in my far-from-perfect ship. The malfunction didn't seem dangerous, though. I'd see to it in the morning.

There were no lights in the bathing unit either, but the scented water worked, and warm air and towels jumped on me out of the wall with their usual terrifying alacrity.

It was very dark, only faint starlight smokily seeping in at the window through blue gauze—I'd forgotten to draw the curtain open, which was odd, for I thought I had. Maybe my poor little overtaxed mind was giving out.

I found the bed, not too easily, tired and bemused as I was, banging my unclothed anatomy on furniture, and uttering oaths resplendent in their inventiveness and squalor.

I sank on to the bed, head and body singing like slackened strings. And at once hands had me, turned me. I was gripped and held, firmly yet unbruisingly, close as the earth holds what grows from it, all the length of a male body.

I knew it at once. How not. It had been mine.

The contact was so vital, so instantaneous, so predictably

electric, I could no more have thrust him off than I could resist some painless, potent anesthetic gas.

Skin on skin. He was naked as I was. He didn't caress me or speak to me, simply held me there, letting my flesh find him out, even if my brain refused to do so.

But my brain, submerged, overwhelmed by my flesh, remembered and, remembering, conjured him from itself till we seemed one thing, indivisible. He understood my compliance before ever I put my arms around him, before ever I said:

"Tell me who you really are."

"You," he said into my mouth—his mouth, my mouth. "Who else?"

Later, he was laughing at me. I could see him laugh, for one small light—he'd asked Moddik how to fix the lights—had been allowed to come on. His eyes were sapphire in that dark glow, as my eyes must be too, for my eyes were still the poet's eyes, Esten's eyes. Those eyes would make us look, though all else was different, like children of one maker, one womb.

"Well now," he said, "was I as good as you were when you were me?"

12

Dawn pierced golden-green through the forest leaves, the glacia-view, the blue gauze, and woke us.

"Dearest *ooma,*" he said, "what's that racket?"

"Frogs? Binni-thing-a-mies? What racket? My heart, perhaps, stirred by your nearness."

"Or mine by yours? No. A Kind of humming."

"Nilla in the bath unit?"

"Fool of my dreams. A metallic sound. Robots?"

"Yay in the bath unit? He'll go rusty."

"Do you always get this silly after love?" he asked me.

"Don't you know, *ooma*?"

"Still striving to guess my identity when I tell you we've never met before?"

"Still striving. I'll guess. Maybe I have."

"I don't think so," he said, seriously, with that heart-wrenching, loin-quickening sorrow chiseling his handsome face just as it had once chiseled my handsome face. "You see, whatever else, you're bound to be confused by the sub-conscious permanent notion that I'm really you. It diverts and tangles you up, doesn't it?"

"Yes. I think it's sick and perverted, and we're a couple
of perverts, you to think of it, me to agree to it. And don't go
on looking at me like that or I'll demand further proof of how
much I like it, and you're obviously far too fragile to cope
with so much libido, what with your consumption and all.'

"Balls," said my lover.

"Quite," I said, and got off the bed.

I could hear it now, that humming, very clearly.

I stared through the window, but sun and leaves and the
ravages of lust made seeing out difficult.

"I'm going to investigate," I said.

"You always were a nosy character."

"Whoops," I said. " 'Always were.' Your former relationship with me is showing."

We weren't outside for another hour, of course. When we
made it, both pairs of sapphire-opal eyes with romantic rings
under them, the terrace was alive. Everyone was out, and first
meal was being eaten.

Danor glanced up at us, and never smiled. Or rather, her
whole body smiled, everything absolutely beaming approval,
everything but her mouth, which she very carefully kept
straight. Kam, on the other hand, grinned broadly, and said
something under his breath that sounded like "Cheers."

The Jang were too preoccupied with being Jang really to
notice; only Nilla shot us an evil look, and Esten bowed to
her.

Then a warm, murmurous voice sounded in my ear, and
surprised me: Talsi.

"Moddik has asked us to meet him, just beyond the purple trees, as soon as possible."

"Do you mean to say he's really made nine water mixers?" I asked.

Talsi said, "Very definitely. I think the dear creature
wants to show them off."

"Why not?" I cried, grabbing up a fruit from the table—
everyone seemed to be eating them now, bar Nilla. Even Naz
had a sun-peach, but he was probably too blasted to realize

what it was, maybe thought it was a syntho-cake or something.

"Come on," I said. "Let's go and see Moddik's water mixers."

The Jang groaned and prised themselves off the angel-food. One good thing, when the provision dispenser had to switch onto pure syntho-basics there'd be no more of that yuk served up on my ship.

Esten, Danor, Kam, and I went first, the Jang tottering after. Glis and Felain had even persuaded Naz into coming. Talsi came last, rather as if shepherding us. Her maternal sex-drive thing again?

We'd forgotten about the humming, Esten and I, and got used to it meanwhile. Now I recollected, because right here was the source.

"Good day," said Moddik, as we emerged on the grass lawn just beyond the grove, and found ourselves facing a semicircle of water mixers.

"Moddik!" I exclaimed. "There are twelve! Do they all work?"

"Of course. Do you doubt the master?"

"Activate them," I pleaded. "Let's get soaked with mixed-water rain. Or shall I press the starter?"

Moddik stared at me, and suddenly he wasn't the same. He looked portentous, somehow. Maybe his achievement had moved him.

"A moment," he said. "Before we do anything, I'd like everybody to listen to something I have to say."

Not one of us missed it. A sort of change in the air, like the change you finally come to recognize in the atmosphere before a sandstorm or before the great rains. In the absolute quiet I said:

"Moddik, has something grim happened? If it has, could you tell us quickly? Because perhaps every second counts."

"Nothing grim," said Moddik. "It may seem so, just for a split. But if we take it calmly, I think we can work it out."

I was so tense, I jumped when Esten spoke.

"Do the water mixers actually work?"

"Oh, yes. They really are water mixers. Have you already guessed, Jang Esten, what I've been up to?"

"No. I'm not certain. You'd better tell us, anyhow."

"Yes, you'd better," said Kam from my right, "and fairly fast."

13

That expression on Moddik's face had an unpleasant familiarity. I couldn't think what it reminded me of. He said:

"Here it is, then. In a nutshell, so to speak. The Committee in Four BEE has no personal grudge against any of you, contrary to what you rather egotistically surmise. The cause for their alarm is only that you may damage yourselves in some irreparable emotional fashion, and others also in more widespread and terrible ways. You are, though you may not properly comprehend the term, anarchists. As such, particularly considering the comparative strength of your numbers—or the strength which your members may eventually attain, since so many in the cities appear to sympathize and lean toward your mode of existence and your ideals—as such, I repeat, you are very, very dangerous. For your own sake and for the sake of those who may misguidedly follow you, you are asked to surrender to us, here and now, and return voluntarily to PD. No harm is offered you. Ultimately, we are acting in your own interests."

"We?" I said. I'm not sure how I managed to say anything. "We?"

"I myself, Talsi, Glis," he said. Talsi and Glis slipped out of our group and to his side. Then I recollected where I'd seen that look before. The Committee Hall.

"You're Q-Rs—you're androids," I said.

Nilla screamed. Even in our extremity, I thought how typical of her that was.

"I thought you were too good to be true," said Esten, "but I couldn't work it out in time."

"You were too intent on the seduction of your leader," said Moddik.

"Yes," I said, "and I on him. And Danor and Kam intent on each other and those fruits you so conveniently found over westward. And Nilla and her garden. And Felain wrapped up with Glis, and Loxi and Phy with Talsi. And Naz ecstasied up to his eyes. Beautifully staged, android. Just *der-isann,* you Q-R turd. I should have got on to you earlier, shouldn't I? Sampling that fruit in the saloon—so human of you, or were you testing it to see if we really could live on them? And that crap about stay-awake pills. You've never needed sleep in your short tubing-and-dial life. Oh, it's too classic for words. Your plane even crashed, didn't it? To make sure I wouldn't turn you away? I'm aghast at your splendid acting. And so clever in overriding my block on the robots—I wondered how you did that. I wondered how you got the monitor computer to do exactly what you said, as well. I know now, don't I? And all that pseudo-history you and those two there flashed about, your Jang circle *rorls* back . . . you even knew Assule, of course, and said what a clot he was because you understood how I'd love it. How well they must have *programmed* you. Hey, Glis, you were right, weren't you? He really *can* understand the brain of a machine. He should, and so should you. You're bloody *all* machines."

"Not quite," he said to me. "No life spark is required to create an android, since we are electronically motivated, but we are grown from cells and possess flesh as you do. Even if a few superior mechanisms do go into our life support. For example, Exile Jang, if I wished, I could pick up your sand-ship and carry it out across the dunes. Let me see you do it, life-spark human.''

I felt sick, partly because I'd liked him, trusted him, admired him. But also because it was finally out, the bare facts of their rivalry, what I had always instinctively felt. Programmed they might be to serve human needs, but in some hidden dark of their personae, they hated and despised us. Give them an excuse for retaliation, and they'd turn it on us like a gun. Dear God, what now?

"So what have you done, super-android?" I asked softly. "There's got to be some threat hanging over us, hasn't there? You know we wouldn't buy your offer otherwise."

"He's rigged something," Esten said. "The water mixers, probably."

"No reason for you to hazard," said Moddik the Q-R. "I'm going to tell you. It *is* the water mixers, also my workshop behind us by the grove of trees, also your robot Borss, currently in the sand-ship, also—must I enumerate further? I put the materials the Committee sent me to good use. The water mixers are particularly nice—real water-mixers that really work, except that at the moment they are mixing something else. Such a touch amused me. You see, we are capable of humor. A moment's rewiring would alter them to their original purpose, of course, but none of you, I think, will be in a position to see to that."

"Don't dress it up," said Kam. His voice was as soft as mine had been, as soft as Esten's voice—as if we were similarly afraid to speak normally in case it precipitated the catastrophe. "*What's* in the water mixers, the workshop, the robot —and everywhere else you've put your hands?"

"Bombs," said the Q-R. "Each on its own big enough to throw this small area sky-high, and higher. Together, quite a pyrotechnic display. Very little is going to be left of your plantation, or your ship. Or, my human friends, of you. Even if you start running now, you won't outstrip the blast, and believe me the perimeter of such a shock is worse than the center.''

"He's lying," said Kam. "You're lying. Activate, and you go, too. Don't you?"

"Just so," said the Q-R, "but I have no—er—soul. This thing that upsets you so much, this thing you call 'death,' is nothing to me. I shall have aided the Committee and mankind at large. The planes from Limbo will collect your remains and you will enter PD as planned. Everything will be as it should be."

"Wait," I said. "You can't harm humanity, can you? Or did your programming slip?"

"Oh, no," he said smiling. "I could plant the bombs, yes, since in their nonactive state they are harmless, and forever would be. I could not, however, depress a switch that would result in loss of human life—murder. But you see in Four BEE I was serviced in a slapdash fashion, deliberately, so that ultimately, at a moment that could be computed precisely, I should malfunction. And it is my malfunction which will activate the bombs, by means of the normal, upper-tonal malfunction alarm signals emitted from my inner circuitry. Do you understand? It's rather neat. The Committee are responsible only for the error in my servicing, not for the bombs. I am responsible for placing the bombs, not for my malfunction. The right hand does not know what the left hand does, so neither hand is guilty. Two parts of a whole, independent of each other, yet they act perfectly as one. But I digress. Maybe I should explain that the moment of my malfunction is several splits in the past, and the signals are already being issued. It will take exactly twelve splits more for them to penetrate the casings of the explosive and trigger the vital nerve. After which there will be something of a bang." He looked at me; his eyes danced, glinted, danced. "If all of you make a run for it, the Jang bird-plane in the grove of trees behind you will get you clear in time, even overloaded though the vehicle will be. I must point out, though, that its controls are set for Four BEE Limbo. The setting, by the way, is irreversible."

"If we agreed to go," said Kam abruptly, "you'd stop the signals, stop these bombs going off?"

"I myself have no power to stop my own signal emission. I would need to be dismantled."

Nilla screamed again.

"I'll go," she screeched. "I don't want to be hurt," and she fled toward the grove and the plane.

"Yes," said Esten. "We'll all leave, won't we? But look," he went toward the Q-R anxiously. "I left some stuff in the ship. Could I just go and get it before—"

It happened too fast for me. Esten flung himself into Moddik. Too fast for Moddik as well. An android is physically constructed like a human, at least externally, so the fist that went into his thorax upset the lung and heart mechanism, and the other fist that cracked on the jaw jarred those hard bones just enough to black-out, momentarily, the steel brain that whirred inside the plastic skull. Moddik fell, crashed full length, and, as he did so, Talsi and Glis fell also. Esten crouched over the Q-R, his face wild, desperate and gray-pale through the desert tan.

"In his workshop," he shouted to me. "Electronic knives—a pane of ice-glass—anything sharp—"

I ran. I'd never run so fast on legs made entirely of lukewarm water. The workshop shelter was a confusion of bits and pieces. I grabbed a molecule-needle knife and ran out again.

"Here," I dived down beside Esten, then turned my head, not ready for the thing he did with the knife, the spurt of completely human-looking blood.

"This is going to be messy," he said, looking sicker than me, but more in control of himself.

"Do you know what you're doing?" I blurted.

I could hear Nilla and Felain screaming from the background. The others just stared.

"Partly," he said. "I read it up, android and robot basics—History Tower. I had an idea they might try something like this—but not yet—not so soon—"

"What can I do?"

"Get one of the robots. We need some kind of liquid spray—water, oil, anything, just to wash this damned red me-

tallic plasma out. I've got to cut through every single nontis-
sue organ to stop that signal.''

I got up and around again, but Kam said, ''I'll do it,''
and ran, as I had, toward the forest area where the robots were
hoeing.

Esten's hands gnawed on the corpse. Glis and Talsi lay as
if dead. Moddik was definitely finished, and, extensions of
him, the two ''women'' had presumably stopped like chro-
nometers once he ceased to be.

Kam sprinted back, the robots clanking after.

''OK,'' Esten said, ''now I handle it. The rest of you get
out, and take those screaming fools with you.''

''We stay,'' said Kam. ''We can't miss it if it goes off,
anyway.''

''You might. Get as far away from the ship as you can,
and climb down into one of those irrigation canals when it's
due. Take a breath and lie on your faces under the water and
stay put. It might work. Now do it, for God's sake.''

The knife sizzled and spat through liquid, more slowly
through steel fibers and hard plasti-rubber. The engines of
android life lay spasmodically bare between the rushes of
plasma and the squirting oil sprays of Jaska and Yay. It was a
somber golden oil. When it met the ''blood'' it turned the
color of Moddik's garnet hair.

''Go on,'' Esten raged coldly, not looking at us. ''You've
got about three splits.''

''All right,'' Kam said.

I felt but did not see them moving, going swiftly to do
what he said. Nilla and Felain were taken too, wailing. Loxi
had started wailing as well. Would they be able to get the
swan down from the roof, or wherever it was? What about the
Gray-Eyeses? What about—?

''You too, you bitch,'' Esten said. I hadn't made a sound,
but he knew I wasn't gone. I don't know why I wasn't. I was
half-dead of fright. I wanted to run screaming like the Jang
girls, run and not stop. But somehow I felt safer there, standing behind him.

''I'd—'' I said, but he cut in as if he hated me.

"Push off. I'm trying to save your shitting land and your stupid hide. Let me *do* it."

So I did what he said. I ran. But not very far. There was a channel quite close—too close, but I couldn't seem to reason it out, and half fell down into it. The water was very shallow, barely reached my ankles. I lay in it, attempting to pull the water up over myself.

I was crying in dry throaty gasps, and trying to count.

But I wasn't counting. I was praying. Like once before. A sort of prayer. Although nobody had answered that one. "No, please no, don't let it—Oh please no oh no oh no—"

It wasn't quiet. There were lots of noises. Animals, breezes through reeds and flowers and leaves. As if everyone were speaking for the last time, hurrying to get out its song of life before the blast tore it in shreds.

Then I heard someone shriek, off to the west. Nilla, maybe. Was it time, and did they know over there?

Now it happens.

Now it comes.

The red wind, the black sound.

Pain and silence forever.

I don't *want* to die. I'm not ready. None of us are ready. I don't want *this* to die, all this around me. I *want* the ache in my muscles from a day's work, I want the ache in my heart from anger or despair. I want every misery and joy I've ever known, and the rest to come. I want them all. They're all precious. And the trees, and the earth, and the sky . . .

Why doesn't it happen? I've bitten through the skin of my hand. Do I have to start on the other hand? It's going to, so let it be now.

Nothing
Happened
At
All.

Kam was hauling me up the bank of the canal, through the pretty weed.

"Kam, are we dead?"

"No," he said, quite reasonably, as if I'd said something intelligent and unusual that deserved a thinking man's answer. "We're OK. It didn't happen. Felain had a chronometer—Glis's chronometer, ironically enough—and I time-checked. Fifteen splits now since it should have happened. All clear."

"Then where's Esten?" I sprang up covered in mud, weed, the complete detritus my position had offered me, and hurled myself past the purple trees, onto the lawn.

Or practically.

He was still there by the Q-R corpse, the knife silent and immobile in his hand. He looked exhausted, literally shattered, as if some framework in him had given way. But then, was that yet another complication of the poet-body syndrome?

"Esten—" I called out, and he shouted:

"Wait—stay back."

"But it's finished," I said. "Fifteen splits since it should—"

"I got them all," he said, "all but one. I got that too, when I found it, but I was over the time. It could be safe. It may not be. Something may still—" he broke off, staring at me, then cried at the top of his lungs: "Down, get *down*!"

Kam was behind me, and pushed me. We fell like desperate lovers together into the grass and the green land smashed us, rising.

The noise was like no-noise, a bang so big it went beyond sound into a sort of clap of deafness.

The sky rained fire and debris. Leaves fell in masses and covered us.

Presently, it was over.

It had only been one water mixer, the seventh and farthest from us at the center of the semicircle. Esten had cut all the signals in time but the last; that last went on long enough to eat through the bomb casing and then peter out. The nerve of the bomb flickered, hesitated, wondering if it were detonated or not. It wondered for fifteen splits. Then decided it was, and blew.

Smoke was clearing in snatches.

I wasn't hurt, but so divorced from myself I could only crawl on my hands and knees. Kam, also unhurt, muttered after me, but I took no notice.

I got to Esten quickly, even that way. I thought he was going to be dead, but I still had to get to him.

He wasn't dead. He was breathing and simply looked like a beautiful poet passed out on some romantic lawn. That was from his left side. When I went around to the other side, the side the blast had been, I saw that he was never going to be beautiful, never going to look as I had looked, ever again.

14

I knew very well what the answer would be, but I had to try. I tried for hours, for days. I tried shouting, pleading, speaking extremely serenely and rationally. I wept and I swore.

The computer simply reiterated its message. We were to use the painkilling drugs we possessed, the antibiodermics, the healing salve. Further supplies would be sent us.

"The salve isn't good enough," I kept saying. "It can't heal that kind of wound—not properly."

The computer said that pain could be alleviated, and infection prevented, that this was the most that we were entitled to, exiles as we were. We knew that new bodies were no longer allowed us, or any form of surgery or replacement.

"But the skin is—the scar will be—"

Rattle click. Rattle click.

Click.

"Damn you," I screamed, "it's your fault!"

Rattle, rattle.

"Your bloody fault—your plot—it didn't come off! Your stinking Q-Rs are melted all over the grass out there—"

Kam shut off the link before I could elaborate.

"No use," he said. "It's on Receive Only. You won't get any more reaction."

"Whatever they send—drugs, supplies—how can we trust them?"

"We'll check everything they send," he said, "as you suggested earlier. But I don't think they'll try again. That point about their programming still holds good—they could only go as far as they did by blinding themselves to it. It's out in the open now. Next time they *would* know. Ergo, they won't."

"Oh, what does it matter, anyway?"

There was a great stillness in the ship. They were mostly sitting in the saloon. Nilla and Felain were intermittently crying, but very softly, holding on to each other for dear life. Naz was generally pacing in the corridor; each time he turned at either end the Jang topaz beads on his trouser hems came together with a little cold clink. We had been going on like this, with minor variations, for five units.

I opened the door of my cabin.

Danor was sitting with him. She was quite motionless, and so was he, but he was at last awake.

I'd been hoping he wouldn't wake up for an indefinite while, though, of course, there wasn't any pain, not with the miraculous drugs, so easy to use and so expedient. The whole of the right side of his face and neck was shielded by a silk-of-ice bandaging, under that the anesthetic foam barrier, keeping the material from actually touching the ruined flesh. The blast had ripped the side of his face open, peeling back the tissues in layers—somehow, incredibly, it had missed the mouth, the nostril, the eye. So it was with two eyes, those eyes that were still mine, that he was able to look up at me as I came toward him.

"Hello, Esten," I said.

"Hello," he said.

The right eardrum had been badly damaged, but that didn't necessarily have to matter. The robots and the machines had already worked out and implanted some sort of miniaturized something or other that would do the ear's work for it—a process they knew, since it was part of their own self-servicing technique.

Danor rose and went out. I didn't want her to go. I didn't want the responsibility of being alone with him, conscious. Unconscious, I had sat by him here four days, four nights, barring my sessions with the monitor computer, when Kam or Danor relieved me.

I'd felt helpless enough then, useless enough. But now. I didn't know what I could say to him. Particularly since—

"Sit down," he said courteously. "I suggest that we should talk."

"Do you feel up to talking? I think—"

"I think you'd rather not talk, and you're putting the onus on me. But I say we have to, and I'm fine, so pull up a float-chair and sit down."

"Very well."

I sat, and I peered at him. I wanted to cry. He said:

"You don't bravely have to stare me out, you know." So I lowered my stinging eyes, ashamed.

"I look fairly grizzly, I imagine," he said calmly, "and when this excellent bandaging comes off, I'm going to look sixteen times worse. Aren't I?"

"Not necessarily. You see, the salve is still very good. And if you keep on using it—it may take a while, but—"

"Shut up, *ooma,*" he said. "You never could lie about anything that really mattered to you. Just listen to me, and then we'll have it straight. I came out to this place to get you, and I got you, and I don't regret it. Neither do I regret saving your greenery from extinction. However, I do see that as your bed mate, with this face, my days are numbered. So, in a little while, Naz is going to bring me in his total hoard of renounced ecstasy and a few other things as well, and I'm going blissfully to overdose myself out of this Ego-Life, into PD."

I jumped—off the chair, backward, upward—

"No," I shouted. "PD is out. Suicide is out. You'd give them the satisfaction of voluntarily doing what they tried to push us into—after *this*?"

"Ooma, it's my life, what's left of it. It's up to me."

"No, not anymore it isn't."

"Please don't squeeze out a host of insincere protestations of eternal affection, or start howling that my irrevocable hideousness will make no difference to you. You'll only regret it, and I shan't swallow a syllable."

Somehow I'd got back to the chair, and flattened myself down in it as if an ogre were after me. Perhaps it was.

"Let me do what I want," he said. "There'll be other males along, you can be sure of that. Run a check to make sure they're human next time."

"Be quiet," I said. I tried to get my breath, and realized I wasn't going to be able to, so I'd have to explain it all to him without breath. "First, I *know* it makes a difference. What else could it do? Every time I look at that scar—oh, yes, there's going to be one bloody awful scar—my guts are going to knot up like a nest of reinforced steel cobras. Not with revulsion, with anger. Anger that it happened to you. What other difference could there be? You're still you—still *me,* you body-thieving bastard. If your hair went white, would I stop feeling anything for you? What does it matter anyway? In Four BEE and BAA and BOO the physical side was, in any case, a joke, wasn't it? If you fell for someone, you fell for *them,* their personality—their—their self, whatever it is—not whatever flesh they happened to have put on that unit. Which is why any true feeling was rare. Oh, yes, the body turned me on, looking like me and everything, but it's you who got through to me, you fool. And this thing that's happened to you—it's something that was *done* to you, not you yourself. You're still *you.*" I managed to get a breath then, and I stabbed the last words out at him as a final cold blow to bring him back to his senses and to me. "Still you—*Hergal.*"

"Oh," he said, quite lamely. He looked as if he might be going to laugh.

"Of course," I added, "maybe you're so effete you can't

live with it yourself. Maybe you don't give a damn about me. You just want to piss off to nice PD and leave me here alone for the rest of my days with your filthy little child to bring up.''

''What?'' he said.

I caught up with myself just then.

''Er, I hadn't quite meant to tell you, like that. Oh, I'm not even absolutely sure. Actually. So, er. Yes.''

''Well, I think you'd better tell me. Again. Quietly and in detail.''

I rose, and then sat on the edge of the bed.

''You see,'' I mumbled, feeling acutely embarrassed for some reason I couldn't fathom, ''Kam and I were near the bomb blast, so we ran checks on ourselves to be sure everything was still in order physically. And it was. But my machine had a little fit and spat out bits of blue tape over me, and it said I was—it's the old word—pregnant. That means that you and I have done what we wouldn't have been allowed to do in the cities, which is, make a child. Only instead of growing in the crystallize tanks, ever so hygienic and safe and everything, the poor little idiot's going to have to grow inside *me*. I'm carrying, fecund, in the club, um, etc. I couldn't work out why, to begin with, but the machine did eventually. It's the 'home-grown' food I've been devouring so rapaciously. Those tubers and sun-peaches and lettuce things. It *has* altered my body chemistry, screwed up the contraceptive properties that apparently linger in our exclusive city diet. So, whoops, we're going to be makers, Hergal, and if you go off and leave me here, I'll never forgive you.''

He just lay there, expressionless. I wondered if he'd grasped what I'd said; I could hardly grasp it myself. Then he took my hand, and he said:

''If you want me to stay, I'll stay. But there's one thing we'd better have clear from here on. I'm not Hergal.''

I gazed at him, and wildly verbalized a list of males who at one era or another had been close: Drar? Rannik? *Lorun?*

''No,'' he said. He looked at me and then he told me.

And I didn't believe him.

"Twelve *vreks* back," he said, "that was the last time you ever really registered me, and not surprising. I couldn't express myself then, particularly not to you. You were like a wall of solid glowing metal. When I was with you, the heat and the brightness shriveled me up. I became all the things you hated most in sheer self-defense. I couldn't say a sentence to you that didn't sound as though it had come out of a rusty mincer. In the end, I instigated for myself a sort of game. I knew you expected me to be a dull, reactionary, clod-hopping lump, with a ragbag of platitudes in place of a brain —a kind of faithful *promok*, who'd dog your footsteps, and creep away when you got bored. Because I could never manage to put over my true thoughts against that glowing wall of indifference, I just used to act out the part you'd allotted me. I'd shamble up looking like Monster-Night, and say: '*Onk*, it's not ethical, but I mustn't grumble,' and blink a couple of my eyes at you, and I could see the circuits engaging in your mind, the right patterns being achieved. A sort of neon sign would light up in your face: Here comes that bloody silly cunt, Hatta. Of course, this was not the way to deal with you, but I'm a defensive man, oversensitive. I can't help it, I need a shell. I got a rather bitter and depressing laugh at the way you had me so wrong every time, and I played up to it. I could tell myself: She doesn't understand me because now I won't let her see me.

"Then they chucked you out of Four BEE, and that was it. I knew I'd got to come after you because you were the only thing that gave any value to my life. I'd been too nervous, too scared before to run on your road. The only time I'd ever put myself on the level, you'd smashed my ego down my throat. But out here there wasn't any other way. Being a monster freak has compensations, but not when there's nothing else you can be.

"To begin with, I had a spell of being female. I was trying to find out something about you, to get over the thing that scared me in you. And I succeeded. It was a kind of therapy I thought might work, and it did. Being a girl is not for me. I'm eighty percent masculine, and stuck with it. But I

found out what makes the clock tick, and high time. To nick
your last male body was pure inspiration. Very disturbing it
was, I might add. More for me, perhaps, than for you when
you initially saw me. That was the first time, or almost the
first time I'd ever had you at a disadvantage. No neon came
up on this occasion. You were just completely nonplussed,
standing out there in the glamorous remains of that jewelry
dress, staring up at me. I'd tried to acquire your manner, your
extrovert qualities, in order to deceive you. The strange thing
is that I took to them quite easily, once I'd got over the fear
of being in the open, not hiding behind six red eyes and eight
legs.''

His gaze never left my face while he said this. When he
stopped, I said:

''Well, it looks rather as if the only one of us two who's
a right *floop* is me.''

He said, ''Now you know who I am, do you still want me
to stay?''

''Hatta—'' I began, but he said:

''No, Esten. Let's keep that the way it is. Hatta is past
tense.''

''All right, Esten, then. You used to say, when you were
Hatta the Horror, that you loved me.''

''Unchanged,'' he said. ''That's what it's about.''

''Well—Esten—I don't know if I love you. But if you
leave me, a bit of me will go with you. Maybe it's just the
clever trick you devised, but you really do seem like a part of
me, myself. And I've got your seed in me, growing, and I
want that child, and I want you. What more can I say?''

''Knowing you,'' he said, ''bloody plenty.''

EPILOGUE

So we sit here on the veranda, Danor and I, like two fecund Gray-Eyeses. In our condition we're obviously too far gone to do much hoeing or digging. In fact I doubt if we could see over ourselves to the hoe.

Danor found out she too had doubled her ego-count some days after I did, but she didn't appear to mind. She looks sweetly lovely and positively scintillates with health, as I do. I suppose it's lucky for us the cities make such first-class body structures. Giving birth with only the knowledge you get from a machine and its library, and no experienced help beyond what a couple of pale and terrified males can offer, is a prospect not without its soul-destroying aspect, but I think we are perfectly built enough that we can cope, and anyhow we'll have to, pangs of cowardice or not. And who cares? It's going to be worth it.

"Mine will be male," says Danor. I surmise she wants to replace Kam's unloving child in BAA. But how can we know what sex our brats will be? A random life this is going to prove, all told.

We've had no more trouble from the cities, despite a sort

of alarm system we arranged, to spot enemy planes and so forth. But so far, over the past *vrek* and a half, twenty new arrivals, each checked out as human, have appeared on the scene—only six of them females, which may create extra difficulties later, and I almost wish we had that android bitch Talsi around. They descend in stolen aircraft, stolen sky-boats . . . Three hijacked a sand-ship and five of the passengers elected to come with them when they saw the valley. They work very hard, though all at various things. We're starting to be able to recognize our own different talents, and channel them. For example, we have four terrific cooks, who can do wonders with the provision-dispenser goo (yes, we're on goo, and checked goo, at that) and even better wonders with the natural food. Fortunately others have robot and me-chanic skills, not like Moddik, but then that's hardly surprising. With their help we've got a complete housing plan on the way, not to mention a reliable contraceptive for those girls who don't want to end up as Danor and I have done, while still enjoying the home-grown edibles. Plus a valley-wide discerning shock wall, almost complete, that discriminates between animals, humans, and *androids*.

Moddik's eleven remaining water mixers—safely re-wired by clever Esten, who read about such things where I absorbed poetry in the History Tower—proudly prowl the Garden in the steps of that mother-of-pearl giant who came first. Except that they go much farther, to the edges of the dunes, in fact. Which is why the valley is green from rim to rim. Green, even over there, where the black crater left by Moddik's last bomb has healed with grass, like a symbol of all healing, of the body, the mind, the heart.

Sitting here, looking out across that landscape of small white homes, half built, the columns of trees, the different-colored lawns and slopes scattered with broken panes of shade and sun; smelling too the perfume that flows off the earth and the flowers, the city I came from seems unreal and forever silenced. Against the stature of those black mountains, against the vault of that blazing sky flashing back at itself like blue-green mirror from the canals, against the music of life, the animal cries, the insects, the din of humans working or arguing or making love or singing out there under the green shadows, it's not only Danor's womb and mine that seem quickened, but the whole defiant womb of our world.

Presently Nilla and Felain will be back from the carving they've started out there in the forest. These two at least won't need the contraceptive, being content with each other for the time being—to the great sorrow of several males. One artistic young man has already painted them as an Idyll. I think he's planning to have a go at Danor and me next as two pregnant tribal princesses. Hmm. Naz is raising some sort of corn over on the west side. He's very enthusiastic about it. Phy and Loxi are somewhere with two girls. In their spare moments they've commenced a hive for the insects, which apparently will make honey. (Sometime.) Esten's dragon has been harnessed to an old-fashioned robot-built plow, and doesn't like it too much. As for my inter-animal-android theories, the swan has been adopted by a family of snakes, and lives with them. Their fur makes it sneeze, but that doesn't seem to matter.

Kam will also be home soon. He'll put his arm around Danor as if she's marked HANDLE WITH EXTREME CAUTION, but she'll make him forget that later, in their cabin. Esten will be next, the color of mahogany, coming up from the forest. From the left he will look like a poet, or a young primitive deity out of the glades. From the right you will see the half-mask of polarized satin.

And when I think now how I almost quoted, not realizing, his own words of so long ago back at him, that day I made him stay alive with me—how the body was a joke, that it was the inner something which mattered . . . well, I've learned your new name, Esten, and I've learned that if I love anybody, yours is the name he gave himself.

Pet, do you hear it, my white pet, buried somewhere out there, over the mountains, under the sand? Do you hear the noise we're making?

The grapes should be harvested soon, and prepared in the ancient fashion. Perhaps I should send a flask of our vintage to Four BEE, with our compliments.

However nasty a drink it turns out, it's going to be better than their lousy sapphire wine.

GLOSSARY OF CONVENTIONS, INSTITUTIONS, AND DEVICES

android   See Q-R.

bee (baa, boo)   A kind of electronic, self-carrying "handbag" used by both sexes. It can contain anything from a bottle of wine to a full-length mirror; and will also run errands and carry messages. In Four BEE these things are known as bees, in Four BAA as baas, in Four BOO as boos.

body change and sex change   The essential element—"life spark" or consciousness—can be taken from one body and replaced in another fresh body, specifically designed by the prospective occupant, via the Limbo Tub at Limbo. The chosen body may be either male or female, depending on the mood of the human concerned. In the earlier part of the autobiography the writer stated that the time supposed to elapse between each body replacement was officially thirty units, but this limit was constantly abused by suiciders.

circle   Jang custom: A circle is a group of friends who more or less stick together as a clique, and are reckoned to do most things as one. Admitting fresh members to the circle is a complex ritual, although not mentioned by the writer. Cutting original members out, however, is easy, and the outcast is traditionally expected to dissolve in tears.

displacement machine   Originally intended for human travel, on the disintegration-reintegration principle, it proved unpopular, since the process tended to make the passengers vomit—according to the writer.

Dream Rooms   The place where citizens can buy and experience dreams previously designed and plotted by themselves— a kind of cerebral Adventure Palace.

flashes   News bulletins, appearing as electrically projected signs in the sky, on walls, etc. They can also be picked up in the home. Nothing much ever appears to happen in the cities, so anything even slightly unusual is worth reporting on, and zoom-scanners and Flash Center bees are constantly on the alert. There is a Flash Center in each of the four sectors of each of the cities.

Four BEE, Four BAA, Four BOO   The three great dome cities. Obviously in size gargantuan, they exist beneath stabilized electricity wave shields—the domes—which protect them from all the hazards of the planet, eruption, storm, earthquake, and so on. Entirely self-sufficient, their inner conditions are made as "natural" as possible, complete with parks and gardens, days and nights, artificial sun, moon, and stars. Outside Four BAA are the lesser domes which contain the breeding-tank farms for the creation of Q-Rs and also glamorous android animals made to delight the populace. Four BOO is famous for the trapping of real desert animals—for pets— and additionally, in point of fact, for fur and other animal products such as scent.

hypno-school   First active stage of city life, where children are taught incredibly sophisticated items, such as extraordinanry forms of mathematics, for which apparently they never find any use afterward. Teaching by hypnosis leaves most of the school activity a complete blank in the child's mind, though knowledge is retained. This phase only lasts one twentieth of a *rorl* (about five years).

Jang   Second stage of city life. Adolescence has become a compulsory part of growing up, lasting anything up to half *rorl* or longer, and is called Jang. Jang have their own customs, culture, traditional modes of behavior (having ecstasy marriage, etc.), and virtually their own language (Jang slang).

Any who depart from the norm are frowned on by all strata of society.

makers Parents. Relevant cells are taken from a male and a female who wish to become makers, and joined in a crystallize tank to make a child. This is supposed to create a bond between the two makers, but evidently rarely does for long. Only one maker is obliged to remain as the child's guardian, and then actually only until hypno-school is finished.

marriage Jang custom. Jang traditionally always marry before "having love"—the sexual act. Sometimes they marry for a substantial period of time—a *vrek*, mid-*vrek*, etc.— sometimes only for an afternoon or unit, in which case the marriage must be paid for both before and after. The marriage "ceremony" consists mainly of one speech, as follows: "I promise to have love with you and no other for the period aforesaid, unless I seek annulment, which may be granted on alternate units throughout the marriage, and which must be paid for." Older People are not required to marry.

Older People Final and longest stage of city life, which can continue more or less indefinitely, until the person concerned, worn out with living and memories, voluntarily seeks Personality Dissolution, in which his current ego is erased and his conscious mind washed clean of all recollection. After this he returns to the child stage once more, this time with a Q-R guardian.

paying There is no monetary system in Four BEE, etc. However, since the cities run on power, emotional energy is taken from the payer and fed into the city power banks. The weird process is accomplished simply by the purchaser entering a pay-booth and going into a hysteria of thank-yous. Ecstasy or other drug stimulants are generally used to ensure the success of this peculiar rite.

Picture-Vision A sort of nonstop TV extravaganza of beauty and eroticism, with no story line.

Q-R Quasi-robot, or android. Grown in the breeding tanks at

BAA, from chemical cells, the Q-R externally resembles a human. Useful circuitry is built into them, however, and even their "blood" is a form of self-servicing metallic plasma. Not being created from male and female tissue and therefore without a consciousness—or life spark—the Q-Rs are brought to life by an electric charge of colossal force.

sabotage   Is carried out by Jang, and is another, though unofficial, Jang custom. It entails breaking into the lookout posts of the cities, damaging the machinery, and thereby disturbing the protective waves of the dome long enough to allow in bad weather, or worse. The dome defenses quickly block the sabotage, and harm of any telling proportion is never done.

suiciding   Literally suiciding—killing the body—but without the normal connotations, since it is only a means to get an off-the-cuff body replacement inside the thirty-unit limit. Limbo robots immediately home in on any suicide or death, and take the "victim" to Limbo, where they rescue the life spark and replace it in flesh.

ABOUT THE AUTHOR

TANITH LEE was born in 1947 in London, England. She received her secondary education at Prendergast Grammar School, Catford. She began to write at the age of nine.

After school she worked variously as a library assistant, a shop assistant, a filing clerk, and a waitress. At age 25 she spent 1 year at art college.

From 1970 to 1971 three of Lee's children's books were published. In 1975 DAW Books USA published Lee's *The Birthgrave*, and thereafter 26 of her books, enabling her to become a full-time writer.

To date she has written 58 novels and nine collections of novellas and short stories. Four of her radio plays have been broadcast by the BBC and she has written two episodes of the BBC cult series *Blake's Seven*. Her work has been translated into over 15 languages.

Lee has twice won the World Fantasy Award for short fiction, and was awarded the August Derleth Award in 1980 for her novel *Death's Master*.

In 1992 Lee married the writer John Kaiine, her partner since 1987. They live in southeast England with one black-and-white and one Siamese cat.

REALMS OF FANTASY

The biggest, brightest stars from Bantam Spectra

Maggie Furey

A fiery-haired Mage with an equally incendiary temper must save her world and her friends from a pernicious evil, with the aid of four forgotten magical Artefacts.

AURIAN ___56525-7 $6.99
HARP OF WINDS ___56526-5 $6.99
SWORD OF FLAME ___56527-3 $6.99
DHIAMMARA ___57557-0 $6.99

Katharine Kerr

The mistress of Celtic fantasy presents her ever-popular Deverry series. Most recent titles:

DAYS OF BLOOD AND FIRE ___29012-6 $6.99/$9.99
DAYS OF AIR AND DARKNESS ___57262-8 $6.50/$8.99
THE RED WYVERN ___57264-4 $6.50/$8.99

- -